Praise for
DragonKnight

"*DragonKnight* is a thoroughly enchanting fantasy where dragons speak, tiny mouselike guardians protect normal-sized folk, and young people search for identity. Woven through Donita K. Paul's carefully crafted world is a strong theme of love, redemption, and the sufficiency of God to see His children through all trials. The icing on this delightful cake is a surprise ending that brings tears of joy!"

    —DOUGLAS HIRT, author of the Cradleland Chronicles series

"Donita K. Paul's inventiveness never ceases to amaze. Fresh ideas for new races of people and unusual creatures keep flowing from her gifted pen. In *DragonKnight,* we meet a few of these and rejoin old friends like Kale, Bardon, Regidor, and the ever-huggable Toopka on a rollicking adventure. As always, this author has a whole bag of tricks up her sleeve—unexpected plot twists, heart-tugging relationships, and captivating characters. 'Classic' is written all over this series."

    —JILL ELIZABETH NELSON, author of *Reluctant Burglar*

"*DragonKnight* swept me into the exciting exploits of Bardon and his loyal friends. The inventive and richly compelling characters quickly drew me into their lives and into a fast-paced fantasy adventure."

    —FAYE SPIEKER, playwright and author of ministry tools for children

"Charming characters in a colorful make-believe world full of beauty and danger. Classic good against evil with wonderful spiritual truths layered throughout and enough twists to keep the reader engaged from first page to last."

    —SANDRA D. MOORE, director, American Christian
    Fiction Writers Association

"Donita K. Paul's new novel examples the skillful weaving of a fantasy story with strong moral lessons and spiritual insights. Throughout her series, Paul has created fascinating characters who battle powerful enemies and learn what it means to live life in the process. As a result, *DragonKnight* is both fun and important reading. Young readers will love the action— and readers of all ages will appreciate the insights."

—PAUL MOEDE, coauthor of *Good News About Your Strong-Willed Child*

DragonKnight

Donita K. Paul

WaterBrook
PRESS

DRAGONKNIGHT
PUBLISHED BY WATERBROOK PRESS
12265 Oracle Boulevard, Suite 200
Colorado Springs, Colorado 80921
A division of Random House Inc.

10 Digit ISBN: 1-4000-7250-6
13 Digit ISBN: 978-1-4000-7250-7

Published in association with the literary agency of Alive Communications Inc., 7680
Goddard Street, Suite 200, Colorado Springs, CO 80920, www.alivecommunications.com.

Library of Congress Cataloging-in-Publication Data
Paul, Donita K.
    Dragonknight : a novel / Donita K. Paul.
       p. cm.
    ISBN 1-4000-7250-6
    1. Dragons—Fiction. 2. Religious fiction. I. Title.
    PS3616.A94D725 2006
    813'.6—dc22

                                                        2006006983

Printed in the United States of America
2006

10 9 8 7 6 5 4 3 2

This book is dedicated to these first readers.
It is so much easier to write
to specific readers than to a general audience.
Thanks for representing a whole lot of readers.

Mary and Michael Darnell
Kristianna Lynxwiler
Jason McDonald
Alistair and Ian McNear
Rachael Selk
Amy Stoddard
Rebecca Wilber
Lindsey Winkler

Contents

Acknowledgments

Because:
"Without consultation, plans are frustrated,
But with many counselors they succeed."
PROVERBS 15:22

Bonnie Aldrich
Alice Brunette
Dudley Delffs
Evangeline Denmark
Jani Dick
Michelle Garland
Dianna Gay
Beth Goddard
Cecilia Gray
Michelle Griep
Jack Hagar
Shannon Hill
Beth Jusino
Christine Lynxwiler
Paul Moede
Sandra Moore
Jill Nelson
Shannon and Troy McNear
Jeanne Paton
Robert Peterson
Cheryl Smith
Armin Sommer
Stuart Stockton
Faye Spieker
J. Case and Eden Tompkins
Ahneka Valdois
Elizabeth and Kathleen Wolford
Laura Wright

Cast of Characters

Ahnek—o'rant street urchin, about ten years old

Captain **Anton**—leader of the guard Sir Dar sends with Bardon

Ardeo—white and gray minor dragon, glows in the dark

Bardon—o'rant and emerlindian, squire to Sir Dar, in training to Paladin since age six

Bim and **Toa**—young twins, sons of cook at inn in Ianna

Blosker—marione rider, works for Hoddack

Bortenmiffgaten—tumanhofer jailer in Ianna

Bromptotterpindosset—tumanhofer adventurer and mapmaker, owns shop in Ianna

Wizard **Burner Stox**—evil female wizard, married to Crim Cropper

Cadden Glas—doneel explorer of the Northern Reach

Wizard **Cam Ayronn**—lake wizard from Trese

Cise—o'rant kindia breaker working for Hoddack

Corduff—owner of a mine near Ianna

Wizard **Crim Cropper**—evil male wizard, dabbles in genetics, married to Burner Stox

Sir **Dar**—doneel diplomat and statesman

Dibl—yellow and orange minor dragon, reveals humor in situations, lightens the hearts of his companions

Lo **D'mon**—not mentioned by name in text, last guard sent with Bardon

Grand **Dost**—grand emerlindian in charge of Bardon's spiritual education during Bardon's time as squire at Dar's castle

Faye—lady's maid in Dar's castle

Wizard **Fenworth**—Bog wizard from Wynd

Filia—pink minor dragon, enthusiastic about all things, collects knowledge, some of it quite trivial

Gallatennodken—dealer in antiquities in Ianna

Gilda—meech dragon once a cohort of Risto, now lives in a bottle to keep from dissipating because of a spell Risto put on her

Gledupkonstepper—sociology professor at The Hall

Greer—Bardon's dragon, purple with cobalt wings, former rider a knight who was killed in battle

Gregger—investigator working for Harbormaster Mayfil

Grupnotbaggentogg—driver of horse-drawn carriage in Ianna

Gymn—green minor dragon, heals

Dame **Hoddack**—wife of Hoddack, her father was original owner of (the rich) farm

Hoddack—wealthy marione farm owner and kindia trader

Holt Hoddack—young marione son of kindia trader

Ilex—o'rant worker on Hoddack's kindia farm

Magistrate **Inkleen**—magistrate in Ianna

Sir **Jilles**—N'Rae's father

Sir **Joffa**—Sir Jilles's older twin brother

Sir **Jofil**—N'Rae's grandfather

Jue Seeno—minneken from the Isle of Kye serving as N'Rae's protector

Kale Allerion—o'rant wizard and Dragon Keeper, former village slave, eighteen years old, has gift of finding dragon eggs

Granny **Kye**—old emerlindian, artist, and N'Rae's grandmother

Harbormaster **Mayfil**—important official in Ianna

Librettowit—tumanhofer librarian to Wizard Fenworth

Lo **Mees**—one of the guard sent with Bardon

Metta—purple minor dragon, sings

Mistress **Moorp**—housekeeper at Ornopy Halls

Scribe **Moran**—Bardon's Tome mentor at Castle Pelacce

Innkeeper **Nald**—owner of inn in Norst

N'Rae—emerlindian girl who was raised by ropma and is searching for her father

Lo **Oh**—one of the guard sent by Sir Dar

Master **Onit**—marione tavern owner in Norst

Master **Ornopy**—o'rant landowner in upper Wynd

Pat—chubby brown minor dragon, fixes things

Lo **Pont**—one of guard sent with Bardon

Regidor—meech dragon, in search of a colony of lost meech dragons, likes fancy things, carries an enchanted meech dragon in a bottle with him

Wizard **Risto**—evil wizard killed by Fenworth

Saramaralindan—Bromptotterpindosset's daughter

Seagram—Pont's dragon

Sittiponder—blind tumanhofer orphan and seer

Taylaminkadot—tumanhofer housekeeper in Fenworth's castle

Toopka—doneel child, under guardianship of Kale and Sir Dar

Trum Aspect—courtier and merchant representative at Sir Dar's court

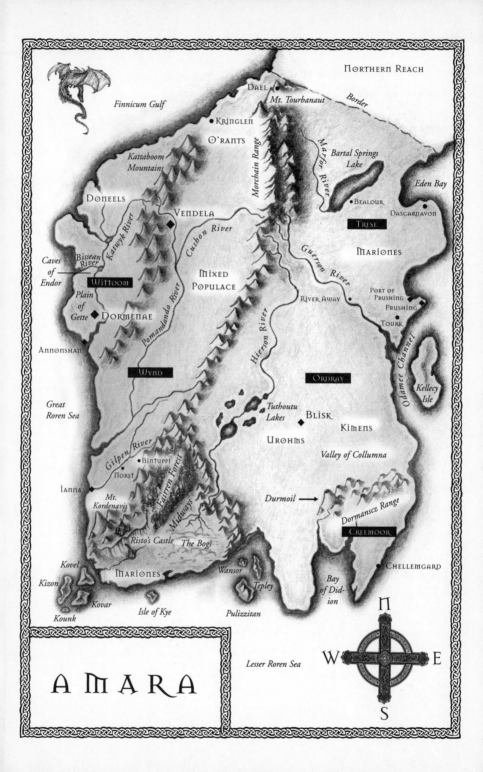

NORTHERN REACH

DAEL

Mt. Tourbanaut

Border

Finnicum Gulf

KRINGLEN

O'RANTS

Kattaboom
Mountains

Morchain Range

Marfor River

Bartal Springs
Lake

Eden Bay

DONEELS

Katwyk River

VENDELA

BEALOUR

DASCARNAVON

Caves
of
Endor

Bissean
River

WITTOOM

Cushon River

MIXED
POPULACE

Gueron River

TRESE

MARIONES

Plain
of
Gette

DORMENAE

Pomandando River

Hierzon River

RIVER AWAY

PORT OF
PRUSHING
PRUSHING

TOURK

Annonshan

WYND

ORDRAY

Odamee Channel

Kellecy
Isle

Great
Roren Sea

Gilpen River

Tuthoutu
Lakes

BLISK

KIMENS

Valley of Collumna

IANNA

Mt.
Kordenavis

BINTUPPI

NORST

Farren Forest

Midways

UROHMS

Durmoil

Dormanscz Range

CREEMOOR

Risto's Castle

The Bogs

MARIONES

Wansor

CHELLEMGARD

Kovel

Kizon

Kovar

Kounk

Isle of Kye

Tepley

Pulizzitan

Bay
of Did-
ion

N

W   E

S

AMARA

Lesser Roren Sea

PART · ONE

PALADIN'S CALL

SABBATICAL

"People. Always too many people."

Only the leathery beat of Greer's dragon wings answered Bardon's observation. Cool air rushed against Bardon's face, blowing away the cares of three intense years of training and study.

He squeezed his knees into the riding hooks and leaned forward across the major dragon's neck. Brisk mountain air rose off the snow-topped mountain and blew his dark hair back from his pale face. Soon he should be able to spot the valley Sir Dar had recommended. He needed time alone. The first part of his sabbatical would be spent in isolation.

Bardon put a hand on Greer's purple scales and communicated his desire to locate a lake shaped like a boot.

Looking down at the forested slopes, he speculated on how many of the seven high races populated the area. A smile spread across his face. It was likely that not one civilized being walked this southern part of the Morchain Mountain Range for a hundred miles in any direction.

He saw a ropma scurry across a rocky stream.

"Don't worry, fella. I won't bother you if you don't bother me. I'm taking a break from everyone, both high and low races."

Greer rumbled in his throat, and Bardon placed a hand on the amethystine scales of his dragon's neck. "No, I'm not running away from you, my friend. And in truth, I'm not really running away from civilization. I just need a sabbatical, a long sabbatical."

Ahead, two peaks stood taller than the rest. Bardon mentally guided the major dragon toward the landmark Dar had given him. He thought about the parting from the wise little doneel.

The room had bustled with activity like all the rooms in Castle Pelacce. Dar had taken Bardon aside to speak words of encouragement and instruction, but the constant commotion intruded on their conversation.

"I'm proud of you, Bardon." Dar's small furry hand had rested on his squire's arm. "You've developed a gracious social presence. I know it's been hard for you, but I consider it one of your greatest accomplishments."

Inwardly, Bardon had cringed when a woman's piercing laugh rose over the clucking babble of a small group of ladies. Squire Bardon glanced at Sir Dar. He couldn't speak of his concern to the knight he admired so much. Every day Bardon underwent a great struggle to project that image of serenity Sir Dar assumed was real.

He thinks too well of me. The young man wrestled with a truth he did not like. *After three years, this knight-in-training is only better at hiding his uneasiness.*

I find the social life Sir Dar thrives on to be overwhelming. Bardon looked around at the gregarious crowd. Sir Dar smiled sincerely at a mari-one's comment as he passed. The squire wished they had chosen a secluded spot for this conversation. But the Castle Pelacce boiled with activity in every quarter.

When does a day pass that someone, important or not, isn't visiting? Dozens of outsiders, along with the bustling staff, roam these hallways.

While his mentor gazed fondly at a group of giggling women, Bardon watched the finely dressed, diminutive doneel ladies and strove to keep his face neutral. *I've given up trying to keep Sir Dar's extended family straight. Are those cousins? I can't remember who's who. There are dozens of families, not just dozens of individuals.*

The uncomfortable memory faded. Bardon put aside the aggravation of court life as Greer passed between the two peaks and headed south. The rough terrain beneath them looked even more uninhabited.

I'm thankful this time of reflection is required before I take my final vow to Paladin. I'm already enjoying the peace of being out of civilization. Noth-ing within the city compares with the beauty I beheld last night as I watched the heavens from my campsite. Even the stars seemed to celebrate my freedom. That comet rising from the southwestern horizon may be my herald of a contented sabbatical.

I can be gone from a month to a year. At this point, I intend to take every day of a whole year to relish the isolation. Searching my soul as I count the cost of this alliance is only part of what I must examine.

Bardon stroked Greer's neck. By using the wordless communication of mindspeaking common to a rider and his dragon, the squire often confided his thoughts to his dragon. The young squire was well aware that his closest companion already knew every detail of his life. Nonetheless, when he talked to Greer, he didn't feel like he indulged in melancholy musings. Friendly chats with the droll dragon often lifted his spirits.

Bardon gazed at the unpopulated mountain region. He would have to guard against falling into self-pity. The solemn reality of his lonely life threatened to accompany him on his chance for a relaxed time of meditation.

I lived at The Hall from the time I was six, he told Greer, *until I was eighteen—a dozen years in a room with five other occupants. Dormitory life doesn't allow much time for solitude. I don't mind telling you, Greer, I crave really being alone.*

Greer beat his powerful wings and rose several hundred feet to soar over a broad mountaintop. On the other side stretched a highland valley, cradling a long lake.

"That water looks to be the shape of a boot." Bardon leaned over the neck of his mount. "Sir Dar said the cabin is on the east side, close to the heel."

Greer banked and headed for the eastern shore at the southernmost end of the clear lake. Clouds reflected in the blue water, and as Greer passed over, an image of the dragon's purple body and cobalt wings glided across the rippling surface.

They landed on the shoreline where stubby grass and tiny, fragrant, white mountain flowers covered the bank for twenty yards before undersized trees erupted in dense woods. The vegetation grew lush because of a long tropical growing season but was short due to the altitude.

A one-level, split-log cabin sat at the edge of the forest.

Bardon swung his leg over the saddle horn, unhooked his other leg, and slid to the ground. With hands much practiced at his task, he unbuckled the straps of the saddle and laid it and the saddle packs on the ground. The young squire stood with his fists on his hips and surveyed the peaceful scene.

Greer stretched out his wings and shook them with a rattle of the thin leather hide. He then tucked them close to his body and rolled in the sweet-scented grass. When his itches were subdued, he strolled to the edge of the lake and took a deep drink. The dragon lifted his head with water dripping from his chin and looked back at his rider.

"Yes," agreed Bardon. "I bet some very big fish swim in these waters."

He picked up two bundles of personal belongings, leaving the other gear to stow later. Right now he wanted to inspect what would be his secluded home for the next few months. He would read the books he'd brought, contemplate life, and seek Wulder's presence, hoping for a clear direction. Should he be a knight after all these years of preparation, or should he settle into a less demanding occupation?

Bardon walked slowly, in no hurry to commence these weighty meditations. He'd been so sure knighthood was his calling. Obviously, his unknown father had desired this future for his son, or he wouldn't have left him at The Hall. But as Bardon trained under Sir Dar, he began to realize that the lofty words *servant to Paladin* actually meant "servant to mankind."

The idea of serving the noble ruler of Amara had a pristine quality to it. In reality, this serving meant forever dealing with the sullied high races. Instead of walking on a more elevated plane than the average citizen, Bardon found himself mingling with and humbling himself for an unappreciative, uneducated, ratty populace.

"People," he muttered. "Way too many people."

He reached the door of the cabin, and without putting down either bundle, he awkwardly lifted the latch. He nudged the heavy wooden plank open with his foot and stepped into the dimly lit room. His nose twitched. He smelled what could have been a hot meal eaten not long before. With shoulders tensed, he lowered his burden to the floor and put a hand on his sword hilt.

The cabin didn't feel right. Abandoned for over a year, the interior should have had a musty odor. Dust motes floated in sunbeams shining through polished windows. A door stood open to a small bedroom.

Bardon crossed the main room silently and peered in at two made beds. A simple dress hung on a peg on the wall. A set of shelves held other feminine clothing folded neatly.

He scanned the room. No one lurked in the shadows. He turned to search the rest of the small cabin. Two other rooms didn't seem to be in use. But it was abundantly clear the kitchen area and the sitting room had accommodated someone earlier in the day.

He marched out of the house and asked Greer if he had seen or heard anyone in the immediate vicinity. The dragon had not, but took to the sky for a scouting trip. The young squire soon had an answer.

What do you mean, 'uh-oh'? Bardon glared at the flying dragon. *Two women, one very old and one young?* He frowned. *What are they doing?*

Bardon didn't appreciate the dragon's comments on how delicious the berries would be when the women returned with two basketfuls.

I doubt they are picking enough to satisfy your appetite.

He turned on his heel and tramped back into the house, snatching up his bundles as he went through the door.

Sir Dar gave me permission to occupy this house, and this is where I am going to stay! These women are certainly not here because they were invited.

He carried his possessions through the sitting room and into the second unoccupied bedroom. He tossed the bags on the bed and went out to haul in the rest of his provisions. In a deliberate surge of activity, he stowed all his belongings. Then, packing a wire, a bottle with a cork stopper, and a hunk of cheese in a knapsack, he went out to the lake. He stopped to whack off a slender, five-foot-long branch from a borling tree, then picked off its smaller limbs as he walked.

The nutty scent of the wood soothed his agitation. Survival skills had been his favorite part of training. He relished the fresh air, the music of woodland noises, and the busyness of living off the land.

I will enjoy these months alone. At this moment, I will focus on what is at hand.

Thank You, Wulder, for Your gift of this time and this place.

A rock outcropping jutted into the water. Bardon clambered over a pile of smooth boulders and sat on a ledge. Settling into a comfortable position with his feet dangling over the water, he pulled out a string and the wire from his pocket. With nimble fingers, he fashioned a hook from the wire and attached it to the string, then the string to the pole. In a matter of minutes, he threw a fishing line with the cork from his bottle into the water.

Greer ambled toward the rocky ridge to sit within a few yards on the grassy bank. Bardon tried to ignore the ripple of amusement coming from the dragon's mind.

"Why don't you go fishing?" he asked.

The dragon stretched his neck over the water.

"Not here!" Bardon jerked his line and jutted his chin out toward the long expanse of shoreline. "Go to the other end of the lake. Sir Dar said the water is quite deep there."

Greer looked to the north and then over his shoulder at the stunted forest.

"No," said Bardon. "I don't need you to stay and help greet the ladies." He paused to absorb the dragon's response. "I am *not* in a foul mood, and I will not catch any fish with you hanging over my shoulder. Go have your dinner and let me catch mine."

Greer spread his wings and abruptly took off, but not before Bardon heard the rumble in his throat that indicated the dragon was laughing at his rider.

Bardon ducked as a draft from the strong, leathery wings nearly knocked him off his rocky perch. But Greer's good humor dispersed the last of his rider's prickly temper. By the time Bardon looked up to see his friend soaring above the mountain lake, a grin had replaced his scowl.

He pulled in his line, reset the bait, and cast his hook into the water. Then he leaned back against the rocky ledge and watched Greer rather than the cork floating in the placid lake below.

The purple dragon circled over the lake. One moment he spiraled in a lazy pattern, the next, he tucked his wings and plummeted into the water. He came out again, stretching his neck skyward, flapping his wings, and leaving a waterfall of droplets cascading from his body. Even across the distance, Bardon felt the satisfaction that pulsed through the dragon as he swallowed his catch.

Bardon's gaze locked on Greer as the dragon repeated the performance many times. The dragon didn't feed every day, but when he did, he ate until sated. With the close connection between dragon and rider, Bardon grew more and more content as his friend satisfied his hunger. He leaned against the sun-warmed rock and sighed. Even if he had to eat hardtack tonight instead of fried fish, he would be immeasurably happier here than at the busy Castle Pelacce in the heart of bustling Dormenae.

Bardon wiggled his foot, feeling as if a muscle in his calf had drawn taut. The cramp intensified. He opened his eyes and sat up. Around the circumference of his lower leg, a writher snake had coiled its two-inch-thick, moss green body.

Bardon held his breath. Writher snakes, though small in circumference, had muscles that were strong like cables, teeth like razors, and a reputation for drowning their victims. Bardon wondered how old this writher might be. Legend said they grew five feet longer every year, but never any thicker. This one's tail still hung beneath the surface of the lake.

With its head lifted, the snake's pale eyes gazed dispassionately at its victim. A black, forked tongue flickered, tasting the air. Hissing with an odd cadence like the humming of a song, the serpent bobbed its head to and fro.

Bardon eased his hand to his waist, where a leather sheath held his hunting knife. The creature flinched and drew back toward the water, squeezing its victim's leg and pulling him toward death. The snake paused, flicked its tongue, bobbed its head, and stared at the face of its prey.

Bardon's fingers inched over the finely braided leather loop that secured the large knife. With no other part of his body moving, he pushed a finger under the catch and freed the blade. He took a slow, steadying breath and tensed for the one attempt he would have to kill the beast. He whipped the blade out in a smooth motion and swung to slice off the snake's head. The snake dodged the knife and struck at Bardon's leg. His boot saved him from the serpent's bite. The tough leather tore, but the teeth did not penetrate.

The snake jerked, tightening its grip, and moved toward the water. As if understanding the threat of the knife, it laid its head along its victim's inner knee, too close to the rock for Bardon to reach without slicing his own leg.

Flipping onto his stomach, Bardon tried to find something to hang on to, something to help him resist being dragged beneath the cold waters. He dug the fingers of one hand and the knife in the other hand against the hard surface of the rock. The stone gave no purchase. He slid farther as the snake pulled.

Bardon knew just when Greer recognized his rider's distress and flew toward the south end of the lake. The amount of fish he'd eaten slowed his flight. His movements would be sluggish, but the dragon would not abandon his rider.

Again the snake yanked backward, and Bardon fell off the rock. Just before his head splashed beneath the surface, he heard the enraged battle cry of a dragon above him and a feminine screech of horror from the shore.

Entangled

Bardon kicked at the coil around his leg with his free foot, trying to pound the snake's body into loosening its grip. Directly above him, the impact of a massive body entering the water announced Greer had come to his rescue.

A cloud of bubbles surrounded the squire, obscuring his vision. A moment later, his descent abruptly reversed. He whooshed out of the lake, dangling upside down, still entangled in the long snake. Greer held the serpent in his mouth and flew toward shore.

Water streamed from Bardon's hair. He swiped at his eyes with one hand and glanced up. The snake coiled around his leg, its head battering the leather of his boot. The length of the writher's body dangled from Greer's mouth. Bardon estimated the creature's body stretched twenty feet between his foot and Greer's teeth. Bardon looked down at the rippling surface of the lake, then at the rocky shore as Greer gained height. The piles of rounded stones did not look like a comfortable place to set down. He desperately hoped the serpent would *not* let go of his leg now.

Seconds later, the dragon banked over the grassy expanse before the cabin. Bardon bent in half at the waist. Still holding his hunting knife, he grabbed the snake's body as if it were a rope and hauled himself up to Greer's head. Clinging to the dragon's neck, he braced himself for the landing.

Thanks, Greer.

In return for his expression of gratitude, Bardon listened to a tirade on the foul taste of writher snakes and the unpleasant feel of serpent scales rubbing against the tongue.

As soon as the dragon's feet hit the ground, he spat the offending reptile from his mouth. Bardon's back struck the grassy bank with a thud, knocking the air out of his lungs. The knife flew from his grasp, landing out of reach. As he labored to breathe, a frantic young woman rushed toward him with an ax raised above her head. He wheezed, struggling for just one breath of air while the snake's hold tightened around his leg.

His eyes followed the young woman's helter-skelter dash toward him with that large ax brandished. He emphatically desired to get away from the snake and out of the path of the ax-wielder, but all he could do was hack and gasp. She stumbled, and the blade of her weapon barely missed his leg.

Sitting up, Bardon finally drew several breaths of bracing air. He tried to move away from the figure sprawled on the grass beside him, but the snake lurched toward the lake and dragged him along.

Greer!

The dragon whipped around, his tail flattening a bush. He examined the situation, gave a huge sigh, and reluctantly placed one large forefoot on the slithering beast.

His dragon friend's surge of disgust washed over Bardon. He thought Greer's abhorrence of snakes would be laughable if he'd been free of the creature wrapped around his leg.

Back on her feet and armed again with the ax, the young woman charged in between Bardon and Greer. She swung the ax above her head and, as it came down, let out a frightful screech. Bardon grimaced and covered his ears. The serpent jerked, the coil around Bardon's leg relaxed, and he shook the body of the snake loose. Dark purple blood spurted from the two ends of the severed flesh.

Greer removed his foot from the twitching snake body and backed away from the creature. The young woman scrambled back as well. Tears ran down blotchy red cheeks, and her chest heaved as she sobbed. An older woman stood by the forest's edge with a serene expression fixed upon her dark face.

Bardon pushed wet locks away from his eyes and studied the emerlindian. *A granny?*

She smiled. *"Yes, a granny. Granny Kye."*

Annoyed that she had heard his thought, Bardon carefully guarded his expression. He could also guard his thoughts after working with Kale on his mindspeaking abilities while they had been on a mission together three years ago. His talent was minimal next to hers. He put the guard in place so that this granny would not know how frustrated he was by the presence of these women.

He struggled to his feet, tried to stamp some circulation back into his numb leg, and straightened his tunic. Chagrined that in spite of all his training, a girl and a dragon had just rescued him, Bardon bent in an awkward bow. The court polish of three years deserted him.

I am not a callow lad, and I will not stutter words I've repeated many times before.

He smiled with all the charm he could muster. "I'm pleased to meet you, Granny Kye."

"And I, you. I have been expecting you."

The younger emerlindian, her pale skin still flushed, turned unbelieving slate blue eyes on the older woman. "Grandmother, you never said."

Bardon almost missed her words as he watched those thickly fringed eyes grow as dark as storm clouds.

Granny Kye chuckled. "I don't tell you everything, infant." She turned to Bardon. "This wild child is N'Rae."

Bardon turned to N'Rae. Her beauty astonished him. Even in plain clothing, she outshone all the fair ladies of court. He straightened his tunic again and managed a more polished bow. "My pleasure."

She glanced away, then down. Bardon decided she was younger than he'd first thought. Probably a little younger than his friend Kale. But where Dragon Keeper Kale Allerion had a determined expression about her eyes and in the tilt of her chin, this fair maiden resembled a lost kitten. Splashes of dark purple blood covered the front of her homespun dress, looking incongruous on someone who radiated such innocence.

Bardon wanted to see the unusual color of her eyes again and spoke softly, hoping she'd glance up at him. "Thank you for saving my life."

She did look up. A moment before, the hue of her eyes had reflected stormy clouds. Now the vivid blue matched the sky above. "I didn't know what to do. I hate snakes!"

Bardon felt a shudder of agreement from Greer's mind, and he glanced over at the dragon to see him giving N'Rae a nod of approval. At the moment, Bardon wasn't too fond of snakes, either. And he'd never been too fond of people. Even a fetching female and a wise old woman were more company than he desired. He turned to the granny.

"I am Bardon, squire to Sir Dar of Castle Pelacce, in Dormenae, Wittoom."

"A squire?" N'Rae almost looked impressed, but she shook her head, causing her long, white-blond tresses to swing. With a sigh that took the stiffness out of her shoulders so they drooped in defeat, she stared again at the ground. "It's a shame you aren't a knight. We could use a knight." Her chin lifted, and she looked to the granny. "Actually, we could use Paladin's army, but Grandmother says we are to accomplish our task with the resources Wulder provides."

The old woman nodded. "And Wulder has provided Squire Bardon."

"Wait." He held up a hand and slowly shook his head. "I'm entering into my sabbatical. I'm charged to devote myself to meditation. I cannot undertake to aid you in any endeavor at this time."

N'Rae turned away from him, gave a little gasp, and pointed a finger at Greer. "Oh dear, that was dinner."

The dragon lifted his nose from the dropped baskets of berries by the forest edge. His long, blue tongue licked the last of the smashed purple goo from his lips. He blinked and focused on his rider.

Bardon frowned at Greer but turned a pleasant face to the two ladies and delivered the message his dragon had impressed into his mind. "Greer wishes to offer his apologies. When it comes to food, he has very little willpower. We have provisions we will gladly share."

His thoughts turned back to the dragon. *Those are my provisions you're offering, and this isn't helping to remove these interlopers from the cabin. Do you have any suggestions on how to get rid of them?*

Greer turned his back on his rider and strolled down to the shore. He launched into the air and headed for the northern end of the lake.

Bardon turned back to the women. "Greer will bring back fish for our dinner. I'll drag what's left of this snake far into the woods for scavengers to dispose of."

He fought the urge to clear his throat before he made his next announcement. "The cabin belongs to Sir Dar, and he gave me permission to dwell in it this summer. I hope this doesn't inconvenience you."

Granny Kye smiled. "Not at all, my dear boy, we shall be leaving on our quest within a day or two."

Bardon deliberately shifted his gaze away from the bright brown, knowing eyes of the emerlindian.

Not with me! he protested. He strolled into the cabin to retrieve his sword. He wouldn't be caught unarmed again. When he came out, he nodded to the women and picked up his hunting knife and sheathed it. With the head section of the snake's carcass in one hand and the long body in the other, he marched into the trees. His stride lengthened as he determined to banish a persistent nagging in his heart.

I am not required to do anything for these females.

THREE!

Bardon dragged the snake's body farther into the woods than was necessary. With every step, he pondered the question of what his reaction should be to these two inconvenient women.

Gracious Wulder, by Sir Dar's example, I know that when someone is in need, that need takes precedence over any personal plan. So, here I quibble. Where it would be expected to set aside a personal plan, it would be unacceptable to ignore a mandate from You. Is my sabbatical a personal plan or a divine assignment?

The snake's body snagged on a bush, jerking Bardon to a halt. He turned and yanked. It didn't budge. He walked back, held the lower branches back with his foot, and pulled. The bush let go, and he trudged on along the narrow path. He entered a forest glade and headed for the other side.

You and I both know that there really aren't two choices, but only one. You wouldn't have put this need in my path if You didn't want me to react as You've taught me. I will do as You require.

The hair on the back of his neck stood up. Bardon unsheathed his sword at the first rumbling growl. He let the dead weight of the snake slip from his fingers and took a step backward. Crouching with his weapon ready, he looked into the cool yellow eyes of a five-foot-long mountain cat. Just within the line of trees, the animal pressed its entire body close to the ground, legs bent, ready to pounce. Golden stripes adorned the animal's tan hide. The cat's tufted ears lay back against its skull. With its lips pulled back, the wild beast's snarl showed pointed teeth.

"I am *really* not in the mood for this, cat."

A growl vibrated through the meadow. The cat's tail swept back and forth across the forest floor.

"Wouldn't you like this snake for dinner? You can have it. My treat."

The cat stepped forward.

"Believe me, the snake would be a tastier, easier dinner."

He inched back. The cat inched closer.

Bardon sighed. He flexed his fingers on the hilt of the sword. The weapon had been crafted by Wizard Fenworth and placed in Bardon's hand by Paladin himself. On the occasions he'd had to use the sword, it had never failed him. Sometimes, he thought Fenworth had embedded special powers within the weapon. Other times, he thought Wulder had blessed the blade for righteousness. But killing a mountain cat over a dead snake did not seem to be a noble cause. Still, being eaten seemed less than a noble end to his career as a knight. He pulled his hunting knife out and balanced the two weapons.

Bardon's lip twitched in humor. Greer would tell him this awkward situation was his own fault. "Never mess with a snake," was the dragon's creed.

"Never mess with a mountain cat" is more apropos at the moment.

Where are you, Greer?

He watched the cat as he listened for the mental connection to his dragon. Greer answered readily, having already placed a large giddinfish on the grass in front of the fair N'Rae. As usual, the dragon's take on Bardon's problem sounded impertinent. Bardon concentrated on the wild animal before him as he responded.

I do not think the cat prefers warm-blooded, fresh meat to cold, dead snake. But I prefer not to test your theory. Could you hurry a bit? I want to be out of here before I become its next meal.

He managed to ease backward a few steps before the cat prowled into the meadow. The feline warily approached the serpent carcass, nose quivering, large eyes on the man, not the snake.

Yes, of course I want a ride, Greer. This is ill-timed humor.

The cat didn't come straight at him, but sashayed in zigzag fashion, always with whiskers trembling and eyes fixed on the man. Bardon held his sword and knife ready but hoped Greer would reach them before he had to fight.

He had plenty of battlefield experience. He'd matched prowess with skilled bisonbeck soldiers. He'd engaged many grawligs, and they were barbarous creatures.

One-on-one with a wild cat involves different skills. Wild beasts fight with a finesse lacking in the savage low races. Still, I've fought a trundle bear and won. Bardon shook his head slightly and clenched his weapons. *But trundles are a smallish bear. Not at all in the same class as this beast.* He looked at the magnificent cat, a creation of Wulder, and willed Greer to swoop in over the trees.

The dragon's grumbling rolled through his thoughts, and he answered.

It's not my fault you gorged yourself on fish and berries… I know you like to nap after a feast… I'm not the one who offered to catch dinner for the women… The sooner you get me out of here, the sooner you can stretch out beside the lake and bask in the afternoon sun.

The cat curled its lip and snarled.

Hurry!

He had succeeded in reaching the forest line. The snake's remains lay in two pieces across the middle of the clearing. The cat stopped and sniffed. The animal's head jerked back, its chin lifted to the sky, and it roared.

Shivers surged over Bardon's arms and back. He flexed his fingers on the hilt of the sword, then the hand that held the knife. The muscles across the cat's shoulders bunched. Its paws kneaded the ground.

"Getting ready to attack, aren't you?" Bardon noted his hands squeezing and relaxing on the handles of his weapons, much as the great feline kneaded the turf. The squire grunted. "Well, so am I! But I'd prefer to just go our separate ways. You go have dinner with the snake. I'll go eat fish with the emerlindian ladies."

The cat licked its lips.

"No, kitty." Bardon kept his voice low and soothing. "This is a bad idea."

A rumble emanated from the cat's throat, and it sprang across the dead snake, launching himself directly at the sword. Bardon twirled out of the way, allowing the animal to fly past and crash into the underbrush of the forest. The cat recovered and thrashed out of the branches, leaving a mangled bush behind. It charged Bardon, who stepped aside barely in time. He pricked the cat's shoulder as it went by.

The feline didn't charge again but circled. Bardon carefully kept turning, sword and knife at the ready.

"I didn't want to do that, cat. But you don't appear to be familiar with the high races and their weapons. This blade hurts. You should avoid it."

Leathery wings beat the air above them. The cat snarled and crouched, backing toward the woods.

Bardon sheathed his weapons and waited. Greer landed in front of him, bellowed at the cat, and flashed his large, sharp teeth. His tail lay flat on the ground, pointed directly at his rider. Bardon ran up the incline of the tail, sat high on the dragon's back, and hooked his feet under the shoulder joints of the wings. He pressed his body against the back of Greer's neck and gripped the spikes that protruded from where the dragon's head joined his neck.

Not exactly comfortable because of the ridges running down Greer's back, Bardon nonetheless felt secure. He'd ridden bareback before in many training sessions.

The dragon spread his wings and lifted into the air. The cat darted into the cover of the trees.

That worked. It'll go off and lick that wound I gave it. Possibly, it has learned to be more cautious of the high races. "To the wise one, a prick on the finger avoids a hole in the heart."

Greer snorted and shook his head.

Yes, I know I don't need to quote Wulder to you. It's habit. For three years,

I've had to back up every action of the day to Scribe Moran at the evening vespers. The girder exercise, you know? An act of will must be consciously chosen with principles to support the deed, and ramifications accounted.

The dragon stretched his wings, caught a thermal, and circled. Bardon knew Greer found the tedious girder ritual boring. But the young squire knew it was necessary. The practice forced novices to order their lives, and the exercise prevented chaos. But Greer would not prolong any conversation dealing with girdering.

Yes, I know you have rescued me twice in one day. Pardon me for not expressing my gratitude more promptly... Of course I'm aware that your loyalty is a blessing of great practical value.

The dragon continued to circle, rising higher. Bardon felt the chill as they climbed. With Greer's droll comments still registering in the back of his mind, the squire turned his attention to Wulder. After years of study in The Hall and under Sir Dar, he still didn't have a grasp of what to expect from his Creator.

You've sent me on sabbatical, Wulder. I know You order my days. What is the purpose of a writher snake, a hungry cat, and these women?

Oh, Greer, give it a rest. Let's return to these two women and find out just what their quest is. Maybe they only need an escort down to the valley to market.

Three? Three! Three women?

4

Big Surprises

The aromas of baked bread and fried fish wafting from the cabin did much to improve Bardon's temper. He slid off Greer's back and strode toward the open door. Getting rid of three females shouldn't be much harder than dispensing with two.

I'll find out what this quest of theirs is, then offer to escort them to the nearest town where they can find appropriate help.

He paused.

Greer can't carry three women and me. That means a hike down the mountain. Three days. Bintuppi is the closest town. A walk across the foothills. Best to follow the Gilpen River. Two days. Time consuming, but doable.

He veered off to the well and pumped a bucket of water. A bar of soap sat in an earthen bowl, and a towel hung on the stone siding. Bardon washed his hands and face. He wanted to change his damp clothing, but the meal smelled as though it was ready to serve.

Bardon smoothed his hair over his ears, rebuttoned his tunic, and walked through the door with a smile on his face.

On the kitchen table sat a brown loaf of bread, a platter of fried fish, a bowl of wild greens…and a tiny table. In the chair beside the fist-sized table sat a gray, furry creature wearing a cape. The material oddly resembled the dress N'Rae now wore. A belt woven from thin strips of brightly colored cloth encircled the creature's waist. A long tail wrapped around the carved wooden chair she sat upon.

A plump figure covered with fur, the creature appeared to be more beast than intelligent race. But her tiny black eyes studied him warily, and her face carried an expression of consideration. Between round, stand-up ears sat a bleached mobcap, white, frilly, and completely incongruous. The maids at the castle wore such hats, and Bardon had never figured out why. The head covering did not keep the sun off, hide unruly hair, or look becoming. On the funny little person, the prissy, starched cap looked comical.

Bardon's eyes shifted to Granny Kye, then N'Rae.

Careful, young Squire. He could almost hear Sir Dar's voice in his ear. *Many a test of your ability to be a knight is not in how you tackle grand endeavors, but how you treat a small circumstance.*

Bardon took several steps into the room and bowed before the tiny woman on the table. "I would like to be presented, Mistress."

N'Rae rushed to the table, taking his arm and giving it a little squeeze. He liked the warmth the contact gave him. The young emerlindian radiated friendliness, and the joy in her expression thawed a spot in his heart.

She nodded to the creature on the table. "This is Jue Seeno. She's a minneken from the Isle of Kye."

Isle of Kye? Bardon's eyebrows shot upward. *How could anyone be from an inaccessible island? And didn't that granny say her name is Granny Kye?* He made a concerted effort to tame the surprise he felt.

"How do you do, Mistress Jue Seeno?"

He heard a squeak.

N'Rae tugged at his sleeve. "You'll have to get closer to understand her words."

Bardon knelt beside the table as if he were kneeling before a sovereign of one of the many provinces of Amara.

"I am well. Thank you," said Mistress Seeno with a nod of her head.

Her high-pitched voice barely reached his ears. He leaned forward slightly and cocked his head.

The minneken smiled. "And you?"

Bardon blinked, and a grin spread across his face. "Pardon me, Mistress, but I am trying to remember every bit of geography, history, and folklore of the Isle of Kye. Until this moment, I thought Kye was the name of an inaccessible island."

"It is mostly inaccessible." Her small, twinkling black eyes moved to Granny Kye. When the minneken smiled, a row of tiny white teeth gleamed between thin lips. The front two were quite a bit larger than the rest. "There have always been members of the Kye family who fly in on the strongest dragons. The air currents are as treacherous as the pounding surf battering our sheer cliffs."

"Am I right in assuming that Granny Kye is a member of that family and has visited the Isle?"

"Partially. She is a Kye of Kye Island but was born on the mainland. I don't think she has ever ventured out to our little paradise."

Granny Kye shook her head and placed a hand on her chest. "Oh dear, no. Never."

Jue Seeno tapped her fingertips together, then folded her hands in her lap. "Very rarely does one of the minnekens leave the isle." She preened a bit, one small gray hand touching the collar of her cape. "I believe I'm the first in over five hundred years." Her beady eyes turned back to stare earnestly at the squire. "Most of what you had categorized as folklore, you may now move under history. In talking to N'Rae, who is a woefully ignorant child due to her upbringing, though we're rectifying that"—she smiled briefly at N'Rae—"I've discovered that the folktales among the seven high races concerning the minnekens are based mostly in fact."

Bardon's ears perked up. "That raises a question often debated at The Hall, Mistress Seeno. Wulder created the seven high races, yet no mention is made of how other races came into being. The dragons are intelligent and could be said to be a race. And now that I know minnekens are more than just fable, I wonder how this race came to be."

The tiny lady tilted her head and looked quizzically at the young man kneeling before her.

"Wulder is the Creator of all," she said.

"I agree."

"The books He has given to guide and instruct deal with this land. There is no reason why they would mention the creation of life in other places."

"What other places, Mistress Seeno?"

"Places too far to imagine." She smoothed her shiny gray fur with tiny hands. "And this is a conversation for after dinner over a cup of tea, under a starlit sky in summer, or by the hearth in winter."

N'Rae stirred beside him. "Now that you are accustomed to her voice, your ears should be able to make out her words from a greater distance."

Bardon stood and faced her. "How great a distance?"

She grinned. "Four, maybe five feet." Then she scowled. "I'm not so totally ignorant."

"I'm sure you aren't."

"My mother and I lived with a band of ropma for many years. My mother educated me. We didn't have books to read, but she told me everything she could remember."

He looked at her gentle face and asked, "You lived with ropma?"

"Yes, I liked them. But after Mother died, they became afraid that I would endanger their band by being with them."

"How could you do that?"

Granny Kye carried a pot of tea to the table. "We'll talk of that as we eat. Sit, children."

After Granny asked Wulder's blessing on their food and fellowship, they passed around the simple fare. Heavy crockery served as their dinnerware. The bowl from which the minneken ate looked like an acorn cap. Her tin drinking cup had no handle. Miniscule eating utensils were also fashioned out of tin.

The tea in Bardon's mug tasted spicy. The dark brew warmed his throat and took the edge off his trepidation concerning these women. He bit into a chunk of bread and savored the sweet, nutty taste. His appetite awakened, and for a few minutes, he concentrated on enjoying the food.

He noticed the silence around the table. He rarely ate alone and expected chatter during the meal. In the palace dining hall, rapid social prattle would have accompanied each repast. Bardon would answer appropriately but allow those more skilled in social graces to carry the conversation. When out on expeditions, the men swapped stories. Bardon listened well.

Shifting uncomfortably, he wondered if he should initiate a conversation. He wiped his mouth with the napkin provided. "So, how long have you been staying in the mountains?"

"We spent the winter here," said N'Rae.

"Alone?"

"Grandmother is never alone for long. We had visitors every week. Sometimes twice in one week. They came through the gateway."

"Sir Dar didn't mention a gateway."

"It's in the cellar. Have you ever been through a gateway? I thought I would suffocate."

Bardon thought Sir Dar had left out several important details about this little cabin getaway. Perhaps one of them was the presence of the ladies. He practiced his court calm and answered civilly.

"Yes, I have. It's uncomfortable but an expedient way to travel across the continent." Bardon slowly ate the rest of his fish, then put down his fork. "I think it's time you ladies tell me what service you require of me."

"An escort to the Northern Reach," stated Granny Kye.

"We're going to rescue my father," said N'Rae.

Oh, is that all? Bardon couldn't keep the sarcasm out of his thoughts. *And what outrageous ideas does this little minneken have?* The squire leveled his eye upon the smallest member of their party.

Mistress Seeno solemnly returned his gaze. "I have been charged to be N'Rae's protector."

His training in diplomacy had, indeed, been effective. He didn't sputter the absurdity of a three-inch-tall, rodentlike lady being anyone's protector. He also managed to stifle an immediate objection to a journey starting at the southernmost region of Amara and proceeding past the northern border into a barren, sparsely populated land. Instead, he posed a question, hoping for a rational answer.

"Who is your father?" he asked N'Rae. "What are we rescuing him from?"

"My father is Sir Jilles. Wizard Risto holds him captive."

"Risto is dead."

N'Rae squirmed in her seat. "Well, yes. We had heard that. But the stronghold is now under the possession of Crim Cropper and Burner Stox. I guess I should have said that *they* now hold him captive. But he was first taken prisoner by Risto."

Bardon crossed his arms over his chest. *If Sir Jilles's capture is common knowledge, why hasn't someone else made an effort to penetrate this stronghold and bring out the prisoner?* "Why have you chosen this time to begin the quest?"

Granny Kye poured more tea into each mug. "The knights have been under Risto's spell for many years. At the end of the appointed time, the spell must be renewed, or they will die. Risto is dead, as you pointed out. However, the spell remains intact until the Wizards' Plume blazes across the heavens and passes beneath the Eye of the North."

Bardon recalled the beautiful new addition he had seen in the sky only the night before. "This Wizards' Plume wouldn't be a comet rising from the southwest, would it?"

"Yes, indeed," Granny Kye smiled at him. "You've seen it?"

Bardon managed a polite smile in return. "Yes, I have." *So much for a harbinger of peace and contentment.*

Granny Kye offered tea to Mistress Seeno, and the minneken declined. "Crim Cropper and Burner Stox may not know the particulars of renewing the spell. They may not even remember that the chamber holds sleeping warriors. They may not care to interrupt their own enterprises to journey to the north. We intend to undo the spell and bring the knights home."

"Knights? There is more than one knight in this chamber?"

Granny Kye nodded. "We don't know exactly how many, but our resources indicate quite a few."

Kale's father! He's been missing for years. Kale's mother said he was under Risto's spell. Perhaps he, too, is in this chamber.

Bardon leaned forward. "How have you acquired this information?"

The minneken piped up. "See, a sensible young man. Thinks things through. Wants all the facts up front." She pointed a finger at N'Rae. "Take note."

Granny Kye patted her granddaughter's arm but spoke to the young squire. "I have been working for years to find the right contacts. You see, Sir Jilles is my son. He was captured by Risto and enchanted. His older brother Joffa went to his rescue. Joffa first intended to transport his own lady and child to a safe haven. However, as the family left their estate, they were attacked, and all were killed."

"So," said N'Rae with a sigh, "Grandmother and my mother lost Uncle Joffa and all hope of saving my father."

Bardon forced himself to remain still. The women's story made him want to squirm. Or maybe it was the instinct to spring to his feet and vow to avenge the loss of this family that made him squirm. He would not jump into their wild scheme.

"Why not give the information to Paladin?" he asked. "Paladin would take interest in your plight and provide a party to carry out the rescue."

The old emerlindian nodded her head. "We have petitioned him, and he gave us permission to rescue my son."

"Gave his permission? He won't send a questing party?"

"The questing party is now being organized."

Bardon sighed his relief and sat back. His curiosity toyed with some of the other aspects of his tablemates' backgrounds.

"N'Rae and her mother were hiding while they lived with the ropma?" he asked.

"Yes," answered Granny Kye.

"I've only met one ropma. His name was Dirt."

N'Rae smiled. "That is a very common name among them. So are Bug, Stick, Rock, and Leaf."

"Um…Dirt possessed a very simple mind."

"They all do," N'Rae agreed. "And they are easily frightened. But they are generally kind and shared everything they had with us."

"They lived in houses?"

"More like huts."

"And clothing?"

"Simple weaving."

"Food?"

"Vegetarian."

"And Lady Jilles protected the band as long as she was alive?"

"Yes."

N'Rae glanced away. "She cloaked our presence so no one could see us except the ropma."

"And you couldn't continue after her death?" Bardon asked. "She didn't teach you how?"

The minneken spoke up in her high-pitched voice. "Singularly untalented, essentially inept, remarkably...clumsy. But we're working on these shortcomings. N'Rae has made admirable progress."

Bardon looked with compassion on the young woman. Being raised among the ropma must have been trying. "How did your mother die, N'Rae?"

Her expression saddened. "She coughed all winter and then into the spring. One morning, she didn't wake up."

That's too much for a young girl alone. N'Rae certainly needs to be reunited with her father. Granny Kye should have her son back. Bardon stifled a sigh of resignation.

"All right," said Bardon. "I'll join you. Who is in charge of your quest?"

Granny Kye patted his hand. "I believe you are, dear."

5

Questions

Wulder, is this a test?

Bardon paced along the shore. Moonlight danced on a path across the lake. Breezes carried the perfume of pines and the sweet mountain flower azrodhan. The vine cascaded over a rocky hillock near the shoreline. Greer dozed, curled up on the grassy bank. And sitting to the left of one of the peaks in the southwestern range, the Wizards' Plume hung as if immobile for the moment in its climb through the night sky.

He could not sleep, although those in the cabin had gone to bed hours before.

Turning away from the taunting Wizards' Plume, Bardon focused on his thoughts. He had too many questions about the design behind this latest turn of events.

If this is a test, what is being tested? Can I exhibit noble instincts when my teachers are not around? Or perhaps this is a test of discernment. Should I recognize this to be an irrational endeavor and avoid it?

Pardon me, Wulder, I mean no disrespect. I'm just frustrated. I'm willing to do whatever You demand of me, but I'm not certain escorting these women to some unknown destination in the Northern Reach is really Your plan.

You know what I'm thinking and even what I am trying not to think. He sighed and thrust his fists deep into his pockets. Looking up, he admired the beautiful starlit sky but avoided looking at the southwestern firmament. Wulder deserved a servant who knew what he was doing.

I want this to be from Your hand. The truth is I'm excited to go on an adventure rather than spend hours upon hours pondering life's choices. In spite of all the noise I've made about this time alone…

He strolled over to the sleeping dragon. Greer snored, ruffling the blades of grass in front of his chin. His breath smelled distinctly of fish. Bardon wrinkled his nose, moved to the back of the dragon's neck, and folded his body to sit on the lawn. He rested against Greer's shoulder. The animal didn't even flinch. Bardon crossed his arms over his chest, noticing that the wrestling match with the writher snake had left him sore.

Tonight he wrestled with a weightier problem.

Wulder, I'm trying to be honest with myself here. You know I was much better practicing weaponry than sitting in chapel. I sat there looking attentive, but I longed for sword practice and archery. I enjoyed digging through the library and putting together a paper much more than listening to a lecture by one of the scribes. I'm more comfortable doing. Physical doing. Intellectual doing. Grand Dost said it was because when I was idle, I delved into my deeper consciousness and that was abhorrent to me. He said that was just why I needed the sabbatical more than the others.

Yes! I would rather go on this quest than stay here and face my own ponderings about my future.

He closed his eyes but still did not relax.

And I shall not discount a definite feeling of pride in thinking You have chosen me to do this impossible task. But have You chosen me? Am I willing to do this because I want to be a hero, or because I want to be a servant?

Bardon chuckled. He leaned his head back against Greer's leathery hide and grinned. He remembered how shocked he had been when Dar announced over a campfire that doing a righteous deed for a wrong reason was not such a bad thing. The two of them had gone to great lengths to track down a widow's foolish son and deliver him home. They didn't do it for a noble reason. They'd done it because his mother was such a pest, constantly accosting them as they rode past her cottage. Eventually, they took a different route to avoid her. Then she had shown up at court to petition aid.

"You see, young Squire," Sir Dar had said as he stirred a pot of magrattin soup, "when we came across the boy, he was tired of his reckless living and really wanted an excuse to go home. We obliged. Now he's accepted his role in life. His mother is happy, no longer lonely. I foresee this young man becoming a good farmer and contributing to the community. And it is all because we went out to do the right thing for the wrong reason."

That had been two summers before, and the young squire had seen on numerous occasions his mentor do the right thing with no proper motivation.

"Wulder is pleased," Sir Dar had said, "when you do the right thing even without the inspiration of a noble purpose. Intellectually, you recognize the righteous rationale. You have the good sense to do the good deed, even if your heart, full of folly, has claimed a less noble basis for action. I doubt that you get the abundant reward that Wulder would have bestowed on you for the same action done with a pure heart. Nonetheless, I'm sure He is pleased at the end results."

Three years of intense training to always choose the more honorable course, and still I have to consciously make the decision to help where help is needed.

He eased his leg into a more comfortable position and rubbed the calf muscle where the snake had grabbed him. He looked up at the multitude of stars and wished the doneel statesman were with him now. The Wizards' Plume now graced a spot a tiny bit closer to the top of that southwestern mountain peak.

"Sir Dar, I would like to hear you say again, 'There can be as many wrong reasons to do the right thing as there are stars in the sky. There might even be more than one legitimate right reason. But there is never a right reason to do the wrong thing. Not ever.'"

He watched the sky for some time, even saw a shooting star. When the mountain air became too chilly for comfort, he rose to his feet and strode to his bed. The secluded house sheltered three women, when it was supposed to be his sanctuary for several months.

Bardon sat on the only chair in his small sleeping chamber and pulled off his boots. He lay down on top of the covers, his hands behind his neck.

What would be a proper principle for the happenings of this day? One readily surfaced in his mind. *"Wulder gives His servants their needs according to His wisdom, not by the reasoning of man." Principle thirty-nine.*

+———+

The next morning, a cloud cloaked the lake and valley. Tiny whiffs of air swirled the white vapor as Bardon made a tour of the clearing's circumference. He found no unusual animal signs, and Greer reported nothing had interrupted his sleep. Of course, that didn't signify much. Bardon had known his dragon to sleep through thunderclaps that woke wine-sodden ne'er-do-wells.

The young man climbed over the rocky projection toward the water. The dragon skimmed the surface of the lake and landed next to him.

"Let's go for a swim, Greer."

Bardon tossed a bundle to the ground. He pulled off his tunic and shirt and sat down to work on his boots.

"No, I'm not changing into court dress to impress the ladies. I'm cleaning up to be more comfortable. I feel like I was dragged through a lake backward."

Greer bobbed his head, and a rumble emanated from his throat.

"Thank you, Greer. I appreciate your evaluation of my comedic attempt. I, too, think my sense of humor is developing nicely."

Having shed the rest of his clothing, Bardon snatched up his bar of soap and dove into the chilly water. Greer followed, wading into the lake. The mist hovered over the water, thinning and eddying and lifting as the sun grew stronger. By the time blue sky canopied the lake from one rim of mountain peaks to the other, Bardon was walking up the grassy slope to the cabin. He presented himself, freshly groomed and dressed in the best he'd brought with him, at the breakfast table. In the back of his mind, he heard Greer chiding him about his gussied-up appearance.

Mistress Seeno twitched her nose at him, her whiskers bouncing. "You don't smell quite so fishy this morning," she squeaked.

Bardon smiled from his place beside her. He felt more confident in clean clothes, when freshly shaven, and with his hair in place. N'Rae brought dishes to the table. He caught her eye and winked.

"None of that," said Jue Seeno. "The girl's too young and senseless to be attaching herself to the likes of you."

Bardon ignored her, and as soon as Granny Kye took her seat, he addressed Wulder.

"We thank You for this food and for the hands that prepared it. We ask for guidance in every step of this day. By Your might and wisdom, may we live and breathe."

They ate turtle-egg brouna and a pastry filled with razterberry jam. The brouna had herbs, cheese, and wild onions folded within it.

"This is delicious, Granny Kye. Thank you," said Bardon after swallowing the first bite.

"I only cooked it," she answered. "Mistress Seeno put it together."

Bardon nodded at the minneken. "Thank you, Mistress."

"You're welcome, I'm sure." She spoke the words formally, preening again, touching her collar in a manner that indicated she was pleased. The minneken nodded at N'Rae. "The girl helped, of course."

N'Rae looked down at her plate, a pale rosy glow rising to her cheeks.

After eating the last pastry and draining his mug, Bardon shoved his chair back from the table and rested his hands on its edge. "We must make plans."

The three women looked to him attentively.

"We need a map and transportation. Greer cannot carry us all. And unless we have an idea of where we are going, there is no sense in departing. We shall acquire the map, then decide the best means of getting there."

The women nodded their heads in agreement.

"Fine." Bardon clasped his hands on his knees. "How soon can you ladies be ready to go?"

"An hour," answered Granny Kye.

"What place does this gateway take us to?"

"The city of Norst, a small tavern."

"I've never visited Norst. Would there be a mapmaker there?"

"No," said Granny Kye. "But I know of a mapmaker in the coastal town of Ianna."

N'Rae shook her head. "What about Greer? He won't fit through the gateway. We can't just leave him behind."

"He'll fly. I'll tell him to meet us near Ianna."

N'Rae followed Bardon out of the cabin. Her head came up to his shoulder. The sun touched her hair, igniting the fair locks so they shone like a candle flame. The hair framed a typical emerlindian face. He thought her large eyes, tilted eyebrows, pointed nose, and small mouth appealing. She had none of the coquettish airs of the women at Castle Pelacce. After all his years of guarding his feelings, Bardon felt strangely comfortable in her presence, even more comfortable than when he was with Kale.

"You can mindspeak?" she asked.

"Only to Greer," he answered as he strode down the slope. "Well, that's not strictly true. I can mindspeak with Kale Allerion." He stopped speaking before telling her that when Kale was around, his abilities multiplied.

"I can't mindspeak at all. Grandmother thinks it is peculiar. Mistress Seeno thinks it is disgraceful." N'Rae trotted a few steps to catch up. "You know the Dragon Keeper?"

"Yes." Bardon shortened his stride so his companion could keep pace.

"Do you think she could come with us on our quest?"

"No," said Bardon with a sigh. Having Kale along would be good, but the thought of perhaps rescuing her father on his own, as a sort of tribute to their friendship, had an appeal. "She's studying under the Wizards Cam Ayronn and Fenworth. I doubt she has time to go on a quest."

"You didn't have time to go on a quest. You were supposed to decide whether you will become a knight or not," she said. "Grandmother explained to me just what a sabbatical is. But you're going on the quest instead. Maybe the Dragon Keeper could go with us instead of studying."

Bardon stopped and faced her. "Do you have a particular reason that

I should know about? Is there a reason why we would need a Dragon Keeper on this quest?"

N'Rae shook her head, sending her blond hair flying. "No, but I would like to meet the Dragon Keeper."

He started walking again, an image of Kale in his mind. He would like to see her. She must have changed some in three years. They'd each written about six times. The letters chronicled their advances in their respective studies. Kale had included anecdotes about the colorful people she lived with. She mentioned that Toopka never sat still for lessons but loved following Taylaminkadot around doing household chores. Regidor sprouted stubby wings and didn't like being teased. He did his best to hide them. Her mother visited often. Fenworth slept through most days. Cam had trained a fish to jump through a hoop. She didn't say why the lake wizard had bothered to do such a thing.

Bardon had never been able to think of something worthy of relating when he had a pen in his hand. He knew his letters bored Kale. How could they not?

N'Rae interrupted his thoughts. "Are you going to take all of your things with you? You brought a lot of books. I've only seen a few books, but I can read. My mother taught me."

Bardon pressed his lips together before answering. The emerlindian sure had a lot of questions. "I'll leave the books. I shall come back here to finish my sabbatical." Bardon laughed to himself over the optimism of that statement.

"Where's Greer now? Is he fishing again? Does he eat huge quantities of fish?"

"Once he's sated, he doesn't eat again for up to a week. Right now he's flying just because he enjoys flying. He'll come if I call him."

"Can you mindspeak with him no matter where he is?"

"Mindspeaking doesn't work over a long distance." He stopped and looked down at her again. Her endless questions annoyed him, and yet he felt protective of her. Her sweet expression softened his usual reserve. "You had best go back and help your grandmother and Mistress Seeno. Do you have any more questions before you go?"

"Just one." She hesitated. "I noticed right away. Well, when the snake was dragging you toward the lake, and you were all wet."

Bardon frowned. What had she noticed?

N'Rae looked up at him, her blue eyes wide with wonder. "Your ears," she said. "You have emerlindian ears. Why do you hide them with your hair? Why is your hair brown? How old are you? Why don't you have an emerlindian name?"

6

One Part
of Being Prepared

Bardon watched Greer fly out over the western rim of the high mountain valley. He turned on his heel and marched back to the cabin. The ladies, true to their word, were ready in just under an hour. He entered the cabin, closed the front door, and opened a trapdoor in the floor. He had already deposited their few bundles at the bottom of the ladder. Granny Kye went down first, followed by N'Rae carrying Jue Seeno's travel basket. Bardon stepped down, closing the trapdoor behind him.

Common blue lightrocks embedded in the stone walls lit the small room, making N'Rae's pale hair gleam azure. A ripple of distortion outlined the gateway. The first time he'd seen the phenomena, he had thought his vision was impaired. A ring of prismlike lights encircled the entry. Outside them, he could see the wall. He could see the same stone wall in the center. Even through the odd lights, he could make out the cellar foundation. But he knew that once he entered the gateway, he would leave rock and mortar behind. He would travel hundreds of miles with only a few steps.

The cellar's musty air filled his lungs, and he longed to get this part of the journey over with.

N'Rae bounced on her toes, eager to go.

He frowned, remembering the curt words he had hurled at her to cut short her stream of personal questions. He'd caused the hurt that had washed over her face. Her look of confusion had added fuel to his anger, and he'd barked an order for her to return to the cabin.

N'Rae had not mentioned his ears, nor his rudeness, since. She had not sent one look of recrimination his way. She merely sloughed aside what he could not and resumed her cheerful demeanor.

Now she tilted her head at the gateway, looking a lot like her grandmother as she pursed her lips. "Will it feel the same, or will it be easier?" she asked.

Bardon frowned at the portal to Norst. "In my experience, it has to do with the size of the gateway. This one is rather small, so the feeling of being squeezed should be quite profound."

"I've been through this one before," N'Rae explained. "I meant, does it get easier each time you travel through gateways?"

Bardon shook his head. "No. It doesn't."

Methodically, he tossed their belongings through the passage. Each bundle hung suspended for a moment in the light-infused air, then disappeared.

When the last pack had traveled to the tavern in the city of Norst, Bardon turned to the eldest of their group. "Would you like me to go first, Granny Kye?"

Her dark brown eyes met his, and he knew she saw through his assured demeanor and understood his anxiety. Bardon relaxed a mite when he saw her tilt her head, a gesture N'Rae often mimicked.

"Please, Squire Bardon, go first." The old granny's mellow voice filled the cramped cellar. "It will be good to have you greet us on the other side."

He nodded to her, then to N'Rae, and strode through the opening. For one moment the sticky air clung to him, and then the lights exploded, pelting his skin with hundreds of gentle strokes. He felt every bit of his exposed hands and face tapped repeatedly. Pressure bore in on him, and just when he thought he'd pass out from lack of breathable air, he stepped into a darkened room filled with wooden boxes and a scattering of their satchels.

Leaning over, he rested his hands on his knees and drew in deep breaths. Remembering the next traveler would come through the gateway and bump into him, he forced himself to trudge forward a few feet. He sat on an upended barrel and closed his eyes.

N'Rae came through the gateway as if she had been hurled by some mighty force. She landed at his feet, gasping for air. The basket tumbled from her arms, and the minneken rolled out of the open flap.

She squeaked furiously. With his ears still affected by the passage, Bardon couldn't make out her words. He carefully scooped her up and handed her to N'Rae.

Tears ran down the young woman's face. She gulped and looked up at the squire. "Mistress Seeno says she doesn't know why we make such a fuss about going through. She's also disgruntled that I dropped her and her basket."

"It's her size. She isn't affected the way we are."

Granny Kye stepped into the room, breathing a little heavily. To the squire's eye, the emerlindian did not appear to be much affected by her journey through the gateway. Upon seeing Bardon's startled face, she smiled.

"One must relax and trust. You know in your head that the gateway will carry you from one place to another. If you trust in your heart, the journey is easier."

Bardon nodded, a sharp jerk of his head. He knew a half-dozen principles from the Tomes of Wulder that said the same thing, more or less. He also knew he was better at quoting the principles than living them.

N'Rae busied herself, gathering the loose items that had spilled from Jue Seeno's basket. Bardon picked up a tiny cushion that had bounced across the floor and landed by his toe. He crouched beside the young emerlindian as he handed it to her and glanced inside the minneken's traveling quarters.

The wickerwork bed, chairs, and tables remained in place. Upon closer inspection, Bardon saw that lashings secured the furniture to the floor and walls of the small room. Only those things not tied down had scattered over the coarse wooden planks of the tavern storeroom. Jue Seeno ran into her little abode. Her muffled squeaks still sounded like tart protests.

The door opened behind them, and a man with a heavy canvas apron over his clothing started as he saw those inside. N'Rae put herself between the basket and the newcomer, successfully blocking his view.

"Granny Kye," he said. "I wasn't expecting you, was I?" He wiped his hands on a towel as he spoke. "You'd think I'd be used to all this coming and going after five years, but I'm not."

The old emerlindian came forward and smiled at the short marione tavern keeper. "We won't be with you long, Master Onit."

"Shall I prepare you a meal?"

"We had breakfast a while ago, but thank you."

"Um, are you planning to stay in my storage room for long? I have workers coming, and I was just going to hide the gateway."

"A few minutes," she answered, and he bowed out of the room.

Granny Kye immediately turned to Bardon. "I fear we have encountered our first problem, Squire Bardon."

He stood from where he had finished helping N'Rae pass tiny hats in to the minneken. He lifted an eyebrow, waiting to be informed.

"N'Rae and I," Granny began, "and, of course, Jue Seeno have no funds. Perhaps you have money with which to purchase our meals, lodging, and transportation."

Bardon shifted his jaw to the side and back again. "I have a little. I didn't expect to need much currency in a mountain cabin." He rubbed his hand over his chin. "I'll go out and make some inquiries. Does this place have a parlor where you women will be comfortable?"

"No, but the inn across the street does. We will wait for you there."

Bardon pulled a leather pouch from a pocket in the lining of his tunic. "Here are some coins. If I don't return by noonmeal, you may need it."

⇥⊷⊶⇤

Bardon walked through the streets of midtown Norst, sizing up the people and the nature of the city. He made a swift survey of the races represented in the market around him. The mixture of populace contained tumanhofers, mariones, and o'rants, typical of most cities in the southwestern regions of Amara. He saw no small kimens nor any huge urohms. This didn't surprise him. The smallest and largest of the seven high races tended to keep to themselves. He saw two doneels, obviously businessmen by their dress. But no emerlindians walked along the market district.

I wonder how amazed these people would be if they knew of their two visitors. The presence of emerlindians among the other six high races has steadily declined for over a hundred years. And what a clamor would arise if they discovered Jue Seeno!

He glanced around at those on the street once more. *This crowd is representative of the statistics Professor Gledupkonstepper liked to quote in class. "Only three of the high races populate the majority of Amara's average cities."*

The economic situation for the township seemed stable. Open doors with people going in and out indicated that the businesses he passed were thriving. Small donkeys pulled carts over the cobblestone, creating a background beat to the musical quality of the conversations. Friendly greetings, cheerful hawking of wares, and shoppers' chatter as they moved from one store to the next wiped the frown from Bardon's face. Optimism pushed aside his pragmatic temperament.

The question is, How can I find work for a day or two so that I can fill our purse with enough coins to get this quest underway? That comet is not going to wait for me to gather funds.

He stopped and read the names of all the shops on a bustling corner. *Grocer, Dressmaker, Music, Barber, Books, Furniture. Not one thing I could lend my hand to and earn a significant amount of money. I shall have to look further.*

He strolled down one street, looking for a busier tavern than the one that held the gateway. The Rafters filled the bill. He crossed the threshold and scanned the crowd for a likely looking group of men. He headed for a half-dozen workers eating a hearty meal. They must have been up early and labored hard to be downing such a large quantity of food at midmorning.

Ordering a tall mug of Korskan tea from a passing maidservant, Bardon sat down at the long plank table where the men ate.

"I'm looking for work," he announced.

The men nodded their heads and continued to chew.

"I'm squire to a doneel in Wittoom and find I need some traveling funds."

They nodded again. Bardon waited.

One of the marione men took a draft of his ale, wiped his bearded mouth on his sleeve, and looked at the stranger.

"Corduff is hiring mine workers. Good pay if you live."

"Naw, don't send him there," said a red-headed o'rant. "Gallatennod-ken is looking for a scholar to translate a parchment brought in by one of his treasure seekers. Said it was in some ancient doneel language. Maybe he can help there."

A tumanhofer lifted his head from the soup bowl he held to his lips. "Heard he found a linguist two days ago."

Except for slurping and smacking of lips, the crew at the table fell silent. The maid delivered Bardon's drink, and he gave her a coin. The cold tea tasted good, having a citrus tang that cut the otherwise sweet brew.

"There's Hoddack," said the red-headed o'rant.

The other men remained silent.

"Hoddack's looking for someone to break six young kindias. Their training time is running out."

The tumanhofer removed his face from his soup bowl again. "Tell him what happened to the last breaker. Only fair."

The o'rant snorted. "Got stepped on is all. The job is to stay on until the animal is biddable. The breaker didn't do his job."

Bardon's fingers, encircling the glass mug, tightened as he looked deep into the tawny brown liquid. He'd ridden kindias as part of his training. Taller and wider than horses, the beasts could travel at incredible speeds through rugged terrain. Their backs sloped down from their muscled necks and powerful shoulders. This slant encouraged gravity to pull riders off their backs. Kindias would not carry any burden other than one passenger on a specially designed light saddle. But the ride was incredible. Bone-jostling at tremendous speeds. As dangerous as flying, without the pleasures.

An unbroken kindia would spin and buck and even roll to remove the pest on its back. The most common way to tame one just required stamina and agility. Six to twelve uninterrupted hours in the saddle, and the breaker usually broke the kindia to accept a rider.

Bardon had never done it, never witnessed it, but he'd read about the process. His eyebrows rose as he heard the words form on his lips.

"Where do I find Hoddack?"

7

Breaking a Kindia

When he saw the six unbroken kindias, Bardon thought first of his dragon friend.

I am so grateful Greer isn't around to add his insightful thoughts on the folly of this endeavor. If I can avoid his ever finding out, my peace of mind will be preserved. Otherwise, I'll never hear the end of it.

The kindias grazed in a large field surrounded by a ten-foot-high, wooden slatted fence.

Hoddack looked first at the young squire, then at his valuable animals. "Five hundred grood for each one you break. I don't pay for fixing you up or the time you spend out of work if you're injured."

Bardon nodded.

"When can you start? They're going to be two-year-olds in three weeks. If you know anything at all about kindias, you know if you don't break 'em by two, you might as well turn 'em loose."

Bardon nodded again and forced his voice past the lump in his throat. "Heard that."

"Well, do you want the job or no?"

"Yes, I'll start now."

"Never done this before, have you?"

"No. I've ridden several, but never broken one."

"Remember, I don't provide care for you if you're busted up."

Bardon nodded.

"You want a drink or something? I don't recommend eating. Likely make you sick."

"I'm fine. Where's the saddle?"

Hoddack pointed out a tall, brindled kindia as they walked to the barn. "That's Mig. She's the oldest, and the one that tossed my last breaker into the fence. Best start with her so the others know you mean business. I got other things to do. I'll get one of the boys to sit on the fence to haul you out should you take a fall. You don't get paid 'less you finish the job. Remember that."

Hoddack sent an o'rant named Ilex down from the main barn. The man helped Bardon corner Mig and get the saddle on.

"All I'm going to do is sit on the fence and watch," Ilex explained. "I thank you for the time off from real work." The older man grinned, showing two teeth missing from a crooked row. "Hoddack's a hard man, but he won't let a man break alone down here. Someone needs to be on hand to pick up the pieces when the breaker comes off."

"Nice of him." Bardon stroked Mig's neck. He had to reach up, since his head came to her shoulder. *Seems to me the kindias in Wittoom were shorter.*

Her muscles quivered beneath his hand.

Bardon lengthened his stroke. Her smooth coat felt silky beneath his fingers. "There, there, girl, this isn't going to be so bad."

She jumped away, and he brought her back with the reins.

Ilex scrambled up the fence, away from flying hooves. Once he settled on the top, broad plank of wood, he took out a stick and a whittling knife. "Don't be surprised if some of the other boys wander down here whenever they got a minute. Hope you don't mind watchers."

Bardon thought of the few tournaments he had participated in. *When you're busy trying to keep from being killed, you don't think much about who's watching.*

He just nodded to Ilex. The other animals in the field had moved away, as if to distance themselves from the upcoming battle between man and beast. If the stories were true, the others would do their best to overlook the captivity of their fellow herd member. Bardon sighed and turned his full concentration on the kindia at his side.

Still grasping the reins, he took hold of the saddle horn with his left hand. He moved back toward Mig's head, stepped forward, and vaulted into the saddle, turning in midair to face forward. His legs landed with knees in the saddle hooks. If he'd missed the hooks or been slow to clench his leg muscles, he would have flown from the saddle as quickly as he'd found it.

Mig danced in a circle, bouncing on all four legs one minute and heaving her hind legs into the air the next. She bounded sideways and reared so that Bardon had to throw himself forward to keep from sliding off her back. She then spun in a crazy circle, switching directions so that Bardon's head snapped.

The agility and stamina that would serve the beast well when she raced over countless miles of desolate territory kept her moving for more than two hours. Bardon clung to the saddle with his legs and eventually threw his arms around Mig's neck to keep from being hurled to the ground. After a grueling campaign to rid herself of her rider, the beast stood still, flesh quivering, chest heaving, nostrils flared and blowing, but still.

Bardon knew better than to loosen his hold or try to get off. He had not won the battle yet. Instead, he crooned to the wild kindia, stroking her neck, and even scratching the top of her head right behind each ear. Fifteen minutes later, Mig kicked up her hind legs. When the nuisance on her back did not sail into the air, she commenced another round of gyrations designed to destroy the rider. The second wild dance lasted just over an hour.

A row of men lined the fence closest to the barn. After a brief interlude where she regained her breath, Mig lowered her head and charged them. They scrambled up to safety, but the maneuver had apparently given Mig an idea. She proceeded to try to scrape Bardon from her back by running into the fence at an angle.

Bardon's body felt like scrambled eggs. Now Mig seemed intent on crushing him. First one leg and then the other took a beating against the wooden slats. Bardon held on.

The contest lasted until dusk. Mig's bouts of fury shortened in length, but never in ferocity. When at last she'd been calm for an hour, Bardon used the reins to direct her. She responded sluggishly at first and then caught on to the gentle pressure he used to guide her. He brought her up to the fence, and Ilex handed him a bottle of drink. He downed it gratefully, then rode the newly broken kindia around the circumference of the field. As they passed the rest of her herd, the kindias turned their backs and ignored the two, rider and mount.

Bardon again went to the fence by the barn, and Ilex passed him a sandwich.

Ilex looked grim. "You be sure to get your pay tonight. Hoddack might just be counting on you being too sore to come back for your money tomorrow. Then again, he may take a likin' to you and treat you fair. Hard to tell with that man."

Bardon bit into the sandwich. "Thanks for the warning."

As he ate, he circled the field again on Mig. When he got back to Ilex, he asked, "What do we do with her now?"

Ilex grinned. "I'll take over from here. I'll bed her in the barn and treat her like royalty all night. She'll get groomed and fed. I'll do everything but rockaby her till morning. By dawn she'll be convinced it was her idea to enter this life of luxury. Funny thing about kindias, once they is broke, there ain't no better mount."

Bardon shook his head. "I ride a dragon. Believe me, Greer is the best."

Ilex led the way to the barn and opened the door. Bardon rode inside, and the worker closed the door behind him. He dismounted.

"Lead her in here." Ilex opened a stall.

Bardon found his legs wobbled a bit, and he laughed at himself. Grinning at him, the worker took the reins and escorted Mig into her new home.

"You coming back tomorrow?" Ilex called from the stall.

"If I can walk," answered Bardon.

"Go up to the main barn. There's an office in the southwest corner. Hoddack will still be there. Get your money and go home. Soak in hot water, but don't drown. Have somebody wake you up should you doze off. I'd like to see you tackle the other five."

Bardon groaned as he turned and headed out the door. He looked through the twilight at the bigger barn.

Was that barn so far away when Hoddack brought me down here? And I don't remember there being a hill between the two barns. He put one foot in front of the other. *And I don't remember the hill being this steep. Oh, what a gift it would be to have Kale's healing dragon, Gymn, right now.*

Hoddack glared at him as he counted out the five hundred grood, but he also handed him a bottle of liniment. Bardon tucked the large gold coins into his pocket and carried the bottle on the long walk back to the inn. *I wonder if the bonus of a bottle of liniment means Hoddack's taken a "likin'" to me.*

Lanterns of lightrock illuminated the darkened streets by the time Bardon entered the inn. He asked for his traveling companions, and the sturdy marione innkeeper ushered him to a private parlor.

"What happened to you?" N'Rae sprang to her feet and came to greet him. "You're filthy."

"And in pain," added Granny Kye. "Innkeeper Nald, bring up a tub and hot water to the young man's room. And a good, hot meal."

"For you two ladies, as well, or just the young man?" asked the tumanhofer.

"I think we're all ready to eat," answered Granny Kye.

The innkeeper bowed. "I can have a meal here in a trice. The gentleman can eat while his bath is prepared." Nald backed out of the room as he spoke, then closed the door.

N'Rae tugged at Bardon's sleeve. "What have you been doing?"

"Breaking a kindia for a marione named Hoddack. I earned five hundred grood. There are five more of the beasts waiting. By the end of the week, we should have three thousand grood, enough to get us started."

N'Rae frowned. "How did you break this kindia?"

"The usual way. I sat on her until she decided I wasn't a danger to her."

"How long did that take?"

"A little more than eight hours."

A knock on the door announced dinner. N'Rae opened the door, and several servants brought in trays of food and drink. They laid the food out on the table and left. N'Rae brought out Jue Seeno's basket and set up the minneken's tiny table and chair so she could eat with them. Granny Kye prepared a medicinal tea for Bardon's aches.

Bardon hesitated to sit with the ladies.

N'Rae, sitting next to the minneken, giggled. "Mistress Seeno says you may be sweat and grime all over, but you labored for us, so you may sit at the table."

Bardon nodded to the imperious little matron and sat. He enjoyed the delicious food, and the minneken decided to regale them with tales of the Isle of Kye. The squire relaxed. The tea eased his discomfort. The food filled his stomach. And the company was pleasant, not taxing his poor social skills. He noticed N'Rae held her tongue and wore a pensive expression.

"What's wrong?" he asked as they ate crisp lemon daggarts for dessert.

"Nothing," she answered.

"You're thinking about something."

She blushed. "I would like to go with you tomorrow."

"To Hoddack's?"

She nodded.

"Whatever for? Watching a kindia being broken may be exciting for the first fifteen minutes, but from there on out, it's just repetitions of the same thing, over and over. You'd be bored. And it's hot and dusty, and there's nothing but a railing to sit on."

With her eyes downcast, N'Rae whispered, "I may be able to help."

Help. Did she say help?

Bardon looked to Granny Kye. The old emerlindian nodded with a twinkle lighting her brown eyes. The squire looked at Mistress Seeno.

The minneken lifted her chin. "She does have one talent. But when she saw through the chicken's eyes, I told her just what I thought of such an ability."

"Saw through chicken eyes?" Bardon asked as he turned back to N'Rae.

She looked up, met his eyes, and looked down. "I can communicate with most animals." She darted a glance at Jue Seeno. "The chicken didn't have any thoughts, but I could see exactly what she saw. It was interesting."

"But useless!" exclaimed the minneken.

"Yes," agreed N'Rae, "useless."

Granny Kye scooted her chair away from the table. "Taking the child with you may yield unexpected results. She can always come back to the inn if nothing comes of it."

N'Rae now looked at Bardon, obviously waiting for him to pass judgment on the scheme. "If it takes you five more days, the comet will be much higher in the sky. If I can help, perhaps we can leave sooner."

"Why not?" he said, wanting to please her. "I can't see that it could do any harm."

8

A Fine Talent

The next morning, N'Rae hovered close to Bardon's side as they walked through the bustling streets of Norst. Her expressive eyes displayed many emotions—fear, awe, and dismay chief among them. The squire kept her hand in the crook of his elbow and patted it reassuringly whenever she flinched at the noise and confusion surrounding them.

"Have you never been in a city before?" he asked.

"This one." She leaned close to him rather than yell over the noise. "But we came in the middle of the night, went straight to the tavern, and left through the gateway."

"That certainly didn't give you much time to get acquainted." Bardon swung his hand in front of him, indicating the people and shops along the street. "This is a very nice city—clean, prosperous, and populated by mostly genteel individuals. Some cities are much uglier, both in appearance and in the way people behave."

"I don't think I want to go to one of those."

"N'Rae, you will learn that a quest, by its very nature, generally takes you to a lot of places you would rather not go."

N'Rae stopped short and pulled her hand away from his light grasp. "You think I'm pretty stupid, don't you?"

Oh, great! I didn't mean to be so condescending. It's a trait Kale tried to hammer out of me. And Sir Dar. And Grand Dost. And Scribe Moran. Now, I've offended N'Rae. He considered her indignant expression. *How do I get out of this? Apologize or explain? Or both?* "Not stupid, inexperienced."

Her hands went up to rest on her hips in tight fists. Her mouth flattened into a stubborn line. "I have plenty of experience, just not in the things you seem to deem important." She glowered at him. "How many babies have you seen born? I helped my mother deliver babies when I was six. Not high race babies, of course. But Mother said ropma babies arrived in the same manner as an o'rant or a doneel or any of the others."

Bardon spoke in a calm voice. "You're right, N'Rae. I have never been at the birthing of a baby. I've seen a litter of kittens born. Does that count for anything?"

"Not much." She still glared. "And I can forage and keep myself alive in the wilderness."

"Now, I can do that." Bardon smiled, trying to get past her anger. "I'm sure we will be very useful to each other as we trek across Amara."

"I know medicinal plants and how to use them."

"I only know a few of the most common ones."

N'Rae relaxed a bit at that remark. "I can hide, and I can track."

"Again, very useful."

"Are you patronizing me? Mother always said patronizing the ropma was rude, even if they were like little children."

"Not in the least. It's good to know in which areas I will be able to depend on you."

She studied his face for a moment, as if trying to read his true feelings. Bardon's years of keeping his expression neutral served him well with this prickly young emerlindian.

She looked away. "And I have very acute hearing."

"Probably developed by conversing with Mistress Seeno."

Her head whipped back so she could see his face. After only a glance, a twinkle came to her eyes, and she laughed. Smiling broadly, Bardon took her hand and tucked it back in the crook of his arm. They walked out of the market district, through a well-kept residential area, and into the country. Hoddack's farm was only a mile out of Norst on the road to the sea.

Less than an hour later, they bypassed the larger barn near the farmhouse and went directly to the expansive paddock where the five young kindias still grazed.

N'Rae glanced at the animals and at the sod that the angry kindia had churned up with its hooves the day before.

"May I see the animal that did this?"

"I should think it would be all right. Her name is Mig. Follow me."

The dark, cool barn smelled of hay and saddle soap. Only a faint, earthy odor of animals rose from the clean stalls. Bardon and N'Rae passed a half-dozen empty stalls before coming to the only one with an occupant. Mig thrust her head over the door and blew a welcome through her lips.

N'Rae walked up to the kindia and put her hand on the animal's cheek. "She's glad to see you."

"Me? I'm the culprit who ruined her day yesterday."

"No." N'Rae protested with a vigorous shake of her head. Mig objected to the flying locks of blond hair. She backed away from the stall door.

N'Rae reached toward the frightened kindia. "It's all right, girl. Come back to me. I'm sorry I startled you."

Mig stood indecisive for only a moment before sauntering back and pushing her head against the emerlindian's hand.

"She *is* happy to see you. She counts you as the one who brought her in out of the cold, provided her with fresh water and good food, and the man with strong hands, who rubs her coat." N'Rae sighed. "She is so *very* content."

Mig relaxed her neck, and her head hung close to N'Rae's face. The emerlindian put her forehead against the animal's broad nose.

"What are you doing?" asked Bardon.

"Gathering images. She doesn't think in words, but in patterns of pictures."

"You're mindspeaking with an animal?"

"You do it with Greer."

"That's different."

"Shh!"

Bardon stood silently for a while, then sat on a bale of hay. Occasionally, the beast would toss her head, but she lowered her face to N'Rae's again each time. He watched the silent interchange. N'Rae's concentration fascinated him, and the kindia's apparent response to the girl amazed him. He had seen the meech dragon, Regidor, do incredible things, and Kale had shown Bardon talents of the mind that defied explanation. He wondered how extensive this communication was between beast and young woman. Did it come close to what happened between Greer and him?

Once N'Rae had patted Mig, told her she was a good girl, and turned away, Bardon sprang to his feet.

"What did you two talk about?"

She shook her head. "We didn't talk. We just understood." N'Rae raised her hands, then let them drop. "It's too hard to explain. Let's go see the others."

"They're wild." Bardon followed her quick steps out of the barn into the paddock. "And dangerous."

"We'll see." She started toward the far side of the fenced area where one kindia grazed alone. "I think I understand the pattern of their thoughts. I'll try to show them what Mig already knows about the inside of the barn. They may want to join her without going through the struggle first."

"That would suit me. If it weren't for Granny Kye's medicinal tea, I'd be back at the inn, stretched out on a bed."

N'Rae gestured for him to stay behind and approached the lone kindia. She stopped ten feet from where it stood. It raised its head from grazing and stared toward the fence, refusing to look at this woman who invaded its territory. Its ears twitched, the only signal that the kindia disliked the presence of a person.

Bardon watched N'Rae's back. She seemed to be doing nothing more than breathing, a deep and slow rhythm. In a few minutes, the beast turned and looked at her. Then it trotted to where she stood and lowered its head, just as Mig had done in the barn. N'Rae stroked its cheeks and neck with both hands. Bardon held his breath as she turned away from the kindia and led it right past him and toward the barn. He fell in step beside her.

"What did you do?" he whispered.

"I gave him the images Mig had given me." N'Rae's face beamed. "Once he'd seen the wonders of the barn, he gave up his independent desire to stand out in the cold, eating grass and drinking muddy water."

"You convinced him with mind pictures?"

"I didn't do much convincing." She reached up to pat the kindia walking sedately beside her. "He's intelligent enough to accept a better life." She grinned at Bardon. "You still have to ride him."

Together they put the saddle and bridle on the patient kindia. Bardon rode the circumference of the field twice and then into the barn. They chose a stall next to Mig, removed the riding gear, groomed the kindia, and gave him food and water. Ilex showed up as they worked with the second kindia that morning. N'Rae stood near the animal while Bardon hung back.

He saw the farm worker and strode over to the fence.

"We already have one in the barn," he said.

Ilex nodded. "I saw that. I didn't even expect to see you until late in the morning. You're moving kinda free for someone who broke a kindia yesterday."

"I used the liniment Hoddack gave me, and my friends have a tea that's helpful." Bardon rubbed his hand across his chin. "What's wrong? Why do you look like you've been stepped on by one of these kindias?"

Ilex jerked his chin in the direction of the young woman who now stood face to face with a reddish-brown kindia. "She's an emerlindian, isn't she?"

"Yes."

"Not sure how the master is going to react." Ilex clicked his tongue and shook his head. "This ain't the way he's used to breaking his stock."

Bardon studied the man sitting on the fence. "Why would Hoddack care as long as the animals are fit to be ridden?"

"I think I've mentioned before that Hoddack is a tricky one to get along with."

"I don't see your point."

"Just expect him to be ornery, and you'll be better off. She's leading that kindia over here. What do you two do next?"

"I'll saddle and ride him, then put him in the barn."

"Well, I'll go back to coddling the two that are in there. They like to hear me sing, you know." He slipped off the fence and meandered into the barn.

By late afternoon, the barn held six contented kindias. N'Rae moved from one to the next, stroking their soft fur and looking deep into their eyes.

Hoddack marched through the open doors with Ilex following.

"I want to see this!" he shouted. "This is some kind of trick."

Instinctively, Bardon moved so that he stood between the blustering man and N'Rae. "I assure you, it isn't."

The huge doors at both ends of the barn opened to the cool wind and the fading sun. Enough light poured in for the owner of the farm to inspect his stock. Hoddack stomped up and down the breezeway between the two rows of stalls. The animals watched him curiously. He slowed and came to a halt in the middle of his barn. The kindia trader removed his hat and ran his fingers through his hair. He put the hat back down on his head with a thump and pointed a stubby finger at Bardon.

"I hired you to sit on these animals until they broke. You haven't done what I hired you for."

"You offered five hundred grood for each kindia broken. Six are broken. You owe us for five. That's twenty-five hundred grood."

"I can do the arithmetic. But this isn't right! How do I know this breaking is going to take? I give you the money, and tomorrow they're all as wild as the day before yesterday."

Bardon shook his head. "I've never heard of that happening. A tame kindia gone wild? Never."

Ilex spoke up. "I haven't either, Master Hoddack."

The older man spun around and shook the same stubby finger at his hired help. "You keep your nose out of this."

Ilex squinted, spat out of the side of his mouth, and jerked a nod.

Hoddack put his hands on his hips and glared at Bardon. "I'm not giving you the money tonight. If these beasts are still broke tomorrow, I'll pay you. I'm a fair man, but I won't take the chance that you're not."

With long, angry strides he reached the door and turned. "And another thing! How do I know these beasts will still run? How do I know that girl didn't zap all the vitality out of them that makes them good stock? If they're as meek as lambs, I'm not going to get a good price for them, and my reputation as a supplier will be shot, to boot. Come back tomorrow. We'll see if you earned the money."

Ilex waited until his master was out of hearing. "Come back at the crack of dawn. He's planning a trip, and it would be convenient for him if you didn't get here before he left."

"Thanks, Ilex."

"It's nothing. I enjoyed working with you." He tipped his hat to N'Rae. "Nice to have met you, Mistress. You have a mighty fine talent with the animals."

"Thank you," N'Rae answered, with a pleased smile brightening her face.

As they walked back to the inn, N'Rae chattered about the day. Bardon didn't really listen but let the light babble wash over him like a merry piece of music. One phrase caught his attention.

"—so I think it should change."

"I'm sorry, N'Rae. What should change?"

"Breaking the kindias. It should change to gentling, or taming, or even convincing, but breaking is too harsh. When we were finished with the kindias, they weren't broken as if destroyed. They were happier, almost like they had realized their purpose and embraced it."

"You are being quite the philosopher."

"You don't have to go to school to be smart. You do have to keep your eyes open, though. My mother always said I had good eyes." She paused and sighed. "I wonder if Mistress Seeno will approve of what we've done today."

9

THE RACE

The next morning as he topped the hill with N'Rae, Bardon saw Ilex pacing in front of the well-lit barn. The crisp dawn barely supplied enough light for him to make out the other figures moving from the big barn near the main house to the smaller barn holding the newly broken kindias.

As they stepped into the circle of light thrown out from the open door of the barn, Bardon spoke to Ilex. "Is this the preparation for Hoddack's trip?"

The older man jumped. "Didn't see you coming. No, trip's canceled. Hoddack had an idea in the middle of the night. He roused everyone a couple of hours ago. We're going to have a race."

"Why?"

"Hoddack thinks the kindias you broke won't make it through the first mountain pass. Then he won't have to pay you."

"When does the race start, and who's riding?"

"Eight o'clock, and the workers here on the farm. They're all experienced kindia riders."

"I want to speak to Hoddack."

Ilex jerked a thumb over his shoulder toward the barn. "In there."

"Thanks." Bardon strode into the barn bustling with activity. N'Rae followed like a shadow. Every stall had a kindia in it. Bardon counted fifteen. Men groomed the kindias and checked saddles for any signs of weakness.

N'Rae touched his arm. "May I visit with the animals?"

Bardon nodded his assent.

Hoddack came to him from the other end of the room.

"You heard about the race? I have men establishing their bonds with the kindias now. It's a ten-mile run into the mountains, over Old Man Peak, and down the other route that lands them in rocky, no-good territory before they get to the clean run back to the farm. Should take five to six hours. A minor test of stamina for a kindia."

"I'd like to ride, Master Hoddack."

"In the race?"

"Yes."

The gruff owner of the stables looked him over. "You want to be along to see there's no foul play, don't you? You think I might tell my boys not to push the kindias, to hold 'em back. Think I might pull something sneaky. Don't blame you. I'd be thinking along those lines if our places were reversed."

The older man slapped Bardon on the back. "Sure, you can ride. Just pick a mount." He turned and shouted. "Ilex, give Squire Bardon any kindia he chooses to ride for the race. Men, I want you each to give an all-out effort to win this race. Therefore, the winner receives one thousand grood. If the squire here wins, he has to split it with the man who gave up his mount so he could race."

A cheer rose from the men attending the kindias, followed by some good-natured joking.

Hoddack looked Bardon in the eye. "Now you see that this race is in earnest."

"I admit you've confused me, Master Hoddack. I thought you didn't like to part with your money, and this race was to save you the fee you owe me for breaking the five kindias."

"I'm a businessman. I go by what's fair, and sometimes, I have to make others operate under the same code. I got no way of telling whether you and that girl are charlatans or not." He slapped Bardon on the shoulder as if he had not just cast aspersions on the squire's character. "Now, last night, I got to thinking that when the countryside hears about this race and the circumstances that brought it about, they'll be clamoring for one of my stock. Prices'll go up." He frowned. "And if your kindias fall way behind, throw their riders, and take off for the wild, then I only have to pay the winner a thousand grood, saving the fifteen hundred more I'd have to give to you."

"And if one of the kindias we broke wins?"

"Well, then, I'm out a lotta coins, but my reputation is not only safe but doubled, maybe even tripled. Your kindias break down, they'll say how shrewd I am not to let you cheat me. Your kindias prove out, then I'm a shrewd dealer with the best stock in the country." Hoddack grinned and went off to speak to one of the other men.

N'Rae came back to Bardon's side as soon as the owner moved off. "The kindias are excited. The ones who have raced before can hardly wait. They want the people to quit fooling around and get them out to the starting line."

"How about the ones you broke yesterday?"

"I didn't break them. I told you, that's an absurd term."

"The kindias you introduced to the barn, then. How are they doing? Nervous? Scared by all this hubbub?"

"They were at first, but I explained to them what's happening, and now they're eager to run."

"Hoddack has given me permission to ride. Which one of our kindias would be a good mount?"

"You're asking me?"

"Of course! You would know."

N'Rae's mouth hung open for a second. She snapped it shut, then pointed to a pale kindia with a dark mane and dark stripes on his legs. "The men call that one Ten because he has ten stripes on his legs. The other animals admire him and consider him their leader."

"Then I shall ride Ten."

+>===<+

Ilex explained the route twice.

"I want you to win this race, boy," the old farm worker said. "It's been a long time since I rode in one, and it would feel mighty good to be backing the winner. And I'm backing you. Remember the turn at the giant monarch tree leads to a sudden decline. It'll be like sliding down the hill on the kindia's rump."

Bardon nodded as he continued to stroke Ten with his bare hands, giving the animal a chance to become familiar with the new rider.

"And remember," continued Ilex, "the starting rope takes about two seconds to hit the ground. Don't spur your mount until you count to two. You'd be surprised how many races are lost with the kindia's front feet tangled in the rope. You better hope the kindias on either side of you have smart riders too."

N'Rae stood at Ten's head and seemed to be lost in an exchange of ideas. Bardon's mouth quirked at the corner as his kindia nodded as if replying to something the young emerlindian said.

A trumpet blast from the main house signaled for the men to bring their mounts to the starting line. A forty-foot rope stretched from the porch of the big house to the large barn. A crowd continued to gather from the town and neighboring farms.

Bardon looked over the throng. *Hoddack's going to get the publicity he wants.* As he walked with Ten, he watched the men around him leading their kindias up the hill. *These animals certainly don't act like horses do before a race. They're plodding toward the starting line as if they were going to nothing more than another stable. Yet N'Rae says that each one is excited.*

At the top of the hill, they stood with the kindias as Hoddack gave a speech about riding fair and a brief description of the route.

Now I'm glad Ilex told me which trails to take. Hoddack's description doesn't amount to much.

A magistrate from the town ordered the riders to make ready. They climbed into the saddles. Bardon, without thinking, vaulted onto Ten's back as if mounting his dragon. He heard the stir among the onlookers and deliberately focused on getting Ten to a place along the rope.

Two burly marione men untied the starting line and held it taut. The magistrate called for silence. The crowd hushed.

"On the count of three, these men will drop the rope. Let this be an honest race, honoring the fair city of Norst. One."

Bardon leaned over Ten's neck.

"Two."

He squeezed his knees against the saddle.

"Three."

The rope fell. Bardon counted to two and dug in his heels.

On either side of him, racers plunged forward. He vaguely recognized a kindia several mounts down rearing up instead of charging forward. Whoops and hollers covered the clamor of hoofbeats on the dry road. But the racers soon left the uproar behind.

The first stretch of the race followed a meandering road through the foothills. At various points along the way, small knots of people stood waiting for the racers to pass. They cheered, waved their hats, and jumped up and down. Bardon held second place and hoped to stay there. The rider in front of him certainly knew the racecourse. He never hesitated at a turn. Bardon followed, planning to urge Ten to pass the leader on the last stretch.

They rounded a bend and nearly ran into a farm cart. Ten sidestepped the wagon and kept going.

Now, here's a big difference. Greer and I would have been hundreds of feet or more above that obstacle. But Ten seems to know what he's doing. Bardon chortled. *That makes one of us. I don't have to win this race. We and the other kindias N'Rae tamed just need to make a good showing.*

He looked over his shoulder. *So far, so good. Our kindias are in the front half of the pack.*

They turned into a rocky canyon. No more pastures lined the way. The kindia took to the pathway like a mountain goat being chased by a high-country cat.

As Ten climbed behind the lead kindia, Bardon bounced in the saddle. Several times the kindia jumped from one large, flat boulder to the next. With each landing, Bardon felt like his teeth would be jarred out of his mouth and his bones would crack.

Riding Greer is a breeze compared to this. Where's the soothing stroke of his strong wings? Where's the smooth glide and steady pace?

Ten scrambled down into a gully, following the kindia in front of him. Bardon no longer consciously directed his mount but rather let the beast decide how best to keep on the narrow pass.

Leaning almost flat on the animal's neck, Bardon spoke words of encouragement. "You're a good kindia, Ten. You're beating all the rest with no help from me."

They left the jumble of rocks and entered a forested area. The trail narrowed and twisted back on itself, zigzagging up the steep mountain. Several times Bardon looked over the edge and saw the heads of riders below him.

Ten didn't appear to mind the height. Bardon, on the other hand, who usually soared among the clouds when traveling, began to feel dizzy whenever he looked over the edge. To keep nausea at bay, he stared between Ten's two long ears.

They crested Old Man Peak above the timberline. Here the wide path allowed the riders to juggle their positions. Another kindia and rider passed Bardon and Ten. Ten snorted, and Bardon laughed out loud.

"It's all right, boy. We'll barrel past those two when we get on the homestretch."

The weathered rock didn't offer much for the kindia's hooves to grip. They mostly slid down to the tree line.

This is rough. And Ilex said it got a little steep after the giant monarch tree.

The older man's words came back to him. *"After that, boy, just hold on for all you're worth and petition Wulder to keep your saddle intact. There's no pride or style in riding down that mountain. You just lie back against the high cantle and hold on! You might even want to close your eyes. Ten will know which way to go, and you couldn't turn him anyways. Blessed thing is, it don't last long. Maybe twenty seconds of going straight down. After that, Ten will prance through the crumpled pile of boulders at the bottom and then along the dry creek bed. Kind of sandy there. Then the rest is easy."*

They raced through the thickening forest along a switchback path. Loose rocks fell on the first riders as the riders behind plunged along the trail above.

Down below, Bardon saw a huge tree with the distinctive upswept branches of a monarch. Beyond that it looked like one section of the mountain had fallen away, leaving a bare escarpment.

Bardon clenched his jaw and did exactly as Ilex had instructed him.

Wulder, protect me and this beast. Protect the men and animals before and after me. And keep this saddle in one piece and on Ten's back.

Two kindias and their riders still led the way in front of Bardon and Ten. They rounded the monarch and disappeared. Bardon followed and closed his eyes. Not out of fear, but because dust and gravel flew into the air from the other animals' feet. He wondered if Ten had closed his eyes as well.

He heard a rider shout behind him, and a torrent of loose rock pelted them. Something whapped them from behind. Ten pitched forward and rolled. Bardon fell from the saddle and tumbled beside the kindia. They stopped at a broad ledge littered with crumbled shale and granite gravel.

Bardon sat up and shook his head. Ten stood prancing, as if to say, "Come on." The two riders who'd been ahead of them were down, as well as two more who must have been directly behind. The men staggered to their feet, brushed the dust from their faces, and ran to jump in the saddles. Bardon left the lower ridge in second place.

At the bottom, they zigged and zagged and hopped through the pile of rocks that had tumbled from the mountain. Bardon sighed his relief when they hit the riverbed, then realized how hard Ten worked to gallop across the soft, dry sand. Even though trees lining the way provided shade, sweat soaked Bardon's clothing, and lather flecked Ten's coat. A kindia Bardon had not noticed managed to pass them.

When they climbed the embankment, the road they had raced down on the way out reappeared. The last leg of the race stretched before them.

"Well, Ten," Bardon shouted behind the animal's head. "Do you want to come in third or first?"

Ten extended his long neck. The muscles in his powerful shoulders moved in an accelerated rhythm under Bardon's knees. They passed the second rider and came up on the right side of the leader.

A multitude of people lined the roadway. Their roar assaulted Bardon's ears. The colors of clothing and waving pennants blurred in his side vision as he set his eyes on the red ribbon stretched across the finish line.

He leaned forward, shifting his weight to his lower legs. Crouching over the saddle instead of sitting in it, he finally found the rhythm that kept his bones from absorbing all the pounding. The distance between him and the leader of the race narrowed. He heard both animals gasping, and he felt Ten surge ahead. The second kindia pulled ahead and then fell back. The ribbon trailed from Ten's ample chest as they crossed the finish line.

The contestants slowed and circled back to the front porch of the big house, cooling the animals. More riders came in, late but finishing. All six of the kindias Bardon and N'Rae had worked with completed the race.

The crowd pushed in on the circle of first runners. Bardon searched the faces until he spotted N'Rae with Granny Kye beside her. The mass of people made it impossible for them to come together. People jumped and cheered, laughed and pounded each other on the back.

The only one who didn't look happy stood on the porch. Hoddack scowled at the people on his property. His eyes met Bardon's, and the young squire saw trouble brewing.

10

CHOICES

Swinging his leg over the kindia's neck, Bardon dismounted.

"I'll take him," said Ilex, removing the reins from the squire's hand. "I've got a fine bed of hay, a bin of bossel, and clear water waiting for him in the barn. This boy is going to have a rubdown, too, and I'm going to sing him the songs my pa sang to me."

Ilex patted Ten on the neck, reached up to scratch behind the animal's ears, and led him off, chuckling to himself. Bardon watched as they pushed through the crowd, and the old farm worker greeted those eager to heap praises on the winner.

Bardon eased between mingling farmers and townspeople, edging his way to the porch. Hoddack pointed his finger at one of the revelers, a neatly dressed young marione with a thick thatch of slicked-down, golden hair. Hoddack hooked his finger in a "Come" gesture and pointed to the front door. Then the kindia breeder turned abruptly, signaling with a wave of his hand for Bardon to follow. He marched into his house without looking back to see if his silent commands were obeyed.

Now what?

Bardon's boots thumped the wooden steps as he climbed to the porch. He met the summoned young man at the top of the steps. The marione's jaw angled just like Master Hoddack's, and he had the same deep-set eyes and large, straight nose.

Bardon slowed, allowing the young man to go first. *Hoddack's son? First Hoddack looks as though he has swallowed a drummerbug, then he calls for his son to join us. I hope this isn't going to be unpleasant.* He shook his head as he tried to determine the type of person the son could be. *He doesn't look as contrary as the father. In fact, he looks rather soft, as though he isn't used to laboring beside the farm workers.*

The son held his shoulders straight, but they weren't as broad as his father's. He wore tailored clothing without one grubby mark on him. Instead of commonplace boots, he wore shiny brown shoes of tooled leather.

He looks as though he enjoys his father's success but doesn't help with the business of running this kindia farm. But then, all this is supposition. "Judgment passed before facts are known judges the judger." Principle sixty-eight.

Inside, the refined décor of the home surprised Bardon. Hoddack had disappeared, but the young man led the squire into a side room. An older woman sat in the dim light on a brocade-covered settee.

"Mother, may we disturb you for a moment?"

She lifted her chin and smiled toward the voice. "Of course, Holt."

He took her extended hand and raised it to bestow a kiss.

Her other hand came up to briefly caress his cheek. "I suspect you've brought one of the riders to meet me. Perhaps, the winner?"

Bardon stepped forward with the assurance of years in Sir Dar's court. He bent over her hand and brushed it with his lips.

"I beg your pardon, Dame Hoddack, for coming into your presence in such a state. I must smell like the kindia I rode. A fine animal, but not one that should be brought into a lady's parlor."

The genteel woman wrinkled her nose delicately and chortled. "And with my sight gone, my sense of smell is most keen. But I am glad Holt brought you to meet me. Are you the same young man who tamed the kindia in such an unusual manner?"

"Not exactly." Bardon looked over to Holt, who nodded his approval of telling the story to his mother. "I spent the first day convincing Mig to accept a working relationship, using the common procedure. My friend, N'Rae, has a gift for dealing with animals. She tamed five in less time than I took with one."

"The lovely emerlindian girl?"

"Yes." He hesitated. "Excuse me, Dame Hoddack, but how do you know of her?"

She straightened the lace shawl draped over her shoulders.

"I have many visitors, and most of the servants are aware that I enjoy knowing what goes on beyond the walls of this house." She'd answered almost immediately, but Bardon detected a slight shuttering of her open friendliness. "I'm glad Holt brought you in. I am very interested in this N'Rae."

"It is my turn to beg your pardon, Mother. Father will be waiting for us in his study."

She reached for him, and he gave her his arm, which she patted. The pleased smile on her face transformed a weary expression to one of loveliness. "Yes, go, dear. See what he wants." She turned slightly toward Bardon, and the mask of the grand lady slipped back in place. "Good luck to you, young man."

"Thank you, Dame Hoddack." Squire Bardon followed Holt to another room on the ground floor.

Hoddack sat behind a large desk cluttered with papers. A sack of coins spilled across the top. Seven neat stacks of five shiny gold pieces, each large coin worth one hundred grood, lined up across the front edge of the desk. A thick, dark purple rug muffled their footsteps, but the kindia breeder's shaggy head jerked up as they entered.

"Took your time."

"We went to see Mother."

Hoddack grunted and waved an impatient hand, urging them closer. "Have a seat, Squire Bardon. I have an additional proposition for you."

Holt took a chair, lounging with a look of disinterest on his handsome face. His fingers played with the fringe sewn into the armrest. His foot silently jiggled.

Bardon remained standing. "My companions and I are on a journey. We've delayed long enough."

"This won't take much of your time, and what I have to offer might make your trip less taxing."

Bardon wanted nothing more than to collect his earnings and leave the crotchety old kindia breeder to stew over whether he'd been shrewd in their interchange. Or, whether he appeared a shrewd businessman in the eyes of the populace. Bone-weary and uncomfortable in his sweaty, dirty clothing, the squire wanted a bath, a meal, and to begin arranging for the transport of his companions down the river to Ianna. He sat on the leather chair next to Holt and waited to see what the farmer had in mind.

"I'm interested in the emerlindian." Hoddack leaned his stocky frame toward his visitor. "If you have an arduous journey ahead of you, you don't need to be encumbered by females."

Bardon remained silent. The sooner he had the money in his hands and got away from this man, the better. He noticed that Holt had ceased fidgeting. He stared at the tip of his shoe, but his stillness belied his lack of concern.

Hoddack picked up an empty money purse and a stack of coins. Through the wide opening, he let each grood piece drop into the soft leather sack. The first coin landed silently, but each one after clinked against the others.

"My son is of an age to marry. As is our tradition, I will arrange for a suitable bride. I find your emerlindian to be suitable."

Bardon clenched a fist, but he voiced his words in calm tones. "Her name is N'Rae, and it is not our tradition to arrange marriages. Furthermore, I am not her guardian."

Hoddack picked up a second stack of coins. "Then you shall propose my offer to the granny."

Bardon stood. "I think not."

The money ceased dropping into the purse. "Why? This alliance would bring her comfort and prestige."

Holt came to his feet, hooking his thumbs into his finely crafted belt. "I don't understand your sudden desire to marry me off, Father."

"You have nothing to do with it." Hoddack snarled his contempt for his son. "It's a matter of business. Do you realize what this emerlindian girl can do?"

"She tames kindias."

"Yes, and we want her to tame kindias for us, not for a competitor."

Holt's hands came away from his waist, and he clenched his fists. Propping them on the desk, he leaned across the clutter of paper and stacks of money. "That's preposterous! Why not just hire her?"

"Hired hands can walk away."

"And a married woman is trapped."

Hoddack stood and glared, his stance mirroring his son's. Inches separated their red faces. "It's business," Hoddack shouted. "Cool, calculated business without the niceties you and your mother prattle on about."

Bardon scooped up two stacks of the money and dropped them into the spacious pockets of his tunic. "No need for a family argument." He smiled at them both as he pocketed two more piles. "N'Rae has a plan in mind for her immediate future, and it does not involve romance, kindia farms, or business." He plucked the leather purse out of Hoddack's hand and gathered the last coins. "It has been interesting, if not a pleasure, doing business with you, Master Hoddack. I wish you well in your endeavors. All those that do not include me or my companions."

He turned on his heel and marched out before either father or son could make further comment.

Granny Kye and N'Rae waited for him in the front yard of the stately farmhouse. The younger emerlindian carried Jue Seeno's basket hooked over her arm.

"You look angry," commented N'Rae as she fell in beside his quick step.

Granny Kye ambled along behind them, seemingly more interested in the scenery than the young people.

He slowed. "Hoddack is an unpleasant marione, insensitive and prone to think first of money and not of people at all."

"His son is nice."

Bardon cast her a quick glance. "You met him?"

"There was little to do all day while we waited for the race to end. Dame Hoddack ordered a feast with roasted pig, duck, and goose. The neighbors brought all sorts of food, and Holt Hoddack made sure Grandmother and I had full plates and plenty to drink in the hot afternoon. He brought cushions from the house for us to sit on in the shade."

Bardon stopped and turned to face her. "So, do you want to go look for your father or stay here and dally with a farmer's son?"

N'Rae crossed her arms over her chest, swinging the basket recklessly. A squeak of protest came from within. "I want to find my father, of course. You can be so prickly. Whatever happened to 'Maturity wears well in soft words and even temper.' Principle thirty-something?"

"How do you know the principles?"

"My mother taught me. I told you I wasn't ignorant."

Bardon stomped down the lane toward the smaller barn. N'Rae and Granny Kye had to hurry to catch up. "We need a few basic supplies, transportation to Ianna, and that map."

"You need," spouted N'Rae, "a bath and clean clothes."

Bardon turned abruptly into the barn.

"Where are you going?" asked N'Rae.

"I owe a man some money."

"Our money?"

"His money. If it were our money, I wouldn't owe it to him." He paused inside the door. Several farm workers busied themselves with taking care of the kindia stock. "Ilex?"

"I'm here." Ilex stepped out of Ten's stall, a brush in his hand.

"Where can I find that man who gave up his chance to ride in the race?"

"Blosker. His cabin is down the east road just past the puny monarch tree. It drops a limb every time there's a wind. He ought to cut it down."

Bardon touched his forehead in a gesture of goodwill. "Thanks."

He turned to leave, but Ilex had one more thing to say.

"You'll be passing Cise's place as well."

"Who's Cise?"

"The breaker Mig broke."

Bardon looked into the old man's eyes for a moment. "I'll see to it." He walked more slowly out of the barn.

Ilex called after him. "There'll be a passel of kids in the yard and a swaybacked, piebald horse tethered under a trang-a-nog tree."

Bardon waved without turning. Not far from Hoddack's gates the road came to a crossing.

Bardon paused. "I have some errands to run before I go back to the inn. You ladies needn't walk the extra way. You can go back to Norst, and I'll be along in a little while."

"I want to come," protested N'Rae.

The older emerlindian nodded. "A walk is good for the soul."

Bardon cocked an eyebrow at the basket N'Rae carried.

"Perhaps Mistress Seeno is tired of being jostled."

"She sleeps when we travel," N'Rae said. "In fact, she sleeps more than anyone I've ever met."

Granny Kye touched her arm. "You've met very few outside of the ropma, infant."

"That's true. But isn't it also true, Grandmother, that Mistress Seeno sleeps a great deal?"

"I think she sleeps when we are awake, and she stands guard while we are sleeping."

"Really?"

"Of course. She is your protector."

N'Rae nodded. Bardon shook his head. He still found it absurd that the tiny minneken thought she could defend anyone. He led the way down the darkening road, beneath ancient trees rattling their leaves in the light gusts of air.

A clutch of o'rant children clambered in and around the trang-a-nog tree and over and under the swaybacked, splotchy horse.

Bardon asked the group in general, "Is your father at home?"

"He's sick-a-bed," answered one.

"Can't get up," said another.

"I'll fetch Ma," said a scrawny boy whose twin nodded vigorously and then raced the slightly smaller child to the door.

The slender woman with graying hair took the five hundred grood gratefully.

"It's half of what I won in Hoddack's race today," explained Bardon. "If Mig hadn't trounced your husband, he might have been riding the winning kindia."

She wrapped the coins in a scrap of cloth and tucked them into her apron. "You could step in for a bit of supper," she offered.

Bardon smiled. "Thank you, Mistress, but we have another errand and then some work to be done in town."

As they walked away, N'Rae said, "The horse and the dog were content but hungry."

Granny Kye looked back over her shoulder. "I imagine the children are the same."

"Did you not mindspeak?" Bardon asked the granny. He knew Kale might have used her talent to gather as much information as needed from the poor family.

"As little as possible. The older I get, the more I'm inclined to think it's often an invasion of privacy."

In memory, Bardon heard his own voice repeating a principle to Scribe Moran. *Draw the boundary of the mind that keeps you whole and respect the boundary drawn by another.*

Not much farther, they passed a woebegone monarch tree. Many rough stubs showed where limbs had cracked and fallen. Uneven patches of good growth revealed the heart of the tree to be sound. A man and his dog came out to greet them. Blosker took his half of the one-thousand-grood prize money readily.

"I knew that would be one whopper of a race," said the man who'd given up Ten so Squire Bardon could ride. "I've done that course plenty.

It's punishment for rider and kindia." He grinned and bounced the sack of coins in the palm of his hand. "It's good to have the money without the soreness you're going to feel tomorrow."

Bardon laughed and agreed. Already his muscles ached for a hot bath.

"Why did you come home?" asked N'Rae. "Why didn't you wait at the finish line to get your money?"

The weathered man pressed the bag of coins against his chest and pondered for a moment before answering. "Why, to give your friend here a chance to do the honorable thing. Then again, Hoddack might not have given the squire here the purse to carry to me. Then the old man himself would have a chance to show his core is aboveboard even if his style of dealing with folks makes you think otherwise.

"Master Hoddack's a strange boss," added Blosker. "Prides himself in being honest because his own family weren't known for being straightforward. When he married to get the farm, everyone thought he would be a stain on the neighborhood. But he's honorable in his begrudging way."

Blosker tossed the bag in the air, caught it, and slipped it inside his shirt. "The dame's father ran the business with a smile. It was right prosperous. Hoddack's kept it making a profit, but he doesn't have the genteel feel about him. Works hard, just doesn't know how to relax and enjoy what he's worked for."

Drummerbugs and crickets sang as the three walked back toward town.

"What did you learn, infant?" asked Granny Kye.

N'Rae shrugged.

"I won't take that for an answer." The old woman spoke softly as if she did not want to disturb the music of the night air. "Think of the people you saw today. The seven high races have much in common. All are prone to err. Not one of the high races is more righteous than another. Without fail you may count on individuals to sometimes make mistakes and sometimes do things right when dealing with their lot."

Bardon thought N'Rae would not answer, but eventually her small voice mingled with the cool breeze. "Hoddack does not enjoy his life and seeks to better it. The children of the injured man enjoy without having much. The mother sought to share what little supper she had. It's choices, isn't it?"

Granny patted her arm. "Yes, choices."

Bardon wondered what choices Hoddack would be making. He couldn't get the last thing Blosker said about the kindia breeder out of his mind.

"Hoddack holds on to an idea like a bodoggin. Once he's thought of a plan, he don't give up."

BE PREPARED

Bardon managed to escape the women to have supper and a bath in his room. Too weary to master his thoughts, he lay in the tub of hot water and drifted from one scenario to another. In one half dream, Paladin arrived and took over the care of the three women, ordering Bardon to return to the mountain cabin. In another, N'Rae's father strode through the inn door and announced he'd been shipwrecked and just managed to return to Amara. In the last, N'Rae declared her undying love for Holt Hoddack, and the farm boy took over the expedition to the Northern Reach.

He could think of no principle that would allow him to indulge in these fantasies.

"'A meager man looks to his own comfort first,'" he recited as he hauled his aching body out of the cooling water.

"'The straight path to easy living is fraught with deception, the worst being in the heart of the man who looks neither right nor left.'" He toweled himself dry with a vigorous rub.

"'A man moves forward faster if he doesn't have to look over his shoulder.'" He rubbed in the last of Master Hoddack's liniment and put on his nightshirt.

The mattress cushioned his sore muscles in a most satisfying manner. Bardon stretched carefully under the weighty covers and stared at the pine-beam ceiling. When a knock resounded on the door, he thought the manservant had come to haul off the bath water. Still, responding to training, he reached for his hunting knife and laid it alongside his leg, on top of the blanket.

"Come in."

The doorknob turned hesitantly. A narrow line of light appeared as the door creaked open an inch. Bardon's hand tightened on his weapon. *This is not the way the servant would enter the room.*

"It's me," said Granny Kye, a second before she pushed open the door. "I've brought you tea to ease your aches and help you sleep."

Relaxing, he sat up awkwardly in the bed to receive the mug.

"Thank you, Granny Kye."

"You're welcome, son. I know that not only your overworked body would give you trouble tonight as you try to sleep but also your keenly felt need to do what is right."

Bardon sipped the tea and chose not to answer.

Granny Kye took a step back but did not turn to leave. "It's hard to be wise." The humble woman stood peacefully beside his bed. Her dark eyes gleamed in the candlelight. "I shall tell you something about myself that is unusual for an emerlindian."

She remained silent, and Bardon wondered if he was required to say something. "Yes?"

"I did not darken as one of our race usually does. People would think I was much younger than my years because of my pallor."

Her shoulders drooped, and she folded her hands at her waist. "I did not learn from my mistakes. I could not reason out a problem. I could not remember what had been told to me the day before. It was not until I realized that Wulder gave me a different gift of wisdom that I began to mature, to darken." She sighed and looked the young squire in the eye. "You won't be able to depend on me to know the answers, to guide you on this journey."

"You knew there's a mapmaker in Ianna."

"Because Paladin told me so a dozen times in the past year." She spread her hands in a gesture of helplessness. "He also gave me funds for the quest."

"And you lost them?"

"Oh no! I would never be so careless. I gave them away." Her face did not reflect any qualms about her misuse of the money.

"If Paladin gave you funds for a specific purpose and you used them for another, don't you think you have done wrong?"

A whimsical smile lifted the corners of her mouth, and her brown eyes flashed with amusement. "He said they were for needs as I would meet them. Unfortunately, I continually meet people whose needs are greater than my own."

"Remind me not to let you carry the purse."

Granny Kye chortled. "See? You already prove that you're wiser than I am."

"The coins I left with you on our first morning in Norst?"

"Gone."

"Gone?"

"Before the day ended." She paused. "The wheelwright had a need for a new hammer. The kitchen maid has a poorly mother. The boy delivering milk needed sturdy shoes."

"I see."

"Also, anything requiring memory is troublesome. However, I am good with herbs, though I sometimes make mistakes."

Bardon stopped before taking the next sip.

"Oh, the tea's all right," Granny Kye assured him. "Jue Seeno helped me."

He let out a gust of pent-up breath and took another soothing swallow.

"What area is your wisdom in, Granny Kye?"

She beamed. "Painting."

Bardon considered this for a moment. "You don't happen to paint murals, do you?"

"No." She tilted her head and looked curiously at him. "Why?"

"Kale Allerion has seen two murals which turned out to be prophetic."

"How odd. No, I do portraits, mostly."

"Portraits? And how does your wisdom show up in portraits?"

"I paint the people as I see them. But when I finish, there's more there. While I'm painting, the expressions on their faces and the colors around them become clear in my mind. Some people say that the finished picture looks like the inside of the person instead of just what is seen on the outside."

Bardon nodded. "I had a friend who saw colors around people, and he said they reflected character and inner conflict."

"He saw them all the time?"

"Yes, but he said he had to focus especially on the colors to read them correctly."

"I don't see them with my eyes even when I paint. But some part of me does, because they always end up on the canvas." Granny Kye still stood relaxed in the same position. "Where is your friend now?"

"In Bedderman's Bog, at the home of Wizard Fenworth. He's training to be a wizard. You said 'mostly,' Granny Kye. What else do you paint?"

"Landscapes, houses… They rarely turn out very well." Her face brightened. "Once I painted a neighbor's house, and in the painting, we saw an odd object under a bush. We went to look, and there was the bracelet she'd lost months before."

"So you saw something while you painted that couldn't be seen just by looking?"

"Yes!"

"I agree with you, Granny Kye, that's definitely a type of wisdom."

The old emerlindian's expression clouded. "Not one that's very useful in the normal way of things. I understand N'Rae much better than most people would, though. She, too, does not fit the typical image of an emerlindian."

"Mistress Seeno would prefer that she did."

"Jue Seeno is devoted to N'Rae, but her mannerisms are somewhat abrupt. And you make her a bit nervous."

"I make her nervous?"

"Decidedly so. Now, are you finished with that tea?" She held out her hand. "Give me the mug. I'll leave you to your sleep."

Taking the mug with her, she swept out of the room, saying over her shoulder, "Don't fret. Trust!"

Amazingly, he put his head down on the pillow and fell into a deep sleep. In the middle of the night, he rolled over and opened his eyes. For a moment he thought he saw a mouse sitting on the windowsill in the moonlight. But he blinked, and it was gone.

Jue Seeno? No, she wouldn't be out and about disguised as a mouse. He grinned at the very idea and went back to sleep.

When golden sunlight, instead of the pale glow of the moon, poured through the curtains, Bardon got out of bed stiffly, stretching his muscles with slow, deliberate movements. By the time he shaved and dressed, he could walk without wincing. He joined the ladies for breakfast in the private parlor, and a cup of Granny Kye's tea finished the job of alleviating the discomfort in his body.

"May I go with you to find passage to Ianna?" asked N'Rae. "We'll go on the river, won't we?"

"No, you may not come. Yes, we shall go by the Gilpen River, but the docks are no place for you." Bardon saw her look of disappointment. "If I find a ship quickly, I'll return and take you to the market streets." He turned to include Granny Kye and Mistress Seeno. "Wouldn't you ladies like to look for some new clothing? You should have something new for everyday wear and perhaps garments suitable for rough traveling."

He was rewarded for his suggestion. N'Rae's face took on a flush of pleasure. "Grandmother, can we? Does this mean I'll get to wear britches?"

"Yes." Granny Kye watched Bardon stand and push his chair back under the table. "Do you have sisters, young man?"

"Not that I know of. Why?"

"Because you seem to know a lot about what makes young women happy."

Jue Seeno squeaked, and Bardon bent closer to the table.

"It could," the minneken said, "also mean he spent a lot of time pleasing the ladies at the Castle Pelacce."

Bardon straightened abruptly, his face burning. He heard N'Rae giggle as he left the room.

What a pleasure it will be to visit the docks where none of the men have manners, none of the men have bathed recently, and none of the men giggle! He hurried through the hall and out onto the cobblestone street.

As he approached the riverway, the houses became less well groomed, as did the people. He stopped in a tavern to have a drink and listen to the news. He heard of a small vessel departing the next day and headed out to find the captain. He soon had made arrangements for them to board the ship that night. The *Morning Lady* would weigh anchor before dawn the next day.

The shopping trip with the women tried his patience. He had managed to secure information and passage in less than an hour. The women spent that much time just deciding which street of shops they would visit first. Then they discussed whether Jue Seeno would accompany them or wait at the inn. The prospect of a servant finding the basket and, out of curiosity, peeking inside terrified them. They decided the minneken would go with them but stay in her basket and wait until they returned to view their purchases.

After making the mistake of entering the first haberdashery with the lady shoppers, Bardon waited outside the other stores. He tried to admire the stamina and cheerful attitudes of the two women as they tramped from one establishment to the next and back to compare the quality and price of certain merchandise. He smiled politely at the citizens of Norst who noticed the unusual sight of two country-dressed emerlindians touring the shopping district. By midafternoon he decided he wasn't as wise as Granny Kye had intimated. *Surely, a wise man would have avoided this expedition.*

He gladly toted the packages back to the inn when Granny Kye said they had purchased the few items they would need. The women inspected their purchases, showing the new clothing to Jue Seeno. Bardon thought the little minneken showed a far more pleasant demeanor as she gave her opinion.

"A woman may appear to value things above all else, but don't try to steal her offspring, friend, or mate." Principle eighty-seven. And this, Scribe Moran said, was what made women so hard to interpret.

After they ate a quick supper, Granny Kye insisted they could walk to the pier, but Squire Bardon ordered a horse-drawn vehicle to be their transportation. After a short ride, they boarded the *Morning Lady,* a passenger ship also hauling a cargo of textiles.

Bardon settled his charges in their cabin and then retired to his own. When he pulled the bunk down from the wall, he could barely turn around. Backing into the bulkhead, he scraped his shoulder. The rough wood left splinters in the cloth of his shirt.

Shouldn't that wood be painted? He tried to reach over his back to assess the damage and bumped his head on the shoulder, a brace of wood that joined the bulkhead to the overhead. Rubbing his head, he mumbled, "I now know for a fact that I've been spoiled by venturing out to sea on one of Sir Dar's sloops. The ceiling in this hold is too low, the walls are too close, and the light is abominable."

He fished book two of his Tomes of Wulder from his pack and began to read, finding comfort in the succinct wisdom of the principles and in the ritual of setting his heart to uphold those principles. The real purpose of this exercise was not to refresh his memory of the written words, but rather to regain his focus. In the past several days, he had found himself so busy dealing with problems that he had often proceeded without tagging each action with an appropriate principle.

The scribes and mentors said that one day the words repeated with the mind would be ingrained in the heart, and the need for constant rehearsal would diminish. Bardon thought that would never happen for him.

After reading until the candle guttered, he blew out the sputtering flame, put the book on the table, and scooted down into the covers. The air over the water permeated the small cabin and chilled him. He pulled the blanket up to his chin. The inn's accommodations had definitely been more comfortable.

At least the ladies have a finer cabin, but I bet they're cold. Curled slightly for warmth, he listened to the creaks of the wooden ship and the faint lapping of the water.

Peaceful for now. But soon we will embark on a quest. I have never heard of a peaceful quest. If I expect giant serpents, evil minions of the devious Wizards Cropper and Stox, and perhaps interference from a troop of bisonbecks, will I be better prepared?

Wulder, I ask that You keep me alert, ever prepared to meet the challenges of this journey, and capable of protecting these ladies. And then I ask that You allow nothing to cross our path that would test my alertness, preparedness, or capabilities. Thank You, Wulder, for Your gift of this time and this place.

⊹≻═≺⊹

A skittering sound roused him from his slumber. With eyes open, he lay still, for he felt certain the noise had come from within his cabin. His hand moved to embrace the handle of his hunting knife. He slipped the finely honed blade out of the sheath.

A slight thump on the mattress puzzled him, and he almost quit breathing in order to listen.

Mistress Seeno's small voice whispered in his ear. "Squire Bardon, get up and arm yourself. A quiss has come on board."

12

A Renegade Quiss

"Meet me on deck when you're dressed," Mistress Seeno said as she jumped to the floor. Her gray blue cape fluttered around her chubby form as she scampered across the wood planks and slipped under the door.

One quiss? I thought they traveled in hordes. He pulled on his britches and stuck his feet in his boots. *I suppose it is possible a quiss could be this far inland. It could have become disoriented and followed the river. But alone? I thought they came out of the ocean en masse every three years.* He buckled on his sword belt, stuck his hunting knife in its sheath, and grabbed a short quiver full of darts. *Don't quiss harass the northeast coast, not the southwest?* He opened the door and entered the dark hallway. *Perhaps it isn't a quiss at all.*

He crept up the ladder and surveyed the deck before stepping out of the open hatch.

How am I supposed to find a little minneken before I find this intruder?

A movement along the wall caught his eye. Jue Seeno emerged from the shadows, scurried across the wood deck, and leapt for his leg. He found it disconcerting to have her scramble up the outer seam of his britches, up the side of his shirt, and onto his shoulder.

She panted. Tiny puffs of hot air tickled his jaw line.

"One dead. Around the corner. Very unpleasant sight." She shuddered. "I believe the quiss has gone to the stern, toward the quarterdeck. We must hurry if we are to save lives."

Bardon had never seen firsthand what the ocean creatures could do, but he'd come across accounts in books and heard tales from seasoned warriors. As one of the seven low races, quiss rivaled the blimmets in their ability to quickly destroy a target. However, blimmets fought with more vicious, mad-animal vigor. Quiss moved slowly. The danger lay in their numerous, boneless arms. Quiss encircled their victims with these muscular appendages, each having three rows of suction cups running from shoulder to tip. In the center of each cup, a sharp and hollow tongue the size of a large needle squirmed, tasting the air, searching for flesh to penetrate.

Bardon edged to the corner and cautiously peered around. On the deck a heap of clothing marked the spot where a seaman had gone down in the clutches of the intruder. Nothing moved in the area, so Bardon crept toward the figure. At first sight of the dead man's face, he swallowed to keep the bile from rising in his throat. He no longer doubted that a quiss lurked somewhere on the ship.

The victim's flesh and blood had been sucked from his body. An empty bag of skin draped the skeleton. Pinpricks in the center of inch-wide, red circles lined the corpse wherever skin showed.

Bardon tried not to breathe. His ears strained to hear the slight swish of an almost entirely boneless body. Only two appendages from the trunk of the body contained enough cartilage to be used as legs. He remembered gruesome tales told in the dormitory. They usually ended with a quiss arm writhing out from a dark corner and snatching a helpless boy.

Once a victim fell into the clutches of a quiss, the thousand tongues stabbed. Hopefully, the last thing the unfortunate soul felt was the pricks of the beast's tongues. The quiss then injected its poisonous saliva, which broke down flesh into a soft mush, and sucked all the soft tissue until the skin was nothing more than a sack for the bones.

Each hair on Bardon's arms and the back of his neck stood on end as a tremor of horror ran across his skin. He turned away from the sailor, blinked, swallowed, and took a deep breath.

"Which way did you say it went, Mistress Seeno?"

"Look down, to your right."

In the eerie light of a half moon, he saw a dark, sketchy trail like a mass of inky lines entangling solid footprints. The beast walked upright on two legs with its many arms trailing. With another shock of revulsion, Bardon realized the dark lines would be red in the sunlight. The creature oozed the fluids of its last meal.

"Don't touch that," warned Jue Seeno.

"I know." Bardon held his breath. "I know it's poisonous."

"Even the smell will become toxic soon."

"It'll smell worse than this?"

"Definitely."

"Let's get rid of this creature. I'm already tired of his company."

Bardon drew his sword and followed, careful not to step on the slimy trail. The sound of a man struggling put an end to his caution. He ran from the shadows of the quarterdeck with his sword raised, ready to strike. Jue Seeno squeaked and leapt from his shoulder, landing on a barrel and shouting a cheer, "Skewer it through and through, young man! Don't let it get the best of you!"

"To arms!" Bardon shouted. "To arms!"

He did not wait for an answer to his call for help but sprinted across the deck. The quiss, with its bulbous head and flailing arms, all but covered a small, wiry man. With a downward swing, Bardon sliced open the back of the creature. The ease with which his sword penetrated the body of the quiss surprised him.

I'll have to be careful not to cut through this beast and into the sailor.

A brief glimpse of the seaman's face as the quiss twirled toward its attacker told Bardon he need not worry about the man's fate. His sword could no longer injure the sailor.

Behind him, Bardon heard the heavy footsteps of men, shouts of dismay, and the voice of the captain issuing orders. He hoped Jue Seeno had made it below deck without being seen.

The longer, heavier arms of the quiss squeezed its victim. The shorter, more limber appendages whipped out at the young squire. Bardon swung his sword in an arc and lopped off the closest threatening arms. Pulling back, he placed both hands on the hilt of his weapon and with a lunge, skewered the beast clean through. The force of the blow pushed the speared quiss and sailor back against a rail. The sword tip stuck in the wood. The remaining smaller arms thrashed the air. The larger arms continued to embrace the dead man. Slowly, the violent thrashing of the creature subsided. Its body quivered.

Bardon stepped back. He left the sword impaling the quiss and the corpse. A crowd now stood upon the deck. Hushed murmurs rustled behind him, but the young squire did not take his eyes off the tangled mass of squirming tentacles. Instead, he drew his hunting knife as if the creature would somehow escape certain death, free itself from the sword, and spring at him.

It opened its eyes and focused on him. The small orbs looked strangely like those of one of the high races except for the lack of hair on the brow and lid. Its expression filled Bardon with sorrow.

The eyes shifted to something beyond the squire. Bardon turned slightly to find N'Rae standing beside him. A nightgown and a voluminous shawl swathed her slight frame. She stared at the dying creature. Bardon knew that look. He put his arm around her quaking shoulders. In a moment the creature closed its eyes. Its body became still.

"He's dead," N'Rae whispered.

After sheathing the hunting knife, Bardon stepped forward and wrenched his sword from the two corpses. They fell as one to the deck.

"Bardon." N'Rae's voice trembled. "Take me away from here. Take me back to Granny Kye and Jue Seeno."

With his arm around her waist, he awkwardly guided her through the crowd. He didn't want to put the soiled sword into its scabbard.

The first mate intercepted them. "I'd be honored to clean your weapon for you, Squire Bardon. The captain said to extend his thanks. He's busy now calming both the passengers and the crew, and setting up a more vigilant watch. Never heard the likes of this." He shook his shaggy head in wonderment and held out his hand for the sword. "I'll return it to you in a trice. We're blessed you were aboard when this happened. Can't imagine such a thing taking place this far up the Gilpen River."

Bardon handed him the sword and then continued with N'Rae, seeking the sanctuary of Granny Kye's cabin.

The old emerlindian greeted them and took N'Rae in her arms, hugging the pale girl tightly before sitting her on the edge of the bunk bed.

She patted Bardon's arm and nodded toward a shelf, where Jue Seeno sat at her small table, sipping from a cup. Even the minneken looked shaken.

"Mistress Seeno told me," said Granny Kye. "What is the world coming to when one of those creatures ventures out by itself? It was an unnatural act, and you can be sure those two, Crim Cropper and Burner Stox, are behind it."

N'Rae sobbed. Granny promptly sat down beside her and pulled her close. "There now, infant. We're not likely to meet another of its kind once we get to the Northern Reach."

The young emerlindian nodded and tried to speak, but only a garbled, throaty wail came out.

Granny continued to pat. The minneken squeaked.

"What was that?" asked Bardon as he moved closer to hear.

"Give her some tea."

Bardon looked around and saw the kettle on a small iron stove. He went to pour the hot water on tea leaves already in the bottom of a mug, but he found the kettle needed to be centered on the hot plate and reheated. He searched the cabinet for a spoon and sugar. His hand rested on a glass jar filled with white crystals, but N'Rae's voice stopped him before he lifted the container.

"It spoke to me."

Granny Kye gasped. "The quiss?"

Bardon turned to see the young emerlindian nodding her head so forcefully her hair flung about her.

"What did it say, dear?" asked Granny Kye.

"It was miserable. So distraught. Not about dying. It wanted to die."

Bardon crossed the room and knelt before N'Rae. He took both her hands in his and looked up at her tear-stained face. "Why was it here?"

"It was trying to get away—away from an evil man and an evil woman. The picture in its mind was of hundreds of quiss, herded into an underground cavern full of water, trapped in the dark, and taken one by one to some unknown place of terror. And always, the evil man and woman glaring. The man had knives. The woman laughed."

13

Down the Gilpen

Bardon hated to press, but she knew more. The haunted look in her eyes told him so. "Is that all you saw, N'Rae?"

She shook her head and took a deep breath. "It was young. In his mind, he referred to himself as one of the young ones. He hurt, and all the young ones born in the man's laboratory were suffering.

"I saw them gasping and writhing in pain. I felt the pain. They had lungs that the old ones did not, and the lungs hurt." N'Rae hugged herself, curling forward, and rocking as if she felt the agony of the quiss.

"I saw images of the gills of the young ones and flashes of gills on the old ones. They were so close to being the same, but the gills on the young ones gaped and became oozy."

Her face twisted as she remembered, and she touched her neck as if she could feel thin slits that would allow her to breathe underwater.

"I saw young ones flailing about in the dark water, being pulled down by two malformed appendages. The old ones walked on land once every three years when those leg things grew rigid." She shook her head. "The young ones could walk on land at any time, but the 'legs' hurt."

She squeezed her eyes shut. "And this quiss was ravenously hungry, always hungry, driven to find food even after it had just eaten. It ate so much that the surplus oozed out of its skin, and that hurt too."

Bardon remembered the slimy dark trail on the deck and suppressed a shudder.

"Anything else, N'Rae?"

"The quiss had begun eating each other in the confines of the small cavern they were in. The man ordered them to be separated into smaller caves and vats of water. This quiss escaped while being transferred to a different prison."

She opened her eyes and reached out to take Bardon's hands. "They understand when people talk. It understood what the man said. It knew they would all die, but the next batch the man would have born in his laboratory would live. The man said so. And the woman laughed. It hated her laugh."

Bardon patted her hand. "Do you have any idea where all this took place?"

"No, just that it swam away from the morning sun and toward the evening sun for many days."

Bardon nodded, thinking the quiss must have come from somewhere in Creemoor. When they reached Ianna, he would have to get word to Paladin. Two things he wanted to relay. He'd write a report of the lone quiss boarding the *Morning Lady.* That would be astonishing in itself. But N'Rae's encounter bewildered him. He knew Paladin would send warriors to investigate the facts. The squire couldn't help but be skeptical of the quiss's story.

How much of this plight of the quiss is true? I'd rather it all be the wild imaginations of a twisted mind. Amara does not need another evil army to combat.

He stood and looked down at N'Rae. She still wept, enveloped in Granny's tender embrace. A string of principles streamed through his consciousness. Only a few seemed appropriate to comfort the young emerlindian. He wrestled with which ones to repeat aloud.

" 'Turn your thoughts to Wulder. Your praise will strengthen you.' 'Let not images of evil dominate your thinking. They distort the truth.' " He sighed, trying to think of words that would help in *this* situation, not words that applied to life in general. "N'Rae, dwelling on the misery of the quiss will weaken you. Paladin calls us to a quest. You must be physically and mentally ready."

The words didn't help him. Why should they help this girl?

He paused before leaving the room to pour hot water in the mug.

Here he stood next to the shelf where the minneken sat at her table, nibbling on a piece of cracker and cheese.

"Thank you, Mistress Seeno, for alerting me to the danger."

She cocked her head at him. "Didn't believe me, did you?"

He smiled and considered how to answer. Before he had the right words in order, she laughed. "I didn't believe my own eyes, so I guess I can't blame you for being skeptical." She shook her head, a big smile brightening her usually somber expression. "And I did enjoy seeing you wield that sword. My! You've been trained well. Couldn't have done better myself."

Bardon felt his eyebrows rise and brought them down again before the testy matron could see them. He tightened his jaw for a moment to block the laugh that threatened to burst forth. Sir Dar would counsel courtesy, and Squire Bardon had mastered the semblance of courtesy. "You have a sword, Mistress?"

"Of course." She bristled. "What kind of a protector would I be if I had no sword?" She chewed on her cracker, swallowed, and took a sip of tea. "I also carry knives, darts, a bow and arrow, and all I would need for ministering to the wounded."

This time he could not keep his eyebrows from shooting upward. *And what kind of damage can you do to an enemy with a sword the size of a needle?* He bit back on the discourteous question and chose one more suitable. "Where do you keep all that?"

She stirred her tea with a tiny spoon. "Oh, I have secrets, you know."

Bardon remembered the cape she'd worn that night. "A moonbeam cape!"

Jue Seeno's face twisted in disgust. "Yes, if you must know."

"Where does one get the fiber to weave a moonbeam cape on the Isle of Kye?"

Jue Seeno stood and placed her tiny hands on her round hips. "Young man, Kye is a very civilized place. We have butchers, bakers, blacksmiths, lawyers, lamplighters, legislators, doctors, dancers, ditch diggers, schools, churches, and a university. We grow crops, manage businesses, and practice the fine arts. And in the woods, we even have moonbeam plants from which we take the fiber and manufacture cloth. It comes in very handy when an occasional bird of prey gets past the violent currents of air that buffet, and thereby protect, our shores."

Bardon felt a twinge of guilt. The tiny woman had truly been heroic this night, and still, he dismissed her ability to serve just because of her size. *I must make a more concerted effort to respect her for who she is.*

He cleared his throat. "Excuse me, Mistress Seeno. I didn't mean to imply that the Isle of Kye was uncivilized."

She folded her hands across the fancy braided belt encircling her plump waist. She gazed at some distant point across the room and tapped her foot.

Bardon waited. He couldn't say much after he had already apologized.

Her foot stopped. She sat down in her comfy chair, looked up at him, and cleared her throat.

"I am sorry for my tirade. I seem to be a bit out of sorts in this large world of yours…and truly, the quiss did disturb me greatly." She chuckled and took up her cup. "That tea you made for N'Rae will be crawling out of the mug and walking if you don't see to it soon."

Bardon stirred in the sugar and presented the mug to N'Rae.

"Would you like tea as well, Granny Kye?" asked the young squire.

"Yes, thank you." She stroked N'Rae's long blond hair away from her face. "Sip it slowly, infant. Those are heavy tea leaves and will stay at the bottom if you don't stir them up by gulping the brew."

Bardon returned to the stove to fix another mug for Granny. Jue Seeno motioned him closer once the water was poured.

"I like you, Bardon," she said, casting a glance at the emerlindian women. Granny Kye hovered over the girl as she put her to bed in a sitting position to drink the tea. "I shall count it a pleasure to work with you in the charge to protect the girl."

Not knowing what to say, Bardon merely nodded.

"Although it goes against the grain to do so, I place myself under your authority. I should have done so immediately, for Granny Kye said it was obvious that Paladin had arranged for you to lead our quest." She blinked, glanced down, and then directly into the squire's eyes. "Frankly, I have a bit of a problem with pride." A twinkle came to her eyes, and a smile quirked her thin lips. "You can help me with that."

"I would be honored to assist you, Mistress Seeno."

She leaned forward and whispered. Bardon had to bend quickly to get his ear close enough to hear.

"I hate being mistaken for a rodent." Her eyes darted from side to side. "A mouse." Her expression hardened, and she stiffened, standing erect. "Should you ever hear someone refer to me by that name, skewer him!" At Bardon's jolt of surprise, she added, "At the very least, persuade him he is mistaken."

Bardon cleared his throat and worked to keep his expression bland. "And if the mistaken person is a young girl who leaps to stand on a chair as you pass, should I skewer her?"

The minneken's tail twitched, and her eyes narrowed. She pointed a finger at him and wagged it. "N'Rae told me not to mention your ears because it causes you distress. I would appreciate the same sort of courtesy returned to me. This is not a matter to be taken lightly."

Bardon wondered if all three women had discussed his ears. He frowned but realized talking about the matter would further confirm the minneken's impression that his ears were a point of contention.

What would Sir Dar say? He'd say to be polite. It never damages your objective to be polite. Outmaneuver your opponent with manners.

"Yes, Mistress Seeno. I understand. I shall endeavor to be more sensitive to your concern. But surely the problem will not arise. Aren't you to remain hidden? I assume you are not in favor of the general populace learning that minnekens do, indeed, exist."

"Quite right, but at some time on my reconnaissance, I could inadvertently be seen."

"At that time, wouldn't it be more convenient to be mistaken for a mouse?"

Her mouth popped open and then slammed shut. Her whiskers quivered, and if her eyes could have done damage to his person, he would have fallen to the floor. Quite without warning, Jue Seeno dropped into her chair and started chuckling. She then began to laugh and ended up wiping tears from her eyes with a tiny handkerchief.

"Oh, lad," she gasped, "you have a hidden streak of mischief. This quest will be a most surprising venture."

Bardon turned back to the stove and reached for the container of sugar.

Mischief? As in humor? I thought it was a very practical suggestion that she let people think she is a mouse. He remembered the mouse he thought he had seen sitting on the windowsill of the inn. *Perhaps she does on occasion lurk in the shadows as a mouse. Ah well, it might be one of her little secrets. But why would she pretend to be a mouse when she has the moonbeam cape?*

People, even minnekens, are too complicated to be understood. Sir Dar thinks I have acquired social skills. Jue Seeno thinks I have a sense of humor. And I think there are too many people in the world. Way too many people.

He finished the tea and handed it to Granny Kye.

"Is there anything else I can do for you ladies tonight?"

N'Rae gave him a wan smile and shook her head. The minneken squeaked. Even though he did not actually catch what she said, she didn't look like she was at all interested in him anymore. She had a long strip in her hands, and he realized she was weaving yet another elaborate belt. Granny Kye shooed him out of the room with a wave.

He moved to the door. "Try to get some sleep. Drink the tea," he said in parting.

In his small cabin, he lit the lantern, folded up the bunk and latched it to the wall, then sat on the floor to write his missive to Paladin.

The first mate came to Bardon's cabin and returned the polished sword.

"What has the captain done about the incident?" Bardon asked.

"He took the bodies ashore and informed the dock manager, who informed the constable, who informed the mayor. Quite a to-do, and for good reason. That thing could have gone ashore instead of boarding the *Lady*. The word'll spread quite readily." He squinted at Bardon. "Do you know if the beasts attack during the day as well as at night?"

"According to the books, they do. But our intruder did not do things according to the books."

The first mate scratched at his stubble-coated chin. "That it didn't. Hope this was just a fluke, and there are no more of them quiss lurking about. We'll keep a close watch." He touched the bill of his cap. "Sorry to disturb you, but I figured you'd rest easier with the weapon at your side, considering…" He shrugged and headed down the narrow hallway.

By the time Bardon finally crawled into bed, he could hear the sailors in the predawn preparing to lift anchor and take the river vessel down the Gilpen.

Later in the morning, the squire sat on one of the crates lashed to the deck and leaned up against another. He held a book in his hands and read from it sporadically. As time progressed, everyone began to relax. Nothing unusual occurred to mar the beautiful, cloudless day.

Granny Kye and N'Rae strolled the deck to get some air in the afternoon, avoiding the stern area where the two sailors and the quiss had died.

That evening, Jue Seeno announced she would not be patrolling outside the cabin.

"There's an abundance of crewmen out there searching the water as if an invasion of quiss is imminent. I'll be on watch here, though. I do not intend to neglect my charge."

The uneventful night and the next day eased the tension even more. The journey downriver to the seaport took two days. The crew went about their business, but with many anxious glances at the railings around the deck. As they traveled, they passed houses on the shore and boats on the water. The people in this area seemingly went about their business in a normal way. No threat of quiss appeared. An hour away from Ianna's dock, Bardon let go of the wariness that kept him on guard.

As they drew near the sea, a salty tang sharpened the dank smell of the river. Traffic on the waterway became congested. Small boats used for transporting people short distances joined the bigger vessels used in commerce. Barges, ferries, and packets chugged along. Voices cried out from ship to ship and from ship to shore. No one mentioned quiss or mysterious disappearances or gruesome deaths. Apparently all was well in Ianna.

Bardon carried their meager baggage above deck, and they all stood at the rail, watching and enjoying the bustle of the harbor.

As they came alongside the dock, Bardon saw an unwelcome sight.

"Look!" cried N'Rae and pointed. "That marione sitting on the cargo bales on the dock. Isn't that Holt Hoddack?"

Granny Kye glanced at Bardon behind the girl's back. She winked at him, and he turned abruptly away. He heard her calm voice, deep and smooth.

"Yes, infant. It is."

14

LANDING IN IANNA

The ship slid into its mooring, but the sailors had not yet lowered the gangway when Holt jumped off his perch. He strode to the edge of the dock, waving at them.

N'Rae waved back. "Hello, Holt. How did you get here?"

"By kindia, of course."

His upturned face, filled with laughter, caught the rays of the sun. Two dimples framed his happy expression. The sea breeze tossed his blond hair.

"Why are you here?" asked N'Rae, smiling and still waving.

"To see you. Why else?"

N'Rae dropped her hands to clutch the railing and bounced on her toes. The minneken's basket on her arm swung sharply, and Bardon wondered how Jue Seeno fared within.

He rolled his eyes, shook his head, and picked up the heavier pieces of their belongings to be taken ashore. He headed to where the sailors hefted the gangway into place. As soon as the wood scraped the pier, Holt bounded up, passed Bardon, and greeted the two emerlindian women. He took Granny Kye's fragile hand in his two square ones and shook it while expressing his joy in seeing them again. But when speaking to N'Rae, the marione took both her hands and held on much longer than Bardon thought necessary.

N'Rae laughed at something the marione had said.

The squire scowled. *You silly little widget. You're all smiles now, but this bounder will crush your happiness. I should warn you off of bestowing your friendship on someone who wears his charm like a pretty garment to make himself look better. Sir Dar's gallant behavior is to ease another's discomfort. How do I explain the difference to this infatuated child?*

But then again, it's no business of mine if she gets entangled with this spoiled youngster… Well, not really a youngster. I guess he's just a year or two younger than I am.

Bardon's fists tightened. *But N'Rae's been entrusted to my care for some inexplicable reason. Master Hoddack is a wily man whose concept of valor certainly falls short of mine. I thought Holt didn't want to have anything to do with this pursuit of N'Rae. So why is he here? Is he a pup, a dog, or a cur?*

N'Rae giggled. The sun made a halo as it filtered through the loose strands of her light blond hair. Holt flung a hand out in an expansive gesture accentuating some story he related. He looked friendly and innocent, like a bothersome puppy.

Bardon bottled behind clamped teeth the command he wished to blast at Holt. He also fought the urge to physically remove N'Rae from the smooth marione's guile. *She is so incredibly naive. Someone should be keeping an eye on her.*

He looked at Granny Kye. The old emerlindian gazed about her with a smile on her face, obviously enjoying the sights of the harbor and unaware that Holt was a potential threat to her granddaughter's happiness.

I am beginning to think it's true. This granny will not be a help on the quest. Who ever heard of an incompetent emerlindian?

Bardon felt the back of his neck tighten. "We have a lot to do," he observed. "I'll inquire after suitable lodging and find transportation."

Holt stood straighter. "Let me help."

Bardon thought the farmer's son even puffed up a bit.

Holt beamed at the ladies. "I've found a modest inn, clean and uncrowded. And as I waited for your boat to come in, I scouted around the dock. I'll be back in just a few minutes with a vehicle for hire." He hurried away before anyone could answer.

"A most accommodating young man," said Granny Kye.

"Yes," said N'Rae, her eyes glowing as she watched the young man disappear in the crowd. She turned to Bardon, took his arm, and squeezed it. "Isn't he nice? And isn't it nice to have friends?"

Bardon put his arm around her shoulders and gave her a little shake. His response to her joy confused him.

He sighed, sent up a quick petition to Wulder for guidance, and gently squeezed N'Rae's shoulders. "Be careful with whom you make friends, little one."

"I know," she giggled. "'The friendship of a viper is not worth the spit on his tongue.'"

Bardon released her and laughed. "Yes, that is one of the pithier principles."

Granny Kye nodded to where Holt could be seen walking in front of a cart pulled by an old horse. Big chunks of dull paint had chipped away from the cart's chassis. A gray and muted-red striped canopy shaded the passenger seat. The upholstery looked handmade, faded but clean.

Bardon picked up most of their personal belongings. With the ladies following, he carried the baggage and bigger parcels down to the pier and onto the broad wooden platform that ran the length of the docks. He set the pieces down. Granny Kye and N'Rae stopped on either side of him. Bardon glanced at the younger emerlindian and saw her eyes trained on the handsome marione. Squire Bardon deliberately turned to study the horse instead of the irksome young couple.

The harness hung on the roan's bony frame, and someone had put an oversized straw hat on her head. Her ears stuck through holes in the wide brim, and colorful flowers almost hid them.

Holt hurried forward. "Let me help with the luggage. N'Rae, may I carry your basket for you?" He reached for the minneken's traveling quarters.

"Oh no, Jue Seeno's quite light."

Holt pulled back his hand, and a slight frown pinched his features. "Seeno?"

N'Rae's face flushed red. "I-I s-see no reason for you to carry it. The basket is quite light." She tittered. "I guess I'm excited. I've never been to a harbor city. I tend to talk too fast when I'm excited."

Bardon heard Granny Kye's chortle as he handed the bewildered marione two heavy bags. "Here, Holt. I appreciate the help."

The marione quickly regained his smile and took the luggage. He headed for the cart, with the others following. Bardon carried the smaller bundles in his arms. As they approached the horse, he heard N'Rae's soft exclamation. She plopped Jue Seeno's basket into his arms, where it rocked precariously on the cloth-wrapped parcel next to his chin, and then she drew near to the old roan.

Jue Seeno's high-pitched inquiry reached his ears. "What is that girl up to?"

"It looks like she's intent on having a conversation with the horse." He spoke, barely moving his lips for fear someone would overhear him talking to a basket.

"I can see that, Squire. That's why I prefer to travel in a basket rather than a box. I can see through the woven reeds. And, of course, the air is always fresher. And I can hear better. But what I meant is, what purpose is there in communicating with a horse, *this* horse, at *this* time?"

"I think," said Granny Kye, "that N'Rae likes meeting animals as much as some folks like meeting people." She nodded at Holt, who nattered away with the driver.

The tumanhofer driver paid particular attention to Granny Kye, treating her with respect and assisting her into the passenger seat before he started with their belongings. Strapping the luggage to the back of the light cart took a few minutes. He took his time to do it properly, all the while regaling his customers with news of the town, the weather, the approaching festival, and suggesting places to visit while they stayed in his fair city.

Since Granny Kye already sat in the coach, the driver had to leave the bags every time he thought of something else he wanted to relay to her in particular. He spouted all sorts of tidbits of information, one of those things being that his wife had found a shop with very good bargains on

Canal Street at the northern end of the city. He also mentioned that a small tavern nearby had excellent soups, which might come in handy, as the weather predictors said cold air would soon be turning their days chilly.

"Now, what kind of prediction is that, I ask you?" He laughed and waved a hand at the sky, where light clouds whisked over the city. "It's still spring. More often than not, we have quick cold spells before winter fully lets loose of us and allows summer to take over. You have the wind up high there." He paused to point at the clouds scuttling overhead. "But only a slight breeze down here. That means a change is coming."

He went back to work.

Bardon gazed up at the azure sky and suddenly missed Greer. Flying in this type of weather challenged their skill. The smell of rain on the wind and the sudden shift of air currents invigorated them both. And whatever it was that would later make lightning skittered across their skin as if to say, "Wake up and live."

Fenworth could explain what happens in the sky. Bardon chuckled to himself, remembering "wizardry" lessons under the old man's tutelage. Fenworth would try to explain and get it all garbled. Later, Librettowit would untangle the supposedly simple explanation given by the wizard. *I miss the old wizard and his librarian.*

He watched N'Rae as she communicated with the horse. Both she and the animal looked content. *I miss Kale, too. I wonder if she can talk to animals. She never writes about the skills she's acquired, only that life is exciting and the details of what everyone else is doing.*

Bardon smiled as he remembered the contents of Kale's letters, the tales of friends he hadn't seen in too long. *They've all changed so much. Toopka is reluctantly learning to read and is a wonderful cook. Regidor has become as clothes-conscious as Dar, but since he doesn't have tailoring in his background, he makes frequent trips out of The Bogs to shop and "see the world." Gilda comes out of her bottle to visit with them all in the evening. How I would like to sit in the castle's cozy common room and listen to those conversations.*

"That does it, then," said the driver as he cinched and buckled the last strap. "Young lady, will you be riding with your granny?"

N'Rae flashed him one of her charming smiles and came to the little box he'd put down for her to step on. "Your Sadie-Up is a very happy horse, Grupnotbaggentogg."

"Here now," said the driver. "You know my name because it's on the side of my carriage. But how do you know my horse's name?"

Bardon stifled a laugh that this glorified cart would be called a carriage.

"Sadie-Up told me," answered N'Rae as she hopped up and settled herself on the wooden bench beside Granny Kye.

"Well, she told you wrong. Her name's Sadie, just Sadie. And why she'd be happy, I can't tell you. She's old enough to be retired and living peaceably in a field somewheres, but I can't afford to get a new horse, and I don't trust nobody to treat her kindly. She can be stubborn."

"She likes the rubdown you give her in the shade of a trang-a-nog tree at noonmeal…and the feed bag. She likes your grandchildren who climb all over her and give her a most thorough and unorganized rubdown every evening in the sanctuary of her cozy stall. You give her an apple, a parnot, or a carrot every morning. And she loves your wife's fried mullins."

"What? Who's been feeding her those? They aren't good for her digestion at her age!"

Bardon handed N'Rae the minneken's basket. "What was the name of the mapmaker, Granny Kye?"

"Oh dear, I don't remember that."

"It was Bromptotterpindosset, Grandmother," N'Rae said.

"Old Bromp?" The tumanhofer clapped his hands together. "He's right on our way. Last time I talked to him he was complaining of itchy feet. We'll stop by on our way to the inn, and if he's not gone off to take the cure, we'll find his shop open and ready for business."

"And if he's gone off to take the cure?" asked N'Rae.

"Well, then, he'll be gone for months!"

Grupnotbaggentogg jumped onto his seat. The two young men scrambled to find a place on the small cart. They stood on the narrow running boards and clung to straps suspended from the awning over the ladies' seat.

The tumanhofer clucked his tongue and jingled the reins.

"Sadie-up," he called.

The cart jerked and rolled forward, heading for the busy street.

15

The Mapmaker

They passed through a warehouse district, maneuvering around lorries and wagons but few people. Then they entered the market, where many citizens walked in the streets as well as on the sidewalks directly in front of the shops. Grupnotbaggentogg turned the ramshackle carriage into a narrow street with much less traffic. Halfway down the lane a dark and light brown ball hung from a wooden beam jutting out from a storefront. The globe turned at a lazy pace, stirred by the gentle breeze. Bold red letters read *Bromptotterpindosset's Maps, Charts, Atlases, and Globes* on the first line of a dark sign above the rafter. Yellow letters stretched across the second line, saying *Emporium, Bazaar, Galleria, and Thrift Shop.*

Grupnotbaggentogg drew up Sadie's reins.

"Here we be." He looked over his shoulder at his passengers. "The shop is open, but that don't mean he's here. His daughter and son-in-law mind the place when he goes off for the cure."

Holt and Bardon hopped off the running boards as the old tumanhofer scrambled down the side of the cart. Holt had been on the sidewalk side and beat Bardon to the task of handing down the ladies. The squire frowned when the marione put his hands around N'Rae's waist and lifted her out of the cart and onto the wooden planks beside him. Holt smiled into her eyes for a moment before letting her go.

A polished wooden door with a large pane of glass had an Open sign dangling from a hook above the window.

Bardon stepped in front of Holt and put a hand on the young marione's broad chest, stopping him from following N'Rae to the door. He spoke softly so as not to disturb N'Rae and her grandmother. "Holt, the business we conduct here is of a private nature. I ask that you give the ladies a chance to make their inquiries without an audience. Could you perchance be persuaded to watch their belongings, protecting them from thieves?"

Holt bristled, then suddenly relaxed. The easy smile spread across his face. "Certainly. I serve in whatever capacity most benefits N'Rae and her grandmother."

Bardon glanced at the ladies. They were perusing the maps, charts, and assorted merchandise in the shop windows. The trinkets from far-away ports caught Granny Kye's attention. N'Rae examined a spangled hat from some distant city.

Under his breath, he addressed Holt. "I don't trust you. After we get the ladies settled, I wish to have a talk with you. I would like to know why you followed us here. What are your intentions? Are you here on your own accord or at the bidding of your father?"

He patted the fine fabric of Holt's coat. "I will expect you to tell me the truth."

Grupnotbaggentogg turned the brass knob and entered the shop to the jangling of bells.

"Bromptotterpindosset," he called. "Bromp! Are you here?"

A young woman came from behind a curtain covering a door to the back. Her thick blond braids wrapped her head like a crown. Bright blue eyes dominated her square face. Her nose and mouth were small for a tumanhofer. She wiped her hands on a white apron that covered the intricately woven blue, green, and gold cloth of her dress. She smiled at all the customers who'd entered the shop but spoke to the driver.

"Master Grupnotbaggentogg, what brings you here?"

"Brought some people looking for a map. Has your da gone off again?"

"Well, he's gone off to get his noonmeal, but I reckon you meant had he gone off for the cure." She shook her head and lowered her voice. "I'm expecting him to leave any day. His feet are driving him to distraction. Miserable, he is." She softened her voice to just above a whisper. "And grouchy, he is. As much as I'll miss him, I can't wait to see the back of him disappear over the horizon."

The old driver patted her shoulder in an awkward gesture of comfort. "It'll be better, Saramaralindan, once he's gone and comes back. Better for a decade or two, until the itch comes upon him again."

She smiled and nodded. "Will you introduce me to your passengers?"

"This be Granny Kye and her granddaughter, N'Rae."

Saramaralindan bobbed a curtsy.

"And Squire Bardon."

Bardon stepped forward. "We require a map of the Northern Reach."

N'Rae came to his side and added, "The western part."

Saramaralindan frowned and tapped a finger on her chin while she surveyed one section of the wall of bookcases.

"We don't have much in the way of inland maps for the Northern Reach. The seacoast is well charted." She crossed to a stepstool and pushed it to where she wanted to examine the shelves. Climbing up two steps, she reached for a couple of rolled parchments. She tucked them under her arm and descended. On a large table in the middle of the shop, she unrolled the first one, putting small, elaborate, wrought-iron weights at the corners to keep the scroll open. The table was the height most comfortable for tumanhofers. Bardon had to bend to examine the parchment.

"This one has great detail of the coast, including rock barriers under the water that would sink a ship." She unrolled the other and shifted the book weights. "This has some sketchy references to inland topography, but we are not certain as to its accuracy. Are you planning to travel in this region?" She waved her hand over the scantily marked territory.

"Yes," Bardon replied. "But I had hoped for a better map."

"If you return this way, would you stop and give us information about the area? Could you keep notes and maybe draw sketches of what you see?"

Granny Kye tugged on Bardon's sleeve. "I could do that."

The door opened, the jangling bells announcing a newcomer.

"It's you, Bromptotterpindosset," said Grupnotbaggentogg in warm welcome.

"Humph! Aye, it is," said the neatly dressed tumanhofer without enthusiasm. He looked younger and wealthier and much more sour than the driver. He scowled at the older tumanhofer through wire-framed spectacles, and a glimmer of mischief sparkled in his eye for only a moment. "And it is you, Grupnotbaggentogg. Do you need a map of Canal Street, or perhaps a chart of Blecoe Warren?"

Instead of being offended by the shopkeeper's gruff tone, Grupnotbaggentogg laughed and slapped him on the back. "Nay, I brought travelers on their way to the Northern Reach. They need a map, of course."

Bromptotterpindosset studied each of his customers in turn. His scowl did not break, even when he gazed upon the fair N'Rae.

"Daughter!" The word rattled the silence. "Get me the chest in the back room."

"Which chest, Father? The room is filled with chests."

The tumanhofer growled in his throat and his whiskers shook. "The one in green leather. The one with rusted clasps. The one under the Dabotnore volumes. That one!"

"The one that hasn't been moved in ten years or more?"

"Yes, of course," he bellowed. "What other one would I want when we speak of the Northern Reach?"

Saramaralindan rolled her eyes and shrugged her shoulders. "I can't imagine. I'll get it for you, Father."

She was gone with a whoosh of the heavy curtains.

Bromptotterpindosset moved to the table and studied the parchments unrolled there. The muffled sounds of heavy objects being shifted came through the doorway.

Bardon responded to a grunt from Saramaralindan. "Perhaps I should assist your daughter."

The shopkeeper waved his hand as if it were no matter to him. Bardon went through the curtained door. He soon returned with a chest covered in decaying, green-dyed leather in his arms. He set it on the table.

Bromptotterpindosset blew over the top and dust flew. He opened the clasp and tilted the lid upright. A small book, several scrolls, and a sextant rested among cobwebs and bits of torn paper.

The tumanhofer pulled out the navigational instrument and set it aside. He picked up the scrolls, one at a time, and brushed them off on his sleeve. Almost with reverence, he lifted the small book in his hand. He held it up, and his gaze went from one face to the next around the table.

"This," he said, "is the diary of Cadden Glas, an adventuring doneel. He chronicles his exploits, complete with notations about flora and fauna, geographical discoveries, observations of the populace, and information about landmarks, rivers, and other descriptive details on how to get here and there in the Northern Reach. He explored the region for decades. The book, however, is written in the language of the meech. Do any of you speak meech?"

They shook their heads.

"Understandable. It is a difficult language to speak…easier to read. Do any of you read meech?"

Again negative shakes of heads met his question.

Bromptotterpindosset grinned. The smile—a set of teeth that were big, white, and numerous—separated his mustache-laden upper lip from the beard dripping off his chin. Bardon couldn't remember ever seeing a grin so magnificently absurd.

"Then I must inform you that most certainly, without a doubt, it will be necessary for you to take upon your journey to the Northern Reach someone who does speak and read meech. Fortunately, I know of someone who is capable of both these endeavors. And it just so happens that he is in the position to do some extensive traveling at this time."

"Ha!" Grupnotbaggentogg threw back his head and echoed his own exclamation. "Ha! So you're off for the cure, eh, Bromp? Well, just remember your age and try to get back in three or four years. You're not as young as you used to be, even if you are a generation or two behind me."

†oo Mαny People

Jue Seeno did not like the addition of the tumanhofer mapmaker to the questing party. And she said so as soon as they sequestered themselves in the room taken at the inn for N'Rae and Granny Kye.

Bardon felt uncomfortable in the tiny guest chamber. The agitated women all talked at once. The emerlindians' voices bounced off the low ceiling, and the squeak of Jue Seeno's tirade punctuated every pause.

The last inn had provided a spacious room with a sizable sitting area adjacent to the sleeping quarters. This room had only the bed and one chair, with no room for N'Rae's pacing up and down. She gestured wildly as she talked, her arms whirling about as she alternately expressed enthusiasm and dismay. Bardon found a place to plant himself, hopefully out of the way. He stood at the foot of the bed, one hand wrapped around a pillar of the gigantic four-poster. N'Rae insisted that the whole quest would be so much safer with another male along. As she brought both arms above her head and swung them out and down to indicate just how greatly this concept encompassed their venture, she came within an inch of poking Bardon's eye out.

He fumed. *It's the bed! This room should have a bed half this size. And that girl should have a hall, a long empty hall, in Castle Pelacce in which to express her views.*

N'Rae sashayed by him once more, knocking him with an elbow. He leaned closer to the post.

Impractical bed to put in such a tiny room!

The younger emerlindian had placed Jue Seeno's basket in the middle of the mattress as soon as they entered the room and the door to the hall was closed. She'd opened the top, helped her tiny protector out, and closed the lid. The outraged minneken stood on her traveling abode, waving her fist in the air.

Granny Kye, of course, sat in the chair.

The afternoon sun streamed through a window, and a chill breeze blew the white curtains about, but the heated oratory in the confined space made the room extremely unpleasant. Bardon sought a reason to escape, even as he appeared to listen attentively to all three women.

Mistress Seeno's agitated voice rose to his ears.

"First, we have that marione farm boy snooping around—"

"Holt has been very useful," Granny Kye cut in.

"But why? Why has he been useful?" shrieked the minneken.

"Because he's been brought up well?" The old emerlindian looked to N'Rae, who nodded her head. The young woman went to the window and parted the curtain to stare out at the street.

Jue Seeno waved her arm in the air, and, for a moment, Bardon pictured her brandishing a shining sword. "We don't need an adventure-seeking tumanhofer nor a ne'er-do-well marione muddling up our perfectly respectable quest. The boy is an inconvenience. The mapmaker is a disaster."

"Jue…" Granny Kye's low voice contrasted to the frantic squeak of the minneken. She spoke rapidly, and enthusiasm shone in her eyes. "The mapmaker is a necessity, and the farmer's son turns out to be handy. He procured the cart for our transportation. And this inn is very reasonably priced. We shan't waste our money here. Everything is falling nicely into place. How like Wulder to take care of every little detail. You know, I've never been on a quest. I think I am going to enjoy it."

The minneken hunched her narrow shoulders, pulled a long shawl more tightly around her, and frowned fiercely at the granny emerlindian. "As for those two interlopers being Wulder's doing, I'll wait on pronouncing that to be fact. As for us not wasting money here, that might be true, unless the mistress gives you a sad tale about needing new linens."

"I'm carrying our coins," put in Bardon.

"Well, that at least is sensible." Her whiskers quivered. "These two men are not a good idea. What should happen if I am discovered? What protection can I be to N'Rae if everyone and their nefarious uncles know about me?"

N'Rae turned away from the window. "Whose uncle is coming?"

"There, there," said Granny Kye. "You can still scout. You can still gather information. You can still stand guard."

The minneken did not look encouraged.

Granny Kye continued, "Master Bromptotterpindosset will be so busy translating the diary and drawing his maps, he won't notice you."

"Not notice a minneken!" Jue Seeno dropped to a sitting position, kicking her feet as they dangled off the side of the basket. She shook her head. A tiny felt hat between her ears slid back and forth. Bardon wondered what anchored it. And he noticed the pink and orange headgear matched the belt she wore. She looked forlorn in spite of her colorful attire.

"I can't do much about the mapmaker," said Bardon, "but I shall try to dissuade Holt from any further prying. Perhaps I can send him home to his loving family."

"Prying?" N'Rae marched to his side and poked him on the arm with a sharp fingernail. "That's unfair. He has been nothing but helpful."

"I don't trust him, either," yelled Jue Seeno. "I'm your protector, and I say he's a wild card. We don't know what he's up to."

Bardon nodded his agreement. "I don't trust his motives. His father may have sent him to discover what our quest is, just in case it should be a profitable endeavor. Or, Hoddack wants his son to bring back a bride who tames kindia."

"That's unfair as well!" N'Rae planted her fists on her hips. "Holt already told his father he didn't want anything to do with such a plan."

Jue Seeno and Granny Kye continued to argue over whether or not to trust the tumanhofer and the marione.

Bardon kept his attention on N'Rae and his voice calm, responding to Sir Dar's training to be a diplomat as well as a knight. "Then why is he here?"

N'Rae's pale complexion colored a bright red. Her lips thinned as she pressed them together. She frowned and looked down at Bardon's chest. "He said he came to see me."

"And you don't quite believe him," Bardon said softly.

She shook her head. "Not quite."

"I'll go ask him. Then we will both know."

"He's out in front of the inn, talking to a man. I saw him out the window."

Bardon left the room, determined to get some answers from Holt. He took in a deep breath first thing after the door closed behind him. Even the stuffy air in the hallway felt refreshing after the heated atmosphere of the tiny bedchamber. He breathed in again, feeling the tension ease from his shoulders. He'd much rather talk to a man.

Women are a tangle of emotions. Pull the wrong string and look out!

A threadbare rug muffled his footsteps in the hall, but as he went down the wooden steps, his boots hammered a swift cadence. He crossed the empty entry hall and stepped out into the sunshine. He stood for a moment, letting his eyes adjust to the bright light.

None of the neighboring businesses looked any more prosperous than the hostelry. Only a few people walked the narrow sidewalk on either side of a rutted street.

Where's Holt?

Bardon stood on the stoop of the inn and searched both directions. The farmer's son was nowhere in sight. Bardon spotted a tavern and headed in that direction. Even if the marione hadn't stepped in for a cooling drink, the squire thought a tall, bracing glass of Korskan tea would be welcome.

As he passed an alley, he heard a grunt. Stopping, he heard heavy breathing, and the thud of fist against flesh.

Another grunt. "I told you I don't have it." Holt's voice.

Bardon stepped into the alley. In the shadows, he saw a tall o'rant holding a shorter, broader man against the wall.

The squire used the same calm voice he'd used with N'Rae. "Let him go."

Three thugs emerged from the shadows and fell upon him. Bardon sidestepped one assailant lunging from the right and grabbed the man by a shoulder and wrist. Twisting the attacker's hand behind his back, Bardon then used the man as a weapon, ramming his body into the brute charging from the left. The third man jumped on Bardon's back. The squire tucked his head and rolled forward over the man he held, slamming the one on his back against the ground. He let go of the first man, continued his somersault over the body of the other, and sprang to his feet.

One of the men charged him again, but Bardon pivoted, swung a booted foot up, and side-kicked him in the stomach. The second man had regained his feet and came at Bardon, only to be kicked twice, once in the kneecap and once in the face. The squire used an elbow to break one man's nose and a backward kick to disable another as the ruffian hurled himself at Bardon's back. The assailants took off, one man helping a badly limping comrade. The o'rant clutching Holt didn't enter the fray. He dropped the marione and ran.

Bardon watched them go, breathing deeply, but without a mark on him from the fight. He went over and helped Holt to his feet.

"Thanks." Holt groaned. He held his arms around his middle. Sweat poured down his face even in the chill shade of the alley.

"What did they want?" asked Bardon.

"What do ruffians usually want? Money, I guess."

"I heard you tell him you didn't have it. That sounds like an answer to a specific question. I don't think it's a good idea to lie to me, Holt."

"I didn't lie. I asked a question and then answered it."

"Prevaricating. That's lying with finesse. Tell me the truth."

"The truth is they wanted money." His face twisted as he swayed and leaned against the building.

"There is still the 'it,' implying something specific. You didn't say, 'I don't have any.' You said, "I don't have it.' I'll ask you one more time to tell me the truth, and if you don't"—Bardon maintained the cool tone of casual conversation—"I may lose my temper. You hurt now, don't you, Holt? You'll hurt more when I'm finished." He paused and looked over the pale, gasping marione. "Do you feel like hitting the dirt with considerable force again? It might jar those aches you already have." Bardon shook his head as if he were weighing the possibilities. "I don't think a shove or two would normally bother you, but I'm not in the mood for a genteel wrestling match. I'm in the mood to hear the truth… Well, it's your decision."

Holt's eyes sizzled with hatred. "All right. I owe a man money. These men work for him."

"Gambling?"

"Some. But the worst of it was I offered to trade five kindias for what I owed him plus six hundred grood. Then Father decided the kindia were not mine after all. They were to be my payment for traveling to Bintuppi and handling a business transaction. The deal went sour. I had no kindia to deliver, so I left town."

"You didn't happen to already have the man's six hundred grood, did you?"

"Yes. I said I needed the money up front to handle the transportation of the beasts from upriver—the men, the special crates, the boat."

"And your father wouldn't help you out with the debt?"

Holt laughed and groaned. "Not again."

"So you decided to follow N'Rae?"

"It was convenient."

"And you think it would be convenient to go on a long quest."

Holt breathed easier now. He stood a little straighter, moving away from the wall that had been supporting him.

"Actually, no. I'm not interested in getting into any dangerous situations, but I wouldn't mind sailing north. Perhaps I can find a way to make some money, and when I have enough to pay my debts—"

"Debts? As in more than one?"

A half grin twisted the marione's mouth. "Yes, quite a bit more than one."

"What makes you think we will sail north?"

"You're going to have to teach N'Rae discretion." Holt snickered. "She chatters like a dorker, but she's quite a bit prettier than those noisy birds."

"So your plan is to sail north with us. Why not just sail north on your own?"

"They will be inquiring after a lone male passenger, not one of a party of five."

"And you plan to separate from us once we reach a port at some distance from here."

"Correct." He paused. "You can't keep me from boarding the same ship, you know."

"Oh, I probably could. But N'Rae would be displeased with my methods." He rubbed his hand over his chin. "If you happen to board the same vessel that takes us north, I would appreciate your leaving N'Rae alone. She's too naive to recognize a cad when she sees one."

"A cad?" For a moment, Holt seemed affronted, but he chortled and grinned. "All right. I'll not turn the young innocent's head. When do we leave?"

"I have to visit a friend in the country first. You can make the inquiries to find the fastest ship going north for our party of five tomorrow. I should be back by sundown."

"Deal," said the marione and stuck out his hand.

"I won't shake with you, Holt. From what you've told me, it is not likely your honor backs your handshake. I wouldn't want you to get the impression I trust you."

The shorter man let his hand fall slowly to his side. The easy and charming smile faded from his handsome face.

"If I didn't need a cover for leaving this region, I'd part ways with you now," Holt said.

Bardon shrugged. "It would be inconvenient for me to put off visiting my friend to deal with the matter of arranging passage first. But you may leave our company now if you wish."

"You'll allow yourself to associate with the likes of me so that you can see him a day earlier? Your friend is that important to you?"

"He is, indeed."

17

A Friend

Rain drenched the city during the night. Bardon listened to the drum of heavy drops on the windowpane and wondered if he'd have to ride through the torrent to find Greer. He barely heard the town clock strike eleven through the splatter of rain and the claps of thunder. But he heard the midnight toll underscoring a gentle shower. Sleep muffled the lone peal of one o'clock.

He woke in the morning, sprang out of a lumpy bed, and opened the window. The sun rose in the eastern sky, casting an enchanting glow on wisps of clouds as they broke apart and trailed away in puffy filaments. Warm, playful breezes rustled the spring leaves in a tree at the side yard. Chickens scurried about, pecking and scratching in the dirt. Skittish brown thornsnippers twittered from the tree, and plump waistcoaters cooed from the eaves of the buildings. The earth smelled damp and rich and full of promise.

The squire dressed and ran down the back steps to the kitchen. He charmed a few biscuits stuffed with bacon and cheese from the busy cook and stood by the hearth as he ate. He also downed a mug of warm, fresh milk. As soon as he'd tipped the cheerful woman and audaciously planted a kiss on her ruddy cheek, he left the inn.

He'd arranged for the use of one of the inn's horses the night before. Riding at a brisk clip, he made his way to a location directly east and three miles beyond the last cluster of houses that could have been called part of the city. He tied the horse securely to a woody bush, climbed a hill, and surveyed the surrounding pastures.

This turned out to be a good place to meet. A few farmers, a few stock-men. Not a crowd by any means. That will please Greer.

He sat on grass dried by wind and sun. The smell of the heated, rich green blades acted as a soporific. He yawned, stretched, and lay on his back. A stir of thought not his own passed through his consciousness.

"You haven't got a chance," he said out loud, knowing that the thought would go to Greer. "You haven't been able to sneak up on me in the three years we've been together. Not even in the beginning when I wasn't all that great at receiving your messages."

Too lazy to get up, he turned on his side and shaded his eyes with a hand, looking to the south. A large black dot skimmed over the horizon. With each breath he took, he saw the shape grow larger and more defined. From experience, Bardon knew he breathed in time to the dragon's wing beats. This unconscious physical synchronization came as part of the bonding between him and his mount.

When he could distinguish purple body and cobalt wings, he stood and waved an arm in greeting. As Greer landed, Bardon knelt and covered his head, shielding his face from the debris blown up in the air by the force of the major dragon's wings.

As the dust settled, he rose, a grin stretching his mouth until his cheeks ached. "I am not groveling before you, you old, overgrown bat!"

He went forward and put his arms around the dragon's neck, resting his forehead against the sleek scales. A warm thrum passed between the two, each relishing the friendship of the other. When Bardon had settled in to wait on the hill, he knew the bond between them would bring Greer as surely as a trained waistcoater would find its way home.

I have had a most unsettling week, Greer. Ideas and images poured out of his mind. He didn't have to organize his thoughts to present them logically. The dragon took possession of the information with the same interpretations that Bardon had placed on each relevant fact.

While he communicated, Bardon removed a large pack strapped to Greer's back. The leather bundle contained his riding saddle, empty panniers, and assorted cloths and brushes for grooming. Bardon removed the cloth and some balm. He proceeded to rub the salve into the place where the pack rasped the dragon's skin. He then buffed Greer's scales. While Bardon groomed him, Greer relaxed, hummed deep in his throat, and stretched out on the grass.

Occasionally, in response to a part of Bardon's continuing narrative, the dragon made a sympathetic grunt in his throat. Once, during the recounting of the quiss tale, Greer gasped. That brought the smile back to Bardon's face. He stroked the dragon's neck, right behind the ear, glad he had someone to confide in.

"Yes, that was pretty gruesome, and the implications of what Stox and Cropper could be cooking up is horrific... Yes, *horrific* is a word."

He went on to describe the reappearance of Holt Hoddack into their lives. Now the rumblings from Greer's throat sounded suspiciously like laughter. Bardon left the subject of the aggravating marione and went on to the acquisition of a mapmaker as well as a map for their expedition. He glossed over the brouhaha in the tiny bedchamber and gave a full accounting of the addition of a debt-beleaguered marione farm boy to their ranks.

"Yes, *beleaguered* is a word... I do *not* use big words when I'm upset. And I'm not upset... I contend that it will be easier to keep an eye on that scalawag Holt if we know where he is."

Greer had settled into a reclining position during this long explanation of what had passed during the days they had been separated. Bardon finished the grooming and repacked the bag. It lay on the ground by Greer's tail.

Bardon leaned back between Greer's forelegs against the dragon's chest. To get his mind off the mess that awaited him back in Ianna, Bardon asked what his friend had been doing.

Greer told of flying over the countryside, basically taking in the sights. He'd hunted chigot deer in the forests. And during another flight, he'd caused quite a stir, flying over a field full of children playing astiket ball.

"I guess you're right," answered Bardon. "People in the southwest region aren't as used to seeing dragons as those in Wittoom and Ordray."

Greer lowered his chin to the top of Bardon's head and gently rubbed it back and forth.

"You're messing up my hair," the squire objected halfheartedly. "People?" He stood and looked down the hill to a valley where cattle grazed. Several men dressed in country togs marched along the road. It looked as though they intended to see why a dragon had landed in their territory.

"Let's fly, Greer." Bardon sprang onto his back, settling into the dip where Greer's neck joined his shoulders. The dragon stretched his wings and took to the air.

The wind rushed against Bardon's face, lifting his hair back and exposing his ears. Usually, he wore a hat. Every day, he used a pomade to stiffen the hair and keep the sides in place. Of course, that wasn't enough to keep his ears hidden in the wind.

Most people didn't notice the slight point that topped each of his ears. One had to look closely to see the peak in their otherwise o'rant shape. Kale had noticed, and N'Rae. He'd caught Kale staring at his ears. She never said anything, but of course, he knew she knew, because they had a special, mystifying bond.

Not only could he mindspeak with Kale, but when he was near her, he could also communicate through his mind with others. Away from her he had no such talent.

He didn't count communicating with Greer as mindspeaking. A subtle difference existed in communication between those of the high races and between rider and dragon.

To my way of thinking, Kale knows too much about me. I'm glad our studies prevented us from being in the same place.

He pictured her serious face as she tried to understand something new Fenworth explained. He saw her eyes twinkle at one of Dar's jests. He heard her scolding one of her minor dragons. He saw the look of shock on her face when they both thought the same thing at the same time. And of course, they knew it had happened. They never figured out why.

He didn't need Kale Allerion distracting him.

Kale had never quizzed him about his obvious halfling blood.

N'Rae asked questions. And N'Rae discussed his ears with Granny Kye and Jue Seeno.

He looked down at the men trudging up the hill.

We left the saddlebag, Greer… No, I don't think they will steal it. What would they do with dragon tackle?… Yes, we have to go back anyway. Where should we meet next? I wish we could fly north together and keep an eye on the ship from a distance. But I don't trust Holt to keep away from N'Rae's tender heart… Granny Kye? Oh no. Jue Seeno is a better guardian than our rather scatterbrained emerlindian… Getting back to the next leg of our trip, Greer, how would you like a seashore vacation?… The fishing would be good.

Greer banked, and Bardon gripped with his knees. He clutched two raised scales along the dragon's powerful neck.

Take up a post north of Ianna on the coast. When you sense I'm on a passing ship, fly over, and I'll give you the location of the first port we will visit.

They circled the fertile valley and returned to the hill.

I guess we better see what the good citizens of this rural community have on their minds. Bardon and Greer descended, landing with a flourish of wind that sent the half-dozen watchers to their knees.

The men turned out to be curious farmers wanting to talk about the unusual sight that had interrupted their routine day. Bardon introduced himself and his companion. The men were as impressed with a squire from Wittoom as they were with Greer.

Greer whispered in Bardon's thoughts that he wasn't very impressed with men who thought another two-legged beast with a minor title was as interesting as a dragon. Bardon hushed him, telling him to be civil. Greer responded with a laugh, and Bardon chastised him.

Yes, I expect you to be a great deal more civil than "not eating them."

He cast the ornery dragon a look of disgust. *When have you ever eaten one of the seven high races? I bet you haven't eaten any of the seven low races either. Be quiet! I'm trying to follow the conversation here.*

Several of the older men reminisced about dragons working together with men.

"I was a wobbly brat, just up on my pegs, when the last family with a dragon left the valley for the high country." The farmer looked with admiration at Greer's muscled shoulders. "I don't remember it myself. Just remember my folks talking of it. They said, in years long ago, each farm had a dragon bonded to the family."

"Where've the dragons all gone?" asked one of the oldest men. "Seems like there're fewer dragons, fewer emerlindians, and I have never seen a kimen in all my days. Of course, you hear tales from those wandering fellows. There was a big to-do in Trese a few years back. That will be legend when my grandkids tell stories to their grandkids."

"I think," said Bardon, "that there used to be a lot more commerce between the different provinces of Amara."

One of the men shook his head. "Don't pay to send your products anywhere but close." He gestured toward the Morchain Range, rising to the east. "You go over the mountains, you have to deal with large, uncouth, smelly grawligs. The rivers, lakes, and wetlands reek with hideous mordakleeps who will take away all your senses. They say in some foreign places, the remnants of Risto's military bisonbecks walk the streets with the high races. I know we don't venture out as much as we used to, but it's safer."

"We do some trading by sea." A farmer broke off a tall blade of grass and stuck it in his mouth.

"That we do, but it's not the bulk of our income." That man shrugged as if it were no matter.

"We produce what we need," said the oldest. "It's not so bad being off to yourselves." He nodded to Greer but spoke to Bardon. "When you leave, would you circle the valley again so the youngsters can get another gander at the dragon?"

Bardon smiled. "I'm going back to Ianna on horseback. I'll ask Greer to put on a little flying show for the children, though. To tell you the truth, he's a bit of a ham and won't be put out at all."

For that flagrant impertinence, Greer butted the center of Bardon's back with more than an easygoing bump. The farmers laughed and kept up a steady stream of talk as Bardon secured the saddlebag onto Greer's back and sent him off with a brief farewell.

The boring ride back exasperated Bardon. The horse stopped to graze anytime he wasn't prodded along. The road became crowded with people and carts either going to market or returning home. Bardon chafed at the slowness of his progress.

Did Holt find a ship? Did Granny Kye give away our belongings to some worthy cause? Was the minneken discovered? Is N'Rae admiring Holt's handsome face and ignoring his smudged character? Has the old tumanhofer finished his preparations for the journey? How did I ever get caught up for a quest with this unlikely crew?

He pulled the horse up short and took a minute to watch the people around him. O'rants, tumanhofers, and mariones. Men, women, and children. Mostly common folk with just enough coins to live on. At this time of day, after the duties and strains of their work, they plodded along to their destinies without much apparent pleasure in their journeys.

I haven't thought of a principle all day. He saw a young child asleep on his father's shoulder, being carried home. *"The body grows weary, the mind will tire, but the soul dances before Wulder in the evening of life."*

He tapped his heels against the horse's sides. Even as the sun lowered to the horizon, signaling the end of a day, he hummed the tune to a sunrise chant. The music sparked the joy he felt in knowing Wulder cared for him and the quest he was on. He began to sing,

"The hour's a gift. The road's a grant.
Enjoy the journey as you see His hand
cover your errors,
wipe your tears,

straighten the way,
straighten the way."

*Scribe Moran would say the first "straighten the way" is an observation,
and the second is a request.*

Wulder, I petition You to straighten the way.

The sight of the quaint inn reminded him of the quest he had become embroiled in with two naive emerlindian women. His sabbatical had been shelved for the time being while he performed his duty.

He stabled the horse and gave the boy working there a coin to groom the animal. He entered the inn through the kitchen with a much heavier step than when he had left in the morning.

"Oh," said the cook when she saw him, "then you've already heard the bad news."

Bardon frowned. "What bad news?"

"You haven't heard, then?"

"No."

She wrung her hands in the apron hanging from her waist. "Best you hear from your own people. Last I heard, they were in their room. Well, the girl and the gent."

N'Rae and Holt!

Bardon bolted up the stairs and slowed halfway up for a moment as he remembered that Jue Seeno would act as chaperone. He hit the next step at full speed, thinking what good could a three-inch-high chaperone be.

He burst into the room to find N'Rae sitting in the chair, her eyes rimmed in red. Holt stretched across the bed on his back, snoring.

N'Rae jumped to her feet when she saw Bardon and ran to grab his arms. Her sharp fingernails dug into his flesh.

"I think Holt drinks," she exclaimed. "He's been useless. He came back after he had been here, and all he did was say we should wait for you. Then he fell on the bed and went to sleep."

"After who had been here?"

"The constable."

Holt snorted and twitched.

Bardon ignored him and frowned at N'Rae. "Why?"

"To arrest Granny Kye."

"What?"

N'Rae nodded, tossing her blond locks. "For thievery."

18

THE JAILHOUSE

"Can't let her out without the magistrate's order. Can't see the magistrate without a registry permit. Can't register to see the magistrate until nine o'clock tomorrow. Office is closed. Been closed for hours."

Bardon turned away from the dirty little man in his squalid little office and bumped into N'Rae.

"What are we going to do?" she asked.

Bardon turned back to the jailer. He glanced at the nameplate on the table. Greasy chicken bones on a folded newspaper testified that the man had already eaten his dinner. The squire's nose wrinkled at the mixture of unpleasant odors in the room. He identified one smell as the rank clothing on the jailer's back.

This is beyond ridiculous! According to N'Rae, they arrested Granny Kye this morning. She's been here for hours. What do the prisoners eat? Have they even fed her? He clamped down on his anger. He wanted cooperation from this ill-bred tumanhofer.

"Look, Bortenmiffgaten, we would like to see Granny Kye. She's old and probably scared."

The man leaned back in his chair and studied the ceiling. "I can let you see her if'n I have some guarantee you won't be blabbing to all that I was derelict in my duty."

"And what would the guarantee be?" asked Bardon.

"Half an ordend." He spit the answer out under his breath. His eyes still scanned the cracked plaster above him.

Bardon shook his head. "I'll not participate in the giving or taking of bribes, Master Bortenmiffgaten."

The front legs of the jailer's chair hit the floor with a whack, then screeched as the small man pushed back. He stood. His chin came to the edge of the table.

This office must have been furnished by his predecessor, Bardon observed as the jailer raised a fist to shake at him. N'Rae scooted behind Bardon as if the diminutive bundle of outrage intimidated her.

"Just who do you think you are?" ranted the tumanhofer. "Ain't nothing wrong with those who have the ready giving a coin to those who do not."

Bardon nodded. "I am Squire Bardon, in service to Sir Dar of Castle Pelacce, Dormenae, Wittoom. And I agree with you that giving you a coin is not a bad thing, but purchasing illegal entry into the jail is."

The little man's fist had come down, and the glower on his face changed to a look of puzzlement. "Sir Dar?" he whispered. "A fancy-dressed doneel? That's your Sir Dar?"

"Yes."

"I'll let you in."

N'Rae gasped and peeked around Bardon's arm. "Why?"

The jailer frowned and mumbled, "Sir Dar did a kindness to our family. Not to me, mind you. But to my sister's children. I've got no use for do-gooders and don't believe in those high teachings some people prattle about. But I'll let you in."

He patted several pockets and came up with a key. That key unlocked a door in a cabinet behind him. Keys inside dangled from a row of hooks. The jailer selected one and carefully put the padlock back in place. He crossed the room and unlocked a door. Bardon and N'Rae started to follow him. Bortenmiffgaten held up a grubby hand stained with tobacco juice.

"Not yet," he said. "I'm just getting another key."

He disappeared behind the door. They listened as several things opened and shut.

Drawers? Cabinets? More doors? Bardon wished he could see.

After more rattling around in the room behind the partially closed door, Bortenmiffgaten returned, jingling a key ring the size of a dinner plate. Two keys swung from the rusty metal hoop.

"This way." He gestured for them to follow him down a flight of stairs. At the bottom he turned right. He jumped to snatch a torch from the wall. As he passed unlit torches, he gave a little leap and swiped his burning one across the next dark stick. Instantly, a flame burst forth.

This underground hallway was cleaner and smelled better than the jailer's office.

Bardon sniffed the damp but pleasant air. *Someone else must be in charge of this area.*

The hall branched off several times, but the tumanhofer kept walking. The underground path ended in a room with one door in front of them. A heavy padlock hung from a metal latch.

Bortenmiffgaten stopped and looked up at them, a smile on his face. In the flickering flame, Bardon thought the flash of yellowed teeth looked evil.

"I'll let you in," said the jailer, "but you have to leave your boots, coats, and that basket out here. Can't have you carrying in weapons."

N'Rae twisted her face as she slipped out of her shoes and placed her folded shawl atop them. Her toes wriggled against the cold flooring. Bardon left his sword, boots, tunic, and knife. He plucked his bag of coins out of the tunic to carry with him. Although the jailer had shown goodwill in admitting them, Bardon doubted the tumanhofer would be able to resist the temptation of an unguarded purse.

"You got food in that basket?" Bortenmiffgaten asked, licking his lips.

"No," whispered N'Rae.

The jailer frowned. "What then?"

"A doll."

"A doll?" He stomped over. "Let me see."

N'Rae slowly undid the little cord that held the lid shut and opened the basket.

Bortenmiffgaten looked inside and snarled. "A lot of fancy stuff for a rag doll." He headed for the door with his key in his hand. "Leave it here."

N'Rae sighed and carefully put the basket next to her shoes and shawl. She smiled tentatively at Bardon.

He glanced at the jailer, relieved that the man had his back to them.

This is absurd. N'Rae practically shouts she is lying about the doll with her sigh of relief. The jailer is dishonest. Despite his sudden change of heart, I don't trust him. He has a hundred keys, and I could have bashed him on the head at anytime. I still could and instigate a jailbreak. I must get Granny Kye out of this place. I'm tempted to tie up Bortenmiffgaten in his own cell and leave him there. But have I ever seen Sir Dar circumvent the law? No. How frustrating!

The door creaked open. Inside, not one but three cells banked the walls. Women occupied them all, Granny Kye in the middle one.

N'Rae rushed in and flung herself against the bars making up the wall between her and her grandmother. "Oh, it's like being in a cage!" she cried.

Bardon stopped at the door and bent to whisper to the jailer. He allowed a growl to underscore his words, a trick he had learned from the meech dragon Regidor. "If any of our things are missing when we come out, I will have to retrieve them from your pockets, since there are no other pockets to search."

"Shh! Shh!" Granny Kye hushed a wailing N'Rae. "You'll wake the children." She sat on the floor with several urchins around her. One slept in her lap. Another rested his head on her knee.

"Are you all right?" whispered N'Rae.

"Oh yes. Dinner was a bit sparse and underseasoned but adequate."

"What did you steal, Grandmother?" N'Rae sounded curious and not in the least bit condemning.

"The children were afraid to take the food from the forager bin. Not a very tidy forager bin at all, but holding plenty of good vegetables and fruits. A few bits of bread and pastries, too."

"So you took them and passed them out?"

"Yes, and the owner of the produce stall came yelling and fussing. Said it wasn't a forage bin at all but his garbage, and he sold it each day to a pig farmer…and I was *stealing*." Granny Kye patted a child who stirred. "Imagine that, N'Rae. Apparently, they don't follow Paladin's edict to feed the poor in this district. The constable told me no one sets out food for the orphans."

Bardon shifted in the doorway. He'd been listening but also keeping an eye on the jailer. He glanced at the ragged group of children and counted. Six. He'd have to get them out of jail, as well. "Will you be all right for the night, Granny Kye? Do you need more food? Fresh water? Blankets?"

"Blankets would be nice. The floor is clean, but hard. Quite a nice jail, in fact. The women workers who were here earlier in the day were a nice lot, proud of their work and cheerful."

Bardon shook his head. "How many jails have you been in besides this one?"

"None," she replied. "But I have *imagined* a prison on several occasions, and I didn't imagine that they would be as nice as this."

"I'll take N'Rae back to the inn and bring blankets. Anything else?"

"Bardon, dear, will you be able to get the children out of here when you free me?"

"I think I can."

"And"—she looked up at him with tears in her eyes—"we can take them with us when we go on our quest, can't we? They've no place to stay and no one to take care of them."

"No!" The word exploded from his lips.

"Shh!" said N'Rae as Granny Kye frowned, shook her head, and said, "Quiet, dear."

Bardon glared at them both.

Granny Kye smiled, the expression lifting the worry from her brow. "You can think about the children, Squire Bardon. Consult Wulder and your principles. I know you will come to the right decisions."

"I'll be back in an hour," he said. "Come on, N'Rae."

On the street, he hailed a horse-drawn cab. The dark streets prohibited their walking to the inn. Once inside the small, enclosed carriage, N'Rae opened the basket.

"What do you think of all this?" she asked the minneken.

Bardon snorted. "Yes, what *do* you think?"

"I think it is very undignified to lie in a lump like a rag doll," she answered. "But we are all called upon from time to time to do things we do not want to do."

19

Taking Care of Necessities

The four-poster bed where Holt had last been seen was empty. Bardon sighed his relief.

"I'm going down to the kitchen," he said to N'Rae and Mistress Seeno. "I'll get some food to take to Granny Kye and the children. I'll also get those blankets to take back."

Jue Seeno gestured for him to lean close so she could be heard. "You better take food for the women in the other cells, or Granny Kye will just give hers away."

"Right!"

He bought blankets from the innkeeper and also a basket filled with cheese and bread, fruit and boiled eggs.

"That ruins my plans for breakfast, young man," said the cook. She threw a couple of handfuls of flour into a large bowl, then doused it with a big splash of milk.

Bardon winked at her. "I have every confidence there will be a splendid repast on the table tomorrow morning."

"You do talk fancy." Without measuring, she used her fingertips to sprinkle salt over her concoction, then added sugar.

"Have you seen or heard of Holt Hoddack's whereabouts, Cook?"

"Aye! He came down asking for a potion to settle his stomach." She didn't look up from her work, where she kneaded the mixture into a stiff dough. "Likely he needed something for his head, I'm thinking. I gave him water I'd boiled the vegetables in. Of course I added a generous tablespoon of vinegar and mixed it up good. He said it tasted nasty enough to do some good."

"Did he say anything about finding a ship for us to book passage on?"

"He didn't." She turned her head to holler over her shoulder. "Bim and Toa, come help the squire carry this to the jail for the granny. Maybe you'll earn a pip."

Bardon smiled as the twin kitchen boys scrambled out from under a table against the back wall. No dirt ringed their necks. They smelled of soap. Only a spattering of freckles darkened their identical faces. They resembled the cook—clean, round, and cheerful. Green pants came down to midcalf. Brown shirts covered a tight-fitting undergarment of printed material. Their scruffy hair hung in their eyes, but it didn't hide their eagerness to be off on an adventure an hour after they'd been ordered to bed.

The cook grinned. "They're ten, sturdy and willing." Her wide smile revealed her obvious pride in her boys. She waved them toward the supplies on her kitchen table. "You each grab a stack of those blankets, follow the squire, and mind you, do exactly as he tells you."

"You'll earn a pip apiece," Bardon said. "One more thing, Cook. Do you know where the Hoddack fellow is now?"

"He refused a good meal and went out again. No good will come of that." She smacked the dough with the palm of her hand, and her sons looked knowingly at each other.

Bardon tucked the rest of the blankets under one arm and grabbed the basket with the other hand. "Thanks again, Cook. I'll have your boys back in an hour."

She nodded and glanced at her sons. The look said they had better be a credit to her, and both boys nodded with understanding.

They went through the inn to the front. Bardon wanted a buggy to take them to the jail. If they were set upon by footpads in the night, he would be hard pressed to defend them all with his arms loaded down.

As they approached the vehicle, Bardon glanced at the southwestern sky. He could see the Wizards' Plume above a housetop.

That's not good. We're running out of time. I could move so much faster if I didn't have to take N'Rae and Granny Kye along. Of course, I would be making great time to an unknown destination. I'm not sure the granny knows where it is from all her tidbits of information she's gathered. I don't know if Bromptotterpindosset can get us there. From all appearances this is a wild-goose chase.

The boys' excitement at riding in the horse-drawn vehicle amused him. So did their sober expressions as they watched the jailer's ritual of retrieving the proper key. But amazement touched his heart as he watched them push the blankets through the bars and compassionately hand food to those in all three cells. They spoke softly to the children on the other side of the iron door.

Bardon placed a hand on each head and roughed their hair as they walked back up the stark corridor. He would be sure to tell Cook how graciously they did their task.

When he reported the incident, she beamed and scooted them back to bed.

She stood with her hands on her hips, a berry-stained wooden spoon poking out of one fist.

"They're good boys," she said. "Their father's a sailor and gone too much, but I teach them the ways of Wulder, not like most in this province. And their father tells them the wonders of Wulder he's seen all over the world. They know the truth, they do. They'll be all right in this life."

Bardon next reported to N'Rae that her grandmother was more comfortable. Then he sought his narrow room, his narrower bed, and a time of reflection. His thoughts became a long petition to Wulder to make right the chaos into which his life had fallen.

⊱────⊰

Gray clouds obscured the morning sun. N'Rae already waited at the bottom of the stairs when Bardon came down. She carried Jue Seeno's basket on her arm.

"What are we going to do?" she asked.

"We have three appointments on our agenda today," he answered, heading for the common room where breakfast would be served. "We must see to securing a place on a ship going north. We must find a reliable transport of my dispatch to Paladin. And we must free Granny Kye and the children from the jail."

"The last one first, please."

Bardon patted her shoulder and then turned her toward their breakfast. "Fortunately, all those problems may be solved by one man, if he is willing."

"Who?"

"The harbormaster."

"He can do all that?"

Bardon nodded and pointed to a table with two chairs. "Along the coast of Amara, the harbormasters wield great power."

They sat, and Bardon handed N'Rae a basket of small, fragrant, sugary breads.

"I'm not hungry," she protested.

"I am."

"We must hurry."

"We won't be able to get anything done until the clock strikes nine and the business day commences."

"If this harbormaster is so important, will he see us? We aren't very important at all."

"No, we aren't. But Sir Dar is, and I'm his squire. Hopefully, that will open some doors for us."

N'Rae picked at her food, but Bardon ate a hearty breakfast and told Bim, or maybe it was Toa, to tell his mother she had lived up to his expectations.

A light rain greeted them as they peered out the front door of the inn. Bardon sighed. "Well, we'll take a carriage once again. I have walked less in this town than in any other I have ever visited."

"Is that bad?"

"You get to know a town and its people better when you stroll through the streets." He laughed.

"What?"

"Sir Dar loves to explore, and he has led me on many a merry chase in towns to the north of here. He is a hard one to keep up with."

"You like him, don't you?"

"Yes." Bardon stepped out from under the stoop's awning and hailed a passing vehicle. He helped N'Rae negotiate a puddle and climb into the closed carriage.

"The office of the harbormaster," he instructed the driver as he climbed in beside her.

"Is Sir Dar a friend?" she asked.

Bardon nodded. "And a mentor."

"Is Greer a friend?"

"And a companion."

"Am I a friend?"

He looked at her, trying to read her expression. "Yes."

"And?"

"And…a pest!"

20

Lost and Found

"You can open that dispatch," said Harbormaster Mayfil, "and add a dozen more deaths by quiss between here and the Southern Turn." The tall, red-headed o'rant, with more weight on him than most men of his race, stood next to a row of windows in his office. Behind him, ships of all sizes could be seen moored at the piers, docking, and sailing in or out of the busy harbor.

Bardon felt N'Rae shift beside him and understood her impatience to get to the matter of Granny Kye. But the port official had his mind on the threat to his harbor. Of course, the captain of the *Morning Lady* reported the incident upriver and Squire Bardon's part in slaying the beast. The crewmen spread the tale along the wharf. Bardon had not had to use Sir Dar's name to get past the clerk outside the office of the most influential man in Ianna.

Harbormaster Mayfil listened to the three things Squire Bardon requested of him. He waved his hand in the air and said, "The *Tobit Grander* sails tomorrow. That's the boat you need."

About Granny Kye's predicament he said, "Hmm? We'll contact Magistrate Inkleen."

But Mayfil sunk his teeth into the subject of quiss and would not let go.

After they stood for several minutes while the harbormaster fired questions at the squire, Bardon unobtrusively offered N'Rae a seat.

Either the man has no manners or he's forgotten them in his fervor to discover all he can about the quiss.

With his hands behind his back and a glower on his face, Mayfil rocked back and forth, heel to toe. "My brother fought several quiss invasions in Trese. He was a military man, rose to full major lee. I heard many wild stories about the swarms of sea creatures walking on land in bands of a hundred to a thousand. He said they weren't particularly hard to slay, but the sheer number caused problems. And when the battle went against the quiss, the beasts never turned and ran. They just kept coming." The harbormaster shuddered.

Though truly interested in the man's story, Bardon took the opportunity to steer the conversation back to where it would be useful to their immediate plans. "I would be glad to include your observations of quiss activity in this area in my report. Do you have the name of someone who will carry the document to Vendela?"

Mayfil stroked his chin. "There aren't many pledged to Paladin in these regions. Not that they are disrespectful of the calling. We're more interested in practical matters. But my brother was one to follow, and he has a grown son I can send with your papers."

N'Rae surprised Bardon by speaking up. "You refer to your brother in the past tense, sir."

"Yes, he died in a battle at Bartal Springs Lake. Risto's bisonbeck army was defeated, but at a terrible cost."

"Should the battle not have been fought, then?" asked N'Rae.

"There are many here who think not. But I had the advantage of hearing my brother's firsthand accounts of the evil he encountered. He'd say that unless a wound is cleaned of the festering, rotted flesh, the whole body will sicken and die. My wife once objected and said the body was *their* body—she was talking about the Creemoor Province at the time—so it was *their* problem and not ours."

He shook his head. "The look of sadness on my brother's face when my wife said that stunned me. I did not know him as a man of much emotion. He had plenty of military bluster. He'd get heated up about his views of politics. Otherwise, his demeanor was cold, rigid, what you would expect from a military man. But that night he looked as though the sorrows of every man lost under his command weighed heavily on his heart. I thought he would agree with her out of his pain. But he said, 'You are wrong, my dear. And you do not know Wulder's heart.'"

Harbormaster Mayfil sighed deeply. His hands, hanging by his side, lifted briefly and fell again. "And now the infection comes to us to knock us out of our complacency."

"We must send a message to Paladin," Bardon said.

"We have ignored Paladin for centuries." The powerful official sounded lost in his despair. "Why should he respond to our need?"

"Maybe you have forsaken Paladin," said the squire, "but Wulder has not forgotten you."

Mayfil sighed again and moved to his desk. He picked up a quill pen, pulled a piece of paper close, and bent to write. "We shall send the dispatch to Paladin and see what happens." He straightened, folded his note in half, and went to the door. Mayfil spoke to his clerk for several moments and then returned to his desk.

"My nephew will come to pick up your papers, Squire Bardon. You may use my desk to add to your account while you wait. I'll send in Gregger, the man I've had investigating the various reports. He can fill in the pertinent details.

"The purser from the *Tobit Grander* will come here to make arrangements for your passage. And if you will allow me to accompany your young friend, we will go visit the magistrate to see about freeing her grandmother."

Three hours later, Harbormaster Mayfil returned alone. Bardon had just sent a sealed document off to Paladin, confident that it would be delivered within a week. He'd booked passage for four on the *Tobit Grander* over an hour before. The sense of satisfaction that resided in his thoughts slipped away when he saw Mayfil's scowl.

"Something wrong?" Bardon asked.

"She wasn't there."

"Who wasn't where?"

"Granny Kye was not in the jail. If Inkleen weren't such a good friend, I would have been embarrassed beyond all measure. I call an important man away from his duties. We go to rescue a poor old woman and orphans from the jailhouse, only to discover when we arrive that there has been a jailbreak. Our old lady and street urchins have escaped."

"How did she do it?"

"No witnesses."

"No witnesses?" Bardon paused, and with an effort, he restored calm to his tone of voice. "Both cells on either side of her held numerous women."

"They are not talking. Seemed to enjoy us looking like fools." He waved a finger in the air. "I fired that lummox of a day jailer and left a message for the night man that he was fired too."

"For allowing prisoners to escape? How do you know which one is at fault?"

Mayfil stomped around his desk and threw himself down in his chair. "No, not for that. I fired them for filth. Most disgusting civil office I've ever seen."

Bardon frowned. "Where's N'Rae?"

"She was most distraught. I took her to the inn. We thought her grandmother might have gone there. But she had not. A young man of your acquaintance, a fellow named Hoddack—I know of the father, a kindia trader—took over with N'Rae. They were going to search the marketplace."

"The market?"

"The girl thought her grandmother would want nicer clothes for the children."

Bardon nodded in a numbed state. "Yes, yes, she would."

"I sent out a runner to the constable stations. They'll be on the lookout for her."

"She'll be arrested again?"

"Well, yes, but I still think old Inkleen will let her out. He thought the whole fiasco was quite amusing."

Bardon sank into the chair N'Rae had sat in earlier.

What is the logical course I should pursue? I don't think there is a logical course.

The harbormaster cleared his throat. "Ahem. Isn't there something you should be doing, Squire Bardon?"

"I should be miles to the north of here, on the back of a faithful dragon, on my way to right a wrong, pleasantly ensconced in the execution of a quest of noble purpose."

Mayfil looked a bit confused. "I thought you might want to join the search for the fugitive granny and her accomplices."

"Yes." Bardon stood. "Thank you, Harbormaster Mayfil, for your co-operation. I'm sure your nephew will return with an answer from Paladin. We have our arrangements for our departure, and I appreciate your efforts to extract Granny Kye from her legal entanglements."

"Yes, very well said." Mayfil stood, put a hand on Bardon's elbow, and guided his visitor toward the door. "I can tell you've been spending your time in those fancy higher courts in the north. Why don't you find that girl's grandmother so I can finish the job of having her exonerated?"

The harbormaster left the squire outside his office. Bardon stayed where he had been deposited.

What is the logical first step? To look where she was last seen. Bardon started forward and stopped. *I have to find N'Rae.* He paused. *Logical. I have to find Granny Kye first.*

Rain still sprinkled the streets when he emerged from the three-story office building onto the wharf. His nose caught the unfamiliar odors of the sea, brine and fish, sodden hemp ropes and sun-bleached sails.

He bolted across the wet wood planks and into the stone street. Traffic posed no problem as he made his way across a third of the city. Most people had enough sense to stay out of the rain. Bardon did not doubt that he would eventually find the old emerlindian drenched and happy.

She is almost always content, and she doesn't have the sense to get out of the rain.

At the jailhouse, he found no jailer but two women cleaning the office. Without speaking to them, he went to the desk cabinet. An easy blow to the latch with the side of his hand opened the door. He took out a key and went to the door where the tumanhofer had kept the next set of keys.

He heard one scrubwoman speak to the other. "Do you think he should be doing that?"

"Don't worry about it, dearie. Even soaking wet, you can tell that one's important."

"He does look somewhat like a prince, doesn't he?"

"It's the fine clothes. Maybe he is a prince."

Bardon crossed the room with the large, rusted key ring in his hand. "A knight, ladies. I'm to be a knight, not a prince. And I'm only a squire now." He entered the opening to the stairway.

"That explains it," said one of the women. "A knight would have the right to be messing about with the keys, don't you think?"

Bardon raced down the steps and didn't hear an answer. Walking much more quickly than they had the night before, he reached the end of the underground passageway. He unlocked the last door and swung it open.

"What are you doing here?" he asked, not bothering to keep the astonishment out of his voice.

"I was arrested, Bardon." Granny Kye sat on the floor of her cell, combing a girl's wet hair. "Surely you remember. You came last night and brought us food and these blankets." She gestured at the folded piles. Three of the children sat on the small blanket towers. Two lay stretched out on the floor, playing a game with sticks and small stones. Bardon strode across the entryway and grasped the iron bars.

"You weren't here. The harbormaster came to get you out, and"—he paused and spoke slowly, distinctly—"you were not here."

"He came to get us out? How nice."

Bardon sought to calm his voice, soften his voice, remove all vestige of emotion from his voice. Finally, he spoke. "Where were you?"

"Giving the children baths. Those nice women who were here yesterday were here again this morning. We all agreed the children needed washing. So we took them to the prison laundry room and bathed them all, including their clothing." She went back to combing the urchin's wet locks. "I think we should get them new garments, Bardon. Perhaps we can go to the market on the way back to the inn."

Bardon dug his fingers into his hair and pulled. "N'Rae is at the market with Holt."

"Those two really should be chaperoned, young Squire. Of that much, I agree with Jue Seeno. I don't think Holt is a bad boy, but natural, healthy attraction does happen between young people. Perhaps you'd better go find them."

"First I must go back to the harbor and disturb Mayfil once more on your behalf."

Granny Kye merely nodded.

Bardon ground his teeth. "Do you think you could stay here long enough for me to get you out of here?"

She tilted her head. "Does that make sense?"

"Perfect sense," he answered. "I want to get you legitimately released so you won't be arrested again for breaking out of jail."

Granny Kye laughed. "What a ridiculous thing to say!"

"Will you stay here?"

"Yes, of course."

Bardon turned to leave. Granny Kye's voice stopped him. "Because I worry, dear…on your way to the harbor, would you go through the market to see if you can find N'Rae?"

Bardon faced the prisoner again and bowed, stiff as usual and without the grace of Sir Dar. "Yes, it would be my pleasure."

21

A Slippery Encounter

Rain drenched the city. Bardon splashed through the market, not bothering to look closely at the few people out on the streets. N'Rae wouldn't be strolling through a downpour. Holt would not want to be uncomfortable and, therefore, would have holed up someplace warm and dry. As Bardon neared the docks, the torrent increased. Water poured off his head, down his neck, and dribbled under his tunic. His soaked socks squished inside his boots. However, he dashed through fewer puddles as he neared the wharf.

Better drainage. A nursery rhyme came to mind, one that must have been planted in his ear before he was six. He couldn't remember anyone chanting nursery rhymes at The Hall.

Drip, drip makes a drop
Tiny raindrops never stop
Flowing to the ocean
Downhill, downhill
Never standing still.

Not exactly great poetry. No wonder children's ditties were not required reading.

He stopped under an overhang of a warehouse building. In a few more steps he'd be on the wooden planks that ran the length of the waterfront. The sheet of rain blurred the outlines of ships docked at the closest piers. He couldn't see beyond a hundred feet. Just ahead of him, it looked as though someone had dropped their bundles and run. Not a soul could be seen in either direction.

Odd… There isn't anyone about.

He waited. The spring rain definitely had a chill to it, and a shiver ran up his spine.

I'll be drinking one of Granny Kye's tonic teas tonight. That is, if we get her out. At least Mayfil's office will be warm, and the rain is letting up.

He dashed across the remaining cobblestones and leapt onto the wharf.

His boots slipped. "Whoa!" he hollered and caught himself before he fell. He headed toward the three-story building that housed the office of the harbormaster. With his head ducked to keep the rain from pelting his eyes, he could see little but the boards under his feet. He caught sight of the abandoned bundles in front of him and only had a moment to wonder if they were rags or mops before the mass split into two forms and lurched to stand.

Quiss! Two quiss!

Neither of the creatures stood taller than the squire, but the quick motion to stop and retreat landed Bardon on his back. The beasts towered over him, waving their tentacles. His feet scrabbled against the slick wood as he propelled himself backward.

I can't let them touch me!

One leaned over him, and Bardon rolled toward the street, falling off the platform and landing three feet below on hard cobblestones. He ignored the shock to his body, rolled farther away, and sprang to his feet. He had difficulty pulling his sword from its wet leather scabbard. But by the time the ungainly quiss had managed the drop to the street, he was armed. With a knife in one hand and a sword in the other, he faced the approaching quiss.

He charged, passing on the left and swinging his sword through that beast's squirming appendages. Before the creatures could react, he circled back and lopped off the outside tentacles of the other beast. He discovered he was most likely to slip when his sword first impacted the creatures. He took care to be prepared. The last thing he wanted was to go down at the feet of a quiss. Since the bold charge worked, Bardon put his knife away and made several more passes, swiftly dismembering the creatures until only a few remaining arms waved over their stiffened limbs. On the next charge, Bardon held his sword parallel to the ground and sliced one quiss in half.

As he turned to finish the last beast, his foot snagged on something. He looked down. A severed quiss tentacle wrapped around his boot. With the point of his sword, he peeled it off and hurled it across the pier. He danced out of the mass of appendages writhing in the puddles around his feet. A grunt warned him of the surviving beast's approach. He swung his sword in the direction of the noise, missed, and on the backswing slashed the quiss's upper body. It recoiled, and he thrust his sword through the creature's bulbous head. It fell.

Bardon surveyed the ground around him. For the first time since the battle began, he noticed the rain had slacked off to a light shower. The corpses and dismembered appendages seeped blood into the standing water. Those tentacles severed first had ceased to writhe. The others moved sluggishly. The pavement glowed red.

He closed his eyes and breathed deeply, as he had been trained to do, to replenish his taxed supply of life-giving air. The swordmasters claimed the exercise purified the soul from the defilement of taking life and re-paired damage done to the muscles by excessive exertion. The squire's lungs filled with the smell of death and the acrid fumes of rapidly disin-tegrating quiss. His stomach lurched, and he ran for the edge of the wharf to heave.

Leaning against a thick piling, he breathed in shallow, quick gasps. He glanced around, wondering when the dockworkers would reappear. A few feet from where he recovered, another quiss grasped the pier's deck and hauled itself up. The quiss breathed with a hiss of air taken in through wet, spongy flesh.

Bardon pushed away from the support and studied the beast. A scrap-ing noise from behind jerked him around to face the other direction. Four more quiss climbed out of the harbor water.

You know, Wulder, I could use some help here.

"Argh!" Bardon charged the nearest quiss and thrust his sword through the beast's middle, then dragged the blade off to the side. He ran on, and turned back to see the beast fall. He shuddered. As he'd rushed past, the quiss's arms lashed out at him. Several had grasped at his sleeve. He wouldn't try that again.

That was too close. Better to methodically disable the beast and then go for the heart. I know very little about the anatomy of these things. I assume the heart is in the massive chestlike area beneath the head. He kept his eyes on the blundering beasts as they stumbled a bit before getting used to standing. Bardon remained cautious, knowing their clumsiness did not make them any less deadly.

Bardon circled the small, bumbling group, seeking a plan of action. *It would be a good idea to attack now before they become less awkward. One at a time. Yes, foul creatures, I prefer to battle you one at a time. Would one of you be so kind as to stagger away from the others?*

One did sway, stumble, and lurch across the wharf platform to fall on the street. Bardon took advantage and attacked as the creature struggled to its feet. Three downward blows and a thrust through the chest finished it off.

Panting, Bardon turned to pick his next victim.

Oh no! Where there had been three quiss, there were now six. The original three stood solidly on their legs. The additional three still swayed unsteadily.

He heard shouts and saw a line of men pouring out of the harbormaster's building. They ran to join the fight. Bardon cheered and then looked closely at their weapons. They carried long chains and clubs tied to ropes. One man had what looked like a heavy teapot at the end of his rope.

He soon saw the effectiveness of this odd weaponry. Two or three men would surround a beast, well beyond reach of the dangerous tentacles. They then twirled their chains or bludgeons. Bardon watched the man with a teakettle. He held the end of the rope above his head and swung the pot around and around, gaining momentum with each circle. He edged closer, and the kettle smashed into the creature's head. The head exploded much like a large, soft gourd hit with a sledgehammer. Messy, but effective.

Bardon remained on the street and watched the men slay the beasts. The slosh of a foot dragged through a puddle, the slurred breathing, and the heavy smell of seawater warned him. He whirled to find a giant quiss a few feet behind him. This creature stood at least seven feet tall. He had never seen nor heard of a quiss this size.

The beast reached for him, and Bardon swung his sword. The arm fell to the ground between them. Without so much as a flinch or a grunt, the animal extended another tentacle. Bardon lopped it off, this time backing away. The creature followed. It became a rhythm of sorts. The quiss reached, Bardon cut off the arm, he stepped back, and the animal followed. They repeated the macabre dance several times until Bardon realized he'd allowed himself to be pushed against a building wall. The arms threatened at a faster rate, and Bardon concentrated to keep up the pace.

The lack of room to swing the sword presented another problem. It took a great deal of skill to produce a short swing, draw back, aim, and swing again. Bardon realized his reflexes were slowing and that each successive arm was thicker and harder to slice through. The writhing arms at his feet whipped his boots. He thought perhaps he would chance dodging to one side or the other, hoping he could spring far enough away to miss getting caught by one of the remaining appendages. He gathered his strength.

The monster before him burst and fell. Bardon looked at the heap of mangled flesh at his feet and then to beyond where the beast had stood.

Holt smiled at him as he wound up the rope of his weapon. "Thought you might appreciate a helping hand."

"Yes," said Bardon. "Thank you."

"That was a big one."

"Yes, it was."

"I think that's the last of them."

Bardon looked over the scene. "Yes, it would seem so."

The rain had completely stopped. N'Rae came running down the steps of the harbormaster's office, the ever-present basket bouncing on her arm. The slight girl zigged and zagged to get through the increasing crowd. She reached Bardon, threw her arms around his waist, and hugged.

"We could see from the building. Master Mayfil organized the men and helped them find weapons and showed them how to use them. It all took so long!" She sobbed, let go of him, and wiped her eyes. An uncertain smile quivered on her lips. "I thought you would die."

She looked up at him, and suddenly her eyes widened, and her lips parted with a little gasp. With both hands she grabbed his head by the ears and forced his face down toward hers. She kissed him soundly on the cheek and then allowed his head to bob back up, but her hands still cupped his ears. Slowly, her fingers moved away, but Bardon felt her placing his long, wet hair over his ears as she released him.

He heard Holt's short bark of laughter.

"Trying to hide the halfling's pointed ears? Too late, N'Rae. They've been seen."

22

Problems Multiply

Holt glanced over his shoulder. Mayfil stood among his men, shouting cleanup instructions.

"We must dispose of the bodies immediately," barked the harbormaster. "They will putrefy within the hour." He wrinkled his nose. "Already the stench is formidable. The fumes are poisonous. Take precautions against lengthy exposure. Shovel up the remains and transport them by wagon to an open space. Burn them, cart and all."

The marione farmer's son looked from the decaying quiss to the men who would have to dispose of the bodies and screwed his face into an expression of disgust. He turned his attention to Bardon.

"What's so bad about being a halfling?"

Bardon forced himself to relax. "It opens the door for impolite people to ask prying questions."

Holt laughed. "You've got no reason to take umbrage at my words, Squire. I'm a sort of halfling myself."

N'Rae scowled at him. "How is that, Holt? Both your mother and father are mariones."

He smiled at her, and Bardon saw her frown melt under the warmth of the young marione's charming expression.

"My mother is a lady, and my father is a boor. Thus you have"—he used his hand to sweep down in front of him, indicating his own person—"a boor with beguiling manners."

Keeping his face in the careful, noncommittal mask he found useful, Bardon waited. He felt certain that Holt would continue to press him. He was not mistaken.

"So, Squire, you are emerlindian and o'rant. Was your father the o'rant?"

Bardon's jaw hurt. Underneath the calm expression, he raged. He'd been channeling the tension inward by grinding his teeth together. He relaxed and breathed, then answered in a level tone. "I have never been told."

"Aha!" Holt smiled sympathetically at Bardon and then with charm at N'Rae. "You see, that is the problem. Not that uncouth fellows like me—rather half-uncouth, half-polished louts like me—ask questions, but that there are no answers to the questions. That would gall anyone. May I make an observation?" His eyes twinkled as he looked again at Bardon.

It would be such a pleasure to punch this young dorker in the nose. Bardon screwed the corner of his mouth down before countering, "Can I stop you?"

A good-natured laugh pealed from Holt's throat. "I propose that you accept your mysterious background and build a persona around it. Use it to increase your appeal, your stature as a knight."

It's a wonder his nose is still straight. I think someone should have broken it for him years ago. Bardon cleaned his sword on a rag and sheathed it. "Holt, I don't deliberately calculate actions to project an impression on the people I meet."

"Of course you do."

Bardon tightened his fists.

Holt chortled again. The sound grated on Bardon's nerves.

"See?" said the marione. "You are doing it now. You are working to appear calm, when you really want to give me a sound thrashing and perhaps even toss me in the harbor."

N'Rae's head swiveled as she watched the two young men. Bardon saw her swallow and knew the prospect of a fight between two men she trusted frightened her.

He looked Holt in the eye. "Tossing you in the harbor is an extremely attractive idea. I hadn't thought of it." He let a small smile touch his lips. "But there is something fundamentally wrong with your analysis of my feelings. You see, I don't endeavor to appear calm for those around to observe. I endeavor to be calm for my own benefit. *You* employ courtesy to make the way easier for yourself. I have been trained to employ courtesy to make the way easier for another."

He offered his arm to N'Rae. "I have found Granny Kye. We still need to rescue your grandmother from the jail. Shall we approach Harbormaster Mayfil?"

She grabbed his arm and squeezed it. "I knew you would. At first I wanted to search the market. But Holt kept looking at things instead of people, and then it was so wet. I thought you might still be at the harbormaster's office, so we came here." She bounced on her toes. "Where is she? Is she all right?"

"She's in the jail cell she's supposed to be in. Earlier, she was in the prison laundry room—"

N'Rae held up a hand. "I can guess. Washing urchins and their clothes?"

Bardon laughed. "Exactly."

They started toward a knot of men. Harbormaster Mayfil stood in the center.

"I still say," Holt called after them, "that you should add your halfling status to your image of aspiring knight. Romance, glamour, mystique, all that. Take my advice, Squire. I'm a lot more familiar with the world than you are."

Bardon stopped. He patted N'Rae's hand resting on his arm. "Excuse me. This will only take a moment."

He turned and walked back to Holt. The marione's face took on a wary look. Without a word, the squire grabbed him by the front of his shirt and the back of his pants, lifted him into the air, and hurled him off the dock. The splash as he hit arced upward, and the water fell on the boards at Bardon's feet. He put his hands on his hips and watched the churning water.

N'Rae ran to peer over the edge. "Oh, Bardon, what if there are still quiss swimming around down there?"

His head jerked up, and he looked at her.

Didn't think of that. That's what I get for acting on impulse.

Holt's head broke the surface of the water. "Help! I can't swim." He sputtered.

"Bother!" exclaimed Bardon and picked up the bludgeon on a rope Holt had dropped. He slung the weapon over the edge of the dock. "Grab hold. I'm certainly not coming in after you."

Up and down the wharf, men stopped what they were doing and came to watch. Holt latched on to the lifeline, and Bardon hauled him to the side. The marione climbed the rough pilings and cross timbers. Those above could hear him coughing and making guttural noises, snorting and cackling. Two men grabbed his arms and helped him over the edge. He lay on the wooden planks and laughed. He rolled and held his sides and roared. He wiped water out of his eyes, part from the sea and part his own tears.

Without knowing the source of his mirth, the men laughed as well. Bardon remembered one of Kale's little dragons, Dibl. Dibl used humor to strengthen the questers. A shared joke brought men closer together. A laugh helped to heal both body and spirit. Seeing the funny side of a situation made the situation easier to bear. Bardon grinned at the memory.

"Coarse humor corrupts, but light laughter elevates." Principle twenty-six.

He watched Holt try to control his laugher, and fail. N'Rae giggled beside him. Bardon laughed. He reached his hand down to Holt and helped the marione to his feet.

"We're going to rescue Granny Kye," he said. "Do you want to come with us?"

"Delighted to join you," Holt answered with a bow. "I'm sorry I missed the hullabaloo this morning when she escaped their tidy little jail."

"How did you know they have a tidy jail?"

"Oh, I've visited Ianna before."

"And the jail?"

He nodded and winked. "And the jail."

He offered N'Rae his arm at the same time Bardon did from the other side. She giggled, transferred the minneken's basket to hang between Bardon and herself, and took both arms.

"I see now why Grandmother and Jue don't trust you."

"Jue?" Holt cocked his head at her.

"You," she answered, coloring. "You as in Bardon. I see now why Grandmother and Bardon don't trust you. But I still like you."

"Thank you."

"But now I don't trust you either."

He nodded his head. "Very wise of you, young lady. Never trust a scoundrel."

Harbormaster Mayfil did not have time to go with them on their errand, but he assured them Magistrate Inkleen would still accommodate them. The magistrate's secretary said he would not be available until after the day's court session, which would be several hours.

"I want dry clothes," said N'Rae after the clerk to the secretary showed them out the door. "And you two smell disgusting and look worse. We should have gone to the inn first."

Bardon guided them past a group of businessmen crowded around a town crier reporting the attack of the quiss. "The idea was to get your grandmother and the children out of jail as quickly as possible."

Holt chortled. "I somehow get the impression that Granny Kye is comfortable no matter where she is."

N'Rae nodded. "She is, you know."

Back at the inn, the mistress of the establishment firmly refused to launder the men's blood-splattered clothes.

"I'll have the stable hands burn them for you, but I won't make my washermaids put their hands in a tub with the likes of that."

Bardon felt better in a clean set of garments but decided he had better shop for something to replace the lost clothing before they boarded the *Tobit Grander.* Holt apparently had no problem producing something else to wear. N'Rae wore the second gown she had purchased in Norst.

She'll need to go shopping as well. And Granny Kye will want new things for the children. Our purse is going to be depleted before we even set foot in the Northern Reach.

They arrived at the magistrate's office at four and, therefore, had to sit politely through the afternoon ritual of umbering. Umbering was practiced all over Amara in different styles. In Wittoom, the small repast included fancy treats of small number. In Ordray, the break for nourishment looked more like a full meal. Here in Ianna, the slow, ceremonial serving emphasized the importance of relaxing rather than the food.

They drank heated juices and ate small daggarts and crisp, fresh vegetables cut and layered with a creamed cheese. Bardon's appetite reflected a skipped noonmeal. The delicacies impressed N'Rae, and she asked many questions about the types of vegetables and the different ways they could be prepared.

"Goodness, girl," said the magistrate with a laugh. "Where have you lived all your life?"

Bardon moved his foot under the table and managed to connect with her shin before she proclaimed she had lived with ropma. He was proud of her when she smoothly answered, "We lived deep in the country where there wasn't a great variety of food, but still plenty to keep us healthy."

Finally, they made their way through the busy streets to the jail. The office shone from its recent scrubbing. A new desk and chair replaced the battered table and stool. A decent young o'rant stood to give them assistance when they came through the door.

"Quite," he answered stiffly when the magistrate asked him if he was aware of the mess of misunderstanding that the former jailers had managed to tangle around a simple matter.

"Good, then," said Inkleen. "We will release the emerlindian woman and the children. She now understands the customs of our people and will not repeat her mistake."

The young jailer didn't know to whom he should offer the lone seat, the lady or the magistrate. Bardon saw the confusion on his face as he fingered the back of the chair. He caught the man's eye and looked pointedly from the chair to N'Rae. The jailer's face relaxed, and he nodded.

"Miss, would you like to sit while I go fetch your grandmother?"

Again, Bardon witnessed the training her mother must have given N'Rae even as they lived among the primitives.

N'Rae curtsied and turned to the elderly magistrate. "I do not wish to be seated. Magistrate Inkleen, would you like the chair?"

He nodded and sat in the humble wooden chair as if it were his elaborately carved seat behind his judge's bench.

Bardon noted the jailer only had to go directly to the small room off to the side of the office to retrieve the key. After all the events of the day, the quiet interlude while they waited seemed too quiet and too long.

He heard laughing and giggling and the soft tread of bare feet. The six children seemed to be in high spirits. They made plenty of noise in the underground corridor. The jailer came first through the doorway from the stairs. The children poured in after him, and Granny Kye brought up the rear. In her arms, she held a baby. The children hushed and stared at the men.

"I thought you said six," Holt said under his breath.

"I did," answered Bardon.

"There are more than six."

The squire nodded. "I counted. There are fifteen, not including the baby."

"I can explain," said Granny Kye.

"I'm sure you can."

"Please do," encouraged the magistrate, not bothering to keep the amused smile from his face.

"The six children had brothers, sisters, and friends."

"I'm a cousin," piped up a curly-headed moptop.

"And cousins," added Granny Kye.

The same child tugged on the granny's sleeve. "I think I am the only cousin."

"And one cousin," the old emerlindian corrected.

"And," said the magistrate, "when torrents of rain made the day uncomfortable on the streets, they broke *into* jail."

"You are so right." Granny Kye beamed. "You must be the magistrate, since you are the one with such a clear way of thinking."

Inkleen nodded his head wisely. "And the other two men who have come to your rescue are known to you, so they could not be the magistrate."

"Yes, that too."

"Granny Kye, I hereby bestow upon you the charge of these children."

The emerlindian's smile grew wider.

"But—," said Bardon.

"You," interrupted Magistrate Inkleen, "are a resourceful young man. You'll manage." He stood. "There now, that is settled. I wish you a pleasant journey." The man left.

Bardon's posture remained rigid as he recounted the children.

N'Rae picked up one of the smallest urchins.

Holt leaned against the wall and howled with laughter.

23

Sailing

The children all wore bright red or yellow shirts. The girls wore blue skirts. The boys wore tan britches. Most of them raced hither and yon over the deck of the *Tobit Grander.* N'Rae, who had never been on an ocean-going vessel, seemed to think they were all in imminent danger of falling overboard. Granny Kye, who had chosen the outfits so the children could be easily spotted, seemed to think that no disaster could befall her charges. Bardon stood somewhere in the middle of the two views.

Granny Kye sat on the deck, holding the baby and watching the activity around her with glowing eyes. N'Rae held the hands of two small children and roamed the deck, urging the boys to be more cautious. Holt had looked over the situation and decided the mapmaker would be a better companion than anyone who remotely had anything to do with children. The marione and the tumanhofer sought the ship's navigator and the blessed peace and quiet of studying maps.

As the ship rounded the last point of land and moved into the open sea, the wind caught the sails with a snap. N'Rae and some of the girls squealed. As the sails billowed, cracking with each shift, the young emerlindian gathered the more timid children and hustled them down below.

A seaman hollered at another lad, snatched him from off the rigging, and none too gently shoved him down the hatch. Bardon caught two younger boys and dragged them below.

As he passed the captain, he said, "There are five older boys left on deck. I won't object to any duties you assign them."

The captain grinned, tipped his hat, and nodded. "I'll see to it right away." He continued through the passageway with a light step, whistling a sea ditty.

Ignoring the pleas for freedom from his captives, Bardon watched the captain's departure.

You've got to admire that man. He took on a party of four that expanded overnight to twenty-one. He doesn't seem to be weighed down one bit by the extra bother. Of course, his purse is heavier and mine quite a bit lighter. That could be the source of his contentment.

Bardon trudged deeper into the bowels of the ship, hauling his recalcitrant burdens. He had marched with outstretched arms while holding weighted bags as one of the exercises for sword training. The torture produced muscular arms and stamina. Bardon thought he might write a letter to his old sword master, suggesting they substitute squirming boys for the heavy bags.

The ship could not provide cabin space for so many. Between bales of cotton, barrels of blackstrap molasses, and crates of fruit, Granny Kye had arranged pallets. She and N'Rae intended to sleep here with the children. Toward the back, she had the older boys push together a pen of sorts, made out of bits and pieces of cargo. Here she kept the goat she'd acquired to give milk for the baby.

Bardon glanced at the goat and her crowd of admirers. One raven-haired little o'rant girl brushed the nanny. An older, heavily freckled marione girl handfed her. Another girl, a tumanhofer, had her arms draped around the gray animal's neck and appeared to be singing in the goat's ear.

That's going to be one spoiled nanny goat by the time we dock in Annonshan.

He set the boys on their feet, and they scrambled toward the hatch ladder. Bardon snatched the backs of their shirts, twisting them around to look him in the eyes. "You are forbidden to be on deck until further notice. If you behave, I'll take you up myself. If you don't, you won't see the sun or the moon and stars again until we dock at Annonshan. Understand?"

The boys nodded. As soon as Bardon let go, they scampered over a pile of crates secured by heavy ropes and disappeared.

He found N'Rae sitting with several children as they arranged brand-new rag dolls on a secondhand blanket from the inn. "Will you be all right down here, N'Rae?"

"Oh yes, I like taking care of children. And this place feels cozy to me. Ropma cave dwellings felt much like this, dark and musty moist. And their huts were sparsely furnished with crates and logs."

I can't imagine living in a ropma hut. How different her life must have been from mine.

He opened his mouth to ask a question but heard Granny Kye calling from behind him.

"N'Rae! N'Rae! Where are my paints?" She swept past Bardon without a word to him and handed the younger emerlindian the baby.

"My easel, my palette, my paints," she muttered as she rummaged through the bundles lined up and stacked against one bulkhead. "Here! Here!" she exclaimed as she grabbed a duffel wedged in among heavier parcels. "N'Rae, help me pull it out."

Bardon saw N'Rae looking for a place to put the baby, and he stepped forward. "I'll help, Granny Kye. Stand over here a little bit."

"That one." She pointed unnecessarily. "The one with hard sides covered with blue canvas. Yes, that one."

No sooner had Bardon shifted the other luggage and pulled that piece free than Granny Kye had her hands on it. She laid it on its side and undid the latches. The children crowded close, waiting to see what was inside.

"What are you going to paint?" asked N'Rae.

Granny Kye answered absent-mindedly as she opened the lid. "Everything. The sky. The sea. The sails. Everything."

She set aside several brushes and a box containing bent tubes smeared with dried paint. Next she lifted out a flat square wrapped in cloth. Inside, blank canvas stretched over a wooden frame. Granny Kye's face beamed as she looked at the grayish white surface. She held it up for all the children to view.

"What do you see here?" she asked.

"It's blank," said one.

"Sorta white," said another.

"Nothing," said the smallest boy.

The granny snatched that child into a tight hug. "No, no, no." She laughed, then turned him around to sit in her lap and look at the blank canvas. "Quite the contrary, young man. You say there is nothing here? No, no, no. This picture is not empty, but full of possibilities."

She gathered her painting tools, handing various items into small, eager hands. Those children who were allowed on deck trailed behind her, helping to carry her equipment. She set up her easel and canvas in a place somewhat protected from the wind. Most of the children lost interest as she went through the long preparation of getting the canvas ready.

<hr />

In the days that followed, Bardon's party took up a routine. The younger children played among the crates in the hold with N'Rae supervising. Holt swapped stories with the seamen and harassed the mapmaker for tales of his adventures. Bromptotterpindosset preferred to spend his time with the officers of the ship or the captain's maps and logs. Granny Kye painted.

The older boys discovered Bardon doing his forms, the morning exercises that most warriors repeated daily to keep in fighting shape, on the deck early in the morning. He did several sets of a fixed order. The procedure for muscle toning that prepared him to use his body as his weapon looked almost like a ceremony. The ritual generally bored most of the boys except one. Ahnek, an o'rant of about ten years, stood beside the squire and mimicked his motions, quickly picking up the intricate positioning and rhythm of the exercises.

The next set required Bardon to roll, leap, balance, and perform acrobatic feats. More of the boys joined him for this, and he ended up instructing the most eager ones. Not only the boys, but also the sailors enjoyed watching Bardon parry and thrust with an imaginary opponent as he went through his last regimen for the day. By the second morning, all the boys had acquired roughly made wooden swords so they, too, could fight the unseen enemies.

Each morning, after Bardon finished the serious business of his scheduled regimen, he good-naturedly coached the boys. He even instructed some of the small ones on how to best use their weapons. He brought out his darts, and they set up a makeshift bull's-eye.

"Are darts really a weapon?" asked Ahnek.

"Yes, they are." Bardon hefted the slim wooden dart, then tossed it. Even with the wind and the roll of the ship, he hit the center of the target. "They won't bring down a bisonbeck or a grawlig, but they can be used to distract the enemy. Worry them. Get them off balance."

Bardon divided the boys into age groups and set up a tournament. They had to move their game to a hold below to avoid the wind, but the children threw their hearts into the competition. Even the girls decided to play. Again Ahnek showed the most promise.

Two of the boys took to their sea duties with a passion. Bardon figured when they reached the next port, the boys would ask permission to serve on the ship. And, according to the captain, they would be accepted as cabin boys.

Each evening, Bardon stood on the forecastle with the ship's navigator. Most nights they could measure the progress of the Wizards' Plume. On the nights that cloud cover obscured their view, Bardon stewed.

The navigator chided him over his impatience. "The comet will not move but a few degrees each night."

"Each night it moves toward the death of noble knights. I cannot relax my vigil."

Each morning, Granny Kye set up her easel. By the third day, Bardon resented the time she spent at the canvas. N'Rae looked paler than usual and haggard. The baby didn't take to the sea or the goat's milk. N'Rae didn't know which. Jue Seeno offered advice, and the tea they brewed for the infant seemed to help some of the stomach distress. But the minneken also made problems for N'Rae. Mistress Seeno insisted that no one know of her existence. Consequently, Bardon had the small friend in her basket hidden in his cabin most of the time.

In the afternoons, the squire took some of the younger children by turns up to the deck. He watched them run wild with excess energy fueling their helter-skelter games. Even as they plummeted past the old emerlindian granny, she scarcely noticed. The unfinished work before her claimed all her attention. To Bardon's untrained eye, the picture held no particular splendor, just white puffy blobs for clouds and odd, curving lines at the bottom in a muddy green hue. A mess of darkness in the middle might have been the ship. But Bardon couldn't imagine how she could paint the vessel she was sitting on.

On the fourth afternoon, he took below the last three children he'd been watching for their hour of freedom. He didn't bother listening to their vehement protests. He knew from previous days that a couple of crackers, a drink, and a blanket would provide enough comfort to have them snoozing in a matter of minutes. The rocking of the gentle waves provided a cradle effect.

Before he reached the temporary quarters in the cargo hold, he heard the baby's wails. He passed into the dim light and saw N'Rae gently bouncing the little one as she paced back and forth in the restricted area. Shuddering gasps broke into the babe's cries. Bardon knew that meant he was winding down and would soon, out of sheer exhaustion, sleep.

The squire gave the three he'd been watching a drink and the crackers. He shooed them to their own pallets and, because he had once made the mistake of singing to them, had to meet their incessant demands to do so again.

He didn't know many lullabies or nursery songs, so he sang ballads he'd learned mostly from Sir Dar. He liked the way the bulkheads of their small quarters made his voice sound rich and more resonant. His mentor's songs represented the best of Amaran folk tunes and also some classical music.

Bardon sang several easy melodies. With the last one he sang, he was certain that everyone except N'Rae napped, worn out from the business of being children. He studied the peaceful scene, knowing that it could be destroyed in an instant by the entrance of one of the rough rapscallions who also counted themselves among Granny Kye's orphans. Luckily, the five older boys remained above, helping at jobs they found thrilling.

The baby nestled in N'Rae's arms as she sank to the blanket-padded crate and leaned against another. Ten children sprawled on their pallets, scattered in an uncertain order around the unlikely nursery.

Bardon tiptoed to her side and whispered, "I think I shall have a talk with Granny Kye."

N'Rae stifled a yawn. "What about?"

"It isn't right that you should have the responsibility for all these children."

"I don't mind."

"You're worn out."

"I'll nap now if you go away and quit pestering me."

"Pestering?"

She grinned. "It is so easy to ruffle your feathers."

He glowered at her. "It was my impression that I was offering to assist you in making the workload equitable. I wasn't aware I was pestering you."

"See?" She slipped down onto the floor and lay down, careful not to wake the baby. "Now go away and don't pester Grandmother, either."

"She's left you to tend fifteen children and a baby by yourself."

"Nonsense! Mistress Seeno helps. You help. And five of the fifteen I never see, they're so taken with being sailors."

"Granny Kye could help."

N'Rae relaxed, her head resting on her arm. "Yes, she could, but what she's doing is important."

Bardon scoffed. "Painting a picture?"

N'Rae's sleepy voice drawled over her words. "Her pictures are wonderful."

"Have you seen it?"

She smiled with her eyes closed as if she viewed a dream. "Just wait and see, Bardon. You'll be surprised."

She snored, a petite and ladylike whuffling as she breathed out.

I see that further protestations will be useless. The one I wish to persuade has found a way to unequivocally ignore me.

He stood and froze, tilting his head to concentrate on a slight nudging in his mind, the indication that his own thoughts were not the only thoughts dwelling there. He grinned and rushed from the room, heading for the upper deck.

The sun flashed within the foam, marking the water in long lines where the gentle waves crested and melded back into the sea. The smell of salt and seaweed and the fish caught for their evening meal filled his nostrils. The breeze tangled in his hair and whipped it away from his face. He no longer used the pomade, and it would have been a useless attempt under the circumstances. The wind across the seawaters constantly freshened the sails of the ship, billowed the men's shirts, and fluttered the clothing of the people on deck.

Bardon had given up trying to keep his ears out of sight after Holt had made his comments. He wanted to prove the marione farm boy wrong. As he worked among the crew and openly practiced his forms each morning, the sailors showed no interest in the slight point atop each of his ears. Their lack of interest at first surprised him. Then he felt chagrin for having thought that his ears would cause a downpour of condemnation. He'd been wrong.

After Bardon had gotten over berating himself for being a fool all these years, he remembered Dibl. The minor dragon roused an awareness of the absurd in those around him. While Bardon traveled with Kale on their last quest, the little orange and yellow dragon had delighted in making Bardon laugh at his own foibles. Just the memory of Dibl landing in his hair and scratching his scalp with tiny claws made the squire smile.

And then he sobered as he analyzed the great difference between his life now and his previous life within the confines of The Hall. Grand

Ebeck had been right to throw him out of those hallowed walls. In the outside world, the petty digs of immature boys meant little. As a youth in The Hall, they had devastated his morale.

Eying the busy workers around him, he allowed that feeling of separation to settle in his chest for a moment. He sighed heavily, remembering the anguish of being a lonely child, too different to fit in and too shy to use his difference to his advantage.

I wonder what Holt Hoddack would have done under the same circumstances.

The presence in his mind laughed, jarring him out of this melancholy. Greer laughed with the joy of connection. Bardon strode to the forecastle and mounted to the highest point. In the distance he saw the black silhouette against the sky.

"Ahoy!" The call came from the crow's nest. "Dragon, due east."

"No cause for alarm." Bardon raised his voice for all to hear. "He is Greer, a friend."

Yes, I know where we shall go ashore. Annonshan... You aren't surprised? Why would I think you would be? You are always two steps ahead of me... And just how did you know about Granny Kye's acquisition of all these children?

Bardon gasped and scanned the waters. *A sea serpent? Since when are you friendly with sea serpents?... No! I'm not implying that your distant relatives are an inferior breed... Could you, for once, answer a question without all this falderal?... Of course, there was a question!...* Bardon chuckled. *No, I guess I don't remember it either. But yes, we are going to Annonshan, and from there we go to Dormenae. Sir Dar will have a solution to our sudden overpopulation in the questing party... Yes, I also wish to acquire dragons for the rest of our journey. I am tired of the clumsy conveyances on the ground.*

He grinned. *I concede, you bothersome beast. I am all kinds of a fool for leaving you behind. You are a far superior mode of transportation.*

You have a message for Sir Dar and Paladin as well?... From the sea serpent?... What were you doing talking to this overgrown snake? I thought you couldn't abide snakes of any kind... Sea serpents are one of the reasons you find snakes disgusting? How is that?... Unsavory relatives are a part of life, Greer. Most people do have branches of their family who are less palatable than others... Hmm? I've never thought of it that way, but I suppose being abandoned at The Hall does have the advantage of having no distasteful relatives.

Getting back to the subject, Greer, I also suppose this message from the exceptionally well-mannered sea serpent is about the quiss... Yes, Greer, I figured that out all by myself. I do have a head on my shoulders and occasionally use it... My head had nothing to do with acquiring a herd of children! Granny Kye collected the children... I am in charge of the expedition, Greer. I have a perfectly good plan for getting rid of the children... No! Your eating them would not solve the problem, and you don't eat children. Although I might tell them you do, if they get out of hand... Ha! You haven't got a reputation to spoil.

24

Danger from the Deep

Clouds rolled in from the open sea, the wind picked up, and the *Tobit Grander* rocked between billowing waves. The inclement weather added a day to their journey, having pushed them away from the coast. Bardon had experienced rough seas before when sailing with Sir Dar, and the rolling deck beneath his feet did absolutely nothing to his stomach. Granny Kye, N'Rae, and Holt hung over the rail, though, losing their dinners overboard, and then took to their beds.

Bromptotterpindosset stepped in to help. The practical tumanhofer brewed tea and served it to those who lay groaning on their pallets or, in Holt's case, a bunk. Most of the children hopped, skipped, and jumped around the hold. The swaying of the ship provided more fun. Bromptotterpindosset ordered them to sit, and they acknowledged the man's sharp tone by scrambling to their own spots to wait for his next command.

Pulling a deck of cards from a huge pocket in his cowled, knee-length jacket, he sat down in the nook that also housed the nanny goat. He pointed to one child and then another until he had a group of youngsters gathered around him. Shuffling the cards with a flourish, he instructed them on the rules of a lively game.

When this group became engrossed in the card playing, he stood and called the others to follow him to the more open area. He charged the older ones to keep the youngest ones out of trouble, and then he produced a dozen balls out of his voluminous coat.

Bardon tilted his head at the tumanhofer. "A mapmaker keeps balls in his pockets?"

"Orbs," he answered gruffly. "Technically, they're orbs."

A green orb sailed past Bardon's ear and ricocheted off a crate, hitting the ceiling and rebounding toward a group of children.

"Bouncing orbs?"

"I juggle," announced Bromptotterpindosset without a trace of embarrassment. "I learned while visiting Himber." He cocked an eyebrow at the young squire. "You've heard of Himber?"

"On the Herebic continent? I have. We study geography at The Hall." He pushed aside his annoyance that the mapmaker thought he knew nothing of the world beyond Amara. His education had been more than adequate, but he admitted he had a lot to learn. The tumanhofer would be a good source of information if he could be persuaded to open up. Bardon determined to use Sir Dar's diplomacy and ask intelligent questions about the man's expertise. "I thought the Himbernese were not a friendly nation."

The mapmaker shifted his glasses up on his nose. "A little standoffish, but most people warm up to you if you express an interest in their customs." His eyes brightened as if he shared an unspoken joke with the young squire. "They juggle to relieve stress and as a means to focus their attention during meditation. I got quite good at it, actually."

Another orb flew between the squire and the tumanhofer. A child chased after it, bumping into the sturdy mapmaker and careening away much like one of the orbs glanced off the crates.

"Not all the orbs bounce," said Bromptotterpindosset. "And the different patterns of the juggle, the order and color of the orbs, have significance. A fascinating study."

"The orbs, then, are valuable?"

"Quite."

"And you allow the children to play with them?"

The tumanhofer squared his shoulders. "In all the cultures I have studied, I have noted that children are less troublesome if they are occupied. Contented children are valuable, as is the peace that surrounds them."

"Energy directed is energy of use." Principle seventy. "A child on his own has only one chance in four of heading the right way." Principle fifty-six. Bardon nodded but had little to say about peace where children were concerned.

A burst of laughter filled the cramped space.

Bardon smiled sardonically. "Peace?"

"Laughter is but one tone of peace." Bromptotterpindosset moved to the pallet of one of the few children stricken with seasickness and offered a crust of bread. The little girl took the bread to nibble on, and the tumanhofer sat on the floor beside her, holding a small bucket and speaking quietly.

"Would you like to hear what children living in Tastendore do when the rains come?" he asked.

The child's eyes grew big, and she nodded.

Bardon moved on to urge N'Rae to sit and sip cooled tea.

Once the clouds and wind moved on and the ship ceased rocking violently, the patients recovered. First the few stricken children found the strength to get up. Then N'Rae forced herself off her pallet. Bardon said she rose from the brink of death just because she had realized he and the tumanhofer were in charge of the children.

"We did very well without you, N'Rae," he teased her. "None of them fell overboard, and all of them are still well fed and clean."

She snorted. "Well fed on what? Hardtack and candy? Clean by whose standards? A grawlig's?"

Granny Kye climbed out of the hold soon after. Holt was the last to appear, and he still looked pale. The passengers on the *Tobit Grander* gathered on deck to bask in the warm sun.

"Squire Bardon," said Ahnek, "Granny Kye's painting is finished. Come see."

A small crowd stood behind the emerlindian sitting on her wooden stool. Bromptotterpindosset, Holt, N'Rae, and several children looked over her shoulder at the canvas on the easel, admiring her work and making enthusiastic comments.

At first, Bardon saw nothing remarkable about the seascape. But the others pointed out images blended into the more obvious forms. When looked at carefully, a cloud became a hand releasing a flock of birds. A wave curled over a finger. The ship rested in a giant palm. Light seemed to radiate from a fingertip touching the sun. Bardon blinked, and the hidden images disappeared. He concentrated, and they came back into focus.

"I don't like the eyes," said Ahnek, his voice breaking with a squeak.

"Neither do I," said N'Rae. "They look evil."

"What eyes?" asked Bardon and Holt in unison.

"There," said Bromptotterpindosset pointing to a crest of a wave. "It's a sea serpent. The tail is over here."

"It's huge," exclaimed N'Rae.

Holt rubbed his chin. "Perhaps there are two. The head of one here, and the tail of another over there."

Ahnek put his hand on the older emerlindian's shoulder. "Granny Kye, what do you think?"

"I think it is stalking us." She reached for N'Rae's hand. "Is it there now, dear?"

The younger emerlindian looked out across the gently swelling waves. After only a moment, she gasped.

"Yes!" She looked around her at the children. "You must go below. All of you! Now!" She pushed the little girls at her skirts toward the hatch. "Hurry now. Get below!"

Bardon ran to gather the youngsters playing on the forecastle. Holt whistled to the boys following after the sailors. Bromptotterpindosset and Granny Kye quickly collected her paints and tossed them in the canvas carrier. She held the wet painting away from her as she hastened after N'Rae. The tumanhofer carried her stool and easel as he hurried her toward safety. He stood at the top of the ladder while Holt and Bardon ushered the last of the children into the hold.

"What is this all about?" asked Holt.

Bromptotterpindosset shook his head and gazed out at the sea. "Legend says that sea serpents prefer tender flesh. In other words, children."

Bardon stood with his hands on his hips. The fingers of one hand wrapped around the hilt of his sword. "Greer said a sea serpent gave him information about the migration of quiss. He didn't indicate that the serpent had evil intentions toward our ship's passengers."

The tumanhofer shifted his load and put a foot on the top rung of the ladder. "There is more than one serpent in the sea, Squire Bardon."

Holt looked down to where the top of the mapmaker's head was disappearing. "In your travels, have you ever encountered a sea serpent?"

"Yes!" declared Bromptotterpindosset. "And I don't wish to do so again."

"What's this commotion?" barked the captain as he strode across the deck. "My crew is whispering about a serpent. Is it true? Did the emerlindians spot the head and tail of a giant?"

"Not exactly," said Bardon. "Both ladies have unusual talents. You can be assured the threat of attack is real."

The seasoned captain nodded his head. "The important thing is to keep it from wrapping around the ship and pulling us down. The last third of its tail has no spine. You can slice through the muscle with your sword." He nodded at Bardon's weapon. "As the body comes over the deck, you need to sever the spinal cord. No need to hack all the way through. A point thrust into the vertebrae is your best defense."

Heavy steps and grunts heralded the return of the tumanhofer. He hoisted himself out of the hold with a double-bladed battle-ax on his shoulder. He addressed Holt. "Do you have a weapon, boy?"

"No," said Holt. "Not one that would count. I have a small knife. That's all."

"Come with me," said the captain. "I'm breaking out arms for my men, and I can provide you with something more dangerous than a stickpin."

With a nervous glance at Bardon and then at the water, Holt went after the captain.

"He'll do all right," proclaimed the tumanhofer. "The instinct to survive is strong in that one."

The hours that passed during the long afternoon reminded Bardon of the time spent on the *Morning Lady* as they cruised down the Gilpen River. The seamen went about their business, but with many anxious looks to the water around them. Tension mounted. Every stir in the water caused the people on board the *Tobit Grander* to grab their weapons.

The wind stilled, and the sails hung limply from the yards. The captain ordered the men to strike and furl the sheets. The sun sank toward the western horizon, turning orange, then red, casting an eerie hue across the glassy surface.

"Blood sea," muttered a sailor as he passed Holt and Bardon.

A dark wave rose out of the crimson water.

Several calls raised the alarm. The mound sank beneath the surface, only to rise again twenty yards farther to the east.

"It's coming at us now," said Bromptotterpindosset as he came to stand beside the two younger men. "It'll circle first. Then the tail will rise up beside the ship and slap down hard across midship."

"Fore and aft," yelled the captain. "Arms at the ready. Steady, men, we only have to worry about the part that's on board. Likely we'll never even see the head."

"If you look into its face," said Bromptotterpindosset, "you are looking at your own death. Sea serpents don't show their heads up close until they know they've got the ship in a death grip."

Bardon, Holt, and the tumanhofer moved to the stern of the ship, as did half the crew. The other half stood ready across the bow.

The beast showed sections of its long body as it undulated through the briny waters in a circle that grew smaller with every turn. It changed course and went under the hull, passing without making a strike.

"It's toying with us," said Holt.

"I wouldn't be surprised," answered Bromptotterpindosset. "They are more clever than one would think."

The serpent made another pass under the ship. In the distance they saw the head rise from the sea, a black silhouette against a blazing sky. The creature disappeared, and Bardon watched for that sinuous, dark form to surge upward and fall down into the water. Nothing showed.

Either it is swimming deep, or it has gone away. I bet it hasn't gone away.

Water showered down on them from one side as the beast's great tail thrust into the air. It poised there for a second before slamming down on the vessel, splintering the wooden rail and cracking the deck. The captain and his first mate ran forward and sliced through the serpent as it lay over the crushed railing. The others surged to grab the severed tail and slide it off the deck into the churning water.

The serpent sped away from the ship, leaving a red foaming trail.

"Will it die?" asked Holt.

"Nay," said the captain. "It'll grow another tail unless it's killed by us or some other creature of the deep. I doubt it even feels the wound." He turned to his men. "Step lively. Back to your posts. We haven't seen the end of this sea devil."

The second attack resembled the first. This time the blood of the creature mingled with the splash of seawater. Bardon and the others ran forward and hacked at the serpent's flesh. The squire thrust his sword deep and hit bone, but whether he connected with a massive nerve running through the spinal column, he could not tell.

The beast swam on, and the heavy body scraped across the wooden deck and fell into the ocean.

"At least one of our blades struck true," said the tumanhofer. "It's lost movement below the part we attacked."

"Will it give up now, Captain?" asked one of the younger crewmen.

Before the captain could answer, the beast struck the hull of the ship, causing the vessel to shudder and rock. The blow knocked the men off their feet. They scrambled to get ready for the next assault and waited. Only a sliver of the sun remained above the horizon. The scattered clouds glowed red in the distance. A deep purple canopy hung overhead. Stars serenely shone in their appointed spots in the dark eastern sky. A breeze whispered among the tall, bare masts.

Out of the darkness, a speeding hulk sailed over the ship, landed, and continued to slide. Its coarse hide rasped the wooden planks. The ship tilted. The movement of the beast stilled, but the muscles beneath the shining black skin rippled.

"It'll be pulling us down," screeched one of the men.

The cry broke their stunned inertia. All hands surged forward and began stabbing, hacking, and piercing the body of the serpent. None of the men stood taller than the width of the beast's mammoth body.

"Go deep, boy," ordered the mapmaker beside Bardon.

His own battle-ax repeatedly bit into the animal's flesh. The sound of cascading water brought Bardon's attention to the side of the ship. The serpent's head hovered over them as if it were merely curious as to what these puny creatures tried to do to its body. A long, black, forked tongue flicked out of a lipless mouth. Gleaming yellow eyes caught and reflected the fire of the dying sun. The head bobbed as if it were pleased with what it saw.

Bardon sheathed his sword and pulled out a handful of darts from a pocket in his tunic. He ran toward the beast and leapt to stand on a pile of crates. Aiming at the bobbing head, he let fly the first dart. It landed in the serpent's eye. The head jerked and turned to glare at the man on the cargo.

As it hissed, Bardon sent the second dart through the air and hit inside the beast's nostril. It flicked its head and dislodged the tiny weapon. As the face came closer, the squire threw in rapid succession his last four darts. Two pierced an eye, one bounced off the hard hide of its cheek, and the last sank into the corner of its mouth.

Bardon jumped from his perch just as the serpent made an open-mouthed strike. He grabbed a running block and swung out and around the serpent's head to land on its neck. He sank the sharp hook of the block into the beast's flesh so he would have something to hang on to as the serpent tossed its head.

Holding the rough rope with one hand, he pulled out his sword with the other. The creature writhed and started to submerge. Bardon put the point of his blade against the base of its skull and fell forward, driving his weapon deep.

The serpent's head dropped onto the deck on top of the mutilated section of its own body.

"Stand back," yelled Bromptotterpindosset. He hoisted the battle-ax above his head and swung downward, smashing the blade between the eyes.

For a breathless moment, everyone waited. The beast did not move.

The captain came forward to stand by Bromptotterpindosset. Bardon pulled his sword from the animal and jumped to the deck. A breeze blew over the ship.

"What are you waiting for?" demanded the captain as he looked over his crew. "Get this stinking carcass off my ship. Hoist those sails. We're a day late to Annonshan. I don't intend to be another."

The mapmaker worked his ax up and down until he could yank it from the skull. He, Holt, Bardon, and several seamen pushed the head off the side. It slipped beneath the water with only a slight splash.

"You know," said Bromptotterpindosset, "serpent meat is considered a great delicacy in some cultures."

Bardon cleaned his blade. "I've also heard there are great, thick, wet forests where people eat caterpillars as big as your thumb. I'm not going to introduce worms or snakes of any kind into my diet."

"I don't know," said Holt, slapping the mapmaker on the back. "It depends on if you have a recipe. Did you bring a cookbook in all that luggage of yours, Bromp?"

"Nay, I didn't." The man shook his head with a look of intense sorrow on his face.

Bardon looked at the exposed flesh of the serpent. "Sir Dar is a famous chef. I suppose you could bring him a cut of the meat. But it's three days over land to his castle."

Holt crossed his arms over his chest. "We'd have to get ice to transport it."

"Hard to come by, this time of year," answered Bardon.

"Salt?" suggested Holt.

"I doubt the galley has an adequate supply. We could get some in Annonshan, but by then, the meat would be ripe."

Holt nodded. "Salted meat never has the taste of fresh, anyway."

The tumanhofer perked up and nodded at the squire. "We could get his dragon to carry it ahead."

Bardon shook his head. "Greer is squeamish. He hates snakes of any kind."

"Just a hunk of meat," said the mapmaker.

"Wouldn't do it," insisted Bardon.

Holt shook his head as well. "And they would have to cook it right away. It would be gone by the time we got there, if it tasted good, that is."

The tumanhofer's shoulders drooped once more. "Aye, doesn't look like we'll feast on serpent."

"Don't take it hard, old man," said Holt. "Probably tastes like chicken."

Wittoom

It had been such a simple plan. How could anything have gone wrong? When Bromptotterpindosset mentioned sending the serpent meat ahead with Greer, Bardon seized on the idea of going ahead himself to prepare the way for the questing party plus fifteen children and a baby.

Wittoom was the safest province in the country. The road between Annonshan and Dormenae bustled with benign travelers. Not one lonely stretch, where one might be waylaid by bandits, existed on the entire route. He arranged for a reputable company, Wittoom Coastal Transport, to oversee the trip, providing wagon, driver, and assigned inns for overnight rests. Mapmaker Bromptotterpindosset would see that they wouldn't get lost. Holt decided he would like to visit Sir Dar's court, so that made an extra male escorting the entourage. N'Rae was too tired from chasing children to flirt with Holt. How could anything have gone wrong?

Bardon paced the dragon field on a hill above Castle Pelacce. Greer reclined on the grass with his chin resting between his forefeet. His eyes followed his rider's movement back and forth. The squire stopped to search the road winding off toward the western hills. He heard Greer sigh behind him but did not turn.

Sir Dar sent out riders with homing waistcoaters. The birds will bring us a message if Dar's men locate our party. Blast it, Greer! I don't see anything but dorkers, finches, and mountain sky birds.

He resumed his pointless walk to the end of the field and back. He made three passes, then stopped in front of Greer.

What good would it do to fly the route once more? We saw nothing last night. And nothing again this morning. They've disappeared off the face of the earth... He slapped his hand against his thigh. *I know they were a bother-some lot—*

He shook his head as if to rid himself of a nasty idea. *Are, Greer, not were!—but they* are *my responsibility.* He looked down at his feet. *I have not worn a path along the top of the hill... All right, you win. It does make more sense to be traveling over the countryside searching for them, than traveling the same patch of ground where I can only see to the next ridge.*

With long strides he crossed the knoll to a well-built shed. He had no problem locating Greer's saddle in the dim light. Greer had followed him to the tack house, and in a matter of minutes, they were airborne.

This time let's travel one mile north of the Annonshan road instead of directly over, Bardon suggested.

Less than halfway to the coast, Bardon spotted something unusual in a small village.

Greer, look at the side yard of that tavern. Isn't that horse wearing a caparison in Pelacce's colors?... A roan horse in green and yellow? It must be one of Sir Dar's riders. Let's go down and find out if he knows anything.

They landed in an open field, the crop of corn already harvested. Bardon covered the distance to the tavern quickly on foot. A young boy walked the horse.

"Is the rider inside, lad?"

"Yes sir. He's from Dormenae. One of Sir Dar's men. He let loose a waistcoater 'fore he went inside, and it took off to the east. Man said it would go right to Sir Dar and give him a message tied to its leg."

Bardon said nothing in response. He wanted to know what was written on the small scrap of paper. He rushed into the inn and located the rider sitting at a table and having a meal. The man stood when he recognized one of his master's squires.

"What news have you, man?" asked Bardon.

"They were seen here by a couple of children at a farmhouse several miles east. And that's where the trail ends."

Bardon nodded and left. As he hurried out the back door, he started to call for Greer, but the dragon's huge form already cast a moving shadow over the yard. The squire sprinted to the road. While the boy walking the horse watched in awe, the man and dragon synchronized the pickup with the precision of much practice. Greer circled and landed in front of Bardon. He ran up the tail and leapt into the seat before Greer took off again.

They flew back along the Annonshan road on the south side. Thick forest covered much of the terrain. Greer spotted smoke and circled low. In a clearing backed against a sheer cliff, a large passenger wagon sat unhitched. The horses grazed nearby. As they dropped down, Bardon saw a man in the livery of the transport company get up from the fire. He slipped on his hat and coat before Greer landed, then came walking toward them.

"I figured someone would come looking for us," he said as Bardon dismounted.

"What happened?"

"First, that tumanhofer mapmaker had to go down this road because it wasn't on his map. Well, it's hardly a road, is it?" He gestured toward a break in the trees. "But he's going on about signs of it being an ancient road that's been forgotten. Says it's on older charts of the countryside."

He shook his head, removed his cap to run a hand over his gray hair, then resettled the hat on his head. "Then the granny decides it's a good place for the children to run for a while. She has me build the fire, the younger one starts fixing food and hot drink, and the children scatter. The tumanhofer and that Holt fellow are walking around looking at the ground, uncovering the rock, pulling the grass away so they can see the dirt better." He shook his head again and did the same little maneuver involving his hat and rubbing his hair. "Then the younger emerlindian calls the children to eat. They come running, only when a count is made, three are missing. There's a bunch of calling. I forget the names of the ones they were calling. Bep was one. And those young ones just don't show up."

He sighed and reached for his cap, but stopped as if he was aware of what he was about to do and rubbed his hands together instead. "Then the most peculiar thing of all...the young one looks like she's talking and listening to the horses. Then she speaks to the older woman and points to the rock face over yonder." He pointed vaguely toward the cliff. "Then she, the older one, sits down and draws a picture. Everyone gets excited. The tumanhofer tells me to stay put, that they'll be back. The granny tells me not to leave until they get back. The younger one tries to leave the baby with me, and I say not today or tomorrow will I be watching an infant. They have this big discussion about who is staying and who is going. They all decide to leave, and the marione Holt tells me not to move the wagon no matter how long it takes for them to return."

The driver let out a long, hard breath. "So here I am. And here they are not. That was yesterday about noon. And I knew someone would come looking for me and my passengers because Wittoom Coastal Transport is a reputable company, and we don't lose our freight or our passengers."

"But you've lost yours?"

The man shook his head. "They went that way, toward the cliff. Went around those overgrown bushes and never came back. I've been over there, and I can see where they trampled down the grass, but once they got to the rock wall, they didn't turn right nor left. But they aren't there."

He shook his head again, took off his cap, rubbed the top of his head hard, and put the cap back on.

Bardon stood with his hands on his hips, staring in the direction his questing party had last been seen. He looked over his shoulder at Greer and nodded, then back at the hapless driver.

"Did Granny Kye leave the picture?"

The old man chewed his cheek a moment, then walked to the wagon. The wooden vehicle had a deep box with doors on both sides and a tailgate. Inside, padded seats with backs lined up in rows. Stacked against the back panel that unlatched and swung down, the questers' personal belongings still took up every inch of space allotted for baggage.

The driver opened a side door and stepped up on the riser and into the wagon. He looked around, moved a jacket and a pair of boots, then snatched a paper from under a seat. After a brief glance, he handed it down to Bardon.

"I think that's it."

Oh, Wulder, help me see what they saw.

Granny Kye had sketched the cliff with a bit of charcoal. Around the edges, fingers had smudged the lines. Bardon concentrated on the bushes where the driver said the children and adults had disappeared.

There! I see it. A gateway.

He looked up at the bushes and saw nothing in the rock wall. But on the paper in his hand, the quivering lines arched in a way he recognized.

"I'm going after them," he told the driver. "Would you unsaddle my dragon and give him a rubdown? He'll find his own food." Bardon folded the sketch and put it into his pocket. "I'll be back with them. Don't—"

"I know," said the driver. "Don't leave."

Bardon nodded. "I'll be back."

He started for the cliff. Greer's comment entered his thoughts but did not stop him. He scoffed at the dragon's concern.

I know they said they'd come back and didn't. That doesn't mean I can't handle whatever it is that has delayed them. Don't be such a worry worm. I'll find them, and I will be back.

He waded through the high grass and, like the driver, could see where the blades had been beaten down by many feet all headed in the same direction. He rounded the bushes and stopped in front of the rock surface. The gateway's frame shimmered within the stone.

It's not that hard to see. Why didn't the driver notice?

"It's about time you got here." A high-pitched voice reprimanded him.

He spotted Jue Seeno sitting on a small ledge. She must have just moved because he could see her even with the moonbeam cape wrapped around her. Her furry feet dangled off the side, and she held a parasol over her head. As she glared at him without moving, all but her face and feet began to blend into the rock wall.

The parasol must be made out of the moonbeam fabric as well.

She stood, threw her moonbeam cape back over her shoulders, and dusted off the shiny fur above and below the intricate belt she wore. "They're in trouble, but between the two of us, we'll be able to extricate them."

"What kind of trouble?" asked Bardon.

"Bisonbecks. Landed right in the middle of a bisonbeck military encampment. Well, not actually in the middle, but to the side. Then they were captured and taken to what the beasts are using for a bailiwick."

"Perhaps we should get reinforcements."

"No time." The minneken pulled her sword from her garish orange and purple belt and brandished it. The thin blade of the rapier glinted in the sun as she swished it back and forth. "They're talking of taking them to Crim Cropper."

"How many bisonbecks are we up against?"

"Only ten."

Bardon had fought bisonbecks on several occasions. The brutes stood more than six feet tall, muscled like the giant cats of the forest and thick-skinned like the vicious, toothy reptiles in the rivers of the southern continent. With massive heads, bulky necks, and meaty fists, they were made for fighting. Smarter than grawligs, they formed the evil wizards' army.

"We'll go scout out the situation," said Bardon, "and then decide how to proceed."

"Precisely." With amazing agility, the little minneken scampered down the wall and stood before the gateway. "There's a guard on the other side. I'll go first and prepare the way. Count to ten and follow. I'll have him distracted, doubled over, and wondering what hit him."

Before Bardon could protest, Jue Seeno stepped into the gateway.

26

Plans to Rescue

"Count to ten!" Bardon exploded. "You'll prepare the way?" He drew his sword. "What kind of a crazy minneken are you?"

He charged through the gateway without his usual trepidation and emerged to find a six-and-a-half-foot, three-hundred-pound bisonbeck in uniform on his knees, doubled over, wailing, and holding his ear. Jue Seeno scaled Bardon's leg, jumped to his arm, and scampered to his shoulder.

"Let's get out of here," she said. "Go through those trees. His comrades will be coming from the opposite direction."

The wounded soldier never looked up. Bardon sidestepped around the collapsed bisonbeck and slipped into the forest. The woodland insects made more noise than he did as he moved swiftly into deep foliage. He'd always excelled in this particular training exercise. Even back in his youth, when all the scholars escorted their pupils to the mountains for several weeks at a time, he'd taken to the woods. None of the other boys at The Hall had ever been able to find him when they played their catch-and-evade games.

He crouched and went under low-hanging branches of an armagot tree.

Jue Seeno lost her footing on his shoulder, grabbed a hank of his hair, and hollered. "Watch it! I'm not used to riding on a giant's shoulder."

Bardon slowed to a stop. "I think we're safe here for the moment."

The minneken scrambled back to her perch next to his ear.

A broad root buckling up out of the ground provided Bardon with an adequate seat. "May I lift you down from my shoulder, Mistress Seeno?"

"Make a fist, and I'll sit on it," she commanded.

He clenched his fingers against his palm and placed his hand close to where she stood. She hopped on and settled herself. Bardon rested his elbow on his knee and held the minneken at eye level.

"There are a few questions I would like to ask you."

She tilted her head at him, and he noticed the feather in her hat was bent, and the hat itself sat at an odd angle. As if she noticed his attention to her headgear, she reached up a hand and straightened it.

"I'm afraid," he said, "that your feather is broken."

She made a moue and shrugged her shoulders. "The fortunes of war."

"How did you disable the guard?"

"I jumped on the brute's shoulder and pierced his eardrum with my sword. One quick jab with a twist, and then I jumped clear as he fell."

"Your strategy certainly was effective."

"Yes." She smirked. "It was, wasn't it?"

"I don't believe I will underestimate you again, Mistress Seeno."

One tiny, whiskered eyebrow went up on the little minneken's face. "Oh, I think you will."

Annoyed, Bardon bit back a response. The little woman certainly knew how to irritate him. *"When emotions strangle you,"* Sir Dar would say, *"stick to business."* "Do you know what part of the country this gateway has led us to?"

"Creemoor, near the eastern seacoast. I overheard two of the bisonbecks discussing how long it would take to deliver our friends to Chellemgard. The captain of their unit said he had orders not to move from this spot, and he wasn't going to. He did send a report of the capture to his superiors."

"Did you hear how long it would be before they had a response?"

"They consider themselves to be forgotten out here and like it that way. Several of the men discussing it were quite irritated that their captain insisted on following procedure. If anyone pays attention to their report, the answer should come by tomorrow."

"Do you know why they're here? Gateways aren't usually guarded."

Jue Seeno shook her head. "No mention was made of the purpose of their watch. They said it was an easy duty, and they didn't want to lose it."

Bardon's doneel mentor had impressed upon his young squire that noticing the unusual could save his life. He remembered Sir Dar pointing out a number of anomalies in a visiting dignitary's entourage. "Always take note of that which is out of place," Sir Dar had instructed him. "Why does the man travel without proper escort? Why did he not bring his own secretary?" On that occasion, Sir Dar had uncovered political trickery and avoided entanglement with a deposed leader of a neighboring principality.

Bisonbeck guards on a remote gateway set off alarms in his mind, but he couldn't figure out why. Right now it was important to rescue his friends from danger.

His eye fell on the frumpy, furry creature preening herself on his fist. He never thought he would be depending on a minneken for aid, let alone one so disheveled, but he now trusted Mistress Seeno to be a valuable ally.

"Your moonbeam cape has hollows," he said.

She wrinkled her brow, and her whiskers quivered. "What makes you think that?"

"Your parasol has disappeared."

She hunched one shoulder. "It is fortunate for you that I am well prepared."

"Do you have a plan to free our comrades?"

"No, but I can slip into the camp and cut the ropes that bind the prisoners when you give the word."

"Now I'm in charge again?"

"You have always been in charge, Squire Bardon."

"Right." He stood. "Where do you want to ride?"

"Where are we going?"

"To observe and evaluate the enemy's camp."

"A pocket. Your shoulder is precarious when you dip and dodge through the trees."

She gave him a precise description of the layout of the ground in and around the camp before she dived into a breast pocket inside his tunic.

Bardon had no problem sneaking up on the bisonbecks and observing them. The tents lined up in a half circle around a central community area. One soldier bent over a fire, stirring a pot that probably contained their dinner. The squire's nose said it was a meat stew with lots of spices.

A larger tent stood with its flaps pinned back. Inside, several men sat around a table and were engaged in a discussion that held their attention. At one end of the encampment, the prisoners huddled in a circle with their backs to each other. In the center, Granny Kye sat on a log with a sleeping baby in her lap.

Bardon pulled one side of his tunic open and whispered, "Come out."

Jue Seeno scurried to her perch on his shoulder.

"I don't see how we can do this without revealing your presence, Mistress Seeno."

"I, too, have come to this conclusion. I don't mind telling the children. And Holt is bothersome, but I've come to believe he has a good heart beneath that rascally exterior. But that mapmaker..." Her tail twitched, her whiskers trembled, and a shudder shook her small frame. "That mapmaker is the real threat."

"Bromptotterpindosset? He seems harmless to me."

"You don't have a home that has been a carefully guarded secret for centuries. None of us on the Isle of Kye want to be put on the map. Tourists! There might even be tourists invading our home."

"They can't get to it. You said so yourself. Only occasionally, a very strong dragon or some other flying creature makes it through the natural barriers."

"No one has had a compelling reason to reach Kye before this." She sighed heavily. "Well, if doing right in the eyes of Wulder exposes us to the outside world, then Wulder will provide the means to deal with the consequences."

"Doing right for the wrong reason," Bardon muttered.

"What was that, Squire?"

"I was wondering what my mentor would say to this situation. He lectured me on doing right for the wrong reason."

"You've lost me, son. And now is not the right time for philosophical debates. What are we going to do to free our comrades?"

Bardon nodded and looked over the camp again. "We need a distraction."

Silence fell between them as they both thought for a moment.

Jue Seeno cleared her throat. "Would fireworks help?"

"You have fireworks?"

"Small ones. Firecrackers." She patted her cape. "Skyrockets don't fit in the opening of the hollow. You do know that the hollows will hold almost anything as long as they are small enough to fit through the opening."

"I've never possessed a garment with a hollow myself, but my friend Kale has one, and yes, she did mention that."

"So I'll give you the poppers—"

"Do you have a flintbox?"

"Of course!" Jue Seeno shook her head over his foolish question. "I shall give you the poppers and the flintbox. I'll cut the ropes binding our comrades and explain what is about to happen. I think you should stay here until I come back to tell you all is set."

Bardon nodded with a grin.

"What?" asked the minneken. "Why do you have that goofy smile plastered on your face?"

"I'm in charge?"

"Of course you are, silly man. A good leader listens to counsel. You could always veto my plan. This is merely a suggestion, after all."

"I wouldn't dream of vetoing your plan, Mistress Seeno. It is an excellent one."

"Yes, right." She looked at him askance. "Well, then, I'd best be off. Try not to be seen while I am busy in the camp."

Bardon agreed. "I'll try."

The minneken skittered down the front of his arm, hopped onto his knee, slid down his leg, and disappeared beneath the bushes.

Bardon closed his eyes.

Wulder, by Your might and wisdom, may our mission succeed.

27

RESCUE

"We've got a problem," said Jue Seeno as soon as she returned and settled on Bardon's shoulder. "Bromptotterpindosset says the gateway is deteriorating. Each time someone goes through the passage, it unravels a bit. This portal hasn't been used recently and has fallen into a state of disrepair. Crim Cropper intends to come and repair it and then use it to let loose crazed quiss in Wittoom."

"I see," Bardon said. "How did our mapmaker glean all this information?"

"He noticed the state of the gateway when he passed through. In a tightly woven structure, you should feel pressure on your lungs as you exit. Of course, I didn't notice because smaller creatures like me don't feel the pressure."

"Now that you mention it, I didn't feel the usual tightness when I came through. I was distracted by the sight of the bisonbeck and didn't take note." *And that just proves I'm not as observant as Sir Dar expects me to be.* "Do you suppose Granny Kye knows how to weave the border?"

"She says she does not. It takes a wizard."

"I helped Wizards Cam, Fen, and Lyll Allerion once when they were constructing a huge gateway."

Jue Seeno eyed him with a speculative gleam. "Do you think you could do it on your own?"

"Not a chance. I needed the other wizards, Kale, and Regidor to even keep up with the weaving." Bardon looked away from her beady eyes. "What will happen if the gateway unravels before we all get through?"

"Granny Kye thinks those in the passage will be thrown out at different spots along the way. That mapmaker thinks everyone will be annihilated."

Bardon growled deep in his throat. He hated making decisions with only conjectures to consider. "Neither one knows for sure, so it's just speculation."

Jue Seeno spoke softly. "There is One who knows for sure."

"Thanks for reminding me, Mistress. And He is our guide. We will trust Him to show us what to do." He placed her on the ground. "Now I shall take your poppers and lead those men on a merry chase. You usher as many of our party as you can through the gateway. When I've taken those soldiers far enough away, I'll double back."

"The gateway may be in too dilapidated a state at that point for you to come through."

He shrugged and mimicked her moue. "The fortunes of war, I'm afraid."

He loaded his pouch with her supply of poppers.

Jue Seeno handed one string of poppers after another to Bardon as she whispered, "That mapmaker says the Himbernese have developed a way to put the black powder from the poppers into a metal tube with a pellet of iron. When the powder explodes, the pellet is propelled with great force out of the tube. To anyone standing in its way, the strike can be most injurious… This popper dust always irritates my skin." She rubbed her palms over her fur.

Bardon likewise cleaned his fingertips on the rough material of his tunic.

Jue Seeno's whiskers quivered. "Sounds like a fool toy to me. A peashooter is bad enough in the hands of rough and thoughtless boys."

"It sounds like an ominous weapon to me, Mistress."

She tilted her head in thought for a moment. "It does, indeed. And a dangerous thing in the hands of rough and thoughtless men."

Bardon cocked his head, remembering a principle. He decided to paraphrase it instead of quoting. "As is a rock in the hand of one with evil intentions. It is not the rock that is the problem, but the heart of man."

Jue Seeno smiled at him and nodded.

He slipped away from the camp and stole through the forest to enact the plan that Jue Seeno had communicated to the prisoners. He stopped two hundred yards beyond the last tent and lit a half-dozen poppers, quickly tossing them to the ground. At the sound of their explosions, he darted through the trees and ignited another set.

The plan was for the bisonbecks to follow him. At the sound of the first explosions, Holt and Bromptotterpindosset were to watch for an opportunity to grab weapons and deal with whomever had been left in the camp. N'Rae, her grandmother, and the children were to run to the gateway, with Jue Seeno as their guide, while the two men guarded their retreat.

Bardon heard deep shouts from the camp. The crashing of bulky bodies through the underbrush told him soldiers were in pursuit. He ran a short space, exploded some more of the harmless toys, and ran on. He repeated the pattern, sometimes allowing his pursuers to gain some ground in order to keep them interested. When he'd used the last of Jue Seeno's supply of poppers, he made a wide circle and returned to the gateway.

Only Bromptotterpindosset and Granny Kye stood there.

Granny had a sketchpad in her hand and drew rapidly, her concentration on the shimmering gateway. The tumanhofer looked up as Bardon approached.

"We can hope the first managed to go through. Holt was the last, and he entered twice before pushing beyond."

"What happened?"

Bromptotterpindosset picked up a stick and threw it. The leafy piece of wood splatted against the surface of the opening, clung for a moment, and then dropped to the ground. Bardon picked it up. He pushed the stick into the quivering air. It sunk in, and then he could push it no farther. The resistance increased, and Bardon was forced to allow it to resurface on his side of the gateway.

"Any ideas?" he said over his shoulder to the tumanhofer and the emerlindian.

"Granny Kye has been drawing the gateway. Come look."

Bardon moved behind the small woman and looked over her shoulder. The lines on the paper clearly depicted the gateway. Around the edges, Bardon saw the unraveling threads.

He glanced up at the surface. The lights playing in the air had dimmed.

Granny Kye looked at Bardon over her shoulder. "Jue Seeno said you have woven the threads before. She said if you could see them, you could do it again."

"She has more confidence in me than I have. Besides, the colors of the threads are important, and I cannot see the colors in your sketch."

"Put your arms around me so that your arms are draped over mine. Put your hands on the backs of my hands."

Bardon reluctantly followed her instructions. He did not want her help to see the threads. If he saw them, he would be required to make an attempt at weaving, an attempt he was sure would fail.

"You can do this, Squire Bardon," said Granny Kye. "Concentrate on the edges, relax, follow the pattern. I see what needs to be done, and although I have never tried, I am willing. Show me, and I'll follow your lead."

"This is pointless, Granny Kye. I merely did what the others did. I don't remember."

"Relax, son."

More to appease the old woman than with a real conviction that something would happen, Bardon stared at the flowing threads of color. At first the frustration of being put in this position rumbled through his brain. Then Greer's presence seemed so real that Bardon glanced away from the weakening gateway to see if the dragon were really in the glen. The feeling faded immediately, so he turned back to focus with Granny Kye on the threads binding the edge of the portal. Greer's presence returned, and Bardon realized it was in his memory. The likeness and voice of Sir Dar also flitted through his mind.

The next image was of Kale, and the impression strengthened with every breath he took. He wanted to reach out and touch her. He heard her voice.

"It's like the beat of a drum behind the music, Bardon. Just react to the rhythm."

He knew she had said these exact words to him before.

The sensation of his friends being at hand intensified the comfortable state of mind that Greer had started. He saw a loose thread and where the end should pass between two others. The colored line moved of its own accord and slipped into place. He spotted the next errant strand and located its true position. The thread moved. When he aided in the building of a huge gateway in a swampland in Trese, he had acted in response to the arrangement established by someone else. He would never claim it was his own instinct. Now he realized he was the one creating the sequence and beat.

In addition to Kale, Bardon recognized the presence of Cam, Fen, Lyll, and Regidor. He knew these people did not physically stand beside him, yet their proximity seemed more real than that of Granny Kye, who stood within his arms with her back against his chest and her head tucked under his chin.

Out of his peripheral vision, he saw Bromptotterpindosset approaching the gateway. He wanted to call out, to say, "Not yet." But the words would not form in his throat. The tumanhofer stood close to the brightening lights and seemed to examine them. Bardon chose to ignore him. His presence interfered with the rhythm. Bardon did notice when the tumanhofer moved away from the gateway. A sense of gratitude washed over him. He wanted to be left alone with his task. Granny Kye's synchronized assistance made her feel like a part of him rather than an annoyance.

A blow to his back shattered his concentration. He loosed the granny and whirled around to see the mapmaker engaged in a fight with two soldiers. Bardon was surprised to note the coolness of the air, the dim light of dusk. Night hovered, about to take over.

The bisonbecks loomed over the battling tumanhofer. Bromptotter-pindosset wielded a spiked club, obviously one he had picked up in the enemy's camp as he escaped. Bardon drew his sword, and his movement caught the attention of one of the men.

This soldier growled and left his comrade to batter the short, old tumanhofer. Bromptotterpindosset had been holding his own against the two. Now he hurled his body sideways at the remaining soldier's knees and knocked him to the ground. Bardon had no more time to observe the mapmaker's next move.

Bardon's attacker opened his wide mouth and roared as he charged. The beastly man clenched two knives above his head in powerful arms. He seemed determined to plunge his weapons into the squire. Bardon sidestepped and sliced the man's torso as he passed. The bisonbeck bel-lowed. An answering roar sent shivers down Bardon's spine. The hair on his arms stood.

Reinforcements echoed the bisonbecks' war cries. Somewhere in the woods, other enemy warriors closed in on the dilapidated gateway. He and his friends would soon be trapped.

Out of the corner of his eye, he saw the tumanhofer had gained another weapon from his opponent. Bardon ducked a blow from the sol-dier he fought. He vaulted into the air and flipped to come down on the hulk's other side. He kicked a stout arm out of his way, spun, and thrust his sword into the brute's chest. If these warriors had been dressed in battle array, the fight would have lasted longer.

He turned to assist Bromptotterpindosset and found the tumanhofer standing over a downed soldier. Blood flowed from the man's forehead where the mapmaker had planted the club.

A howl arose from the woods.

"Time to leave," said Bromptotterpindosset. He rushed to Granny Kye's side and took hold of her arm. She hadn't moved from the spot where Bardon had left her.

"Oh, I agree," said the small emerlindian. "I've never seen a bisonbeck up close before. They are extremely tall, aren't they?"

"Extremely," answered the tumanhofer and guided her toward the gateway.

"It isn't completely repaired," objected Bardon.

"Neither was it when we came through before. We shall have to chance it." With a firm grip on the old emerlindian, he plunged into the clinging light and disappeared.

Bardon followed. This time he noticed the lack of pressure on his chest, but the lack of resistance made the atmosphere slick. He pushed and felt he made no headway. He thrust a leg forward and it returned to his side. Leaning his body forward, he hoped he could just fall into the meadow where he had left the driver of Wittoom Coastal Transport. A twinge of nausea gripped his stomach, as if a part of him would be left behind when he took the final step. He bent one knee and shoved with all his might against the slippery surface beneath his foot.

A crowd cheered when he emerged into the late afternoon light, a golden hue with a tinge of rose. The children swarmed around him, all talking at once. In N'Rae's arms, the baby pulled at a bottle with vigor. Behind them stood the driver from the transport company. The look of befuddlement on his face hit a chord of understanding in Bardon. He had felt that way many a time in the past few weeks. The young squire laughed.

"No time for jolliment," said Bromptotterpindosset. "I suggest you and the granny unravel this gateway before the remaining eight bison-becks follow us through."

28

CASTLE PELACCE

Squire Bardon watched Sir Dar's expression carefully as he related the events of his "sabbatical." The doneel's face twitched with suppressed humor.

Annoyed, Bardon shifted his gaze to his surroundings. The receiving chamber stretched away in endless opulence.

Surely purple is a bit gaudy. His eyes went back to his host. The dignitary wore satin and brocade, silk and lace. *No, nothing Sir Dar designs is anything less than elegant. If I had put purple on a couch, it would have looked tawdry. He chooses the right amount, the right shade, and the right combination. He does this in all areas of his life…and it is disconcerting. He does it with such ease. He thinks life is fun.*

Dar's furry face still sported a crooked smirk.

"I don't find these misadventures funny, Sir Dar."

His knight laughed out loud. "No, I suspect you don't. But it's so typical of the way Wulder arranges things to challenge our worst weaknesses."

Bardon stiffened. "Wulder has assessed me as being so weak that I cannot handle women and children and self-centered adventurers?"

Dar shook his head slowly. "Bardon, it takes more strength of character to handle the crew you've got with you than it does to face a horde of attacking blimmets."

The doneel waved his hand as if brushing away a fly. "But we must look at the more serious side of your adventures. I'll send a messenger to Paladin about the quiss. And I'll set up a guard beside this end of that derelict gateway."

"I'm sorry we could do no more to block it, Sir Dar. Granny Kye and I aren't proficient in such things."

"No matter. If Crim Cropper and Burner Stox decide to use that portal, they'll repair it despite its condition. You have at least slowed them down." He shook his head, the expression on his face serious. "I can tell you I don't like the idea of these landlubber quiss invading Wittoom."

A memory of fighting quiss on the dock sent a shiver down Bardon's back. Quiss attacking at random threatened more than just Wittoom. "Greer's message from the sea serpent is unsettling, as well."

"To say the least," the doneel agreed emphatically. "A hundred quiss in areas that used to have five and small colonies where there were once no quiss!" He tapped his hand on his knee. "And the news about them climbing in and out of the sea at any time… Yes, Paladin must be alerted, and we must recruit men from the East Coast to train our men how best to fight these creatures."

Bardon shifted in his seat. He had other matters to discuss with his knight.

Sir Dar continued. "I was raised believing they were cold-water animals and that they lived exclusively off the northern coast of Trese. Now they've migrated south and across to the western coast and even up rivers. These are dangerous times. We shall need those knights you go to rescue."

Bardon leaned forward, and Sir Dar cast him a suspicious look. "You wanted to ask me something?"

"Quite a few things, actually," admitted Bardon. "I thought you might like to come along."

"Ah yes, I would. But with the threat of quiss and the need for preparation, I don't feel that it is a good time."

The squire had suspected that this would be the case and went on to his next request. "Would you equip us with dragons for transportation?"

"Lost your trust in Wittoom Coastal Transport, have you?"

"I hardly think WCT would send a party into the Northern Reach."

Dar chuckled. "Yes, dragons and provisions can be donated to your cause. How large is your party going to be?"

"I was hoping to leave Granny Kye, N'Rae, and the orphans under your care. A couple of the older boys would love to be put to work on your ships. They were disappointed when the *Tobit Grander* ended up in dry dock for repairs."

Dar nodded his head. "The boys will be placed to their advantage."

"I don't know if Holt will stick with us. So it may only be Bromptot-terpindosset and myself."

"I'll assume responsibility for the orphans, but the emerlindian women must go with you. This quest is at their instigation. Paladin has approved of their participation. And the marione Holt Hoddack"—Sir Dar's eyes twinkled with amusement—"will most likely go anywhere the lovely N'Rae goes."

"Not if he doesn't have a dragon or supplies."

"Bardon, another young male might come in handy on this venture. He may not be trained, but I bet he does better in a fight than either of the women. N'Rae's assistance in killing the writher snake nearly cost you your leg. And I haven't heard you say one word of Granny Kye so much as tripping anyone on purpose. If you take them, you'll also have the assistance of Jue Seeno."

Bardon smiled. "She did turn out to be a worthy ally, didn't she?"

Dar grinned as he stood and stretched to his full height, just under four feet. "I have never underestimated the fighting power contained in smaller packages."

The comrades in arms exchanged appreciative grins. But Bardon soon sobered.

"I'm disappointed that you will not go with us, sir."

"No more so than I." Dar shrugged his shoulders. "You will have much more excitement than I have organizing the defense of my holdings and urging the Wittoom parliament to take similar precautions." He smoothed the hair on his cheek with a finger, then pointed it in the air.

"Aha!" said Dar. "I've had an excellent idea. I will contact Regidor. He would be someone interested in exploring the Northern Reach. The vanished meech colony is supposed to be there, and he's been looking for someone to help him learn more about his meech ancestry. Your Bromptotterpindosset might be just the man."

Bardon brightened at the prospect. "Regidor would be a welcome addition to our quest. Does he still carry Gilda around in a bottle?"

Dar chuckled. "Yes, in his pocket. She has mellowed in the last three years but is still a very melancholy, moody, distrustful dragon."

"And Kale. Have you seen Kale since I've been away?"

Dar nodded his head, his furry ears twitched forward. "Yes, I visited Bedderman's Bog. Kale's a beautiful young lady now, not the gangly youth we knew. And Fen and Cam argue over who's responsible for her remarkable abilities as a wizard. Fenworth is supposedly retired and spends much of his time as a tree. Still he claims it's his instruction that shines through Kale's more daring achievements."

Bardon pictured the old man and knew exactly how he would twist his face into a scowl as he made his outrageous claims. "And Librettowit is well?"

Sir Dar laughed out loud. "Librettowit married that helpful little tumanhofer they rescued from Crim Cropper."

"Taylaminkadot! If I remember correctly, it was Taylaminkadot who rescued Kale and Toopka from the enemy camp."

"A very resourceful woman, a stellar cook, and an enthusiastic housekeeper. She is the bane of Wizard Fenworth's existence and the joy of his librarian's."

Bardon laughed out loud. As Fenworth's notable librarian, Librettowit had always complained. The tumanhofer did not believe his duties included cooking and dusting. Fenworth assumed they did. He also assumed Librettowit would wholeheartedly join any adventure, which the librarian resisted like a mule being taught to fly.

A hundred more questions tumbled into Squire Bardon's thoughts. *How's Toopka? Dibl? All the minor dragons? Have any more been hatched?* It had been four months since his last letter from Kale. She'd hinted that

Taylaminkadot flirted with Librettowit, but he had dismissed that revelation as a young girl's invention of romance in her rather isolated society. The urge to see and talk to Kale and the others surged strongly in the young squire's heart. Dar's voice interrupted him.

"This is a nasty business," the doneel said as he stood. "I'm glad you're to lead this expedition. If Paladin hadn't chosen you first, I would have. You've grown into one of my most reliable men."

Bardon thrust aside his personal inquiries and followed his mentor.

Sir Dar ushered him to the tall double doors of the chamber. Bardon gave a gentle push to one of the ornate panels, and it swung open.

"We'll dine in my blue room tonight," said Dar. "Privately, with only the adult members of your questing party. You'll find your room just as you left it. If you need anything, just ring."

Bardon nodded and walked out into the massive hall. Clumps of people stood in the hall. Always the hangers-on seemed to know exactly which room Dar occupied. If the doors were closed, implying he did not wish to be disturbed, they waited in the immediate vicinity. Bardon had little patience with these people. But Dar treated them well, with the same genteel courtesy and respect he extended to everyone.

Even me. I'm one of the ones Sir Dar treats with respect, though I don't deserve it. Why do I begrudge the grace that falls on these cadgers when I deserve no better and receive so much more?

Bardon nodded to people as he passed them. He saw the spark of curiosity in their eyes. *They're wondering why I have returned so quickly.*

Then he saw it, a quick glance directly at his ears, accompanied by a start. The woman unfurled her fan, and from behind this small screen, whispered to another in her group. Bardon fought to keep his hand from smoothing the hair into place, hiding his points. *I haven't used the pomade for a long time. In just a few weeks I forgot the necessity. I came immediately to find Sir Dar before washing away my travel dirt and making myself presentable. But their stares are not for my disheveled appearance. It's my ears that draw their snickers.*

A buzz followed him, and he deliberately kept his pace even and unhurried. Hot anger roiled in his chest. *So I was not wrong after all. It is not only petty rich boys in a secluded private school who torment those who are different.*

Sir Dar manages to treat them with civility. I shall do as well as Greer does under similar circumstances and promise not to eat them.

29

The Lovely Π'Rae

Squire Bardon traversed the length of the castle, using corridors he had roamed for much of the three years he spent under Sir Dar's tutelage. During the long walk, he found an empty room and ducked inside. In the privacy of this unused classroom, he ran his fingers through his hair, covering his ears. He wet his fingers from a pitcher of water on the master's desk, then patted the hair down in the style he had abandoned since leaving for his sabbatical.

With a chary look both ways, he reentered the corridor. Deserted halls attested that classes had ended for the day. As he hurried through the wing that housed a small college, Scribe Moran appeared out of a classroom and headed his way.

Great! I haven't thought of a principle all day. I couldn't run through a girder exercise right now if I tried. I haven't bothered to support each action with a principle for weeks.

"Bardon!" said Scribe Moran with surprise. "I didn't know you had returned. You've made your decision so soon? Odd, I would have thought you were one to take the entire year."

"I have not started my sabbatical, Master." Bardon stopped beside the tumanhofer scholar. "I ran across two women who needed assistance. We are on a quest."

"Ah," said the short, round man as he stroked his gray beard. "And you have come to enlist Sir Dar?"

"That would have been convenient, but no, I somehow ended up with a ragtag bunch of orphans and needed a place of sanctuary for them."

"You've found that sanctuary with Sir Dar?"

"Yes, Master."

"And your quest?"

"We continue tomorrow."

The tumanhofer scribe patted Bardon's arm. "You say you haven't started your sabbatical. I wouldn't be so sure of that, my boy."

He chuckled, bent his head, and resumed his shuffle down the corridor.

Now, what did that mean? A sabbatical is supposed to be a time of reflection. I certainly haven't had time to think about what I'm going to do with my life. At least he didn't ask me to run through today's girder.

Bardon went to his room in a foul mood, bathed, dressed, and groomed his hair. Before he ventured out again, he looked in the mirror and made sure his hair covered his ears.

Imagine Librettowit getting married. His face relaxed. *And Dar may be able to reach Regidor and send him to join us.* He smiled. *And Kale is beautiful and talented. I knew that.* His lips parted, and his eyes turned into half moons with laugh wrinkles radiating out.

He nodded to the image in the mirror and left his room. He quickened his step when he finally reached the dining suites. Turning a corner, he nearly ran into a woman being escorted by a courtier.

"Excuse me." He stepped to the side.

"Bardon," the lovely young emerlindian said, "you're going the wrong way."

The squire looked sharply at the couple. The courtier he knew as Trum Aspect, an o'rant dignitary promoting trade with the southern continent. The young lady, he had never—

"N'Rae?"

She smiled, let go of her escort's arm, and twirled. "Isn't it gorgeous?"

Her dress of light blue silk swirled around her and settled again in soft folds starting from a high waist and ending with the hem brushing the toes of satin slippers. The bodice glimmered with tiny blue gems. Her white-blond hair swept up under an elaborate headdress with two sheer scarves draped from the crown. She wore long, white gloves and carried a painted fan. A lace shawl, fringed and beaded, covered her bare shoulders.

"The nicest lady came to my room and helped me dress," she said. "Her name was Faye."

Bardon let his eyes drift over her attire and then gazed at her face. Her eyes sparkled, her smile invited him to join her enthusiasm, her entire being spoke of elegance and beauty. He shifted his gaze to the man beside her and then back to N'Rae.

"You look extremely good tonight. But I'm not going the wrong way."

"Oh, but you are. Trum is taking me to the blue room. I'm to meet Grandmother there."

Squire Bardon looked back at the young o'rant. "He is?"

N'Rae resettled the shawl on her shoulders, not looking at either young man. "Well, of course he is. Why are you being such a dolt?"

Bardon grinned as he took her hand and placed it in the crook of his elbow. "Now, that sounds like the N'Rae I know, even though you look like a princess instead of my comrade."

N'Rae gasped. "Am I really your comrade, Bardon? Truly?"

"Indeed. We take up our quest tomorrow." He nodded at the courtier. "I'll escort her the rest of the way, Master Aspect."

The young man nodded and stepped back. Bardon noted the overly correct stiffness that hid the young man's anger. And that N'Rae was totally oblivious to having been in the company of a cad.

"Thank you, Trum," N'Rae called softly after the departing suitor. "I enjoyed our talk."

"As did I, fair lady."

Bardon tugged gently and started them down the hall.

N'Rae shook her head. "But this is the wrong way, Bardon."

"I lived here for three years, N'Rae." He winked at her. "This is a shortcut."

They passed two doors, turned down a hallway, and entered the first room on the right, stopping in the doorway to survey the scene. The other guests had already arrived. Dinnerware gleamed on the long table. Scrumptious smells of wonderful delicacies filled the air.

"Where was he taking me?" asked N'Rae.

"Probably just for a long, roundabout walk in order to spend time with the most beautiful woman at court this evening."

She squinted at him with a crease across her brow. "Does a pretty dress really make that much of a difference?"

He leaned over and kissed her cheek. "You are a charming young thing and shall have to guard against young men who would love to steal from that beauty."

"How could one steal from beauty?"

"By taking what doesn't belong to them. By encroaching on your youth." He saw the bemusement on her face.

He shook his head and screwed up his mouth. "N'Rae, in plain words, unscrupulous men will want to filch a kiss and more from you. This would give them great physical pleasure and, for some of them, the satisfaction of a conquest as if you were no more than a hunting trophy. You would have lost something that could not be replaced. Your beauty would be less pure."

N'Rae cocked her head. "Does that mean that I can never kiss and cuddle?"

"When you choose a man who will be your life partner, then each kiss accentuates your beauty instead of diminishing it."

A look of mischief came to her eye, and a smile quivered on her lips. "You give sage advice for a bachelor, Bardon."

Bardon felt heat creeping up his neck. He cleared his throat. "It is written in the Tomes of Wulder, N'Rae. I have studied the Tomes extensively."

"Have you ever stolen beauty?"

"No, I have not."

Granny Kye approached them. The basket on her arm looked out of place with the brightly colored robes layered over a straight white tunic. The floating material of the outer garments billowed as she walked. Bardon suspected she couldn't decide which color appealed to her most and so put them all on, one on top of the other.

"We're going to close the doors now that you're here," she said. "Jue Seeno is to eat with us, and the servants are not allowed in the room. She's a bit nervous, as you can imagine."

She handed N'Rae the basket. "Bardon, Mistress Seeno wants you to sit next to 'that tumanhofer' and keep him distracted. Steer him out of any conversation dealing with the minnekens."

He leaned over the little creature's traveling abode. "Yes, Mistress."

Her high-pitched answer could be heard clearly through the woven reeds. "Don't you get smart with me, boy."

When they sat for the dinner, Sir Dar gave thanks to Wulder, ending with "By Your might and wisdom, may we live and breathe."

"Prejudice, that's what it is," said the tumanhofer after several helpings.

"I beg your pardon, Bromptotterpindosset," said Bardon. "I don't know of what you speak."

The mapmaker tilted his head toward Jue Seeno's small table and chair sitting among big tureens of soup, baskets of rolls, and platters of meat.

"She's prejudiced against tumanhofers. Thinks we have no discretion."

"I believe she is worried for the privacy of her people."

"Humph!"

The tumanhofer's grunt reminded Bardon of Wizard Fenworth.

Bromptotterpindosset chewed and swallowed, his fork already stabbing into another chunk of meat. "Did you know there is no foundation for prejudice in the Tomes?" He waved the fork for emphasis.

Bardon thought for a moment. "I haven't pursued that concept in any study I've done."

"Well, there isn't. I've studied Wulder's Tomes as well as other religions of the world."

He nodded. *I was supposed to steer Bromp away from talk of the minnekens. I think he has done it himself. But I'm not sure exactly what we are talking about now.*

The tumanhofer pointed to Bardon's other side, where N'Rae sat. "Your little emerlindian is about to burst into tears."

The squire turned abruptly and caught N'Rae dabbing at her eyes with the napkin.

"What's wrong?"

"Everything," she answered in a small, pitiful voice. "I shouldn't be enjoying this fancy meal and fine clothes and even music coming from somewhere. Where is the music coming from?"

Bardon waved a hand toward one of the walls where the ornate paneling hid a small chamber. "There are musicians behind that false wall."

N'Rae's face took on the expression of a startled deer. She peered at the panel and then at Jue Seeno. "They can't see her, can they? She would be so upset."

"No, there's a black cloth backing the open work of the carving. The sound can penetrate, but the room here is still private."

The girl relaxed but still looked miserable. Another tear formed in the corner of her eye.

Bardon patted her hand. "Tell me, what's wrong?"

"We'll never get to the fortress where my father is prisoner. At this rate, the Wizards' Plume will pass under the Eye of the North long before we even cross the border into the Northern Reach."

"We'll make better time riding dragons, and we leave early tomorrow. Do not give up hope, N'Rae."

She sniffed and smiled wanly. "It's just that suddenly I felt so guilty, Bardon. I was so happy with the dress and this beautiful place. The pleasure of it all seemed wrong somehow."

"In the first Tome, Wulder says, 'Taste now and imagine. For this pleasure is as a grain of salt to what I have prepared for you who follow Me.'"

"So it's not wrong to enjoy this."

"Not in the least."

After dinner, the guests mingled for a while. Bardon spotted Mistress Seeno cornered on the ledge over the hearth by the inquisitive mapmaker. Jue Seeno sent him a beseeching look that begged for rescue. Bardon approached them.

"Bromptotterpindosset," he said as he raised the water goblet to his lips and sipped. "I know Sir Dar's interested in the maps you acquired on the Herebic continent."

"He is?" He turned to find his host in the room, locating him conversing with Granny Kye. "I'll just visit with him now, since our time tomorrow will be short." He bustled off.

"Thank you," said Jue Seeno.

"It was my pleasure."

"The man loves to hear himself talk. He lectured me on prejudice, and in truth, I agree with the man. But I felt like he wanted me to realize how much knowledge he had of all the persuasions of the many cultures he has visited. I didn't really appreciate his topic when it was merely a showcase for his theories." The minneken sighed and sat in her chair, making herself comfortable and picking up her needlework. "My opinion on the subject is based on Wulder's teaching."

"The subject was prejudice? He mentioned that at the table. It must be on his mind."

"He'd taken a more narrow subject, actually."

"He had?"

"Yes, and I couldn't get a word in edgewise to set the man straight."

"And the narrowed subject was…?"

"Your ears."

Bardon felt his eyebrows shoot up.

"Your ears reveal your mixed heritage." Mistress Seeno wove several strands of bright thread together. "Some people scoff at halflings, but why?"

Good question. Why? Bardon reached for a candy mint in a bowl beside the minneken's chair and placed it in his mouth instead of answering.

"Because misinformed people equate the creation of a mixed race with Pretender's creation of the seven low races."

Bardon nearly choked. He sipped from his water glass as Jue Seeno went on without even a glance at her uncomfortable audience of one.

"Wulder does not forbid intermarrying among the seven high races.

Of course, some mixes would not work for obvious reasons. Urohms and kimens, for instance."

With difficulty, Bardon swallowed and carefully placed the glass on the hearth ledge.

"The point is that men, in their infinite wisdom, have decided to make a law that Wulder did not deem worthy of putting in the Tomes. So you have prejudice, founded on misconception and pride."

Mistress Seeno carefully tied off her thread at the end of the row. When she had examined the work and turned it over to bind the edge, she said, "I don't believe Wulder looks down on the seven low races."

"You don't?"

"I don't see it written in the Tomes."

"But the Tomes were written before the emergence of the seven low races. How could there be revelation of how they would stand in Wulder's eyes?"

"Wulder is Creator of all."

"Not the seven low races!"

The minneken lifted an eyebrow but said nothing.

Bardon lowered his voice. "Pretender created the seven low races. They are a travesty of natural beings."

"I believe that Wulder allowed the creation of these unnatural beings."

"Why?"

She shrugged. "Either He is Wulder and in control, or He is not. I believe He is. Since He is Wulder, and the low races were created with His knowledge, then they will ultimately serve His purpose. Nothing Pretender does is done without the overseeing of the Creator. In the end, Wulder will use what Pretender has created for evil to do something good for all."

Bardon paused. He searched for something to say. "I think you have a greater faith than I do."

Jue Seeno stifled a sudden laugh in her throat. "I am just older, my boy, just older. Give your faith time to grow, be strengthened by adversity, refined by trial and error."

Later, in his chamber, he had trouble sleeping. N'Rae's ability to attract males, without a proper education as to what to do with them once she had them hovering around her, bothered him a great deal. Jue Seeno's theories about Wulder's involvement with the future of the low races puzzled him. When he finally did doze off, he slept fitfully.

The corner of his bed sank under a weight. Immediately awake, he lay still.

"It is I, Paladin. You need not fear. Sit up, Bardon. We must talk."

His candle sizzled, and a flame sprang from the darkened wick.

Bardon pushed back the covers and sat up. Paladin sat on his bed, leaning against the tall footboard. In the flickering light, he looked weary.

"You have traveled far, my lord."

"Yes, these are disturbing times."

"You know about the quiss?"

"Yes." He waved his hand through the air in a dismissive gesture. "It is monsters harder to fight than the quiss that trouble me."

"May I be of service, my lord?"

A sad smile crossed the noble features of the leader of Amara. "Yes, you may be successful on this quest of yours. That would be a great service. I could use a dozen or so more knights who understand the code of valor."

"Do you not have an army of warriors who understand?"

"They have been taught ineffectively—a convoluted version of the code. Among them, there are a few who have grasped the truth. But our forces are weakening. 'Variance from the code' is the monster that worries me most."

"I shall do my best to bring the knights back, my lord."

"I know you will, Bardon." He reached into a pocket and pulled out a coin. He handed it to the squire. "I brought you something to help."

Bardon examined the small, round disk. "Kale has one similar to this."

"Yes. Yours will help you to discern the hearts of those you encounter. If it is warm against your palm, you can trust the person. Even if their best is not good enough, their hearts are true to your cause. If the coin is cold, shun the person. His way is not your way."

He rose to leave.

"Paladin?"

"Yes?"

"Is that all? Are there no other instructions? If this quest is so important, could you not come with us?"

"You have all that you need to be successful if you use your knowledge and resources wisely. The quest is important, but Wulder has put me on a different path." He shrugged, and his lips lifted in a genuine smile. "I don't choose my tasks any more than you do, Squire Bardon. But I am content to follow whatever road He lays before me. After all these years, I cannot but trust Him. Even when I misinterpret His meaning, He saves me."

As Paladin walked out of the room, the flame guttered and went out.

He looked so tired. How could one empowered by Wulder look so weary?

30

Additions

Those planning to depart on the quest gathered at the dragon field as the sun peeked over the horizon.

"Oh look, how beautiful," said N'Rae as she and Bardon crested the hill. "Why are the dragons dancing?"

Soft, pink rays of the new morning glistened on jewel-like dragon scales and the dew clinging to the grass carpet beneath their feet.

"They're stretching, getting their blood moving."

"You mean like a lizard or a snake warms itself on a sun-baked rock?"

"Don't say anything like that around Greer. Dragons are not reptiles."

N'Rae giggled. She pointed to Jue Seeno's basket, which she carried on her arm, and whispered, "Just like minnekens are not mice."

"Exactly." Bardon steered N'Rae to the side of the field, where they had a better view.

Six dragons moved with surprising grace in a slow-motion ballet. Their different colors added to the dramatic effect. Two, besides Greer, were purple and blue hued. Yellow and copper scales covered one. The last two belonged to the green cast of dragons, but one had yellow accenting his wings, and the other's underscore color was a shimmering blue.

Bardon enjoyed watching the dragons stir their blood.

"Like many older people," he said, "when dragons first come out of a slumber, they are stiff. Of course, Greer has another theory. He says his body is so huge, he has to do these exercises to remember where the different parts are. He is reminding his brain where his tail is and what he can do by swishing it around. Same with his legs and wings. He says his brain never loses track of his neck or his stomach."

N'Rae laughed, then pointed across the field. "Look. There's Sir Dar."

Sir Dar stood talking to three men and two women. By their uniforms, Bardon identified them as dragon riders. The doneel shook hands with each one and then came to join N'Rae and his squire.

"I've provided you with five dragons and their riders, Captain Anton and his guard," said Dar. "They are under your command, Squire Bardon. Also, I have had several requests from individuals who wish to join your quest."

"A guard?" asked N'Rae. "What's a guard?"

"A military unit," answered Sir Dar. "A captain and four loes. A lo is higher rank than leecent and lower than lehman."

"Is a captain higher in rank or lower than a leetu?"

"Lower," said the doneel. "Why do you want to know of military rankings?"

"Bardon mentioned a Leetu Bends, that's all."

Sir Dar sent his squire a quizzical look. Bardon merely shrugged. He didn't know why his little emerlindian comrade should take such an interest in someone he spoke of once.

"Is that good, Bardon?" asked N'Rae. "To have more people to help rescue Father?"

"That depends." He looked at Sir Dar. "Who wants to join us?"

"Follow me." Dar led them to the other side of the field, skirting the dancing dragons. The five in service to Sir Dar executed their drill in synchronized motions. Greer only just managed to keep up. He usually performed his morning exercises by himself.

Watching his dragon trying to blend in caused Bardon to puzzle over the odd behavior. *Why are you even bothering to join their routine?* The squire's eyes moved to the graceful golden female between the two greens. *Yes, I see what you mean. She is, indeed, a beauty.*

Bardon put his hand on N'Rae's elbow to guide her. Her head was turned so she could admire the graceful movements of the dragons. She had no idea when Sir Dar changed directions and would have walked off the steep decline on that side of the hill if Bardon hadn't tugged on her arm.

Three people, two boys and a man, stood near the tack house. Bardon knew two, Ahnek and Trum Aspect. A surprisingly slender tumanhofer youth stood next to Ahnek. He had a walking stick in his hands and gazed over the dragon field.

Bardon stuck his hand into his pocket, curling his fingers around the coin Paladin had given him.

Sir Dar led him to the courtier Trum Aspect, who had distanced himself from the poorly clad boys, and made introductions.

The coin grew cold in Bardon's hand. He bowed politely. "I decline your generous offer, Master Aspect. We have no need of your estimable talents on this journey into the wilderness."

Aspect held his expression in check and bowed with just the right amount of deference. "Your choice, of course," he answered. He turned on his heel and strode off toward the castle.

When he had passed the end of the field, Sir Dar muttered, "I wouldn't have taken him, either. Shifty. Couldn't figure out why he wanted to go."

"I believe he thinks N'Rae is a valuable commodity."

Sir Dar tilted his head, and his ears lay back. "Emerlindians are becoming scarce, but his investments are usually more commercial."

As they walked closer to the shed and the two boys, Dar said, "Next, we have two eager young adventurers. Ahnek, you know. The other is Sittiponder from Vendela. He has traveled here for the express purpose of joining your quest."

"He must have known of it long before I did."

"He probably did. He is a blind seer."

"Sittiponder?" Bardon spoke the name in a considering tone, then paused. "I think Kale mentioned this lad."

"She did. He's an associate of the street urchin, Toopka."

Bardon clenched the coin in his fist. It held warmth as he studied one boy and then the other. He and Sir Dar stopped in front of the boys. Ahnek looked up with a smile. Sittiponder cocked his head slightly, but his face remained directed to the field he could not see.

Bardon put his free hand on the blind boy's narrow shoulder. "What is your reason for coming, Sittiponder?"

"To serve Paladin, Squire."

"How will you serve him?"

He shrugged. "I haven't been told. I have only been told to come." Bardon considered the answer.

The boy shuffled his feet. "I have a talent that might be useful."

Dar's ears perked. "And this is?"

"I hear voices of wisdom."

Dar cocked his head and nodded. He looked up at Bardon. His squire nodded as well.

"Why do you want to go, Ahnek?" Bardon asked.

"I can be of use, and I desire to train to be a knight. With my background I have no hope of entering service unless I make myself useful." He stopped and looked around as if to find something he could do immediately to show his willingness. He grasped Sittiponder's arm. "I can be this seer's eyes. He will need help. I can do that. Then neither of us will be a burden to you."

Sittiponder carefully removed his arm from Ahnek's hold. "I am not as helpless as you would think."

"Of course not," Ahnek said quickly. "But wouldn't it be convenient for you to have a servant?" A big grin spread across his face. "I'd like that if I were you. Bet you've never had someone at your beck and call. Sounds good, huh?"

Bardon knew something of Sittiponder's history as a street urchin who told stories in exchange for food. He almost laughed at the irony of one boy being servant to the other. But the dignity exhibited by both lads kept him from so much as smiling.

"You shall both come," he said, "and you shall both do chores that fall to you. Sittiponder, go to each dragon and determine who is the best mount for you. Ahnek, accompany him. You will ride with him on whomever he chooses."

Sittiponder chose the largest of the dragons. Named Frost, the blue purple major dragon had wings with a silver shimmer over his sapphire hide. Silver also edged each purple scale. Small blue stones and silver beads adorned his black leather saddle and straps.

"You've chosen well," said Bardon. "He's muscular enough to carry the triple saddle and supplies."

"He's magnificent, Sitti," Ahnek said after describing Frost in detail. "Why did you pick him?"

"He's the only one who talked to me."

"He did?" Ahnek's mouth hung open. "You mean like mindspeaking? Talking back and forth in your head without words?"

A small smile slipped into place on the gentle tumanhofer's face. "There are words, but I hear them in my thoughts, not with my ears. I hear voices a lot. It used to scare me when I was little, but someone told me about Wulder, and from then on, I could tell which voices were good and which were bad. I learned to shield myself from the bad voices."

"For true? What did the bad voices say?"

Sittiponder laughed. "Do you know that hardly anyone ever asks me what the good voices say?"

Ahnek rolled his eyes. "Well, what do the good voices say?"

"They tell me the secrets of the universe."

"Secrets?"

Sittiponder nodded.

"Are you allowed to share the secrets? Say, with someone who is your personal servant and does all sorts of things to make your life more easy?"

Sittiponder's smile twisted at one corner of his mouth. "I suppose…if I knew such a person. I don't know such a person yet. Someone who has actually been of service and not just talked about it."

"Do you have a parcel I could fetch for you?"

"No."

"Are you thirsty? hungry? Can I get you something?"

"No."

Ahnek's shoulders drooped. "This isn't going to be easy."

Bardon laughed. "You boys better get on board. Ahnek, Sittiponder has never ridden a dragon. You will need to describe the way to climb up, and give him a hand."

"Right!" said the young o'rant. "This way, then." He put his hand on Sittiponder's elbow and steered him to Frost's hind leg. He stopped, a look of confusion washing over his features.

"Squire Bardon?"

"Yes, Ahnek?"

"The thing is, I haven't ever ridden a dragon myself." He scratched his head. "I don't suppose you could show us the way up."

"I'd be glad to." Bardon stepped closer to the boys. "First, since this is a dragon you are only briefly acquainted with, the proper etiquette would be to go to his head and ask permission to board."

"I'll do that," said Sittiponder. He moved away from Ahnek and walked deliberately along the reclining dragon's side, directly to Frost's head. Frost looked at the lad solemnly, and his head bobbed. Sittiponder grinned.

He came back to Bardon and Ahnek. "He thought it was funny when I asked if it would be too much extra weight to carry us. He said we were like fleas on a dog, to climb up, and he'd appreciate it if we didn't bite."

Bardon showed them how to mount the dragon and explained the triple seat. One large leather pad lay over the dragon's spine, molded to fit the ridges that rose between his shoulders. Three seats were sewn to the large rectangle. The rider sat forward, and the passengers sat facing the rear. Their legs fit into knee hooks. A padded crest rose between the knees with places either to rest the hands or to grip when the dragon's flight became erratic. Each section had a high cantle to lean against and pouches at the side where food, drink, and blankets were stored.

"It can get very chilly in the higher altitudes," explained Bardon. "If you feel like you might go to sleep, there's a strap to put across your waist. The buckle is over here. You can wear this belt all the time if you like."

"Excuse me, Squire Bardon," said Ahnek. "What does *erratic* mean? Does it mean 'dangerous'?"

"Erratic?"

"You said to hold on when the dragon's flight became erratic. What does *erratic* mean?"

Bardon remembered using the word when he described the parts of the saddle. Ahnek had a very inquisitive mind. The boy would do well in life. Bardon put his hand on the lad's shoulder as he explained. "When a dragon is chasing something or being chased, he will make sharp banks, soar upward, or plunge downward. That's an erratic flight. Also, the belt can be useful when the wind is rather forceful."

"How will Granny Kye fare in such a seat?" asked Sittiponder.

"She'll travel in a basket, as will Bromptotterpindosset. Wizard Fenworth says that old bones don't bend to fit right in a dragon's saddle." He looked over to where N'Rae settled her grandmother in the woven contraption. "The basket has a special name, doohan. It looks like the cab of a single-seat buggy, doesn't it? The doohan is tightly woven out of small reeds. This makes the enclosure warm for the passenger and light for the dragon. It rides on the side of the dragon rather than perched on top like a saddle. This is for the dragon's ease. Usually, it's balanced with an equal load on the other side, sometimes another doohan."

"I wouldn't like to ride like that," said Ahnek. "All closed-up like. I couldn't see."

"I wouldn't like it, either," said Sittiponder. "I couldn't feel or hear or smell."

Bardon laughed. "You shall soon feel and hear and smell a great deal, young Sittiponder. Get yourself settled. We shall depart very soon."

"What's that smaller basket, Squire?" asked Ahnek.

"Homing waistcoaters. Sir Dar wants us to keep him informed of our progress."

He left them to make his way around the field, checking on each rider and dragon. Satisfied that all was well, he bade farewell to Sir Dar.

"Wulder be with you, young Squire."

"And with you, my knight."

He vaulted into Greer's saddle and gave the signal to rise. With huge colorful wings sweeping through the air, the entourage of six dragons ascended into a clear blue sky and headed north.

Nothing untoward occurred during the morning flight. They landed, ate, and rested at midday. During the afternoon, clouds began to accumulate.

What was that, Greer? My mind was wandering… Frost says that Sittiponder says that the voices say there is bad weather ahead? Relay a question to Bromptotterpindosset. Is there shelter nearby?

Bardon waited for a few minutes.

Seagram says his rider, Pont, says that the tumanhofer mapmaker says The Caves of Endor are the closest?… I, too, find our passing of messages amusing, Greer, but I think not as much as you do. Your chortling is jiggling my saddle…

I am *learning a sense of humor, but just now I am leading a questing party into foul weather. I think it imperative to see to their safety… I never claimed to be a people person if that means, as I think it does, that I relate well to people… I've never claimed to be a dragon person, either…*

Oh, enough Greer! Just tell the other dragons to inform their riders that we are changing our course to reach The Caves of Endor. Pont's dragon shall take the lead. Tell Seagram to have Pont secure directions from Bromptotterpindosset.

Greer, my saddle is jiggling again.

31

THE CAVES OF ENDOR

Lightning forced them from the sky, but not before they reached the Plain of Gette, where they could go on foot, following the Bissean River. An hour's trek in sheeting rain got them to the Ledges. The Caves of Endor honeycombed the oversized, natural, sandstone steps. Unusual geological formations covered one hundred square miles of the upper Wittoom Valley. Between the river and the beginning of the Ledges, numerous mud holes bubbled with smelly gases. Steam mixed with cold rain around each one. Occasionally, they heard sizzles and pops as cold water hit hot rocks.

The caves provided crude shelter for travelers. None of the high races lived close by because of the smell rising from the mud holes and because geysers occasionally popped through the crust of the earth without warning. No one wanted to build a house, then wake up in the middle of the night to find the floor swamped with steaming water.

The riders and passengers did not complain as the dragons marched through the unusual terrain.

"We should be close now," called out Bromptotterpindosset.

Bardon called a halt to their caravan. "Holt, Ahnek, men, we shall get down and gather fuel for a fire."

"Won't it smoke something awful?" asked Ahnek.

"It'll cover the smell of the mud holes."

The men descended from the backs of the dragons. "Gather the thick limbs of the portamanca bushes," instructed the mapmaker from his doohan. "They are surprisingly light, and you can peel the outer bark to find a wood core that burns very efficiently."

"What's this portamanca bush look like, Master?" called Ahnek.

"Have one of the riders point it out, boy," barked the tumanhofer. "It's past time you got out of the city. You need a different education than what you got on the streets."

"That's why I'm here," muttered Ahnek.

Bardon stood nearby and heard him continue grousing as he shuffled through the puddles.

"I mean to make the most of my life, and here I am doing it, in muddy water up to my ankles with smelly gases nearly choking me 'spite this blasted cold rain."

Two riders put out a tarp on which to throw the branches of the portamanca bushes. Then they dragged the waterproof canvas as they walked to the caves. The others continued to gather wood.

"How do we know we're going in the right direction?" Ahnek asked Bardon as they met beside the tarp, each carrying an armload of fuel.

"As long as we don't cross the Bissean River, we're going the right direction. The cliffs and ledges angle out from the riverbed. We'd have to turn completely around to miss them."

In just a few more minutes they came to the first ledge. The dragons stepped up easily. They all turned on the wide shelf, lowered their heads, and allowed the walking members of the party to ride up, clinging to their necks. With the four corners of the large canvas tied together, Greer took the bundle in his teeth and carried it up several more layers of rock before they reached a ledge that had huge, gaping, black entries to the caves beyond.

"We're going in there?" asked Ahnek.

Bardon slapped him on the shoulder. "It'll be warm and cozy."

"Right. Just like a warehouse."

"I can't say I've ever slept in a warehouse, Ahnek. But I have slept in The Caves of Endor. Aside from the smell, they're a very comfortable accommodation. If you wish privacy, you can choose your own little cave jutting off from one of the main caverns. I've met other travelers here and shared a community campfire. Music, good stories, and dance. It can be quite a treat."

"Right."

The boy didn't sound convinced but followed Bardon as he led the party into the largest cavern. The riders brought out lanterns from their packs of supplies and soon had a golden glow emanating from the center of the cavity in the limestone ledge. The other passengers dismounted, and Bromptotterpindosset took over the job of building a fire. Holt and N'Rae built seats out of the larger parcels and bundles as they unloaded the dragons. The dragons, one by one, slipped off to nearby caves to curl up and sleep.

"Why did they leave us?" asked N'Rae.

Bardon hooked together a metal apparatus that would hang over the edge of the fire and hold a kettle. "They don't like the smoke and don't mind the smell of the mud holes as much as we do. And, they really only enjoy the company of people in small numbers. In other words, they like their riders, they tolerate passengers, but people in a crowd are bothersome."

The riders prepared food, a potato flat and creamed greens, which all the questing party enjoyed. The smoke from the fire did minimize the stench from outside. After they ate, Bromptotterpindosset told stories of his many travels. Granny Kye got out her sketchbook and drew. Sittiponder and Ahnek sat together with their backs against a soft roll of blankets. In the cave, the warmth of the fire kept the chill at bay.

Eventually, the mapmaker grew tired. "My voice will give out," he said. "Let's have some music."

Three of Sir Dar's riders played musical instruments. That didn't surprise Bardon, who had also been trained to play the flute while in the doneel's service. They chose songs of adventure, ballads of charming maidens and daring rescues, chants of epic quests, and melodies of haunting beauty, which filled the cavern with a mysterious ambiance.

First Granny Kye took herself to a corner of the room, and N'Rae followed to help her lay out a pallet. Holt and Bromptotterpindosset took the boys with them to share a sleeping nook. Bardon went with the riders to check on the dragons and make their campsite secure for the night. The squire assigned shifts for night watch and took the first one himself.

During the first hour, the storm whipped itself into a crashing uproar with flashes of lightning and claps of thunder. Bardon doubted anyone huddled in their blankets had fallen asleep. The worst of the tempest moved south, and only the sounds of rain and distant rumbles disturbed the silence. On the third hour of his watch, the rain subsided to a drizzle. Bardon woke Pont to take the next shift. Before turning in, he circled the room one more time. Everyone slept.

At the back of the cavern, a tunnel reached into the depths of the mountain. He chose the wall next to this opening to roll out his blankets. Stretched out on his back with his hands clasped behind his head, he reviewed their progress.

The first day hasn't been so bad. The riders are helpful and work well with the original party. Holt has pulled his weight and shown no signs of bothering N'Rae. I do wonder why he is with us. To court the kindia-gentler? To escape his debtors? Just to try something new?

Bromptotterpindosset is an asset. Mistress Seeno has made herself scarce. Granny Kye already seems tired. This is too much of an undertaking for one so old. But she wants to find her son. I believe this desire will carry her through. Sittiponder and Ahnek have both contributed in their own ways.

All in all, it has not been a bad first day.

After three hours of deliberate alertness, he found his body unwilling to relax. The light from the flickering flames cast dancing shadows on the walls but scarcely reached the ceiling. To compose himself for sleep, he quoted principles in his mind.

"*Beyond what we see, our fire enlightens or destroys.*" *Wulder, make Your passion to be my passion so that when my actions affect those beyond my vision, the influence will be good and not bad.*

"*A ripple or ring. The rock or the shore. It is no more glorious to be the start or the end.*" *Wherever You place me, Wulder, allow me to be effective.*

"*A man of integrity—*"

A sound from the depths of the mountain echoed through the tunnel by his head. Bardon sat up and put his hand on the hilt of his sword.

Critch. Critch.

He stood, concentrating on the slight scratch of a hard substance against stone.

Pont saw him and drew his own sword. He tiptoed across the cave and stood beside the squire. Bardon held up a finger to indicate he didn't want the rider to speak.

Critch. Critch. The sound moved closer.

Pont tilted his head. His eyes locked with Bardon's. A question clearly lit the rider's expression.

Critch critch. Critch critch.

Bardon pulled his sword.

Pont mouthed a word, his voice not sounding the question. "Druddum?"

Bardon shook his head. The cave-dwelling mammals skittered at high speeds through caves and tunnels. This creature sounded large and slow. Druddums would be no problem. He suspected this beast to be deadly.

Critch critch. Critch critch.

Whatever made the light sound could not be more than a few feet deep into the tunnel. Bardon waved Pont to the other side. They stood waiting with their weapons ready.

Critch.

Bardon took in a breath and held it.

Critch.

He concentrated only on the dark mouth of the underground passage.

Critch critch.

Black, snakelike tentacles waved out of the opening.

Critch.

The body of a huge spiderlike creature stepped into the light.

One more step, you beast.

Critch.

Bardon plunged his sword into a soft spot directly behind the creature's bulging, compound eye. A second later, Pont's knife speared one of the other eyes. The creature thrashed once and collapsed.

Bardon let out the breath he'd been holding and heard Pont do the same. He looked up at the rider-warrior.

"Now, what do you suppose a Creemoor spider is doing in Wittoom?"

32

A Legend

Bardon sent a message by waistcoater at first light: *Killed Creemoor spider in Caves of Endor. B.*

Three of the riders hauled the carcass of the spider onto the flats amid the mud holes and set fire to it. It took most of the morning to burn the body to ashes so that none of the creature's poisonous fluids remained to kill some unsuspecting animal.

Even with the late start, the flight north that day covered more ground than the previous day. Bromptotterpindosset estimated two more days before they would reach the northern foothills of the Kattabooms. The mountain range petered out one hundred miles south of the Finnicum Gulf. From there, they would veer to the east and follow the coast to the northern border. Unless they dallied along the way, they should reach their destination before a week was out.

The mapmaker and Granny Kye sat together in the evenings. She poured out all the bits and pieces of information she had gleaned over the years. He made notes and examined his maps and charts and the diary of Cadden Glas. The doneel's crude maps compared favorably with the more-expertly drawn cartographer renditions of the Northern Reach. However, the adventuring doneel had explored areas that were blank on Bromptotterpindosset's scrolls.

"I'm trusting Glas's recordings to be accurate," he told Bardon as he pointed with a stubby finger to a high mountain valley. "This is recorded in the diary but not on the official charts. Cadden Glas proves close to the mark on the places we can compare. Why should he be imprecise on the areas only he has drawn?"

Bardon examined the map in the diary. "And Granny Kye thinks that this high valley is the location of the fortress where the knights are under a spell?"

The mapmaker nodded with conviction. "It matches the snips of information—a tiny, round lake at the southern end. Two towering peaks to the west. A break in the eastern wall of mountains, as if some giant had pulled out one of the mountains in the chain like a sore tooth."

"Is there a name for this valley?" asked Bardon.

"Cadden Glas called it Broken Cup Valley."

The squire contemplated the peculiar markings on the small page of the diary. "Why do you suppose he chose to write his diary in an obscure language? No one that I know of converses in meech. Except perhaps those dragons of the missing sect."

"Why are they missing?" asked Ahnek as he walked up with Sittiponder.

Bardon and Bromptotterpindosset jumped.

The tumanhofer scowled at the boys and fussed. "I thought little boys were loud, noisy, rambunctious. How is it you two are always lurking about without a squeak between you?"

Both o'rant and tumanhofer child grinned. Ahnek answered, "We're practicing for when we're in enemy territory."

"I know," said Sittiponder.

"Know what?" asked Ahnek, his forehead wrinkled.

"About the meech colony. A small group had lived in seclusion in the Kattaboom Mountains. They kept a distant friendship with the doneels, but only because the doneels were useful to them. Risto sent a force to ravage the little community and steal their eggs. The survivors fled to the north."

"Why didn't they fight?" asked Ahnek.

"Because they believe in a better way."

"What better way?"

Sittiponder shrugged and then grinned. "I don't know. It's just called the better way."

"Who tells you these things, son?" asked Bromptotterpindosset.

"The voices."

The older tumanhofer adjusted his glasses higher on his round nose. "Do you hear the voices all the time?"

"Not so much since we've been traveling. I think I am too tired at night to listen properly. And we are too busy during the day for me to sit and listen." He sniffed the air. "Supper is almost ready. Fried fish. Holt caught them."

The boys hurried off to the cooking fire. The mapmaker put away his precious book and scrolls. He and Bardon joined the others around the campfire. The squire frowned as he saw that N'Rae sat on the same log with Holt. On the ground at their feet, Jue Seeno sat at her table, which was set up on the flat lid of her basket.

Bardon got his plate, filled with fish and cooked wild ostal greens, and perched on a square parcel on the other side of the young emerlindian girl. He didn't speak but silently said a word of thanks to Wulder.

He looked down at N'Rae's most diligent chaperone. Mistress Seeno sipped tea from a tiny cup. His eyes roamed over the rest of their questing party. Not far away, Granny Kye sat with the boys and did not once look to see if her charge was up to mischief. Bardon cast a sideways glare at Holt and began to eat.

The marione acknowledged the squire's presence with a brief nod. His handsome face held a look of congeniality, his eyes a sparkle of merriment. He chewed and swallowed.

"N'Rae, do the fish speak to you?"

"No."

"But I thought you could talk with any animal, even a chicken."

"You don't understand. None of the animals talk. They use images to relay their thoughts, not words."

"None of the animals use words?"

"Dogs and cats use a mixture of pictures and a limited vocabulary. Ropma do the same but possess quite a few more words to express themselves." N'Rae stirred the grain porridge with her fork. "A lot of emotion comes through as a dog communicates. Cats are different. I think that cats actually have a much wider command of words than they let on."

"Humph," said Jue Seeno.

"What was that, little mistress?" asked Holt.

"Oh, don't tease her, Holt," scolded N'Rae. "You know she doesn't like to be called 'little mistress.' And she said she doesn't care for cats. They think too highly of themselves."

"So dogs, cats, and ropma use words?" Holt focused his attention back on N'Rae.

Bardon watched her blush, the color clear even in the flickering light of campfire.

She nodded. A few yards from where they sat, Sittiponder leaned forward, his attention on the conversation.

"How about birds?" asked Holt.

"Pictures."

"And other animals? Pigs?"

"Surprisingly clear images. Quite a few words."

"Horses and kindias?"

"About the same, except horses think deliberately, and kindias' thoughts move in rapid changes of pictures."

"Dragons?"

"Dragons are not animals, Holt."

"They aren't?" He grinned. "Then what are they, fair lady?"

"They are a race from somewhere else," Sittiponder answered abruptly. "They came through a dark hole. Many creatures swarmed at their feet, fleeing whatever was beyond that hole. But not all the smaller creatures adapted to our climate and our food."

Holt looked up, clearly annoyed at the interruption. "I suppose the voices told you this."

Sittiponder shrank back a little at his tone. "Yes," he said meekly.

Jue Seeno abandoned her table and scooted up N'Rae's leg to sit on her knee. She spoke to the girl, and Bardon almost caught the gist of what she said but was too far away to hear properly.

"Oh!" said N'Rae. "Mistress Seeno wishes me to tell you that there is a legend on the Isle of Kye that would correspond to what Sittiponder just said. She says that the minnekens came with the dragons. The meech led the way. It was the exodus."

"Exodus from where?" asked Holt.

Jue Seeno spoke.

N'Rae repeated. "She doesn't know."

The tiny minneken turned and faced the blind seer. Bardon knew from the inflection of her words that she asked a question.

From across the fire, Sittiponder responded. "No, Mistress Seeno, I do not know either. The voices have not told me."

Holt muttered, "He could not have heard from way over there. I can barely hear anything sitting right beside her."

The minneken turned and shook her fist as she spoke to the upstart marione. Her raised voice carried distinctly to Bardon.

"Not all creatures have their own egos stuck in their ears, keeping them from hearing."

Bardon laughed out loud. Jue Seeno had quoted a principle with her own twist to the words.

Holt looked puzzled. Ahnek smiled but did not seem to understand what was going on. The others smiled or laughed.

When Bardon could still his laughter enough to speak, he quoted the principle properly. " 'A man's ego may interfere with his hearing the truth.' "

"Very funny," growled Holt. "I suppose that is written in one of those Tomes of Wulder you drag around."

Bardon nodded. "Right smack dab in the center of the second book. And since there are three Tomes, it is in the middle of Wulder's written word. Some say it is the crux of the whole revelation."

33

NORTH

As they traveled north, the trees showed a less mature green, reminding Bardon that spring was several weeks newer in the northern part of Amara. Cooler nights also reinforced the feeling of a different climate.

They camped one night by the sea, where waves crashed against granite cliffs. Bardon paused in his assembly of the tent N'Rae and her grandmother would sleep in to watch the silhouetted ballet of the dragons over the water. Of course, he knew they were merely fishing, gorging themselves to be exact, but the beauty of six dragons plunging into the waves and then reemerging to soar through the orange-tinted skies took his breath away.

"Oh my!" N'Rae's exclamation at his side expressed how he felt. She turned, her eyes seeking out Granny Kye. "Look, Grandmother. Everyone, come see."

She insisted that each member of the party stop what they were doing and gather at the top of the cliff. Huge, rough boulders served as seating.

"Play," she ordered Bardon and the others who carried instruments with them. "Play one of those slow, haunting melodies."

Pont pulled a piccolo from his breast pocket. " 'He Will Greet the Morning'?"

The others nodded. Captain Anton counted the tempo and raised his hand to begin their impromptu concert.

"I know the words to this one," whispered N'Rae. She began to sing.

"He will greet the morning,
Because He will make each day.

Now He scatters the stars.

He covers the moon.

He draws the light in the blaze of the sun.

"Do not mourn the day's end,

As the sun declines its realm.

Now He collects the stars.

He reveals the moon.

And He allows the sun to stay its course.

"He will greet the morning

And never restrain new light.

Now He governs the stars.

He directs the moon.

As He greets the morning, He orders our world."

They repeated the entire song, then the musicians went on to other melodies. Granny Kye sat on a rock. N'Rae sat on the grass at her feet. Bromptotterpindosset, Holt, and the two boys chose to sit on smaller boulders closer to the cliff's edge. In the distance, the dragons swooped, dove, and rose again as the sky deepened to purple.

When the dragons turned to shore and the musicians put down their instruments, Ahnek stood and watched Sittiponder get up.

"That was nice, but now we have to get everything ready in the dark," said the practical o'rant lad.

Sittiponder grinned. "I'll help you."

"And I'm hungry."

"Me too." The blind tumanhofer turned away from the ocean's roar. "Too bad those dragons didn't catch us our dinner." He scrunched his shoulders as the wind from Frost's wingspan swept over them.

Sshplatt!

Sittiponder giggled.

"What is that?" Ahnek took two steps forward and peered at the ground. "It's a strange fish. It's flat, Sittiponder, and round, as big around as a todden barrel. Can't tell what color it is in this light."

Bardon walked over. He poked his hand in a slanted gill and hoisted up the three-foot-wide, disk-shaped fish. "It's a smoothergill." The fish wriggled, and Ahnek jumped away.

"Feel the skin," Bardon said, holding the fish out toward the young o'rant.

Ahnek backed away, waving his hands in front of him.

However, Sittiponder came forward quickly, with his arm stretched out in front of him. In his haste, he bumped his friend as he passed.

"Hey!" said Ahnek.

"Sorry." Sittiponder touched the fish and stroked its side. "It feels like it's been oiled. I don't feel any scales."

The smoothergill gave an exhausted flap of its tail.

"Good eating," said Bromptotterpindosset. "You want to learn how to clean it?"

Ahnek shook his head. "I have chores to do for Pont."

"Wasn't talking to you, boy," the tumanhofer spoke gruffly. "Sittiponder, come with me." The mapmaker took the fish from Bardon and strolled away with the young tumanhofer following.

"Do you think he can?" asked Ahnek. He took a step to follow his new comrade, but Squire Bardon stopped him with a hand on his arm.

"I'm sure he can," he answered.

Bardon turned back to see N'Rae still standing near the edge of the cliff and gazing toward the western horizon. He walked to her side and put an arm around her shoulders. The Wizards' Plume marked the sky with a bright starlike blaze followed by a short tail.

"We still have time," he whispered and turned her to the camp. "Let's go see what a smoothergill tastes like."

They ate an hour later. The thick white meat of the smoothergill cooked well in a pan placed on rocks at the fire's edge.

Jue Seeno chewed rapidly, her whiskers bouncing. "I admit I thought it would be greasy, but that oil seems to have fried away. Delicious!"

Sittiponder had only one small cut on his thumb from his first attempt to clean and fillet a fish. N'Rae wrapped his wound with a small, clean rag. He wore a huge smile as he ate.

The questing party rose early the next morning and flew all day with two stops to rest the dragons. In the evening they landed in a meadow surrounded by tall rock pines. Beside the campfire, Bardon remembered Kale's story of her first battle with grawligs. He recounted the tale and held a rock pinecone for Sittiponder to tentatively explore with his fingertips. The weighty orbs had barbs that, once embedded, had to be cut out of fur.

The following night they reached an area populated by o'rants. Ornopy Halls had once offered shelter to Kale's first questing party. Master Ornopy and his housekeeper, Mistress Moorp, welcomed them as Paladin's emissaries.

As soon as Bardon crossed the threshold, he smelled Kale. Not that she was there. But a scent of citrus emanates from all o'rants' skin. In this household of o'rants, the aroma floated on each current of air through every room.

He was well aware that his own emerlindian blood stifled the tangy smell rising from his pores. Ahnek needed several baths to erase the odor of the streets from his hide. Once or twice Bardon had caught a whiff of that identifying fragrance about the lad, but mostly Ahnek smelled of dirt and old sweat.

Bardon noticed Sittiponder's nostrils quivering. He put a hand on the boy's shoulder. "It's the fragrance of oranges, lemons, limes, and o'rants."

"It's nice," the blind boy answered. "I like it."

"So do I."

They stayed two days, allowing the dragons to thoroughly rest. At midday on the third day, the small band of questers crossed the border into the Northern Reach. Stretching before them, miles of short, pale new grass rolled over the hills like a variegated carpet. For the most part, only shades of green and an occasional tree made up the landscape. But here and there, outbreaks of splendor spotted a monotonous stretch.

N'Rae exclaimed over patches of wildflowers that puddled the swells and hollows of earth with a melee of color. Bardon noticed the beauty only after the young emerlindian pointed it out. He then saw that Ahnek readily described the scenery to his blind comrade.

Dar would be chastising me if he were here, Greer... Guilty as charged. Again I've been focused on images in my mind of rivers too wild to be crossed, chasms too deep to fathom, and trails too twisted to follow, while Wulder has painted a picture to gladden my heart right in front of me... Yes, I know there are numerous principles to quote about the folly of the mind's eye. You needn't remind me... It would appear that Wulder Himself is doing a good job of reminding me, so you can relax in your duty to keep me in line.

They traveled more east than north at this point. Herds of wild animals scattered as the dragons flew overhead. Streams meandered through the steppes and joined a river crossing the plain. In the distance, mountains rose out of the plains. At the second rest stop for the day, Bromptotterpindosset, Bardon, and Captain Anton decided to make camp and study the charts.

The boys explored. Sittiponder held on to his walking stick and Ahnek's arm. He ran as fast as the o'rant boy and listened intently as the sighted boy described each new wonder. Granny Kye got out her paints. Holt helped with a saddle sore one of the dragons had developed. N'Rae walked in circles around the camp.

Bardon kept an eye on the wandering boys and N'Rae. The lads stayed close, crossing and recrossing the same bit of land, discovering rocks, bushes, and animals that deserved inspection. N'Rae's trail rounded the camp in ever-widening circles.

"Here's where we are." Bromptotterpindosset jabbed a stubby finger at the parchment unrolled on the ground and weighted by rocks. "And here," he said, pointing to a page in the diary, "is the map that Cadden Glas sketched."

"What does the writing say?" The squire crouched beside the sitting mapmaker to look at his book.

The tumanhofer pinched his upper lip between a finger and his thumb. "Hmm. Cadden Glas's handwriting is sloppy, and when he got excited about something, it became a scrawl."

"It all looks like random scratches to me."

Bromptotterpindosset ignored him. "Luckily here, Glas is not disconcerted. He does butcher the meech verb forms, however. This says, 'We traveled overland for ten days and reached our first view of the mountains.' Actually, it says present tense *travel* and future tense *will reach.*"

"Does it say anything useful?"

The tumanhofer gave him a scathing look. "It lists the flora and fauna. I shall have to snag those two boys and compare his notes to what they have found." He turned the page. "There are also sketches of the specimens he noted."

A piercing scream lifted the hairs on the back of Bardon's neck. He sprang to his feet and ran to the crest of a hill where he'd last seen N'Rae. The other riders and Holt scrabbled up the rise behind him.

A cluster of grawligs ran through a gully, splashing in the small stream that cut through the earth. Bardon paused only a moment to see N'Rae draped over the shoulder of one of the ill-clad ogres. The squire raced down the hill.

With powerful legs, the grawligs covered ground quickly. The knot of raiders disappeared around a corner of the deepening ravine.

Greer, cut these beasts off and herd them back toward us.

Mighty wings whipped the air above him, and the dragon's huge shadow skated across the sloping bank. Keeping an eye on the rough terrain, Bardon charged toward the opening where N'Rae had been taken. He heard those following slip and slide as the crumbling soil broke away under their feet. He blessed his emerlindian agility.

A satisfied grin broke the serious expression on Bardon's face as he heard a collective shout from the small ravine.

He stepped aside just as Greer warned him the horde had turned and was about to trample him.

The horrified beasts ran out of the opening to see a living wall—six warriors, armed and blocking their escape. They stopped short and started to turn.

Bardon jumped back onto their trail and yelled, "Eeeyah!"

Greer landed on the edge of the cutaway above them, peering over the cliff at the unfortunate, trapped ogres.

The grawligs shuffled, their massive heads swiveling as they realized they had no way out.

The beast carrying N'Rae abruptly dropped her. She sat up and straightened her skirts around her legs. Glaring at her captors, she remained where she was, with her arms crossed defiantly over her chest and her chin tilted in the air.

"No good." The grawlig grunted and looked at those around him. They echoed his profound statement. "No good."

The spokesman stepped over N'Rae and walked a few steps toward Bardon, who held his sword ready in his hand.

"We go," said the grawlig. "No like woman. No like men. No like… that." He pointed to Greer.

Greer sneered, his lip curled, and sharp teeth clicked against each other.

"Dragon," said Bardon. "Do you not see dragons here?"

"We go."

Bardon waved his sword. "No, you answer some questions. Do you not see dragons here?"

"High in sky." The beast grunted. "Not belong on ground." He puffed out his chest. "Ground belong to hunters."

Greer hissed, and the hunter's chest deflated.

"We go."

"No, you answer some questions first. Do you know of a castle in the mountains?"

The brute's forehead collapsed into deep furrows. "Castle?"

He looked at his cohorts. They muttered, "Castle?" and shook their heads.

"Big house?" asked Bardon.

They repeated their performance of confusion.

A voice from the ridge opposite Greer spoke with deep authority. "You won't get anything out of them."

The horde of grawligs gasped in terror. In sheer panic, they scattered, bolting in every direction, right through their captors' wall of defense as if the warriors held no weapons. Some of the beasts cried out as they encountered the swords but kept on running.

Bardon turned to face the newcomer. Against a backdrop of brilliant blue sky stood a tall, lean figure dressed in black, with a cape billowed by the wind, and a broad-rimmed hat shadowing his face.

"Welcome, Squire Bardon of the Castle Pelacce, Dormenae, Wittoom."

34

An Old Friend

The figure shifted, striding several steps along the top of the cliff.

Bardon smiled and lowered his sword. "Regidor!"

The meech dragon stepped off his perch, dropped ten feet, and landed lightly beside the squire. His tail, glistening, green scalelike skin with a dark ridge down the center, swooped out from under the long cape, then back under. With one forefoot on the hilt of his sword and the other a fist against his waist, he smiled his long, flashy grin. Two rows of gleaming, pointed teeth showed between thin lips. His hairless jaw line extended from a squarish chin with a deep dimple in the center to the almost indistinguishable ears on the sides of his head. Even with the oddness of his appearance, Regidor was handsome.

Bardon considered the seven-foot meech dragon. "You've matured a great deal since last we met, my friend."

Regidor agreed with a downward jerk of his head. "Almost too fast. It was more fun chasing Toopka around and trying to get Librettowit to let me stay up late to read."

Bardon gave a slight nod. *Sounds like a typical, though short, childhood. I have no recollection of the years before I entered The Hall. Wonder if my childhood included chasing friends and reading at night.*

This is awkward. What do I say next?

His comrades inched closer to him and the odd visitor. They still had their weapons drawn and looked ready to pounce should Regidor make a threatening move.

Bardon nodded to Captain Anton. "This theatrical fellow is a friend, Wizard Regidor of The Bogs."

The guard relaxed on their leader's signal but continued to watch the meech dragon, now out of curiosity.

On the crest of the hill, Ahnek whispered earnestly to Sittiponder. A few feet away, Granny Kye stood beside N'Rae, who had gotten up and was dusting off her clothing. It seemed everyone but the minneken had gathered at the gully.

"So." Bardon shifted on his feet as he sheathed his sword. "How'd you get here?"

"Sir Dar sent a message, and I came. I wasn't far. In Dael, in fact."

What in the world would he be doing in the tumanhofer underground capital city? The universities! I bet he was studying.

"Yes, I was."

Now that's not very polite.

Regidor grinned. Bardon responded with a laugh, and the two young friends embraced, pounding each other on their backs. Regidor was more than a foot taller than the squire.

"You overgrown lizard," exclaimed Bardon. "What have you been up to? And I have a hundred questions to ask you about those in the bog. Did you finish your apprenticeship? Are you a wizard?"

"I am," said Regidor. "Best pupil Fenworth has ever trained."

"I bet!"

"Well, considering Fen slept through most of my instruction and Cam Ayronn and Librettowit taught me most of what I know, it is an amazing feat. Of course, the venerable Wizard Fenworth is capable of any task."

A sudden thought struck Bardon as odd. Greer had not told him of the arrival of another major dragon. "Regidor, how did you get here?"

"Sir Dar—"

"No, no. Physically, how did you get here?"

"I floated in on a stiff breeze."

Bardon looked at his friend's serious face for a moment. The expression was almost too serious, as if he were trying to hide an emotion.

No, he couldn't have. But... "You flew?"

Regidor's green eyes gleamed, and he silently nodded.

The squire gasped. "I didn't know it was possible."

"There is very little known about the meech, including whether or not they fly. I figured I had the wings, so I would give it a try."

"And?"

"And I fell off successively higher platforms until I eventually got the coordination down right."

"Ouch!" Bardon laughed. "Are you joining our quest?"

"Yes."

"Then let me introduce you to our party."

The riders stepped aside so Bardon could lead Regidor to Granny Kye and N'Rae.

"Granny Kye," said the squire in his most formal tones, "may I present Regidor."

The meech dragon bowed, and the emerlindian granny curtsied. He took her hand and kissed it. "It is a pleasure to meet you, Granny Kye. I admire the wisdom of your people."

"Oh w-well," Granny Kye stuttered, "you see...well, I kind of missed out...on the wisdom. Took my mother forever just to teach me to tie my shoes."

"That would seem to be a problem of dexterity, not discernment."

Granny Kye took back her hand and propped her chin on it. "Yes, I see your point, but I'm not sure they would." She shook her head. "No, that doesn't make sense at all. Now my fingers are much more clever than I am. I paint, you see."

Regidor nodded his long head solemnly. "Yes, painting requires dexterity."

"Bardon, you will unravel this knot for me at a later time, I trust."

Oh yes.

"And this is her granddaughter, N'Rae." Bardon gestured toward the pale emerlindian. "It is her father we seek to rescue."

Regidor bowed. N'Rae curtsied.

"Charmed," said the meech dragon.

The emerlindian girl giggled.

"A beauty."

Don't.

"Don't what?"

Dally.

"Why not?"

She innocently captures men's hearts and then doesn't know what to do with them.

Bardon cleared his throat. "I'll introduce you to the guard Sir Dar sent to accompany us. Captain Anton will want his riders to get back to their duties."

The captain and his riders were loath to return to camp. None of them had met a meech dragon or knew anyone who had. But their military training won out, so they took their curiosity and returned to camp.

Bardon moved to the next member of their questing party.

"Bromptotterpindosset, this is Regidor." He turned to the meech. "Regidor, our mapmaker friend reads and speaks meech."

Regidor's eyes grew wide. "A rare accomplishment. I do not speak the language of my heritage. I would be honored if you would instruct me."

"Gladly." The tumanhofer beamed with pleasure at such a prospect.

"May I ask, where did you learn meech?"

"On the vast continent of Punipmats, there is a thriving colony of meech in a hard-to-reach area surrounded by tropical forest."

The two would have continued their discussion, but Bardon interrupted.

"We have four more members of our party." He took Regidor's elbow and turned him to face the marione.

"Holt Hoddack is…a riding-animal expert."

As the two exchanged conventional greetings, Regidor snickered in Bardon's thoughts. *"This will be an interesting story."*

Later.

"One of N'Rae's smitten beaus?"

Later.

"And these two youngsters are Sittiponder and Ahnek."

Regidor shook hands with both lads.

Overawed, the boys merely bobbed their heads in response to the meech dragon's deep-throated, "Hello."

"I believe you said four more members, Squire." Regidor looked around. "I see no other."

"Jue Seeno," squeaked Ahnek.

"Jue Seeno?"

Both lads nodded vigorously.

"Come see," said Ahnek. He took the shorter tumanhofer's arm and turned him toward the camp.

"He means come meet her," said Sittiponder over his shoulder. Aside to his friend, he whispered, "Be polite. You don't show somebody to somebody as if one somebody was an interesting cat or dog you happen to have in the barn."

"What are you talking about? We don't have a barn. She's in a basket." Ahnek frowned at his friend as they walked.

Bardon and Regidor exchanged glances, each smiling over the boys' argument. Bardon shrugged, and they followed the two lads.

"You have the manners of a street urchin," Sittiponder grumbled.

"I am a street urchin."

"Not anymore!" He shook Ahnek's hold off his arm and trudged forward, using his walking stick. "You are a member of a questing party charged by Paladin himself to rescue noble knights from an evil curse."

"Now you sound as if you're telling one of your grand stories again." Ahnek stomped alongside Sittiponder. "And I learned to eat with my mouth shut like you wanted. That's manners."

"You still slip up."

"How do you know?"

They stopped and faced each other, oblivious to the grown men who stopped as well.

"I can hear you," shouted Sittiponder. "I'm not deaf, you know."

"It might be easier if you was."

"If you *were,* not *was.* And you don't mean that."

"No, I don't." Ahnek stared at his friend's mulish expression for a moment. He reached out and punched Sittiponder's skinny arm. "Let's go tell Mistress Seeno a meech dragon is coming. Bet she doesn't believe he's real."

"Bet he won't believe she's real."

The boys hooted with laughter, grabbed each other by the arms, and ran ahead.

Regidor turned with a question in his eye, accentuated by one lifted eyebrow. Or rather, the skin that would have sported an eyebrow if the meech had any hair.

"I won't believe this Jue Seeno is real?"

"She's a minneken."

"Aha!" Regidor contemplated this. "He's correct. How refreshing that there should be someone else on this quest who is the personification of myth. I wish to meet such an oddity."

Bardon laughed as he quickened his pace to keep up with his friend's long stride.

35

Temperaments

"My, my," said Mistress Seeno as she tilted her head back to get a better look at the dragon standing beside Squire Bardon. "You cut a dashing figure."

Regidor swept off his hat, passing it over his leg as he made a deep bow. The gallant gesture would have impressed royalty.

Bardon raised his eyebrows.

The meech dragon, now standing straight and tall before the humble basket of the minneken, ignored him.

"I'm honored you think so, Mistress Seeno." Regidor rested his hat against his chest as he spoke to the fur-covered person sitting in her chair on her basket. "It has actually taken quite a bit of effort to acquire a wardrobe that has style, yet minimizes my tail and wings."

"And this was necessary because…?" prompted Jue Seeno.

"Because I wish to mingle unobtrusively with the citizenry of the high races."

"Your height and coloring would still distinguish you."

"Ah yes, but you'd be surprised how much a busy person hurrying down the street, absorbed in his own affairs, will overlook."

"Height and an unusual complexion—"

Regidor nodded. "But not wings and a tail."

Ahnek danced from one foot to the other.

Bardon put a hand on the boy's shoulder to help him contain his excitement. "What is it?"

"We want to see his wings."

Regidor grinned, stepped back a few feet into an open space, and tossed the sides of his cape back over his shoulders. In a great whoosh, large leathery wings expanded behind him, fanning the air and ruffling the hair of his audience.

Ahnek clapped his hands and stomped his feet, then grabbed Sittiponder. "They're green and glistening like I told you his tail is. He's got dark ridges running through them just like Frost, only a different color, of course. Sitti! They must be fifteen feet across and taller than he is at the highest point. They're stupendous."

Regidor brought the wings forward until they touched in front of him so that he stood within a circle of his own making. Then he flashed them back, and Ahnek plopped down with a thud, stunned.

For a moment, the lad just took in the wondrous sight. Then, he reached up and grabbed Sittiponder's hand, jerking him down to sit.

"The underside of his wings is now like oil in a puddle, dark with swirly colors in it."

The others in the camp came to watch as well. Regidor repeated the action. This time his wings gleamed red. Once more he encircled himself, and after a longer pause, he slowly unveiled not only himself but also a beautiful female meech dragon.

She stood in front of him and a little to the side, so they faced the small crowd as a pair. Their smiles reflected amusement at the astonishment they had created. Her blue gray dress contrasted with Regidor's black garb and blended in with his now moonlight-gray wing.

"She's not really there," Ahnek whispered to Sittiponder before he even described the vision. "You can see through her like she was made up of smoke or something."

"No," corrected Bardon. "She is there."

He bowed his head to the female meech. "Welcome, Gilda. I see you still travel with Regidor."

She glanced over her shoulder toward her companion's face, then back at the squire. "He kindly includes me in his daily life. It's much more exciting than sitting on a shelf, I assure you."

A breeze flitted between those watching and the two meech dragons.

The zephyr swirled dust into the air and bent the grass. Gilda's dress swayed as the air stirred. It looked for a moment as if the edges would blow away, like tendrils of smoke. But the scattering substance pulled back together.

Regidor moved his wings around them once more. When he snapped them open, Gilda was gone. He stretched the now-shimmering green appendages out to their complete wingspan, and then with a loud ruffle, they folded and disappeared behind him. He reached to his shoulders and adjusted his cape.

The riders reluctantly turned away. Holt went with them.

Bardon tried to interpret the young marione's reaction. Of those assembled, only Holt seemed disgusted by what they had seen.

What was that? Jealousy? I better find out what is sticking in that young man's craw.

Before he could make any more speculations, he saw N'Rae leave Granny Kye's side and run to Regidor.

"Can I talk to Gilda? Will she come back? She's lovely, isn't she? Is she your wife?"

Regidor gazed down at the excited girl. "No, she is not my wife. Yes, she is lovely. Yes, she will come back. And yes, you may talk to her, but not now. Gilda does not feel comfortable when exposed to the elements."

He put a hand on N'Rae's elbow and steered her back toward the minneken's basket. "I believe my conversation with Mistress Seeno was interrupted."

He glanced over at the two boys. Their heads nearly touched, and Ahnek talked in rushed undertones, his hands waving in small, jerky movements.

Jue Seeno waited for them, standing and tapping her foot, fists on her hips. Bardon had not moved, and so he heard her sputtering even before Regidor and N'Rae arrived.

"Quite a display," she said. "So much for mingling unobtrusively with the higher races."

"This is hardly a town square." Regidor seated N'Rae on a pile of parcels unloaded from the dragons. "Now, why have you turned all prickly on me, Mistress Seeno?"

"Don't worry," said N'Rae. "It's her natural reaction to life. She bristles whenever you don't do something exactly as she thought you would." N'Rae shrugged. "She'll be over it in a trice, and quite often it will be ten or fifteen minutes before she gets all riled up about something again."

The minneken's body stiffened. Her whiskers quivered above a pinched mouth. "You, young lady, are taking on airs, talking like you know more than you do. Kindly remember your place."

N'Rae raised her fingertips to her lips, and her face went from its natural alabaster tone to ruby in a matter of seconds. "I'm sorry, Mistress Seeno. I didn't think."

"Nonsense," fumed the little woman. "Of course you were thinking. No one ceases thinking. The problem is you thought only in one narrow line. Your focus was on this Regidor person with his charming smile and dashing ways. You spoke in a context of two, you and him. But you don't live in a context of two. Your life is intertwined with many more than just two."

Jue Seeno stood even straighter and glared with piercing black eyes. "And I, young lady, am your protector. It is my duty to bristle."

"Here, now." Granny Kye's deep, gentle voice intervened. "Are we having a fuss? Let's have tea instead. It's still some time until our evening meal, and everyone is a bit excited."

She shooed the boys off to help with chores. "I'll call you as soon as the tea is ready and there is a daggart to be eaten," she promised, then turned to the handsome new addition to their party. "Bromptotterpindosset wishes to speak to you when you have a moment."

"You might as well go with him, Squire Bardon," Mistress Seeno piped up. "The three of us can make the tea without your assistance."

Bardon and Regidor inclined their heads and moved off to join the tumanhofer.

When they were a few steps away, Regidor commented quietly, "The question is, Can the three of them make peace without your assistance?"

Bardon chortled. "I believe they can. Granny Kye has a calming influence on Jue Seeno." He paused. "You may think that the little minneken is harsh, but she has a huge responsibility. Granny Kye does little to stem her granddaughter's impulsiveness, so the role of protector falls squarely on the minneken's shoulders."

"So this marione Holt is one of N'Rae's admirers?"

"I'm not sure, Regidor. Would you mind looking at him and seeing what measure he exhibits?"

Regidor searched for Holt and caught sight of the marione bending over the fire with one of the female riders at his side. He studied the young man. "The colors flowing around his person are mostly in harmony. That would verify he is comfortable with his present circumstances. Underneath, he has rifts of displeasure, contrasting tones in one color indicating tension. A lack of uniformity would indicate he is unsettled in his desire and motivation. The serenity of Wulder's influence is definitely missing. His measure is variable, at best."

"So is he a good addition to the questing party or not?"

Regidor shrugged. "I would say that is as undecided as the young man's aspirations."

"I have a coin given to me by Paladin. It is supposed to help me discern whether a person is in direct conflict with the purpose of our quest."

"Interesting." Regidor returned his attention to Bardon. "Somewhat like the metal disk that has already confirmed Kale has found her lost mother and will tell her if she has found her lost father?"

"Yes."

"Useful."

"Not in Holt's case. I've tried it several times and gotten different degrees of heat each time."

"Then I say we keep an eye on him."

36

Tradition

Under a tarp set up to provide shade, the mapmaker had erected chairs and a collapsible table to display his treasures. Books, charts, and maps covered the sturdy table. Bardon sat on a trunk cushioned by a pillow. He could not work up an eagerness to view this hoard of knowledge one more time.

Bromptotterpindosset and Regidor pored over the diary of Cadden Glas and the mapmaker's charts. The meech dragon pointed out mountain ranges he had already explored and made minor corrections to the scale and scope of the sketches before him. The tumanhofer interpreted both Glas's notations on the diary maps and the daily entries.

After an hour, the meech dragon began translating the pages with much less difficulty than his instructor. Bardon laughed at his friend's ability to grasp the nuances of a language so quickly, but the mapmaker stared open-mouthed. He slammed his mouth shut, furrowed his brow in a fierce frown, and shook his finger at the meech.

"What's this? Were you lying to me?" demanded the enraged tumanhofer.

"No." Bardon leaned forward from where he sat watching the two. "He has always learned at a phenomenal rate. Didn't the meech you encountered in Punipmats exhibit incredible mental abilities?"

"They were intelligent, it's true," Bromptotterpindosset admitted. "But I didn't actually observe them learning what they knew." He glared at Regidor, then shook his head and looked back at the map.

"So how is it, Wizard Regidor," asked Bardon, "that you have spent so much time in this region?"

"I'm searching for the lost meech colony."

N'Rae approached, holding hands with Sittiponder and Ahnek. Holt followed, carrying a tea tray. Granny Kye came with Jue Seeno's basket over her arm.

A warrior's battle shield served as the tray, and the cups and plates rattled slightly with a metallic clanking. The teapot was the camp's tall coffeepot. The tea and daggarts, however, smelled like a real treat that might be served in Dar's castle.

"So, Regidor, you are searching for your parents," said Holt as he stood by the table, waiting for Bromptotterpindosset to clear away the scattering of charts. "I'm beginning to feel out of place. I seem to be one of the few on this quest who knows exactly who and where my parents are."

Regidor stood so that Granny Kye and N'Rae could take the bench he had been sitting on.

"There are fourteen in our party, and only…" The meech dragon paused and leaned over the minneken's basket. "Mistress Seeno, are you without knowledge of your parents?"

Regidor nodded at whatever the minneken had answered.

He turned back to Holt. "Only five of our members have little or no information about their parents. It would seem you erroneously claim a position of minority."

"What'd he say?" asked Ahnek, shaking Sittiponder's arm, but his friend ignored him.

"I have a father," said the young tumanhofer.

"You do?" exclaimed Ahnek. "Where is he?"

"Everywhere. My Father is Wulder."

The mapmaker nodded. "A quaint term used in many traditional circles. You are from Vendela, am I not mistaken?"

"I am," answered Sittiponder.

Granny Kye poured a cup of tea and handed it to Bromptotterpindosset. He accepted with an inclination of his head. "I have always considered it odd that the 'City of Enlightenment' clings to the older traditions of the Tomes."

Bardon frowned and reached into his pocket. His fingers found the coin Paladin had given him, and he pressed it against his palm. The cold metal chilled his skin as he watched the mapmaker pass a plate of daggarts to N'Rae.

Bardon exchanged glances with Regidor as the well-traveled tumanhofer talked of various cultures and their similarities.

"Don't be so alarmed, Bardon. He can still be of use to us even if his beliefs are tarnished."

The coin is cold in my hand. Paladin said to shun those people who did not have a heart for our quest.

Regidor's eyes returned to the pleasant tableau of an afternoon tea. *"What are you going to do? Put him on a dragon and send him back to Wittoom?"*

Perhaps. We needed Bromptotterpindosset to translate the diary. Now you can do that.

"Yes, but the diary belongs to the mapmaker. If he goes back, the diary and his maps go with him."

I believe Wulder would take us to the resting place of the lost knights without Bromptotterpindosset.

"In theory, so do I, Squire."

Bardon paused, mulling over the scene his announcement to ban the mapmaker would cause. His nose wrinkled in distaste. *I should challenge Bromptotterpindosset now and make arrangements for his return tomorrow.*

Bardon started forward, but Regidor put a forefoot on his arm.

"Don't act rashly, my friend. Give yourself time to consider what Wulder would have you do."

It seems pretty clear cut to me. Paladin gave me a coin to help me discern the hearts of men. He said to shun those who cause the metal to cool. He paused, rubbing the late-afternoon stubble on his chin. *Regidor, what do you see in this man's colors?*

The meech turned his gaze on the tumanhofer. The mapmaker sat at ease, clearly a man accustomed to sitting at the tables of refined citizens. He held the others' attention with a story of a deity popular among the

Ataradari, a tribe on one of the smaller southern continents. This Ataradar-ian character of folklore rewarded cleverness and beauty from his powerful seat of authority on a mountaintop.

Bardon twisted his lips. *Even a child learning the rudiments of the Tomes knows cleverness and beauty are temporal achievements and have noth-ing to do with lasting contentment.*

"*His colors.*" Regidor's voice interrupted Bardon's thoughts.

What?

"*You asked about his colors.*"

Yes?

"*He carries no dark hues indicative of transactions with Pretender. But none of his colors have clarity, either. All but a very few of these strands of muddy-colored light turn back, inward. They should encompass him in a cir-cular pattern. The lack of symmetry is significant. He is a very self-centered man.*"

Bardon's throat tightened. *We should be rid of him.*

"*Yes, now I see why you are eager to be rid of him,*" remarked Regidor in a steady voice that did much to soothe Bardon's distress. "*He worked beside you to kill the sea serpent, and again, to escape the bisonbecks through the disintegrating gateway. But it was vital to his own personal safety that he do so. I think his decisions would be different should he need to choose between his own life and anyone else's.*"

Regidor placed a hand on Bardon's shoulder but still did not speak aloud. "*I am now convinced that this mapmaker would not choose his path based on the principles of Wulder or the commands of Paladin. Nevertheless, you cannot load him onto a dragon at this late hour. And you would have everyone upset if you announced your intentions. So…*"

So?

"*So, consult with Captain Anton tonight and arrange for Bromptotter-pindosset's transportation in the morning.*"

I worry about his influence on our party. The way he spouts off his phi-losophy is very entertaining.

"*You do your people a disservice. Look at their faces.*"

Of those seated around the mapmaker's table, all but Holt and Ahnek had lost interest. Sittiponder had a distant expression, as if he were listening to an entirely different conversation. N'Rae's brow furrowed as if she could not quite understand what was being said. Granny Kye yawned, covering her gaping mouth with a scrap of linen she used as her handkerchief. Jue Seeno, with her tiny hands and an odd metal instrument in her lap, worked on weaving yet another fancy sash.

Quietly, Bardon and Regidor left the gathering around the teapot and went in search of Captain Anton. The young squire had to double-time to keep up with the meech dragon's long stride.

"Tomorrow," said Bardon as they passed by the cooking fire and the lo who was in charge of the evening's meal, "we shall address the false philosophy that riddles the tumanhofer's tales. Paladin said he was more concerned about the monsters of variance than the quiss."

"Rightly so." With his long legs, Regidor stepped over an outcropping of rock that Bardon had to hop onto before he could jump down to the other side. They were headed for the temporary dragon field where riders and dragons relaxed.

"I've pondered what Paladin said, and I think I understand," said Bardon, breathing heavily. "Slow down, would you, Reg? I can't talk and run to keep up with you."

Regidor complied. Bardon took a couple of deep breaths and went on. "When people are confronted with an outside enemy, they band together for mutual protection. A physical threat unifies."

"Correct," said Regidor.

"But ideas, contrary concepts, shades of differing opinions, theories, these things shatter commonality."

"I agree," said Regidor. "A quiss rises up out of the mist, and one knows one must kill or be killed. A man says over a pint of ale at the tavern that he believes Wulder is one form of universal fable, and who contradicts him? No one. Yet his words are belittling the truth, wounding the strength of our convictions."

Bardon laughed. "We can't slay everyone who doesn't agree with the Tomes."

"Words are powerful weapons, Squire Bardon. False philosophy can be killed with the right weapon. And the weapon is words. And the right words are truth."

Bardon stopped. Regidor paced ahead, then halted his course to turn and tilt his head at his friend.

Bardon pointed back to the main camp. "If what you say is true, Reg, we should go back to Bromptotterpindosset and expose his lies with principles. We should be shouting our opposition."

Regidor grinned. "No, no. I don't believe that's the correct course for this dilemma. You cannot attack a bad idea as you would a savage beast. You don't reason with a bull who charges. You don't shoot arrows at men with ideas." Regidor signaled with his forefoot for Bardon to follow and started off again to the dragon field. "Sittiponder has already raised the flag of truth. Tomorrow we shall discuss Bromptotterpindosset's stories. We will kill the false teachings of an ignorant man. Because...we shall allow each person to wrestle through his or her thinking to reach a personal conclusion. Their decisions will come from within."

"There are men with bad ideas who do shoot arrows at us. What of them, Regidor? Do we reason then?"

"Thinking of Crim Cropper and Burner Stox?"

"Among others."

"Because they wish to kill us, then by all means, let us shoot back. Those we do not kill, we shall capture. Then we can talk their ideas to death, once we have their arrows safely in our hands."

They found Captain Anton sitting between the front legs of his dragon. He held a small, stringed instrument in his hands and played a melody commonly heard in Amara's music halls. He stood immediately as Bardon and Regidor approached. The squire explained the problem with the mapmaker. If the captain thought the solution a bit extreme, he said nothing, merely agreeing to fulfill the orders given to him by his superior.

Bardon chose to sleep beneath the stars that night. He spent a great deal of time talking to Wulder in hopes that a clear answer to his unsettled feeling would emerge.

The problem of the Wizards' Plume advancing across the sky could not be ignored. It hung at about forty degrees above the southwestern horizon. In the north sky the Eye of the North looked down from its ninety-degree position. It seemed that as the Wizards' Plume gained height, it also gained speed. Bardon could do nothing to slow the comet's progress. He spent time staring at the heavenly lights and wondering why Wulder allowed this particular clock to tick away the time. And he pondered an old question. Why did Wulder put each star and planet in intricate synchronization with one another, yet never bothered to send a follower just one clear-cut answer to a simple question?

Have I made the right decision regarding the mapmaker?

In the morning it didn't matter. Bardon got up from his pallet, rolled it and stored it with his gear, and went to tell the tumanhofer he was returning to Dormenae.

Bromptotterpindosset was gone.

37

BOOTS

The young o'rant Ahnek followed Bardon as they circled the area east of the camp, looking for evidence of how and why the missing mapmaker left. Others searched the perimeter as well. Regidor canvassed the north with two leecents. Captain Anton and two riders studied the ground on the west. The last rider and Holt covered the south. Granny Kye, N'Rae, Sittiponder, and Jue Seeno fixed the morning meal.

"How'd old Bromp get past the guards?" asked Ahnek. "Isn't that what they're posted for, to keep people and things from coming into or leaving camp?"

The squire gave his young companion a stern look. "You will refer to our lost tumanhofer with respect, Ahnek. He is Bromptotterpindosset unless he gives you permission to call him by a more familiar name. And that is highly unlikely."

"Do you think he's dead?

"No, I don't think he's dead."

"Then why won't he ever say I can call him Bromp?"

"He just doesn't seem the type to want to be called in a familiar manner by a scrap of a boy."

Rather than being insulted by Bardon's description of him, Ahnek grinned. "So how did Bromptotterpindosset get out of camp without being seen?"

"The guard did see him leave," explained Bardon as he crouched to examine some marks in the dirt beside a large bush.

"Nobody told me," complained Ahnek.

"Obviously." Bardon gestured for the boy to come closer. "Look at this. Someone with big feet covered with a soft material such as well-worked leather stood here for a long time."

Oval imprints overlaid each other in the scuffed dirt.

Ahnek let out a low whistle. "Someone was watching us?"

"Probably."

"Why didn't the guard raise an alarm when Bromptotterpindosset left?"

"It was one of the major dragons, and she saw nothing unusual with one of the men leaving the camp for a few minutes."

"Those guards sure don't like it when Sitti and I go out."

"They probably assume you're up to mischief."

"Well, it was Bromptotterpindosset who was up to mischief, wasn't it?"

"We don't know that." Bardon stood and followed the indistinct tracks as they moved from one bush to the next.

"Do you think whoever was standing here watching clobbered Bromptotterpindosset on the head and hauled him off?"

"Problem is we don't know if these tracks are coming or going." Bardon stopped and put his hands on his hips. He surveyed the terrain around them. "The shape doesn't indicate front or back of the foot, and the ground is too hard to show the indentation of the heel when it hit the dirt first."

"Do you think it was a high race or a low race watching us?"

"Low."

"Bisonbeck, grawlig, or ropma?"

"Grawlig."

"Those that tried to carry off N'Rae or some others?"

"No way of telling."

Ahnek scratched his head. "I can see why someone would want to carry N'Rae off but not that tumanhofer."

"Ahnek." Bardon's voice held a note of warning.

"Mistress Seeno calls him 'that tumanhofer' all the time."

"Mistress Seeno is not a callow lad, who—"

"Uh-oh." Ahnek had stopped in his tracks and stood staring down a steep slope into a patch of bushes.

A scrap of the tumanhofer's shirt snagged by a thorn, broken branches, signs of a struggle in the trampled grass, and small, dark splotches of drying red blood on a rock told an interesting story.

Bardon tucked his lower lip under his upper teeth and whistled, loud, sharp, and clear. Those searching for clues came running.

"It would seem," said Bardon as they waited for the others to gather, "that whoever was standing there watching clobbered Bromptotterpindosset on the head and hauled him off."

Ahnek gave a satisfied nod. "See? I told you."

Regidor arrived first and surveyed the scene. "Grawligs," he said. "Six of them." He looked back to the camp. "By going down into this little depression, our mapmaker took himself out of the line of vision of the guard." He paced a few feet with his eyes on the ground. "It'll be an easy trail. I'll fly ahead and see if I can learn anything."

"I thought you were going to get rid of him anyway," said Ahnek. "I thought he was a hindrance to our quest because he didn't truly follow Wulder."

Bardon and Regidor stared at the boy. Ahnek clamped his mouth shut and became very still, as if he could turn into a mere shadow and not be noticed.

"That's very interesting," said Regidor.

"Where did you come up with that information?" asked Bardon.

Ahnek swallowed. "Sittiponder."

Bardon narrowed his eyes at the boy. "And where did Sittiponder learn of this?"

"His voices."

"Hmm?" Bardon looked at Regidor.

The meech dragon shrugged.

Holt ran up, followed closely by the others coming from various directions. "What did you find?"

Before they could answer, he spotted the site of the abduction. "Oh." He studied it for a moment. "Looks like he wasn't hurt too badly."

As the search party crowded closer to see, they shoved Ahnek next to Bardon's leg.

Holt shook his head and half laughed. "If they knocked him on the head, old Bromp won't hardly have felt it."

Ahnek nudged Bardon at the words "old Bromp." The squire glared at the lad's impertinent grin. The boy tried to control the muscles that lifted the corners of his mouth but failed. He looked away.

A whoosh of air captured Bardon's attention.

Regidor had paced off a few yards and released his wings. "I'll make a reconnaissance flight and bring back information. You might as well eat, then break camp."

His wings spread to their full span and beat the air twice. On the second downward motion, Regidor lifted off the ground. In a moment, he swooped over the hills and soared away. Soon he looked like a large bird of prey in the distance.

The talk, as the group walked back into camp, centered on speculations. Bardon listened but didn't participate. His thoughts centered on this new twist in the plans to find and rescue the sleeping knights.

Ahnek pulled on Bardon's sleeve.

"But why are we going to try to find Bromptotterpindosset?" he asked. "Couldn't this be Wulder's way of taking away the problem of what to do with him?"

Bardon clapped a hand on the lad's shoulder. "Some might think so, but when you read the Tomes, you find that Wulder expects us to treat someone like Bromptotterpindosset with respect, just as we would treat Paladin with respect, or would want to be treated with respect ourselves."

Ahnek shook his head. "What does respect have to do with it?"

"I have two pairs of boots, Ahnek. One pair is new and looks good. The other pair is old and looks bad. I've cleaned my boots and put them on the windowsill to air, because the polish I use is strong and smelly. The good pair looks better. The bad pair looks only passable. It begins to rain, and I retrieve my boots out of the rain. Do I fetch both pairs in out of the rain, or just the new pair?"

"Both."

"Why?"

"Because both pairs need to be out of the rain, not just the good pair."

"Correct. They are my boots, and I will take care of them. We are Wulder's people, and He will take care of us."

"Whether we are shiny and new, or old and stinky?"

"I never said the old boots were stinky."

Ahnek wrinkled his nose. "Old boots just are."

"Well, yes." Bardon roughed up the lad's hair. "And Wulder takes care of His people with equal respect, whether they are old boots or new."

"But Bromptotterpindosset is not one of Wulder's people at all."

"But Wulder has put the mapmaker in our midst. And before we were able to hand him over to someone else's sphere of influence, he fell into trouble." Bardon smiled at the image in his mind. "Bromptotterpindosset is an old boot in the rain, Ahnek, and we must retrieve him."

"B-but he isn't *our* boot, Squire Bardon. And he isn't Wulder's boot either."

"It's one of those hard things to understand, but Wulder is very interested in all boots." Bardon laughed.

They breakfasted on fresh journey cakes and fried wild onions. Bardon thought the sweet corn flour biscuits and crunchy onions an unusual combination, but he didn't want to spoil N'Rae's pleasure in providing the morning meal. She had done most of the cooking herself. Granny Kye had pulled out her easel. An hour later, Bardon urged the old emerlindian to pack up her art. They had completed preparations for departing.

"We are going to follow Regidor and, hopefully, catch up with the grawligs who have Bromptotterpindosset."

She merely nodded.

Bardon went searching for N'Rae. He found her communing with a furry animal twice the size of his foot. He'd never seen one outside of drawings in a book, but he guessed it was a steppesman. The burrowing animals earned their name by the locations of their colonies and the odd habit they had of congregating around an object. As these furry animals sat up on their haunches and chittered at one another, they looked like a group of men discussing something of great import. The creature saw Bardon's approach and dashed down his hole.

N'Rae gave the intruder an exasperated look.

"Was he saying anything important?" asked Bardon as he gave her a hand and helped her to rise from her seat on the ground.

She brushed off her skirts. "I was learning quite a bit about the local weather."

"You were discussing the weather?"

"Not exactly. I was trying to get information about anything unusual around here, like a place where my father might be. But the silly little rodent could only think about sunshine and food."

Bardon patted her arm, not knowing how else to offer sympathy. "I need your help."

She looked up at him sharply. "You do?"

He nodded. "I can't pry Granny Kye away from the picture she's painting. I have requested on numerous occasions that she pack up and get ready. Her only response, if she answers at all, is, 'My landscapes are getting so much better.'"

The younger emerlindian laughed. "Yes, I'll come and help."

"He's coming," yelled Ahnek. He pointed to the mountains.

Bardon shielded his eyes with his hand across his brow. In the sky, flying toward them from the mountains, a shape like a large bird approached.

Greer, is that Regidor?

Instead of hearing his dragon's droll comments, he heard Regidor's voice.

"It is, indeed, I."

You can mindspeak over such a great distance?

"No, I can't. I'll talk to you when I get closer."

Bardon paused for a moment and digested the sarcastic reply. How like his friend to tease him in the midst of a crisis.

Regidor?

"Yes?"

So it was a stupid question. I deserved that jab at my intelligence.

"Stop, Bardon, you are driving me to the end of my patience."

I was merely acknowledging that my remark was spoken without first considering.

"You are being a boring, sanctimonious academician. Just laugh and ask me what I found out."

Bardon didn't laugh. *What did you find out?*

"That these grassland grawligs dig holes like rabbits."

You found where they have taken the tumanhofer?

"In a manner of speaking. I found their village, which is a warren of burrows in the foothills of the mountains you see to my back."

This isn't going to be a simple rescue, is it?

Regidor laughed. "You are correct. 'Simple' is not the right descriptive word. Try 'interesting.'"

38

GILDA

"Carry this." Regidor handed Bardon a blue glowing globe and pulled another out of an inside pocket of his cape.

"You've got hollows," Bardon said as he balanced the palm-sized light in his hand. He tossed it to the other hand and back. "Are you sure of your translation of Glas's diary?"

Regidor nodded. "This warren has burrows crisscrossing under the land for miles in any direction."

"I've always thought of burrows as small, housing rabbits and badgers and the like. These are huge."

"Yes, but what else would you call them? They are tunnels with small chambers dug out for sleeping."

Bardon nodded in agreement but still marveled at the size.

Regidor continued. "This particular tunnel leads to a central meeting place of the local grawligs, a watering hole inside the first range of mountains. It seems reasonable to assume Bromptotterpindosset's captors would take him to this location to show off their prize. The diary describes just such activities when Glas explored the territory."

Bardon nodded. *This does seem to be the most logical place to start our search. However, there is something inherently wrong with using logic to predict the actions of grawligs.*

They sat in the entrance to one of the many burrows that riddled the hills. Out of the wind, Regidor had opened the top of a shapely bottle made from thick glass.

"Do you like it?" he asked. "I think it suits Gilda much better than that clay jar she used to inhabit. I got it at an open-air market in Vendela."

He held the blue vessel in front of him. "Blue is her favorite color. And the silver…well, the silver is because she is precious to me."

A wisp of smoke floated out of the opened top. It formed into Gilda, and the female meech dragon sashayed over to sit on one of the boulders lining the side of the tunnel as if placed there for a purpose. Neither Regidor nor Bardon had figured out the purpose.

This entrance to the warren showed little sign of use, which seemed odd. The map showed this large tunnel to be the most direct route to the grawligs' celebration site.

Bardon had firmly refused Ahnek's plea to come along. And he'd left instructions with Captain Anton to return the questing party to Dormenae if he and Regidor did not return in a day's time.

"You know, there should be some advantage to having a wizard as a friend," Bardon said, still tossing the light back and forth between his hands. "How about giving me a hollow as a gesture of our deep and abiding brotherly affection?"

Gilda laughed softly, and Regidor scratched the ridge above his left eye. "Hadn't thought of the depth of our mutual esteem before. I guess I could make you a hollow to commemorate our bond… Do you want a small hollow or a large?"

"I thought a hollow could hold as much as you put in it. I didn't know they came in sizes."

Regidor pulled out two metal contraptions and handed one to Bardon. Demonstrating its use, the meech fitted the pointed, clawlike clamp over the light. With the sphere held in the device, he could grasp it by a handle or clamp it to some object.

As the squire followed his example in mounting the light into its holder, Regidor reached again into the hollow. "Once the object you wish to store is inside the hollow, it takes up no discernable space. At least, not in this dimension."

Bardon held up a hand. "Stop. Don't explain dimensions to me. Just get to the point."

"I agree with him, Reg." Gilda crossed her legs, shifting to a more comfortable position. "Too often you launch into explanations that are truly beside the point."

"And nobody wants to hear," muttered Bardon.

"More reason to find my clan," said Regidor. "The hope of finding intelligent conversation."

The meech dragon twisted his face into a mask of extreme tolerance, eyebrows raised, lips pursed, and eyes cutting Bardon a look of disdain. "However," he continued as if not interrupted, "the size of the opening to the hollow can severely limit what you collect. If you can't pass the object through the opening to the other plane, you cannot store it."

Bardon nodded. "Like a dragon cannot go through a gateway unless the gateway is sufficiently proportioned."

The meech wrinkled his brow. "Not quite an exact parallel, but close enough."

"At this point," said Gilda, "it would be worth our while to have the little Dragon Keeper with us."

Both men looked at the beautiful, exotic female sitting coolly on her rock.

"Don't look so astonished," she said. "I'm surprised you haven't thought of it before. Those minor dragons are excellent as scouts. She herself is an admirable warrior. And although she has not nearly the expertise of dear Reg, she is a formidable wizard."

"Be that as it may, Kale is thousands of miles away," responded Regidor as he checked his weapons—a sword, two knives, and a pouch of small projectiles.

Gilda's eyes glittered in the blue light of the globes. "These tunnels twist and turn like a maze. You'll be sorry you haven't got Kale and her little dragons beside you."

Regidor did not answer.

Gilda smiled in what Bardon thought was a catlike manner, with her head tilted and a look of superiority on her lovely features. She hunched a shoulder and spoke to Regidor. "Now you're grumpy because you should have thought of her joining you earlier, and didn't."

He faced her and spoke softly, no anger or impatience marring his tone. "Do you want to ride in your bottle or walk with us?"

Her eyes widened, and her lips parted as she took in a quick, small breath. She glanced down the dark tunnel and shivered. Her chin tilted up, and she slid off the boulder. As always, her movements were smooth and fluid. "I prefer to ride in comfort, thank you."

He unstopped the container. She transfigured into her vapor form and flowed into the bottle. Regidor replaced the stopper and put the container in his pocket.

"Can she hear us while she's in there?" asked Bardon.

"She used to be able to, but her powers have diminished over the years." Regidor led the way down the tunnel, holding the light in front of him. "She used to be able to stay out of the bottle for longer periods of time without beginning to dissipate. She used to be able to perform minor acts of wizardry. She used to enjoy a good debate, especially when she thought she'd bested me."

"You're worried about her."

"I think she is dying."

They walked along in silence for a while, skulking through the earthen corridors, listening intently for anyone else who might be in the large burrows.

"Regidor," Bardon said after a long stretch. "Has Librettowit or Fen or Cam been able to uncover any solution? a spell? a recording of a similar circumstance such as Gilda's?"

The meech dragon did not turn but shook his head. "Like the plight of the sleeping knights, Gilda's end hinged on knowledge that apparently passed away with Wizard Risto. He cast the spell that placed her essence in a bottle. Presumably, he knew how to undo his enchantment."

"You're hoping to find something to help her, aren't you?"

"I hope for so much, Bardon, my friend. To free Gilda from her prison. To find other meech dragons who can tell me more of my heritage. To break the spell that put good men to sleep to keep them from fighting for justice and against oppression. And even to serve Paladin in some outrageously heroic deed." He turned slightly and flashed his toothy grin over his shoulder. "Perhaps we are destined to do all these things together."

Bardon smiled back. Odd as Regidor was, he always managed to lift Bardon's spirits.

Regidor turned a corner and disappeared from view.

"Oh, bother." His deep voice rolled back to Bardon. "Gilda was right. We should have fetched Kale to help us."

39

Dragons

Bardon heard Regidor's sword glide out of its sheath just as a sinister hiss reached his ears. He clipped the globe light to the edge of his tunic at the shoulder, drew his own weapon, and leapt around the corner. He landed, ready to fight, side by side with the meech dragon. Regidor's glowing orb floated next to his shoulder.

Of course he doesn't have to carry it. The holding device was for my benefit.

Bardon followed Regidor's gaze to a few feet beyond where he stood. Their globe lights cast a blue radiance on the pale skin of a cave dragon.

What type of cave dweller is this?

The animal guarded a three-way branch in the tunnel. The bulk of its body filled the lower half of all three openings. Both head and tail curled away from the men.

Bardon scowled and tightened his grip on the hilt of his sword.

Is it sleeping soundly enough for us to crawl over without waking it?

Bardon looked to Regidor. The meech appeared to examine the beast blocking their way. He picked up a fist-sized rock, held it shoulder high, and dropped it. The clatter as it hit echoed in the chamber.

The creature stirred.

Glad we didn't try climbing over. Now, we'll see just what type of cave dragon we are up against.

Muscles rippled under the unnaturally pale skin. It rolled to get its feet underneath and push to a stand. As it gained its feet, the neck slithered out from the tunnel where it had been resting. As long as the body, the thin shank supported a small head.

Snake dragon! What do I know about snake dragons? Not enough.

The dragon rocked back and forth on two short front legs as if preparing to pounce. Its serpentine neck swayed to and fro like the head of a hooded cobra. Large eyes, stunted wings, and a powerful long tail added to its monstrous appearance.

The creature hissed and struck at Regidor, mouth open and ready for a chunk of meech flesh. Regidor blocked the strike with his sword but did not injure the beast.

Bardon kept his eyes on the ugly dragon.

You're going to test me next, aren't you? You want to see if I'm as quick as Regidor here. Well, you ugly brute, I'm close to matching his skill, and I'm ready for you.

The creature continued to sway on its front legs and bob its head. Bardon became impatient. "Regidor, couldn't you tell this monster that we're friendly?"

"Already did," answered Regidor. "It's not buying it."

The beast made a double strike, first a thrust aimed at Bardon's leg, then another at Regidor's arm.

Both men protected themselves with precise parries.

Regidor chuckled. "I guess we now know why...umph...there was no sign of activity...in this part of the warren."

Each sentence had to be timed so as not to interfere with their efforts to remain unscathed by the increasingly hostile lunges of the dragon.

Bardon fended off the next blow. The dragon drew back and hissed. "While you're mindspeaking with...this obstacle, you might mention that you, too, are...a dragon."

"I'm as much related to that creature as you are to a goat in a barnyard."

"Then why not just blow your fire breath on it, and let's get on with this rescue."

"It seems to me a shame to slay it for being in its own home."

"Any suggestions?" Bardon jumped to avoid a hit.

"I've given it lots of suggestions. It really just wants to eat us."

The squire looked the snake dragon in the eye. "Sorry. We really don't have time to stay for dinner."

Bardon held off striking the beast in a way that would do permanent damage. He believed Regidor should give the signal. *I hope we don't dally with this creature long enough for it to strike a lucky blow. Better to kill it and get on with our search for the tumanhofer.*

"What makes you think Kale would have been useful in this situation?" Bardon asked.

"She *is* the Dragon Keeper. You would be amazed at what influence she has over animals, especially, of course, over dragons."

The creature slammed the side of the tunnel with its tail, causing a shower of dirt to fall on their heads.

"That does it." Regidor sputtered dirt from his mouth. "Kale might be able to turn you from your wicked ways, but I sure can't." He sprang forward with his arm up, ready for a downward slash. Before the air cleared of dust, the dragon's body lay on the tunnel floor, minus its head.

Bardon sheathed his sword. While Regidor cleaned his before putting it away, the squire unfastened his light and thrust it into each branch of the tunnel. In each opening, the light illuminated several yards.

Bardon peered beyond to darkness. "Any idea which way we should go?"

Regidor pointed at the first tunnel. "From the smell, I'd say that leads to the dragon's lair."

Bardon sniffed. "And it wasn't a very good housekeeper."

The meech pointed to the opposite tunnel. "That one has the freshest air, so I would assume it leads back to the outside after a very short distance."

"So," said Bardon, "the middle one probably stretches deep into the ground, into the enemy's territory, and is, therefore, our logical choice."

Regidor picked up his light orb. "That was my assumption."

Bardon shrugged, heaved a sigh of resignation, and headed into the middle burrow.

Dug out of the earth to accommodate grawligs, the burrows were plenty big, even for Regidor's seven-foot height. Regidor and Bardon, ignoring many narrower passageways that branched off from the central core, kept marching forward.

"Regidor, have you noticed the change in the walls for the past mile or so?"

"I have. We're moving through rock—mountain instead of hills."

Regidor meandered through the large corridors, examining the stone.

When Bardon studied the walls, he saw only long grooves spiraling down one wall, traversing the floor, returning up the opposite, and crossing the ceiling. To him, these markings looked like the impressions left in wood when a screw was inserted, then removed.

What is Regidor up to? Does he see something in this odd pattern etched in the limestone? Are we lost? Would he admit it if we were?

The squire cleared his throat. "Somehow, I don't think we are headed to where the grawligs have our tumanhofer."

"And I don't think these tunnels were crafted by grawligs."

Does that matter? Bardon studied his friend for a moment.

Regidor's mind is engaged on the uniqueness of these burrows and not on our mission. The question is, How do I bring him back to our original purpose without ruffling his intellectual feathers? I'm not sure there is a way.

"Aren't we supposed to be rescuing Bromptotterpindosset?" Bardon asked.

"Hmm? What did you say?" Regidor stopped and raised his orb to scrutinize the wall. "Look at this, Bardon. This is writing."

Bardon came closer, held up his light, and peered at the marks in the stone. "What language is it?"

"Ancient Kere."

"Can you read it?"

"Hmm?" Regidor squinted as his eyes moved back and forth over the lines of writing.

"I said, 'Can you read it?' But it looks like you are doing just that. So you need not answer. That is, if you're too busy."

"What?" Regidor shook his head and turned away from the wall. "Are you being sarcastic? No, I can't read it. I was scanning the text to see if I recognized a word or even a syllable."

"How do you know it's Kere?"

"Saw some in one of Librettowit's old books."

"You don't have a clue as to what it means?"

"Oh yes. I believe it's a warning about a two-headed dragon."

"You said you couldn't read the script."

"I can't." Regidor moved over a few feet and shone his light on another section of the wall. "They drew pictures."

Scratched into the soft rock, elaborate line drawings depicted a party of men fighting a two-headed dragon, losing most of their fighting party, and the few survivors hobbling away. By the size and shape of the men, Bardon guessed they were all tumanhofers.

"This is very interesting, Regidor, but we still have a tumanhofer of our own to track." The squire waved his hand back the way they had come. "We haven't seen a sign of a grawlig. We haven't even seen a drud-dum. I think we should retrace our steps and try another direction to find Bromptotterpindosset."

"I would agree, except we now feel a fresh air draft coming from ahead of us."

"We do?"

"I do." Regidor moved on down the burrow.

Bardon made a face but followed him. "How long ago do you think that picture was made?"

"Hard to say," Regidor answered over his shoulder. "I would guess before tumanhofers began recording their adventures on paper."

"Is it unusual for tumanhofers to write in Kere?"

"We don't know that the message was written at the same time as the picture. The words may have been there before the picture was drawn. In that case, the picture explains the text. Or the picture could have been scratched onto the walls first. Then someone came along to explain the picture with words."

Bardon pondered the possible order of events. He didn't see how the timing made much difference, but it was the kind of thing Regidor liked to dwell on. "Well, it all seems to be done for naught."

Regidor laughed. "Because all that explaining, in one way or another, has left us without any understanding?"

"Uh-huh."

"You are agreeing to keep me from further expounding on the subject."

This time Bardon responded with more enthusiasm. "Uh-huh."

Regidor lifted his hands and let them drop. "What am I to do with you?"

Bardon laughed. "Leave me as I am. Not everyone has a compulsion to understand everything."

"You misunderstand, Squire. It is not the compulsion to find answers that drives me, but rather the contentedness after I fully comprehend that satisfies me."

"Nevertheless, my meech friend, I am content to allow you to know it all while I know enough to answer my immediate questions."

Regidor shook his head. "Someday I will find my meech relatives and have a discussion that lasts for days."

Bardon groaned at the prospect, and Regidor grinned.

They walked on, and Bardon finally felt the slight, fresh breeze that Regidor had detected earlier. The passageways leading off to one side or the other became more numerous. Regidor checked Glas's diary once again and insisted the largest tunnel was the most likely to lead them to the grawligs' meeting ground.

Bardon spotted the next etching in the wall. Upon examination, the picture was remarkably like the first.

"Another two-headed dragon," said Bardon.

"Or the same two-headed dragon."

Bardon shook his head and twisted his mouth. "I'm getting an uncomfortable feeling, Reg. You know, there is the possibility that this two-headed dragon is still roaming around these tunnels."

"The thought had occurred to me as well."

Bardon pointed to the picture. "It looks a bit like the snake dragon you killed at the entrance to this part of the mountain. Except for the two heads, of course."

"Of course. And that thought had occurred to me as well."

"Has it occurred to you that we have not rescued our tumanhofer? We are probably lost in this mountain full of tunnels. There may be a two-headed dragon waiting for us. And our time is running out for finding and rescuing the knights."

"I have thought of all those things."

Bardon quite easily identified the stony mask on his friend's face. He was sure his own face held a similar expression. A person of his rank in society did not allow frustration to contort his features. Nor did he let words explode from his mouth in unrefined anger. The two stared at each other, their breathing audible in the silence.

Regidor scratched the ridge above his eyes. "Do you want to go back?

Bardon pressed his lips in a firm line as he considered their options.

"No," he said at last. "Let's follow this to the end."

The main tunnel curved to the right, no longer carved in a straight line, to some unknown destination.

"I've decided," said Regidor, "that this is an abandoned tumanhofer settlement."

Bardon compared what he had seen here with a visit he had made to the tumanhofer city of Dael. "I think you're right. It must be very old and must not have been occupied for centuries."

"Longer than that. I don't recall seeing any mention of this in Librettowit's history books."

A heavy object—a blur of white—a tail!—slammed down between them as they passed a wide tunnel. The animal sped away, the tail disappearing into darkness.

They had their swords drawn. They listened to the heavy tread of the attacker as it moved farther and farther away.

"What was that?" asked Bardon.

"I think we may have found the snake dragon's big brother."

"Did you get a look at it?"

"Only the pasty white dragon tail." Regidor replaced his sword in its sheath. "I wonder if it has two heads."

"I wonder if it's hungry."

40

LITTLE DETAILS

Traveling through the burrows became a long and tedious task. One tunnel looked much like the last, and the monotony of the walls wore on the squire's nerves.

"I'd much rather be flying," he told Regidor.

"Ah yes. When I first started flying on my own I had no stamina, no endurance. Now I do pretty well at the long stretches."

Bardon nodded, figuring his friend understated the case. He knew Regidor to be extremely agile and stronger for his size than any creature he had ever encountered.

"Here's another drawing and the same type of writing beside it." Bardon pointed to the inscription on the wall.

"Each battle scene is a tad different, Squire." Regidor examined the scratched image. "In this depiction, there are seventeen tumanhofers battling the two-headed dragon. In the one previous to this, there were twelve, and in the first, there were only seven."

"You counted?"

"Well, of course, I counted." Regidor ran his fingers over the unreadable words. "The depth of this carving is deeper than the first or the second. The number of lines are less."

"Anything else?"

"Yes, the dragon has been larger in proportion to the crudely drawn men in each successive picture."

"Regidor, you amaze me."

The meech dragon smiled over his shoulder. "I used to amaze myself, but I am getting used to my genius as time goes by."

Bardon stared at his friend for a moment before he recognized the humor in Regidor's eyes.

Laughing, Bardon sank down to the floor. "I'm ready for a little break." He pulled out his water flask and a packet of food.

Regidor sat beside him. Both of them leaned against the rock wall, and the meech pulled out his own provisions. He handed the squire an extra package.

The squire peeked inside. "Daggarts. Thanks." He shifted to rest more comfortably against one of the spiraling grooves. "Have you thought about what was used to burrow these tunnels?"

"Yes."

"And what was your conclusion?"

"Didn't have one." Regidor chewed a bite of bread. "What kind of cheese do you have?"

"Bordenaut."

"I'll trade you criantem for the bordenaut."

"Deal."

They exchanged hunks of cheese and sat resting while they ate. When he had almost completed his repast, Regidor brought out Glas's diary. He thumbed rapidly through the pages and slowed down when he came to the section about the burrow. He skimmed several pages.

"That's what I thought."

"What?" asked Bardon as he rolled the crumbs of his lunch in the paper it had come in.

"Glas never mentions the two-headed dragon, the pictures or words etched into the walls, or the unusual formation of the grooves in the stone."

"What does that mean? That he wasn't very observant?"

Regidor shook his head. "This section is inconsistent with the careful notations on other pages of his diary." Regidor closed the book and tapped the cover with the claw tip of one finger. "I suspect that Glas was never in one of these tunnels. He probably recorded what someone had told him, not what he had seen with his own eyes."

"That means we have been depending on a map drawn blindly."

"That doesn't mean it is entirely inaccurate." Regidor stood. "Let's move on. The quality of the air is improving steadily. We should reach an opening to the outside very soon."

Bardon stood, stuffed his trash into an inner pocket, and dusted his hands off on his trousers. "I'm eager to get this underground journey over with."

Regidor took the lead. Bardon followed six to ten feet behind him. They passed several tunnels branching off to the right, but none on the left. Ahead there seemed to be an intersection where a tunnel completely crossed the main one. Bardon heard a whoosh like a sudden intake of breath, and then a huge white stone rolled across their path in the junction ahead, blocking the way.

Both men drew their swords. Regidor leapt to Bardon's side and turned so that they stood back to back. They listened and waited.

A scrape across the stone floor gave away the location of whomever or whatever else waited in the warren. The sound repeated, closer.

Regidor sniffed the air. "It is the same dragon who startled us with a whack of its tail some time ago."

"I suppose we are going to find out if it has two heads."

Regidor grinned and nodded. "And whether it is hungry."

The creature approached them from the tunnel they had just passed through.

"Ah," said Regidor as it came closer, but still could not be seen. "It has two heads, and it is hungry. They are quite interested in having something besides druddum for their next meal."

"I had noted the almost nonexistent druddum population in this warren."

"Indeed."

"So interesting that you can mindspeak with our opponents." Bardon breathed deeply, relaxing his muscles in preparation for the fight. He flexed the fingers that held the hilt of his sword. "It would, perhaps, be more useful if they responded to your eloquence by abandoning their intent to devour us."

"The problem with mindspeaking with these snake dragons is they don't join in the conversation."

Two scuffing noises indicated the beast was much closer.

"I," Regidor continued, "make perfectly reasonable suggestions. And I am ignored."

"For instance?"

"I suggest that we taste ghastly. One head tells the other that it will be nice to each have its own body on which to munch. I say we are mighty warriors who will hack their sluggish, overgrown body to bits. It says it needs to approach with greater stealth."

"It's using quite an elaborate vocabulary."

"No, no, Bardon. It is my vocabulary. I am merely interpreting the grisly mental images that I detect in its feeble brains."

"So it isn't a particularly smart dragon."

"Correct. Both heads together couldn't spell *cat*." Regidor pointed with the tip of his sword. "There, in the tunnel, just out of view, it stands, watching us."

Bardon heard the hoarse chorus of breathing from the two heads.

"It was smart enough to block our way, then circle back to attack us."

"Merely copying someone else's strategy."

"Whose strategy?"

"One of the tumanhofer hunting parties."

Bardon considered the ramifications of Regidor's statement. *This must be the original two-headed monster. A descendant wouldn't have memory of a battle with tumanhofers eons ago. Long memory, but not very clever. There must be a way to trick this creature.*

"Regidor, I recall hearing of Wizard Risto doing a particularly clever visual deception. He created an illusion in which he, or several images of himself, stood about the room."

"A good idea, Squire."

Bardon blinked and saw not one meech dragon standing beside him with sword drawn, but two. He turned his head to the other side and saw three more replicas of the original Regidor.

"Now be careful," warned Regidor, "and don't swing your sword through the real me. Piercing one of my fellows would not injure them, but—"

The two-headed dragon bolted out of the dark. In three strides, it loomed over them. Both heads swiveled, trying to pick a target.

"Not identical twins," observed Regidor.

"Definitely not," agreed Bardon.

The skin of the dragon's left neck was wrinkled, with an ugly purple mottling over a greenish tan under-color. Smooth, ebony skin covered the other neck. The left head reminded Bardon of a gourd with a point on top, and it wobbled a bit on its perch. The underbite of this distorted head exposed a row of jagged, crooked teeth with gaps where several had fallen out.

The roundish head of the right side had a crest of burnished copper scales. It sported a strong jaw line and a mouth full of shiny, pointed white teeth.

The well-formed head swooped down, mouth open as it tried to bite one of the Regidor illusions. Its teeth snapped together, holding nothing.

Bardon took advantage of its bewilderment and charged. He slashed the creature's neck and chest, then ran out of reach. He turned and surveyed the situation, looking for his next opportunity. The wound he inflicted on the two-headed dragon barely trickled blood. The squire didn't have an opportunity to puzzle over why his attack had done so little damage.

The weaker head swung wildly through the line of Regidor images. It whipped through three and came in contact with solid flesh on the fourth. Regidor was thrown off balance and fell on his back. He used his position to strike a blow to the underside of the beast's chin. It roared and pulled back.

While the uglier head retreated, the stronger, smarter-looking head glanced down at Regidor. With teeth bared, it struck. Regidor rapped it sharply on the snout with his blade. It reared up as the weaker head came down for another strike at Regidor. The heads came together with a re-sounding thud. The meech rolled to the side and sprang to his feet.

Regidor breathed rapidly, and with every breath, more images of himself appeared. Bardon's eyes widened as he watched. The meech dragon wizard had improved upon his first attempt. The first set of Regidor images had moved in synchronization, all doing exactly the same thing as the original. These images moved around the room independently.

Bardon recognized what each illusion was doing. Forms. In years of training, Bardon had done these same routines himself in a state of mind that was detached from the motions. Now these images of Regidor went through the forms in mindless repetitions.

The momentarily stunned dragon shook its heads and gazed, glassy-eyed, around the tunnel. The head closest to Bardon bobbed, sinking slowly until its underdeveloped chin rested on the ground a few feet from where the squire stood.

"Uh-oh," said Regidor.

"What?"

"The other head is not too happy with what we've done to his partner."

"We didn't do that." Bardon pointed to the unconscious part on the floor and then at the still functioning part looming above them. "It did. It knocked it out with its own hard head."

Regidor laughed. "A concise summary of the circumstances. But to this menacing head it is a minor detail. Unfortunately, the conscious part of the beast does not take responsibility for the injury to its other half. It blames us."

"Well, what's it planning to do?" Bardon eyed the creature.

"It's trying to figure that out. It's never fought solo before." Regidor yelled and jumped to the side as the beast's head came slamming down. "I guess he's not going to bother to do any more thinking." He swung his sword and hit the creature between the eyes. The blade left a deep scratch.

"Our problem is going to be piercing this thick skin," Regidor commented to Bardon as he danced away from the snapping mouth. "You might join me in this fracas. I'm not so conceited that I have to fight this thing alone."

Bardon stepped over the sleeping head and joined Regidor in his defense against the still-active, stronger head. The effects of the collision between heads had worn off this one. Instead of dazed, the creature was enraged.

It repeatedly thrust its open mouth at the two-legged warriors, snapping and snarling and keeping Regidor and Bardon jumping. The men made numerous hits. They battered the dragon with their swords, leaving bloody marks on its face and neck. But the wounds did not inhibit the dragon's fury.

"Aim for its eyes and the inside of its mouth," suggested Bardon.

"I *am* aiming for those tender spots. I believe this beast has a few more years of fighting experience than we do. Ouch!"

Bardon glanced at his comrade. Regidor's foreleg bled from a straight-line wound. It didn't look like the jagged tear teeth would make.

"He bit you?" asked Bardon.

"No! The confounded animal slapped my own sword against my foreleg."

"Not a good idea, Reg. We're having enough trouble subduing this beast without your loaning him the use of your weapon."

Bardon felt something painful clamp down on his calf. He looked to see that the ugly half was awake and active and biting his leg.

The few teeth this head had left were sharp, and they penetrated the leather of his boot, pricking his leg. He had half a moment to think he was glad it wasn't the other head holding his leg. When he attempted to strike a blow, the animal hoisted him in the air and swung him over Regidor's head. The more attractive head took affront at his recovered partner getting in the way. It swung to the side, slamming into Bardon and the mouth holding him upside down.

An opening in the dragon's defense allowed Regidor an opportunity to attack. He flipped into the air. As he somersaulted over the rounder, crested head, he slashed downward, slicing the creature's eye. The meech landed on the weaker head and managed a deep thrust through the eye into the brain. The beast jerked, letting go of its prize.

Bardon sailed up toward the ceiling. He landed with a whump on a

ledge and rolled onto his stomach to peer over the edge. His sword lay on
the floor below. He pulled out his darts and began menacing the brighter
head of the dragon while his meech friend dealt with the other. Bardon
aimed his darts at the eyes.

Regidor withdrew his sword from the other head and stabbed again.
The snake dragon thrashed, trying to dislodge the awful attacker. Regidor
slid down the neck, taking his sword with him. When he reached the
back, Regidor turned and lifted the underdeveloped wing. He thrust his
sword into the tender flesh beneath. Another thrust, and blood spurted.
He'd hit a main artery.

Bardon ran out of darts and sat up. He realized a section of the wall
behind him opened into another room. One look caused his heart to race.
He turned back to shout to Regidor, but his friend still needed to admin-
ister the killing blow.

The meech pushed the dragon's head back and exposed its neck. With
the point of his blade, he pierced the jugular vein. He moved to the other
lethargic head and did the same. Then he backed away from the snake
dragon and let it die. When the beast shuddered and expelled its last
breath, Regidor gazed up to where Bardon sat on the edge of a lip of stone.

Bardon grinned. "Good work, Reg."

"Enjoying the view?" asked Regidor. He looked with disgust at the
blood soaking the front of his cape, shirt, and pants.

"Yes," answered Bardon. "And I've made the most wonderful discov-
ery up here."

Regidor looked up again, tilted his head, and cocked the ridge over
one eye.

"A hole," Bardon answered the unasked question.

"A hole?"

"More like a doorway."

"A doorway?"

Bardon nodded. "To a room."

Regidor sighed noisily. "A room?"

Bardon smiled. "Filled with lightrocks and…sleeping knights."

41

A Castle

Even before they entered the chamber, Bardon heard the roar of falling water. Once inside the stone room, the noise drowned out every other sound. Draperies in rich, dark burgundy covered the windows, so he could not see the waterfall that dominated the room with its din.

Regidor and Bardon circled the vaulted hall without saying a word. The knights stood, sat, and reclined around the room as if they were visiting in someone's home. Only the knights did not breathe, their closed eyes saw nothing, and their skin felt hard like marble and cold like ice.

Twelve. Twelve young knights exiled from their lives.

The room itself looked like the great hall of an old castle, dusty and smelling of mold. Under the layer of disuse, the chamber exhibited age-old elegance.

Regidor plunged into an investigation of everything he saw. He examined books, furniture, the walls, the sleeping knights, the candles, everything, in a rush.

Bardon's second slow walk around the room included a careful study of all the knights. These men did not appear as statues, since their skin tones looked natural. Two urohm knights sat on the floor next to the curtained windows. Their heads leaned back against the wall, halfway to the ceiling. One tumanhofer knight sat in a chair too tall for him. An untouched tea tray sat on the table at his elbow. No mariones, kimens, or doneels had been captured. Five emerlindians and four o'rants made up the remaining knights.

"Look at these two emerlindians, Reg," Bardon called to his friend. "They're brothers, maybe even twins."

Regidor left the picture that had caught his attention and came to examine the two sleeping knights.

"Definitely," he said. "They probably looked more alike as boys. Their lives have marked their faces."

"I wonder," said Bardon, "if they are Jilles and Joffa."

"You said Joffa was killed in an ambush."

Bardon nodded.

Even though both had raised their voices, many of their words were drowned in the noise of the cascading water outside. This roaring water-fall claimed Bardon's attention as the meech hurried off to inspect a tea service.

Long, narrow windows lined one wall. Bardon moved aside a set of dusty drapes to consider thick, beveled glass set in movable frames. He stepped up on the deep ledge of a window and tried to wrench it open. The old frame would not budge.

"Reg, I could use some help here," he shouted.

After Bardon's second call to break Regidor's concentration, the meech dragon pushed a heavy chest under the window. The deep ledge was too narrow for both of them to stand on. Regidor examined the frame and then removed a bottle of oil from his hollow. He poured this slick lubricant down the side grooves where the window stuck in the wooden track. He put two fingers of each hand at the top of the grooves. After a moment, he drew back.

"Try it now." Regidor gestured with his hands as well as shouted. The tumult of falling water obscured their words.

Bardon lifted the window easily. "You're handy to have around, Reg."

The meech just grinned and returned the bottle of oil to the hollow.

"What do you see out there?"

Bardon pushed aside thick vines that had completely covered the opening and peered out. A fine spray of water landing in cold droplets on his face startled him. A cascade of water flowed over the building from a narrow river. The water splashed in what looked like a deep pool at the base of the castle and then sped away in white-water rapids.

"I can see the waterfall. It appears to plummet over the end of the castle. We're at the front of the building, near the top." He leaned out the window. "From the position of the sun, I'd say it's late afternoon and we're at the eastern end of the castle. There's so much growth covering the walls, it's hard to distinguish the mountain from the castle. Both are made out of the same type of stone. Who would build their home so that one end is perpetually wet?"

"Let's explore. We need to find Bromptotterpindosset. Perhaps we'll discover the answer to other questions along the way." Regidor motioned for Bardon to come out of the window and jump down. The meech dragon replaced him on the windowsill. "Let me try something," he yelled.

Bardon did not see his friend do anything, but the sound of the waterfall faded. The roar became distant, as if it were over a mountain ridge and in the next valley.

Regidor jumped down, and Bardon climbed back into the window. The water still cascaded over the rocks and part of the castle.

"What did you do?" asked Bardon, without having to shout.

"I just repaired a sound barrier. I got to thinking that the people who lived here surely didn't listen to that noise constantly." Regidor gestured toward the window. "When I looked outside, I could see the fragmented barrier. It was a simple thing to bind up the loose ends."

He flashed his large and charming smile. "I have a great deal of practice with sound barriers. Smaller ones than this one, of course. But they came in handy with Toopka's constant jabbering, Wizard Fenworth's tendency to fuss, and Librettowit's courting of Taylaminkadot."

"As I said before, old friend, you come in handy." Bardon lowered the window and jumped down. "Our exploration of this oddity will be much more pleasant now that we can hear each other."

Bardon looked at the statuelike knights. "I wonder if they are aware we're here."

"No, I wouldn't think so."

"Do you think any of them resemble Kale?"

Regidor's eyes narrowed. "Yes, I, too, thought perhaps her missing father could be here." He looked carefully at each o'rant's face. "No, I can't say that one looks like our Kale."

"We'd best get busy. We can't do anything for the knights right now."

Over and over again, the empty rooms and the signs of neglect proved their assumption that the castle was deserted. They explored the upper floors and those below. The building consisted of seven floors and three turrets that extended two stories above the seventh floor.

They thought it odd that the chambers seemed to be mostly for entertaining. On the ground floor, a grand ballroom stretched from one end of the structure to the other. A raised platform would have accommodated a small orchestra.

A few smaller, out-of-the-way rooms might have been servant stations where maids and footmen stored supplies and prepared teacarts. But they saw no kitchen, no bedchambers, no laundry, nothing practical or designed for the background functioning of such a huge establishment.

A storage basement sprawled under the entire structure, but aside from a few pieces of furniture, nothing was stored there. Large-leafed, rope-thick vines covered all the windows. Regidor called this lush ivy heirdosh and said it was poisonous if consumed.

The doors to the outside would not open, even with Regidor's wizardly help.

"Warded, I suspect," said the meech after another unsuccessful attempt to get out of the building and explore the grounds.

"Isn't it more customary to place a spell on the entryways to keep people out rather than to keep them in?" asked Bardon.

Regidor raised both ridges over his eyes. "This whole setup is rather unusual." He waved his forefeet at the area surrounding them. "Elaborate dining rooms, but no kitchen. Elegant soiree chambers, drawing rooms, salons, music rooms, and grand halls for entertaining hundreds of guests, but no bedchambers. No library, no study, no housekeeper's quarters. It's almost as if part of the castle is missing." He furrowed his brow as he continued his list. "No stables, no wine cellar, no armory. As it is, this establishment could not function."

After exploring the part of the castle where the air was relatively dry, they ventured into the rooms where moisture clung to the walls and furnishings. Their feet slipped on a marble floor slick with a thin sheen of mud. Plants grew along the walls and cascaded across the floor as if nature had decided to take over the décor.

When they came to what they thought would be the last wall of the castle, they found massive doors. Opening this giant portal revealed another section of castle directly behind the waterfall.

Here they found servants' quarters. Upon further exploration, they identified many different craft rooms where obviously things had been made to accommodate the needs of the people living in the castle. At one time, these halls had produced everything from linen and leather, garments and furniture, cheese and jerky, to horseshoes and armor.

After they had walked from floor to floor, Regidor stopped and leaned against a wall. "This raises even more questions."

"Indeed," said Bardon. "When was this castle inhabited? And by whom? I see evidence of urohms as well as o'rants, mariones, and tumanhofers."

"The herb room looked like it had been run by an adept emerlindian."

Bardon pointed in the direction of the halls holding looms. "Doneels had a hand in the weaving of fabric and fashioning clothes and jewelry."

"Where were the gardens for food, the pastures for the animals?" asked Regidor.

"Was this fortress occupied five hundred years ago or five thousand?"

Regidor tugged on the edge of a tapestry. "If it was five thousand years ago, why hasn't it all disintegrated?"

Bardon put his fists on his hips and slowly turned, surveying the room, still amazed by the overall grandeur of this deserted castle. "If it was only five hundred years ago, why are there no recorded histories, no legends passed down through the generations, and not even a mention of it in the ballads?"

"What is the name of this castle?"

"Why was it abandoned?"

The two warriors looked at each other, shrugged, grinned, and said in unison, "We don't know."

Bardon sighed. "We still have to find Bromptotterpindosset."

Regidor reached into his cape and pulled Glas's diary from the hollow. "The map clearly shows the grawlig meeting field at the end of that burrow."

"It doesn't show a castle?"

"No castle." Regidor shook his head without looking up.

"We must have been in the wrong burrow all along, or we made a wrong turn."

Regidor studied the page in the diary and shook his head again as he contemplated what he saw. "There were not that many turns."

"You said Glas drew that map on hearsay."

Regidor nodded. "But there must be a tincture of truth to substantiate the drawing, or Glas would not have included it. He seems to have been a meticulous recorder of his explorations." He snapped the small, leather-bound volume shut. "Let's keep looking."

"Where and for what?"

"For answers. I suspect," he said, pointing to the west wall, "that there is another set of massive doors somewhere."

"That would lead us into the side of the mountain I could see from the window. It was a vine-covered, sheer cliff face."

Regidor held a finger in the air and started for the staircase they had climbed. "It *looked* like a vine-covered, sheer cliff face. Let's retrace our steps to the doors that lead back to the first part of the castle."

Bardon followed as Regidor bounded down the wide stairs at a rapid clip.

Regidor called over his shoulder, his voice charged with enthusiasm. "I want to get on the outside of this castle and view it from that perspective."

When they reached the massive doors, Regidor walked directly across the great hall and began probing the thick layer of vines.

Reluctantly, Bardon followed. He reached between the palm-sized leaves and heavy stems. His fingers touched smooth plaster. He moved over a foot and tried again. His fingertips brushed carved wood. Exploring with his hand, he came to the conclusion he had found the doors Regidor wanted.

"Right here, Reg."

Bardon got out his knife and began chopping through the heavy vegetation even before the meech dragon confirmed his suspicion. The heavy vines were remarkably healthy. He used his blade to saw through some of the thicker branches. Regidor worked beside him, using a claw to sever each limb. By himself, Bardon would have worked several hours. With Regidor employing some wizard's trick, in minutes they removed the vegetation barring their way.

Regidor also opened the massive doors by some method Bardon did not quite perceive.

In this wing they found the personal quarters of whoever had owned the castle. Bedchambers, a study and library, a solarium, a hothouse, and smaller parlors occupied three floors.

"You will have to repair the sound barrier on this side of the castle, Regidor. I can barely hear myself."

"Let's open a window, then." Regidor's voice came clearly into Bardon's mind.

The view, when they got the window opened and cleared, was exactly like what they'd seen from the other side.

Bardon frowned and shouted. "This castle blends into the mountain so that you can't tell it's here."

"Makes our mysterious castle all the more mysterious." Regidor looked outside. *"The barrier is torn between here and the falls. I'll repair it in a moment."* He turned to the back of the room. *"We have windows on two sides instead of just one. Let's see what is out there."*

Now that they had experience opening the stubborn windows, it didn't take long to throw open the sash. The first window they opened had let in the roar of the waterfall. This window let in the roar of grawligs at play.

42

VIEW FROM A TURRET

"So, we've found them after all," said Regidor as he slapped Bardon on the back.

The squire squeezed to one side so his friend could lean out of the window and examine the courtyards.

Regidor scowled. "I haven't spotted Bromptotterpindosset, have you?"

"Over there, by the fire pit," Bardon said. "I hope that doesn't indicate they've chosen him for their next meal."

"You can never tell with grawligs." The meech jumped down from the windowsill. "We better find a way out of this castle so we can rescue him."

They dashed down the wide, curving staircase and tried the doors to the outside.

"Warded," said Regidor, "just like the doors in the other wing."

"Let's try reaching the top of one of the turrets. You can fly out, and I can probably climb down those vines."

They sprinted back up the staircase and then climbed the twisted steps inside a small, stuffy tower. When they reached the top, they spotted a trapdoor in the ceiling. Bardon climbed the remaining steps built into the stone wall and felt around the edges for a latch. When he found nothing securing the square door, he put his shoulder to it. Surprised when it did not move, he tried again, grunting. The trapdoor did not give way.

"Warded," he said as he stepped off the ladder and onto the last platform at the top of the turret.

Regidor reached up and placed his forefoot on the wood. "Yes, it's warded. But the ward was cast from the ground floor. This is probably the weakest point, being farthest away from the origin. Let me try to break through."

Bardon waited. Twelve tiny windows spaced evenly around the circular wall gave him views in every direction. Out of one he saw the waterfall. Out of another he saw the opposite wing of the castle and had to look carefully to see that it was not just a sheer cliff face mostly covered with heavy vegetation. He saw the sun setting to the west. He saw the grawligs cavorting in the courtyard below, and he saw another stone mountainside behind their festivities.

"Regidor, I believe there is yet another wing to this castle."

The meech dragon grunted. "Busy."

Bardon stared at the wall he suspected to be manmade and not nature's cliff until he could make out a few of the windows. He looked at the skyline, and after some study, he could distinguish the turrets, a battlement, and twin towers.

"That's done," said Regidor as he lifted the door.

The hinges creaked, and dirt, dried leaves, and dead bugs rained down on their heads.

"I'm glad I wasn't looking up," said Bardon.

Regidor sputtered. "I was." He stepped down and slapped at his clothes, knocking the debris away. "It has not been a good day for my wardrobe. Blood and dirt. Unacceptable embellishments to sophisticated attire."

Bardon blinked as Regidor's apparel vibrated at enormous speed. When the activity ceased, the meech was clean.

Regidor swept an open forefoot toward the ladder. "You may go first, Squire."

Bardon, in his grimy clothing, climbed out of the turret and peered over the chest-high wall. Regidor joined him. Below them the grawligs participated in a wild rumpus, beating drums, hooting in what might be considered a song, and dancing that consisted mostly of jumping up and down.

"They're certainly happy about something," Bardon observed.

"The simple pleasure of having stolen one of us away. After their humiliation in the ravine, they needed the exhilaration of pulling off some daring deed right beneath our noses."

"You sound as if you have studied them."

"Oh, we have. Wizard Cam Ayronn and I are writing a book on the mores and cultural structure of the lower races. Of course, so far our studies have only encompassed grawligs, ropma, and bisonbecks."

"Of course." Bardon couldn't contain the smile that broke out on his face. He knew he'd missed any chance he had of appearing serious.

Regidor spotted his smirk and returned a haughty stare. The coldness of the meech dragon's expression melted into a toothy grin. "Never mind, dear Bardon. You were not designed by Wulder to be an academician like Librettowit or Wizard Cam. You were not meant to be debonair like Sir Dar, or persistently friendly like N'Rae, or obnoxiously inquisitive like Ahnek."

"What was I meant to be, Regidor?"

"You don't know?"

"You know I don't. I've always known you see right through me. I don't particularly understand why you still choose to be my friend."

Regidor now scanned the sky as if he expected to see something. "I suppose you're talking about the facade you have created that gives the impression of being all-sufficient."

The smile dropped from Bardon's face. He now had the serious expression he had wanted a moment ago to tease his friend.

"I don't know that Wulder made me with what it takes to be a knight, Regidor. My sabbatical was important. I needed to know if I had enough in me to fulfill the vow I would make to Paladin to follow Wulder."

Regidor leaned against a parapet and crossed his forelegs over his chest. "You are saying that Wulder made a mistake when He designed you?"

"No, of course not." Bardon looked away from his friend's scrutiny and examined the western sky. The sun hovered over the horizon, displaying a red blaze of last-minute glory as it disappeared. "Of course it is

I who am at fault. I have failed to recognize what Wulder wants me to do. I try to be something that is not in my nature to be."

He glanced back at his friend. The meech rolled his eyes and pushed away from the wall. "You have failed to recognize that Wulder wants you to be the knight that is Sir Bardon, not Sir Dar. You are not like any of the heroes of our last quest. You are you."

Bardon looked away again.

Regidor came and put his hand on Bardon's shoulder. "You have also failed to recognize that Wulder fills you with what you need when you need it. What is within you at this moment is not sufficient to meet a need that will not arise until forty years hence."

The squire did not answer. Regidor's words sounded as if they might apply to someone else but not to Bardon.

Regidor clapped him on the shoulder. "Here comes my messenger."

Startled, Bardon looked to where Regidor pointed. A moonbird winged toward them and landed on the same parapet the meech had been leaning against. Bardon had seen kimens smaller than this large bird, whose feathers glowed white with an under-color of gray. Its head swiveled as it looked with piercing golden eyes, first at Regidor, then at Bardon, and back to the dragon. Its yellowish orange talons spread across the rock of the castle. It snapped its large beak together as if asking Regidor a question.

Regidor gazed into the beautiful creature's eyes for a long moment.

I don't suppose I should interrupt his commune with his bird friend, Bardon thought, *but speaking of messages, it would be convenient to send a message to our party.* "Good news—we've found the knights and our mapmaker."

I should tell Captain Anton to hold on for one more day. Technically, he should head back with our party in the morning. But we may be back with Bromptotterpindosset by midday.

Regidor touched the moonbird lightly on the chest, and then the creature flew away.

"Who was the message to?" asked Bardon.

"Captain Anton. Actually, it will go to N'Rae, who will relay it to Captain Anton."

"And the message said we have found the knights and should return tomorrow sometime with our missing tumanhofer." Bardon's anger hummed beneath the words.

Regidor's head shot around so that the two stared at each other.

"I see," said Regidor. "Yes, you're in charge of this expedition. I apologize. Kale's always onto me for being too independent. She says she will someday have me write the definition of *team* in a notebook a hundred times."

The tension drained out of Bardon's neck and shoulders. He wasn't sure if it was Regidor's ready apology that caused him to relax or the fact that Kale also became frustrated with the meech dragon's occasional high-handed manner.

"Um." Regidor uncharacteristically hesitated. "Would you like to outline our course of action?"

Bardon laughed. "Now you're deferring to my leadership?"

Regidor nodded. "Belatedly."

"Oh, Reg, Kale has taught you to do contrite very well."

The meech dragon chortled and managed to look even more sheepish.

Bardon studied the activity below and then crossed to the back of the corner turret. "We'll go down this side and meet by the garden wall. We can follow that with reasonable cover until we are within striking distance of the guards around Bromptotterpindosset. He doesn't look injured and should be able to travel. When we get closer and see what the setup looks like from the ground, mindspeak to him and tell him what is about to happen.

"Hopefully, your sudden appearance will give us enough time to free him and escape through the front gate. You can hold them within the enclosure easily enough to give me time to get him some distance away. Then fly to join us, and we'll determine if any further diversionary tactic is needed. Any questions or suggestions?"

Regidor's pointed teeth gleamed in the moonlight. "You did that quite well, Squire. Are you sure you don't have what is needed to become a knight?"

Bardon sighed and ran the fingers of one hand through his hair. "This is merely delineating a course of action."

"This," said Regidor, "is exactly what a knight does."

Bardon hopped up to sit on the turret wall and threw a leg over. "I'm climbing down these vines. Good-bye."

Regidor released his wings from the tight folds he kept them in as they lay against his back. The air blew Bardon's hair away from his face.

"And I will fly. A lot less work."

Bardon nodded and lowered himself over the edge. Regidor took to the air and glided noiselessly into the back courtyard.

The squire put his foot on a branch, testing it. Finding it strong enough to support his weight, he began a cautious, step-by-step climb down the side of the castle. Halfway down he placed his foot on a branch that seemed to melt under his weight. He moved over to assess another branch. This vine would not bear his weight either.

Bother. I'll have to inch back again. If I move more in this direction, I'll be in sight of the grawligs' little party.

He went up a ways and then scooted over the weak spot.

"Having a problem?"

Yes, Reg. Can you see the vines from where you are?

"Of course," he answered. *"I'm wondering why you are dancing around in that one spot. The vines are thick and sturdy there."*

They give under my weight.

"Odd. They shouldn't. Put your foot on one and push it down. I'll watch."

Bardon reached with his foot, found a branch, and shifted his weight. This vine felt thick beneath the sole of his boot. It had given a little, but Bardon decided to trust it. Still clinging to the vines next to his chest with both hands, he moved the other foot to follow the first.

"Careful, Squire. There's something underneath."

That something wrapped around both ankles and jerked. The vines dissolved in his hands, and Bardon slid into a hole in the wall. An explosion of lights told him he'd entered a gateway. Pressure built up in his lungs too fast to grab a last breath to hold on to. Usually, the sensation of going through a gateway was horizontal, a matter of a few steps, and the traveler determined when those steps were taken. This gateway opened up like the top of a well. Bardon did not walk, he fell. He did not travel a few steps, but down a long tunnel of variegated lights. The atmosphere stuck to him and slowed his descent. The lights dimmed, and he hit the side of the passageway. He realized the shaft had changed direction and now descended as a slope. He began to roll. The flashing lights returned right before Bardon tumbled out onto a planking of a cygnot tree.

Spread out, facedown on the firm weave of branches, he closed his eyes and enjoyed breathing.

A voice from above him brought his eyes wide open.

"Bardon, what are you doing here?"

PART TWO

Wizard's
Call

43

KALE

Kale swung down from one layer of the planking in Bedderman's Bog and sat cross-legged on the next.

"What do you think, Pat?" she said to a small brown minor dragon no bigger than a kitten. "Can it be fixed?"

The little dragon chewed thoughtfully on some bug he had captured and eyed the portal. She listened with her mind to the dragon's assessment of the damaged gateway. Her eyes widened. "Eight or nine thousand years old? Maybe Fenworth made it in his youth. Of course, he claims to be older than that, but I don't believe it. I think it's part of his confusion." She leaned back against the thick trunk of a cygnot tree. "This is such a boring assignment." She picked up a notebook and made an entry. First she marked the location of this gateway on a map of The Bogs, then numbered it. "Number fifty-six, approximate age eight to nine thousand years." She tapped her pen on the page. "You know Fen isn't going to accept such a broad estimation. Oh, I wish Reg were here. He would have this figured out in a trice."

Kale scooted closer to the opening and studied the fibers with which the gateway had been woven. She didn't touch them because they were actually made of a material similar to light. She preferred not to be shocked. And, she didn't want to accidentally fall through.

The task assigned her was to locate and catalog every gateway in The Bogs. It was a tedious chore, and sadly, she saw the necessity.

Fenworth was dying. Not a painful or difficult death, but as he put it, the end of this life and the beginning of the new. Once he had quit this world and stepped into the presence of Wulder, he would no longer be able to assist Kale. And he was leaving The Bogs to Kale. She would be its mistress and must be familiar with all its properties.

"This looks like the pattern woven in the Pordactic Period, and the strength of the fibers backs that up. I'll put down eight thousand, five hundred, twenty-five years. And as to the weaver of the gateway, it was not Fenworth. Fen believes in simplicity, unless it's his stay-at-home robes. Those are elaborate and beautiful."

She glanced down at her attire, black leggings, a smock shirt in a dull green, and, of course, her moonbeam cape. With a grin, she concentrated on the plain pants until they blossomed into loose-fitting silk trousers, shimmering in peacock colors. Her floppy blouse she changed into a fitted blue tunic embroidered with threads of gold. Under the tunic, she now wore a dazzling white long-sleeved shirt with sapphire snaps at the throat and wrists. Still not satisfied, she rearranged the embroidery on the tunic into a scene including a white palace, strutting peacocks, and dragons flying over her shoulder and across her back. She left the moonbeam cape alone.

A second minor dragon scampered out of the hanging moss. He chittered and flew to a branch of leaves above Kale's head. She looked up and smiled. "Hello, Gymn. Your tummy full?"

The green dragon smacked his lips and stretched out in a patch of sun filtering through the dense leaves above.

Kale turned back to her examination of the weave. "Strot. I think it was Strot who made this gateway." She tilted her head. "That's peculiar, though. Why would Strot be here in The Bogs making a portal? This clearly is the initial entry." She wrote her identification in the notebook and tapped the pen against her chin. "Now, where does it go? These broken strands would indicate north, and they were quite long, weren't they, Pat? Now they're so frayed and tangled, it's hard to know what to think." The brown dragon scrambled among the leaves. She put the pen and notebook down on the floor and faced the gateway squarely.

"Let's fix this, Pat. Maybe while we're weaving, we can determine the location of the other side."

The little brown dragon dropped the collection of tiny beetles he had in his forefeet and flew to Kale's shoulder. With the help of the fix-it dragon, she used her knowledge of wizardry to gather together the broken strands, form new matching strands, and work them into a smooth frame for the gateway.

"My," she said as she finished and let out a heavy sigh. "That covered quite a distance. All the way up to the Northern Reach. And the exit at the other end was most peculiar. Where's Filia?"

Almost immediately, a small, rosy pink dragon appeared from within the foliage. The creature looked far more delicate than Pat. Her pale wings, filigreed with silver and gold lines, were almost transparent. "Filia, do you remember anything about the Wizard Strot?… A mountain wizard. Yes, I remember that too… Murdered by Risto? Oh no, I don't think I knew that."

Kale again studied the gateway. "Two things I detect about this gateway, friends. The first is that it proceeds vertically instead of horizontally. Second, there is a device at the other side that literally pulls in anything that comes too close to the entrance." She tapped her pen again on her chin. "To what purpose would that be?"

She closed the book, stuck the pen in a pocket along its spine, and shoved them into a hollow in her cape.

"Now, where is everybody? It's time to go home. I'll ask Librettowit what he knows of this gateway and Strot."

Pat had again gathered a meal. He reluctantly released the drummer-bug he'd been about to devour and followed Kale.

"Metta? Ardeo?" she called.

A purple and a gray dragon came through the planking from the cygnot floor below.

"Dibl? Dibl! Wouldn't you know he'd be the last to come?" She walked to the tree trunk, gave a little jump, latched on to the hole in the flooring above, and pulled herself onto the next layer. Her stylish pants caught on a twig. Annoyed, she carefully unhooked the cloth so it would not tear, and stood up.

"Dibl, where are you?"

The yellow and orange dragon swooped down from the branches above and ruffled her short curly hair. "Oh, cease your antics, you naughty little beast." She laughed but stopped short when she heard a thump from the landing below.

Dropping to her knees, she peered through the hole. In front of the gateway, a halfling stretched out on his stomach. She knew those pointed ears and coal black hair.

"Bardon, what are you doing here?"

44

Joining Forces

Bardon pulled his face out of the planking and looked up, trying to locate Kale. "Where are you?"

"Up here."

He rolled over on his side and peered into the woven branches above him.

Kale giggled. "Here."

He shifted his gaze, following the bright sound of her voice, and spotted her face upside down with curls bouncing around her ears.

"Are you all right?" she asked. "You look kind of stunned. Did you whack your head coming through that crazy gateway?"

She disappeared for a moment, then her legs came through the opening. The colorful material of a wild pair of bloomers fluttered as she swung for a second and then dropped to the floor. A stream of dragons followed her, all small, all chittering wildly in their excitement.

Bardon pushed himself to a sitting position as Kale sprang across the planking to his side.

"Are you hurt?" she asked. She crouched next to him and touched his arm.

"No."

"Where did you come from?"

"A castle in the Northern Reach."

"Strot's castle." Kale nodded vigorously and then looked to one of the dragons, a pink one. "Filia agrees that's the most probable conclusion."

Bardon sat up straighter and inched away from Kale's hovering presence. "Filia, what does that mean?"

"She loves life and is interested in everything, therefore she collects tidbits of information. Her knowledge comes in very handy."

Kale noticed Bardon was staring at her and frowned at him. "Are you sure you're all right?"

"You're different."

"I'm three years older."

"What are you wearing?"

Kale stood up suddenly. "What kind of question is that? I'm wearing clothes."

Bardon struggled to his feet and faced her. "Yes, but what kind of an outfit is that for traipsing around The Bogs?"

"It is a very becoming outfit." She slammed her fists against her waist and stood with her feet apart. "It declares my flamboyant personality. It is functional and flattering at the same time."

Dibl swooped between the two glaring faces and landed on Bardon's head. The squire flapped a hand at the small yellow and orange dragon perched in his hair. Dibl fluttered upward and settled back down on his crown. To preserve his dignity, Bardon refused to flap at the minor dragon again.

Kale's wide-set hazel eyes shifted up to look at Dibl and then refocused on Bardon's face.

An image of the two of them standing almost nose to nose, glowering and fuming, flitted through Bardon's thoughts. He also envisioned the ridiculous dragon pulling with tiny talons on his black hair, and next his mind's eye focused on the peacocks parading around the hem of Kale's outrageous tunic.

He knew Dibl projected the images to him. The minor dragon had a keen sense of the ridiculous and loved sharing his humor. Bardon smiled.

Kale smiled, too, and giggled. Her clenched hands relaxed, and she let them drop from her hips. But a moment later, she crossed her arms over her chest and looked at Bardon, speculatively. "What are you doing, falling out of old gateways, acting dazed, and…"

"Asking stupid questions?" Bardon held both hands up, palms forward. "I apologize for the inappropriate comments about your beautiful ensemble. I'm dazed because this is the last place I expected to be and also the last place I need to be. Although it is very good to see you again."

He paused and jerked a thumb at the portal behind him. "And, before I fell through that ramshackle gateway, Regidor and I were about to rescue a tumanhofer."

"Regidor is with you?"

"Yes, he joined the quest."

"Quest?" She crossed one leg in front of the other and gracefully lowered herself to sit on the cygnot flooring. "Let's talk, Bardon."

"I really have to get back, Kale."

"I may be able to help you with that. Pat and I just repaired that gateway, and you tore some of the strands when you came shooting out. Right now it would be a bit dangerous to plunge back in."

Bardon sighed and sat down. "I suppose you want to know all about the quest."

"Uh-huh." The five other minor dragons landed on Kale and settled in as if they, too, wished to hear this tale.

"This is going to be a quick version, Kale, because I really have to get back to help rescue Bromptotterpindosset."

"You said something similar to that before. If you don't repeat yourself, you will be much more efficient in the telling of this story."

Rather than being annoyed, Bardon found himself grinning at the beautiful o'rant girl before him.

Is this joy the influence of the humor dragon on my head or the pleasure of seeing Kale again?

"Let's say both, and hurry along with this quest tale."

It's rude to read my mind without engaging in conversation.

Kale laughed out loud. *"Yes, it is, and it feels so good to be linked with you again, Bardon."* Her expression settled into one of intense mischief, eyes gleaming, dimples in her cheeks. *"And it's good to know you think I'm beautiful. You'd be surprised how rarely I hear such a compliment."*

Your most constant companions are Wizard Fenworth, Wizard Cam,

Librettowit, Taylaminkadot, and Toopka. Bardon mockingly scratched his head. *No, I'm not surprised.*

She laughed, and the precious sound reminded the young squire how much he'd missed this comrade.

"The story," said Bardon, aloud and firmly.

His companion nodded. "Yes, the story."

"My sabbatical was interrupted by two emerlindian women, Granny Kye and N'Rae. They're searching for knights entrapped in a sleeping spell rendered by Risto. The spell must be refreshed before the Wizards' Plume crosses under the Eye of the North, or the knights will die."

"We noted the Wizards' Plume rising. How long do you think you have before it passes under the Eye?"

"Regidor and the mapmaker have been debating about that. Does it mean when it first touches the perpendicular or when it has completely passed under? Hopefully, there will be more clues in the castle."

"Who are these knights?"

"Granny Kye and N'Rae believe one of the knights is N'Rae's father and Granny Kye's son. We've found the knights in an abandoned castle. But grawligs have captured our mapmaker and may eat him if I don't return promptly."

He stood, and Kale did, too, with dragons taking flight as she moved.

"I'll go with you," she said.

"You can't just come along, Kale. You have responsibilities here."

"I'm a wizard now, and I can do what I please."

Bardon cocked an eyebrow at her.

"I *am* a wizard, Bardon, even if I am not in the class of Regidor. But who could be? Wizard Cam is very well pleased with my progress. Wizard Fenworth thinks I could surpass even Regidor if I just applied myself. Mother says that when she was his apprentice, Fenworth had unreasonable expectations for her as well."

She looked pleadingly at her friend. "Bardon, I'm so bored here in The Bogs. Regidor has always been able to come and go as he wishes, but I have many more restraints upon me." She made a face and used a voice that sounded remarkably like the old wizard in charge of her education. "'You're a female and likely to get into trouble.' Ha! Regidor tells me some of the scrapes he gets into. They should chain him to the castle."

She rubbed Filia's back, who had landed on her shoulder. "I'll send a message to Fenworth's castle so they'll know where I've gone. And I'll return tomorrow, after we have freed your tumanhofer mapmaker and lifted the sleeping spell."

Bardon remained silent.

"Please."

A grin tugged at the corners of his mouth. "All right."

Kale's face beamed, and she reached out to squeeze his arm. Then she whistled, and a thrush winged out of a nearby tree to sit on her finger. Bardon watched, assuming she communicated her message to the little brown bird. It took to the air, and she turned smiling eyes to Bardon. He caught his breath, again startled by the fact that this Kale was no child, but a young, charming woman.

"Shall we go?" she asked.

He nodded. "It seems both you and N'Rae can twist me into doing things I think are not the best ideas."

Kale frowned. "Just how old is this N'Rae?"

He shook his head and shrugged. "How should I know? She's still pale, paler than Leetu Bends."

"Is she like Leetu?"

"A warrior?" Bardon barked a laugh. "No, she is more like an inept kitten. She has a tender heart, but not much common sense. She needs someone to look after her."

Kale's eyes narrowed, and though he didn't quite understand why, Bardon thought he had better change the subject.

He waved at the gateway. "Are you going to fix it?"

"Yes, of course." She stood before the portal but didn't seem to be doing anything. Her shoulders drooped, and she turned to face Bardon. "Pat and the others are giving me all sorts of lectures. Your fall through the opening only caused a small tear in the corner. The possibility of that insignificant, tiny rent in the fabric causing you a problem is infinitesimal. So I lied to keep you here."

She paused. "Oh," she exclaimed as if she had just remembered something. "And I'm sorry I lied."

Bardon tilted his head as he studied her slightly flushed face. "You have six dragons reminding you what is right and wrong?"

She nodded. "And how to do spells, and when I said I would do something like read a book to Toopka or help Taylaminkadot with dinner. They tell me where I left my shoes and when I need to check on Wizard Fen."

Bardon groaned. "Oh, Kale, that's awful."

She nodded. "You know, it really is." Then she grinned. "But I love them, and I scold them right back. We make a wonderful team."

"Shall we go?" asked Bardon.

"Yes."

"I must warn you, this is a rough ride. At least it was coming this way. Longer than most, and you don't walk on your own. Rather, you are hurled along."

"All right. I'm ready."

"And when you get to the other end, the portal is in the wall of a turret. Try to grab on to something as soon as you come out."

"All right. I'm ready."

"You'll come out on the west side of the turret. On the east side, in a courtyard, the grawligs are having a bit of a frolic. Try not to make an excess of noise."

Kale remained silent.

Bardon looked at her cold expression. Just a moment ago she was all eagerness. "Now what's wrong?"

"I'd forgotten how full of details you can be."

"Details can save your life."

"Details may make us too late to save your tumanhofer's life."

Bardon thought for a moment. "Right. Let's go."

45

GRAWLIG DINNER PARTY

Kale struggled to remain calm as the pressure of the gateway intensified. She tumbled head over heels and marveled that she felt as if she were falling up.

Bardon's right. This is a rough ride. I hope the minors are all right.

She catapulted out of the gateway, frantically trying to grab something to hold on to. To her relief, she landed facedown on ground padded with thick, tall grass. She lifted her head and saw statuary blended into the bushes by the shadows of night.

Bardon plummeted out of the gateway and landed on top of her.

"Oomph. Ouch!" Too late, she remembered about being quiet.

The "shh" that followed her exclamation did not come from Bardon. He rolled off of her, and she sat up, looking for the source of the shushing sound.

Regidor sat on a stone bench next to a statue of three dragons. Her minor dragons escaped the confines of their pocket-dens and flew about her head, chittering to one another. Once the six little dragons had determined that Kale was not injured and none of them were hurt, they landed on the statue to examine the artwork.

Cold night air raised goose bumps on Kale's arms. She rubbed her hands over them.

The squire sat, with his hands on his knees, staring up at the turret.

"You were gone long enough," said Regidor in a low voice. "I became intrigued with the idea of moving the entry by shifting the edges along a guide wire. The process was meticulous but surprisingly speedy once I practiced a bit. I had time to slide the gateway down to a safer level."

Bardon stood and dusted bits of grass off his clothes. "Thanks, Regidor. I'm sure you saved us a hard landing." He turned and offered Kale a hand. "Do you know what he's talking about?" he whispered as he pulled her to her feet.

"I believe the process would be something like slip-stitching in a piece of knitting."

Bardon adjusted the scabbard that held his sword on his belt. "I still don't have a clue as to how he did it, but if he is willing to spend more time here, the inside of that passage could use some work."

Regidor shook his head. "No, I came to realize as I was finishing the move that I might have defaced a national treasure, a site of historical significance. That gateway must have been one of the first ever constructed."

The meech focused on Kale. "What are you wearing, Kale? That isn't exactly an appropriate outfit for a rescue."

The material of her outfit shimmered in the moonlight.

Kale smoothed the fancy fabric over her arms and grimaced at her best friend. "Hello, Regidor, I'm glad to see you, too."

He grinned and came to give her a hug. His long, strong forelegs embraced her with brotherly affection. The frown on Bardon's face surprised Kale.

"Why are you looking daggers at me?" she asked him.

I'm not.

He turned away from Kale and Regidor and looked toward the grawligs' playground. "They've settled down somewhat."

Regidor gave Kale an extra squeeze and let go of her. "They've massed around the food, and their mouths are full. They're feasting."

"Not on our friend, I hope," said Bardon.

"No, they've decided to play a game with him. They wrangled for some time over what game and what the rules would be, then decided to eat first. Grawligs are not known for their organizational abilities."

"Then now would be a good time to rescue Bromptotterpindosset," said Bardon. "If his captors are busy with food…"

"Right," said Regidor.

Kale twirled in place, changing her outfit into more serviceable dark green leggings and a brown tunic. Her mother had taught her the twirl technique. In truth the spin was totally unnecessary for the transformation, but Lyll Allerion had a flair for the dramatic that she had passed on to her daughter.

"Besides," Wizard Lyll had said, "the twirl is invigorating, and you need that rush right before entering your more challenging situations."

Before her moonbeam cape stopped swaying from the spin, Kale looked at her companions and said, "Anything you need to tell me before we get this rescue underway?"

"You're a little too enthusiastic, Kale," said Bardon. "Try to remember we're in a life-or-death situation."

Regidor just winked and gestured for them to follow him. They skulked behind a wall made up of stone and almost hidden by vegetation. The minor dragons either rode on Kale or flew beside her. Except Pat. Pat trudged through the grass, kicking up bugs and eating them. Regidor held up a hand for them to stop. He pointed to the other side of the wall.

Kale peeked through the shrubbery wrapped around and over the stones. Most of the grawligs sat or reclined in clusters. Big pots garnered all their attention. They ate cooked meat with their fingers, smacking their lips and squabbling occasionally over the next piece. An untidy stack of bones to the side of the lawn gave evidence that a buck had provided the meal.

A few of the mountain ogres leaned against trees or statues. Statuary seemed to have overrun the place. Several grawligs, who appeared to be some kind of beaten-down, low servants, passed among the others, handing out raw fruits and vegetables.

A very disgruntled tumanhofer sat, bound hand and foot, with his back to a stake. Two sturdy ropes wrapped around his chest and the wooden pole. Another thinner rope secured his neck to the same stake. Two additional ropes looped his neck like leashes and were held by a pair of massive grawligs as if he were a dog.

"We've come to rescue you." She saw him jerk slightly as her words entered his thoughts.

"*Who are you?*"

"*Kale Allerion of The Bogs, Dragon Keeper and Wizard.*"

"*Well, I hope you're a mighty warrior as well. These grawligs are brutes.*"

"*Squire Bardon and Wizard Regidor are with me. They're well noted for their fighting skills.*"

"*Two warriors? There are nearly a hundred grawligs in this encampment. Where's the guard Sir Dar sent to escort us?*"

Kale turned to Bardon. "*Your tumanhofer wants to know where the guard is.*"

Protecting the rest of our party.

"*Granny Kye and N'Rae?*"

And the others. Oh, I didn't mention the others, did I?

A shout erupted from a group of grawligs. Two of them stood and growled at each other. One threw his fistful of meat down. The other stepped closer and smashed his grease-covered hand into the first grawlig's face.

Kale just had time to say "uh-oh" before all the grawligs jumped to their feet and began pounding one another.

One of the grawligs holding the mapmaker's ropes stepped toward the fracas.

"Hey!" yelled the other. "You can't go. You stay here and watch him." He thrust a thick finger at Bromptotterpindosset.

"You stay!" The grawlig turned and beat his chest with one fist. "I am Bor-bor clan. I fight Nastrek." He hurled the end of the rope at the other.

The grawlig grunted when the rope flailed across his face. "I Nastrek clan," he roared, dropping his rope and lunging at the other grawlig.

"*Very* good time to retrieve our mapmaker," said Bardon. He and Regidor vaulted over the wall.

Kale stood up and lifted the hood of her cape to cover her head. She whistled the call of a night bird as an alert and commanded, "Dragons, spit in the eye of any grawlig who sees us."

Regidor and Bardon had been spotted. Five grawligs, who evidently weren't as determined to defend the honor of their clans, had blocked the warriors in their charge to rescue the tumanhofer.

The minor dragons flew to help. They spit sticky, caustic saliva into the faces of the enemy. When the substance struck an eyeball, the grawlig would double over and howl. Unfortunately, this attracted the attention of those who had not been attacking Bardon and Regidor. These abandoned the brawl between clans and joined the attack on the outsiders. The fray, a few yards away from the captured tumanhofer, grew from five grawligs to ten. As one dropped out, two more took his place. The odds against Regidor and Bardon grew more uneven by the minute.

Kale jumped over the wall and stood perfectly still, giving her moonbeam cape a chance to camouflage her. She then took slow steps, one at a time, until she knelt directly behind the tumanhofer. Using her short sword, she cut through the knots that she could not undo with her fingers.

"Give me a weapon," the tumanhofer demanded as he rubbed his wrists and stomped his feet. "It's a good thing those beasts are inept at tying tightly. I've still got the use of my limbs."

Kale pulled a short, heavy sword out of the hollow of her cape. Bromptotterpindosset grabbed it and began swinging as he worked his way from the fringe to the center of the battling circle around Bardon and Regidor.

Rather than join the two warriors and the tumanhofer, Kale chose to keep any more grawligs from joining the conflict. She created a ring of quicksand around the main fight. Four feet across and four feet deep, the mire provided an efficient barricade. The ogres stepped in, sank to their hips and struggled. Eventually, there were enough of the grawligs stuck in the loose, saturated sand that the following brutes just used their trapped comrades as steppingstones. This, of course, enraged the ogres sinking in the sand. They began reaching up to snag those crossing over, pulling them down into the mire.

Kale watched a brawl develop that far outshone the fight inside the ring. Bardon, Regidor, and Bromptotterpindosset incapacitated the last of their attackers and stood at ease, watching the chaos around them. Occasionally, almost by mischance, a grawlig ended up on their island, and they dispatched the poor unfortunate individual with speed.

Bardon called to her. "Kale, did you have a plan for how we're to get from here to there?"

She shrugged. "Regidor can fly."

Bardon indicated his short mapmaker. "Neither of us have wings."

Kale grinned and directed her thoughts to Regidor alone. *"My dear meech friend, shall we help them out?"*

"Of course," he replied. *"The mapmaker first?"*

"Yes."

The tumanhofer rose off the ground and floated. His eyes grew big, his face turned red, and he began to pump his legs as if he could run from whatever it was that had ahold of him. Kale and Regidor passed him over the heads of the scrapping ogres and set him down. Then they seized Bardon, lifted him higher than they had the tumanhofer, and sailed him quickly through the air to land next to Bromptotterpindosset. Regidor spread his wings and took to the air.

From across the courtyard, a chorus of howls drowned out the snarls and gnashing of teeth in the quicksand ring. A thundering pack of wild grawligs charged through the open space. Kale jumped behind a statue to keep from getting run down by this new band of beasts. The swarm surrounded Bardon and Bromptotterpindosset as they passed by the grawligs stuck in Kale's mire.

They ran through the courtyard and out the other side, while Kale ran to where Bardon lay on the ground. The squire sat up and shook his head as if trying to clear it. He looked around.

"Where's the tumanhofer?"

Kale, too, searched the ground around them. She jumped to her feet and looked behind the two statues that were close enough for Bromptotterpindosset to have used for refuge.

"He's not here."

"Those ogres took him," Bardon said as he struggled to his feet.

"Why?"

"Who knows why a grawlig does anything? And you only compound the absurdity when you have grawligs making decisions en masse."

Kale came back to stand next to Bardon. "Where's Regidor?"

"He probably flew after them to see where they go."

"What are we going to do?"

Bardon sighed, picked up his sword, and turned toward the gate. "Follow them."

46

A Friendlier Dinner

Bardon asked Ardeo, Kale's light dragon, to lead the way. He flew close to the ground, and the glow of his skin gave Bardon enough light to see the tracks of the mob that had stolen Bromptotterpindosset. The huge grawligs had beaten a wide path through the underbrush. Kale and Bardon sped after them, slowing only when they came to cliff-like inclines. Apparently, the mountain ogres with their tough hides just slid down these rocky slopes.

Bardon heard the beat of Regidor's wings and put a hand on Kale's arm to stop her. In a moment, the meech dragon landed in front of them, immediately folding his wings and retracting them under his cape. The minor dragons perched on Kale and Bardon.

"Well," said Kale when Regidor didn't speak, "what did you find out?"

The meech dragon looked pointedly at Bardon's hold of Kale's arm. The squire frowned and stepped down the path a few feet.

Kale looked from one male friend to the other. Bardon thought she would make some comment, but she surprised him by staying focused on the rescue.

"Where is the tumanhofer?" she asked.

"Unfortunately, they have taken him back into the warrens." Regidor clapped his forefeet together, producing a table, chairs, food, and drink. "Shall we? I'm sure you're as hungry as I am, and we have time to make plans over a succulent meal."

Fried fish, a large loaf of dark bread, corn, pnard potatoes, and crisp salad greens lured them all to the table. Regidor hurried to pull a chair out for Kale. Bardon stopped to stare.

Now, why did he do that? Of course, I would have done the same in a more formal setting. It's not as if I'm unaware of how to treat a lady.

Kale flashed a smile at Regidor and then frowned at Bardon. "Aren't you coming?"

Bardon sat down without saying a word.

Regidor bowed his head, as did Kale. The squire followed suit a second and a half later.

The meech dragon's low voice rumbled his petition. "Wulder, we acknowledge Your sovereignty, we thank You for our meal, and we ask that You strengthen our friendships, even making them new. By Your might and grace, may all things be done."

Just as he opened his eyes, Bardon caught a look passing between Kale and Regidor.

What is going on between those two? And what did Regidor mean by making our friendships new? Should I ask?

No! We're here to rescue Bromptotterpindosset. We're here to rescue the knights.

The squire knew the meech dragon would rather report on his own time, but he was tired of the delays and all the nonsense that seemed to be interfering with their purpose. "Regidor, what did you find out as you followed the grawligs?"

Regidor wrinkled his nose in distaste but complied with Bardon's request for information. "The band that most recently abducted Bromptotterpindosset were the Gar-hoo. And, they were the ones who abducted him from our camp. The Bor-bor then ambushed the Gar-hoo and stole their prize. The Bor-bor then invited the Nastrek to join in a celebration. To them, successfully grabbing the Gar-hoos' loot is of great consequence. Also, having in their possession an otherlander increases their prestige, so of course they wanted the Nastrek to be witness to their triumph.

"As long as the clans do not lose interest, Bromptotterpindosset is fairly safe from becoming a meal. These grawligs like to play with their food and don't actually cook them until the novelty has worn off and they have become bored."

Kale had buttered thick slabs of bread and placed them on each plate. Now she poured a cool, clear, red juice into tall goblets and passed them to her companions.

"Thank you," said Regidor.

"Thank you," echoed Bardon and tried not to choke on the bite halfway down his throat.

What is this? Some kind of contest? My manners are just as polished as the manners of a meech dragon from a swamp!

He bit into the fish and found it salty, crunchy, and delicious. A savory sauce covered the pnard potatoes. A light dressing glistened on the salad greens and tasted of delectable herbs with a hint of garlic. The fragrance alone soothed Bardon's frazzled nerves. He soon forgot his irritation over Regidor's odd behavior toward Kale, and he ate heartily.

When they each leaned back in their chairs, totally satisfied, Regidor clapped his forefeet, and the whole dinner, dirty dishes, table, and all disappeared. Only the chairs remained.

Bardon looked askance at his friend. "I only had rudimentary wizardry lessons under old Fen, but it seems to me that all things must be created from existing things. That a wizard cannot pull objects out of thin air."

Kale's expression took on the look of a mentor displeased with her pupil. "Now that your stomach is full you think to question where the food came from?" She giggled. "Regidor doesn't pull them out of thin air, but out of well-stocked hollows. Regidor is more a master of dramatic display than most of us. Librettowit says he has a 'flair' for the art of wizardry that hasn't been seen in any wizard for eons."

Bardon smiled. "And Fenworth says?"

"Harrumph!" imitated the two ex-apprentices at the same time.

They laughed.

We have so much in common, the three of us. Not only the crazy old wizard, but also the lack of parents and the desire to follow Wulder. He caught himself before he let his thoughts stray further down such a philosophical path. They had work to do.

"We need to rest," said Bardon, "then find Bromptotterpindosset, send him on his way, and tackle the problem of how to wake up the knights."

"You left out an important step," Kale said as they all stood. She paused and raised her eyebrows. "Removing your tumanhofer from the midst of his captors."

"Ah yes, that should be entertaining," said Regidor. He snapped his fingers, and the chairs they had been sitting on folded in on themselves and disappeared.

They strolled through the moonlight among the jagged rocks toward a part of the warren Regidor thought might be unoccupied. Ardeo flew in front of them, close to the ground, illuminating the shadows in their path. The other minor dragons sometimes flew and sometimes perched on the three travelers.

"We'll look this dirt shelter over carefully," explained Bardon to Kale. "The last supposedly unpopulated burrow we explored housed two cave dragons. One was a small snake dragon, and the other, a massive two-headed snake dragon."

The minor dragons set up a hullabaloo, chittering, scolding, and chirping interspersed with shrill whistles.

"What's that all about?" asked Bardon.

"They're expressing their opinions of what they call degenerate dragons. They consider snake dragons to be very low creatures, indeed."

"Which," said Regidor, "raises the question of why some dragons behave more like animals and some like upstanding citizens of the high races."

"Which," said Bardon, "raises the question of why some citizens of the high races behave more like animals, never fulfilling their potential for nobility."

Kale clamped her hands over her ears. "Stop! I get my fill of philosophical debates when Wizard Cam comes to visit. He and Librettowit can discuss the vagaries of civilization until they are both hoarse from talking."

Bardon laughed. "They had those kinds of deliberations at The Hall, but Sir Dar discouraged them at Castle Pelacce."

"Why?" asked Kale.

"He said there came a time when words lost their ability to accomplish change and just became noises in the air."

"So he didn't believe people should indulge in discussions?"

"Oh no," Bardon shook his head. "He encouraged discussions until they became futile. He used the example of describing an egg. There are only so many words you can use to describe an egg, and after those have been used in every possible combination, the smarter activity is to eat the egg rather than describe it."

When they reached the burrow Regidor had spotted, they found vegetation grown up around its entrance and no sign of anyone having gone in or out for several seasons at least. Both Regidor and Kale used their minds to see if they could detect life within the enclosure. They found nothing larger than a druddum, and those cave dwellers never posed problems other than occasionally startling an explorer by appearing suddenly.

The troop settled in, using blankets Regidor and Kale had in their hollows. Kale volunteered to take the first watch.

Regidor uncorked his elaborate bottle. "Gilda will keep you company. She's safe here and will enjoy the visit."

Kale brightened at the prospect. She smiled at Bardon and explained. "Gilda and I often visit when Regidor stays at Fenworth's castle."

Their voices—Kale's sweet and musical, Gilda's low and breathy—lulled Bardon into a restful slumber.

47

One More Time

"How are you feeling, Gilda?" asked Kale.

"Just tired."

"You're not bored anymore?"

She shook her head wistfully. "I'm too tired to be bored these days, Kale."

"Are you frightened?"

"I'd say I was too tired to be frightened, but that isn't true. I'm not frightened anymore, but it isn't because of the nagging fatigue. It is because Paladin has taught me about Wulder. Because I understand."

Kale nodded.

"And," Gilda smiled the slow, lazy smile that relaxed her face and cast an aura of tranquility over her features, "I am very glad I met Regidor. We've traveled so many places. Do you know why he travels?"

Kale shook her head. "I've often resented his freedom to go places Cam and Fen would not let me go. And although Mother visits often, she never takes me with her to the places she goes."

"Your mother still does very dangerous work for Paladin. She goes places where it is not safe for a young, inexperienced girl."

"You're younger than I am, Gilda, and so is Regidor. Everyone seems to forget that."

"We are meech, dear Kale, and you know that makes a difference whether you want to acknowledge the fact or not."

She's right. Just look at her. She's poised and unruffled and everything I am not. And actually, I would rather not be exactly like Gilda for all her sophistication. Being stuck in The Bogs is infinitely more entertaining than being stuck in a bottle. I'm happy with my lot.

Kale smiled and stretched and leaned back against the earthen wall of the burrow. "I know I'm not a meech. Fenworth often bemoans the fact that I don't learn as quickly as Regidor." She yawned. "Tell me about your travels and make it very interesting so I'll stay awake."

Gilda chortled, the laugh rattling deep in her throat. "I won't need to work at that." She reclined across a broad rock shelf where Regidor had set her bottle. "Where shall I begin? You know Regidor spent a great deal of time visiting weavers and tailors."

"I used to think he was vain."

"He enjoyed teasing you. When you scolded him for wasting his time, he secretly took pleasure in being able to mislead you. He searched for fabric suitable for his adventures and for clothes designed to help him blend into the general populace. It is difficult to be hairless, green, and scaly. It is also difficult to hide a tail and wings."

Kale looked at her elegant friend who also disguised a tail and wings. Gilda used draped veils. Her dresses and swirling capes added to her exotic glamour.

"But Regidor travels for two other reasons," continued Gilda. "He searches with a passion for information about the meech race. The question of where they came from troubles his peace of mind. Equally, he wants to know where the remnants of our race have gone."

Kale nodded in understanding. "And the last reason he travels is you, isn't it?"

"For me. He hopes to find a way to save me." She shrugged as if the solution to her predicament was not all that important to her.

"Don't you want to live, Gilda?" Kale asked.

"I suppose I do, but not with the zeal one might expect. I think it's good that I've spent time with Wizard Fenworth." Her face lit up with a much warmer expression than her usual serene smile. "Besides amusing me, he has instructed me in the gentle art of dying. Without anger or defiance. No desperate clinging to this realm with a fear of the next."

"You wouldn't fight to live?"

"Under certain circumstances. But those circumstances are not mine. I would only cause myself unhappiness to chafe under my situation. I would cause Regidor's anguish to intensify. No, my desire is to enjoy each moment. And should I be granted an unexpected reprieve, I shall rejoice."

Kale shook her head, her brown curls bouncing against her face as they swung back and forth. "I don't think I could be so calm, Gilda. I just couldn't resign myself to die without a fight."

"That's because your circumstances are not mine. I think Wulder expects you to fight and me to comply."

Gilda soon returned to her bottle. The length of time she could spend outside had dwindled significantly over the three years since Risto had imprisoned her. Kale recognized that each time Gilda appeared outside her bottle, her vapor was less dense, her image less sharp.

+==+

Regidor took the next watch. Bardon the last.

In the morning they ate a simple meal.

"Regidor," Bardon said as he swallowed the last bite of mullin, "we should send another message to N'Rae that we'll be delayed."

"N'Rae?" Kale frowned at the squire. "Didn't you say a Captain Anton led your party in your absence? Why are you sending a message to a girl?"

"Because," answered Bardon with excruciating patience, "Regidor delivers the message through an animal. You do remember that I told you N'Rae's particular talent is the ability to communicate with animals?"

Kale hated the tone of voice Bardon used. It reminded her of their early acquaintance, when he was a snooty lehman at The Hall. At that time, he treated everyone with cold disdain. Irritation seeped into her voice. "I do remember you saying something about a chicken."

"Children, children," scolded Regidor as he laughed and tried to keep his face solemn. "Let's not squabble. I'll send a message to Captain Anton via N'Rae. Kale, would you send out your dragons to see if they can pick up a trail for us to follow? Preferably one that leads to Bromptotterpindosset. And, Squire Bardon…"

"Yes?" Bardon growled.

"I think it would be profitable if you were to busy yourself by being in charge. You could plan our attack, or devise a scheme to find our way back to the castle, or you might want to—"

"Regidor." Bardon's voice held no humor.

"Yes, my good friend?"

"Go find a crow to carry your message."

"Yes." He turned on his heel and headed for the burrow's outer opening. "I believe now would be a good time to do that."

It took the dragons less than an hour to locate the grawlig camp. Pat and Gymn came back with news of snoring ogres and one old tumanhofer trussed up again and spitting mad.

Kale recounted what her green dragon, Gymn, had reported. "Bromptotterpindosset has escaped the ropes binding his hands, but a great brute is lying across his legs, and he can't get out from under him.

"Gymn says once we've moved the beast, Gymn and I will have to heal the tumanhofer's legs."

"Have they gone to sleep?" asked Bardon with concern.

"No." Kale sighed over the clumsy, irrational behavior of these beasts. "The grawligs repeatedly dropped the mapmaker while using him to toss in a game of catch last night. His legs are bruised, but not broken. Perhaps an ankle is sprained. Gymn had a hard time assessing his condition, because the grawlig sleeping on Bromptotterpindosset thrashed around a bit."

"Did Gymn say how many there are, and if any are awake?"

"Pat said there are forty-seven, and none of them is conscious. They drank brillum last night."

"Sounds like a good time to go rescue our mapmaker."

Regidor grunted. "One more time."

They followed Pat and Gymn through the burrows. In these passageways, lightrocks illuminated the way.

Kale stifled a giggle as they came up to the cavern where the grawligs sprawled in piles like puppies. These troublesome ogres had celebrated their coup too well. The cacophony from their snores reverberated off the stone walls. Instead of sneaking in on tiptoe, the rescuers walked among the beasts as if they were scattered boulders. Wrinkling her nose and trying not to breathe, Kale followed Regidor. The rancid smell from the grawligs' unwashed bodies made her want to gag.

Bromptotterpindosset opened his eyes, raised his head, and gave a slight nod in recognition of their arrival. He then let his head droop.

"Gymn," Kale called to the healing dragon, *"let's get to work while Bardon and Regidor remove that beast."* She pointed to the grawlig sprawled over the mapmaker's lower half, pinning him to the ground.

Trying to keep her breathing shallow so as not to inhale the putrid smells from around her, she knelt beside the tumanhofer's head, placing her hands on his neck and shoulder. Gymn came to rest on his chest. The hum of healing energy flowed in a circle from the small dragon, through the injured man and Kale, and back to Gymn. Bromptotterpindosset began to breathe easier, his color improved, and his expression lost the pinched look of one in pain.

Bardon and Regidor lifted the weighty grawlig and carried him a few feet to set him down among other unconscious grawligs. Kale and Gymn moved to the bruised legs and completed the healing. Bardon helped Bromptotterpindosset to his feet, and the four walked without incident out of the hotbed of trouble.

"That was too easy," said Bardon as they followed the minor dragons flying toward fresh air. They soon stepped out of the cave and into sunshine.

"I'm not sure," said Regidor, "that it is written as law that every endeavor must be fraught with danger."

The tumanhofer remained silent. He had not spoken at all since they freed him and restored his health.

Kale watched him out of the corner of her eye. "Are you all right, Bromptotterpindosset?"

"I am," he said and kept marching, his head down and his eyes on the path.

She turned to Bardon. "Where are we going?"

"Back to our camp to get the others. We've found the knights, but we must awaken them."

Kale surveyed the area. "These are odd mountains."

Bardon glanced around. "Why do you say that?"

She shrugged and grimaced. "I don't really know, they just... I know." She pointed to a mountain peak ahead. "That mountain"—she turned and pointed behind—"looks like that one." She pointed in yet another direction. "And that one."

The mapmaker stopped. His head came up with a jerk. He looked around, placed his hands on his hips, and looked around again. "We're lost," he muttered, his usually brusque manner subdued by despair.

"We follow the sun," said Regidor. "The sun does not lie."

48

LOST IN ONE PLACE

The minor dragons grew sleepy almost as soon as they started the morning trek. One by one the little dragons crawled into their own pocket-dens in Kale's cape.

"That's unusual," she told Bardon when even Filia, who loved to see new things, tucked herself up in her pocket to sleep.

He held a branch back so she could pass. "They're used to rather a dull life in The Bogs. They'll come out when they've rested."

But the little dragons did not reappear.

Plenty of game, birds, and insects inhabited the area. But the creatures acted in a perplexing manner, seemingly unaware of the strangers. The meech dragon tried to summon birds so he could learn from them something about the land. They refused to come. Kale called to different animals, but none responded. After walking west for several hours, the four travelers came to an impenetrable forest.

Regidor started a fire to warm them as they tried to figure out where they were and how to get to where they wanted to be. The meech conjured up the ingredients, and in a short time, Kale sat stirring a pot of soup.

"Why don't you just fix the meal?" Bromptotterpindosset asked Regidor. "I know wizards can produce banquets out of nothing."

Regidor patted the tumanhofer on his broad shoulder. "That's a misconception, Bromp. And besides, sometimes the preparation of a meal, with its smells and procedures, is comforting. Are you terribly hungry, sir?"

"No, I'm not. Not at all. I don't know why we stopped. We should be covering more ground before the day slips away from us."

"That's just why we stopped. Our desire is to cover the right ground, and we seem to be getting nowhere." Regidor pointed to the satchel that had been returned to the mapmaker. "Shall we look at your maps?"

The men settled down. Bromptotterpindosset sat on a long log, Regidor sat on a rock, and next to the tumanhofer sat Bardon with his back against the rough bark of the log.

Kale's eyes scanned the bushes, trees, and undergrowth. Her mind wouldn't rest but kept pondering what strange power lay over this region.

At times she had trouble hearing, and at others, she would hear one thing almost to the exclusion of the other natural noises. She heard a drummerbug until she thought she would go insane. When she mentioned it to Regidor, he said he didn't hear it at all.

Kale stirred the bubbling liquid and sniffed the fragrance of onions and meat. *I find it odd that I'm not tired. Walking is my least favorite mode of transportation. And I'm not really hungry, either. Bromptotterpindosset doesn't appear tired, and he said he wasn't hungry.*

She peered into the pot and frowned. *When did I put carrots in this soup? Regidor must have put them in. He likes carrots.*

Bromptotterpindosset, Bardon, and Regidor pored over maps and the diary, trying to retrace their steps. They passed the different items to one another. As far as Kale could tell, they hadn't resolved anything during their hour-long discussion. She listened to them speculate and wondered if she and Regidor could build a gateway, choosing a place to go.

Bardon pointed first to a spot on one of the maps and then to a mountain to the east. "If we came into this range of mountains from this direction, then that peak is this one on the map."

Bromptotterpindosset shook his head. "That would mean the scale is wrong. We haven't traveled nearly long enough to get from there to here."

"There is the possibility that the map is wrong," argued Bardon. "I don't believe this area is recorded on any of these charts. None of the drawings match with the configuration of this range. Everything is just a bit off in either size or spacing."

"I agree." The mapmaker folded the map in his hand. "Could we have passed through a gateway without knowing as we traveled through the burrows?"

Bardon scrunched his face. "I've never been through a gateway that didn't squeeze the breath out of me."

"There was the large gateway made by the wizards to transport dragons and warriors to the Battle of Bartal Springs Lake," said Regidor. "That one was less constricting."

"Yes, but the sensation of sticking to air was the same. I don't think we could walk through a gateway totally oblivious to making the passage."

Regidor grunted. "Neither do I."

Kale turned her mind away from the discussion. It seemed to her that they repeated the same argument in a cycle. Soon they would spread out the maps again and try to determine where they were. The minor dragons refused to come out, and she sensed their fear and confusion. Something was not right, but her little friends did not know what.

In the thicket not far from her, a squirrel picked up a nut, scampered along a rotted log, and buried his treasure.

Kale sat up, attending to the small details around her, and waited. Overhead, a bird took off from a limb. The branch shook and three leaves fell to the ground. Kale looked at the fallen leaves in the dirt. They lay in a rough triangular formation.

With her lips pressed together, she watched for more signs of life in these woods. A bee flew to a bush covered with small white flowers, then after a long pause, a bluebird brought a twig to the tree at her left. Her eyes turned to the sky and followed a cloud as it sailed past a mountain peak.

In the thicket not far from her, a squirrel picked up a nut, scampered along a rotted log, and buried his treasure.

Kale nodded her head and waited patiently for the three leaves to fall from the tree after the bird took to the air. They landed, making a triangle on the dirt. In due time, the bee came, and then the bluebird with his twig. She looked up to the mountain and saw the same cloud drift out of sight over the same mountain peak.

"We're in an illusion," she announced, loud and clear.

She closed her eyes for a moment, dreading what she might see when she looked at her three male companions.

They had the same discussion over and over, but they didn't use the exact same words.

She turned her head and opened her eyes.

Bardon, Regidor, and the tumanhofer had stopped what they were doing and stared at her.

She sighed and smiled. "I'm so glad. I thought you might be part of the illusion as well. In which case, I would be alone. But you're not repeating."

Bromptotterpindosset glanced first at Bardon and then at Regidor. "Does anyone know what she's talking about?"

"I think," said Bardon as he stood, "these maps are useless in our present circumstances." He moved toward Kale.

"What does he mean?" the tumanhofer asked Regidor.

Regidor rose to his feet and looked down at Bromptotterpindosset. "If this place is under a spell, the maps will not guide us out."

The meech followed Bardon, and the mapmaker got up clumsily. "See here, I've been around the world, and there has never been a time when my maps failed me. Even if I couldn't determine where we were by landmarks, the stars remain constant to the celestial charts. You, yourself, said the sun never lies."

"Yes," said Regidor over his shoulder, "but is that the sun?"

Bromptotterpindosset glanced at the sky and then sputtered, "Ridiculous! How could the sun not be the sun?"

Regidor ignored him. "Tell us what you've seen, Kale."

She pointed to a limb above them. "That bird will take off, and three leaves will fall to the ground." She pointed to the dirt. "They'll come to rest there, making a triangle."

The bird took to the air, and the leaves landed in the dirt just as Kale predicted.

"Next a bee flies among those white flowers, then a bluebird carries a twig to that tree."

The three men watched the insect and the bird.

"Coincidence," scoffed the tumanhofer.

Bardon and Regidor cast him disapproving glares.

"Next," said Kale, "the cloud goes over the mountain peak."

Bromptotterpindosset shifted in irritation. "Anyone can see which way the cloud is going."

Kale ignored him. "Notice the three leaves are gone."

They looked to where dirt lay in the cleared patch.

The cloud drifted out of sight.

"A squirrel will pick up that nut and bury it over there."

"I'm convinced," said Bardon as the squirrel flicked its tail and grabbed the nut.

"What does it mean?" asked the tumanhofer.

Regidor frowned at the shorter man. "It means we're lost unless we can break the spell."

Kale put her hand on Bardon's arm. "We broke a similar illusion in Risto's dungeon with music. Dar played his flute."

Bardon reached inside his tunic and pulled out his small silver instrument. He played a few random notes. Nothing happened. He played a scale. Nothing. He played the first bars of a popular tune. Still nothing. He looked to Regidor. "Any ideas?"

"We could try interrupting the cycle."

"It's the bee's turn to make an appearance," said Kale.

Regidor stood ready beside the flowers and scooped the insect out of the air with his bare hand. He threw it to the ground and stepped on it.

"It didn't sting you?" asked the tumanhofer.

"My forefeet are covered with very thick skin. But that's beside the point. It didn't try."

A minute later, the bluebird flew by with a twig in its beak.

"So," said Bardon, "the destruction of a bee did not disturb the order of the illusion."

"What do we do now?" Bromptotterpindosset asked, while looking around nervously.

"I doubt that anything is going to attack us," said Regidor.

The tumanhofer's eyes snapped back to glare at the meech dragon. "I didn't expect that something would. It's just"—he shuddered—"this place is unsettling. Nothing's real, isn't that so?"

"Mostly," said Regidor, patiently. "I believe the ground under our feet is real. It perhaps doesn't look like this ground we see, but we are standing on something."

"You're a clever fellow," said Bromptotterpindosset. "You'll figure some way out."

Regidor inclined his head but said nothing.

Kale wiped her hands on her britches. "Could we build a gateway, Reg? You and I have studied them and repaired them, and I helped make one. Bardon did too. Shall we try?"

"It will be difficult, if not impossible. One needs to know one's exact location in order to begin."

After two tries, they gave up.

"Don't quit!" exclaimed the tumanhofer. "Get us out of here."

"I don't see why you're so upset," said Bardon. "Surely you've been in more dangerous situations than this."

"I like to know where I am, that's all." The mapmaker's eyes darted right and left. His eyes latched on the bee as it returned to the flowers. "Let's burn a section. Maybe that will do the interrupting thing you tried to do by killing the bee."

Bardon and Kale both looked to Regidor, waiting for the more proficient wizard to pass judgment on the idea.

"I don't think we can get an illusion to catch fire. But I don't mind giving it a try."

"You got the fire to start to cook the soup." Bromptotterpindosset whined, sounding as if he accused the meech of some kind of trickery.

"I used material from my hollows," said Regidor with a sigh. "You didn't see me gather any wood, did you?"

"Well, no," he admitted. He glared at each of the others in turn and then grabbed a stick from the fire, holding the end that stuck out from the coals.

He poked the stick under a bush, but the branches sizzled to black and then reformed. He tried burning old leaves on the ground, but they did the same thing. In disgust, he threw the lighted branch down in the dirt. It burned for a minute and slowly went out.

Bromptotterpindosset sat down hard on the log. "We aren't going to get out. We'll die here. There's no real food to eat after Regidor runs out of his supply. No water to drink, either. We're trapped."

Regidor sat down beside him. "We're a long way from being dead, my friend. Wulder has not abandoned us."

"Wulder? Wulder! You think a fable can help you?"

"Well, He has in the past."

"I don't believe in your Wulder. He does not exist."

Regidor chortled. "I would be very worried if Wulder said that about you." He spoke in an authoritative voice. " 'I don't believe in Bromptotterpindosset. He does not exist.' " The meech dragon clapped the tumanhofer on the back. "If He said that, my dear friend, then you would not exist. However, your saying such a thing about Him does nothing but make noise in the air. And that noise is soon gone."

"So, is your Wulder going to break this illusion and show us the way out?" The mapmaker rubbed both hands over his face, ending with his palms covering his eyes. He leaned forward, resting his elbows on his knees. "If we must depend upon a myth, then we shall truly perish."

"This 'myth' can turn a stream or a river from one path to another. And He also turns the minds of men to one destiny or another. I would not be surprised if the way of our salvation has not already been established."

Bromptotterpindosset groaned. "What does that mean?"

"It means," said Kale, "that someone is already on the way to rescue us. Or, the collapse of this fancy illusion has already been devised."

"You really believe that?

"Yes."

"If we get out of here in the next hour, or even today, I'll think about your Wulder being more than a figure in a fable."

Regidor stood. "You would still hesitate, even if He clears a way out of this illusion in less than an hour?"

The tumanhofer stood, puffed out his chest, and glared at the meech dragon. "No! By the word of Bromptotterpindosset. If we escape this madness, I'll believe in your Wulder. Or at least, try."

"Even to the point of reading the Tomes and learning more about Him?"

"I'll spend the rest of my days chasing down every fact I can discover about this marvelous myth."

Regidor shook his head, but a big grin broke the solemn expression he'd worn just previously.

"No myth. He's Wulder. And you are going to find out the risk involved in challenging the all-powerful Creator."

A rough shout resounded across the forested region. "There. There they are. Onward, we shall capture them."

Bromptotterpindosset jumped and grabbed Regidor's arm. "Grawligs."

The wizard meech laughed. "Yes, it would be just like Him to use the lowly mountain ogres to do His will, but have you ever known a grawlig to speak in a complete sentence?"

"Here now," the voice from the woods spoke again, "who's put all this muck in my way? Be gone, you falsified flowers. Off with you, you bloodless creatures. Of what use is a sun with no warmth and no place in the galaxy? Good work, though. Must admire the good workmanship of this fantasy. But enough. Be gone."

The colors of the trees dripped into the dissolving bushes. The birds, insects, and creatures faded into nothing. Kale, Bardon, Regidor, and a stunned tumanhofer stood at one end of a large cavern aglow with lightrocks. At the other end stood two old wizards, one leafy and one wet. Beside them, two women, a child, and a librarian waited.

Kale let out a shriek and ran to greet them.

49

More Joining of Forces

"Mother." Kale threw her arms around a tall, elegant o'rant woman.

Lyll Allerion returned the hug, then shook a finger at her daughter. "Young lady, you scared me. I went to Fenworth's castle for a visit and found you were gone. Fenworth had no idea where you were."

"I sent a bird to tell him."

"Yes, but Fen was meditating."

"Harrumph!" The old man interrupted, putting an arm around his apprentice's shoulders. A lizard darted out his sleeve, scampered down Kale's tunic, and sprang to the floor of the cave. Kale didn't even jump. Three years in constant company with the bog wizard and his creatures had inured her to their sudden appearances.

Fenworth squeezed her shoulders. "I was resting, and the bird, very politely, waited in my branches until I awoke. Of course, when your mother started tugging on my beard, I roused from a very pleasant slumber." He cast Lyll a disapproving look.

She smiled in return.

Toopka jerked her hand out of Taylaminkadot's and ran to leap into Bardon's arms. The tiny doneel child, dressed in bright and mismatched colors, squealed. She hugged the squire fiercely around the neck.

"Are you a knight yet? Can I call you Sir Bardon? Did you miss me? Where's Greer? Why did you take Kale away?"

Bardon laughed. "No. No. Yes. I don't know, and she wanted to come."

Toopka stuck out her lower lip, and her whiskers quivered. "I wanted to come, too, and they almost left me until they figured out everyone was coming but me, and they couldn't leave me home by myself. Only they really could have because I can take care of myself." She took a big breath. "But I wanted to come. Wizard Fenworth swirled us to the courtyard of a funny castle that looks like a mountain. Wizard Cam scolded a bunch of grawligs. He shook his finger at them, and lake water sprayed out of his sleeve." Toopka stopped to giggle. "Grawligs do *not* like to be wet. And Wiz Cam told them to clean up *everything*. They'd made a horrible mess. And he dried up a circle of quicksand and let the stuck ones get out, but they had to agree to help clean. And Wizard Lyll fixed their hurts. Isn't she pretty? She is *so* pretty, except when she's tired and then she looks like a very comfy grandma. Then Librettowit said we had to quit fooling around with the dirty grawligs and find Kale." Again she took a deep breath. "I said Kale would be all right, because she was with you." She looked over Bardon's shoulder and waved at Regidor, who waved back. "And if Regidor is with you, almost nothing bad can happen that he can't fix, because he's probably the greatest wizard and the greatest warrior that ever lived."

Librettowit walked over to Bromptotterpindosset and stuck out his hand. The disgruntled mapmaker took it reluctantly, shook briefly, and dropped the friendly gesture as quickly as possible.

The newly arrived tumanhofer seemed not to take offense. Kale knew the librarian Librettowit could be hot-tempered, and she watched with interest. She squeezed her mother's hand, drawing attention to the little drama taking place. But Librettowit's face remained neutral, expressing neither irritation at Bromptotterpindosset's rudeness nor projecting false cheer.

"I'm Trevithick Librettowit."

"Gordonnatropp Bromptotterpindosset. Pleased to meet you."

"I've heard of you," said Fenworth's librarian. "I have some of your maps in our library."

The mapmaker's expression brightened. "This was supposed to be a fact-collecting expedition. I hoped to make new maps and improve some of the old. At least on my part, it was that and nothing more. These others are on a quest to save sleeping knights."

"So I heard."

"And we were trapped in this cavern." Bromptotterpindosset slowly shook his head. "So many things I don't understand. For instance, we walked some distance." He glanced from one end of the cave to the other. "We should have covered miles, and yet, we are still in this one space."

"When trapped in an illusion," Librettowit explained, "you think you are traveling in a straight line, but you are actually going in circles."

The mapmaker nodded toward the two old wizards. "Can they get us out of this mountain? Can they return us to civilization?"

"Oh yes. But first I think their plans include rescuing the knights. They were quite put out when Risto commandeered Strot's castle for his own evil purposes. We all were under the impression the castle-fortress had been destroyed eons ago."

Librettowit scratched his nose before continuing. "I suspect a blinding spell was cast over many written records of the castle and its history. I'll be doing some research when I return." Librettowit's eyes gleamed with anticipation. "And there will be the library in Strot's castle to examine."

The mapmaker's shoulders slumped once again. "I have done a foolish thing."

"What is that?"

"I vowed to accept Wulder's existence and seek a knowledge of His ways if we were rescued."

"Foolish?" Librettowit clapped the man's shoulder. "Probably the most intelligent thing you have yet to do in your life."

"Ha!" The word came from the mapmaker's lips without his typical bluster. "A coincidence has put me in this position. A coincidence and fear and my own stupid words."

The librarian shook his head. "Nay. Do you not realize that Wulder Himself was in pursuit of you?"

The guttural grunt in reply only made Librettowit smile more broadly. "You're still under the influence of years of disbelief. You'll soon see that what you call coincidence was a carefully laid plan devised by Wulder to bring you to a place where you had to accept Him for who He is."

The same grunt rumbled in the mapmaker's throat. "What makes you think so? Why should I change?"

"Initially, because your pride will force you to honor your vow. But more importantly, Wulder has begun a work in you, and He will not abandon you."

"The meech said something similar. He said Wulder had not abandoned us in the illusion."

Librettowit nodded. "Smart fellow, our meech wizard."

Movement inside her cape drew Kale's attention away from the two tumanhofers. The minor dragons crawled out of their dens and flew from one member of the rescue party to the next, chirruping greetings.

Pat dove into Fenworth's beard, searching for a snack of insects. Kale started to call him out, but the old wizard held up his hand. "He's a growing dragon."

"He's growing round," said Kale with a smile.

Fen's eyes wandered around the gathering. Kale felt compelled to follow his gaze and knew her mentor was impressing her with his thoughts.

Regidor stood tall with his tail swishing across the ground. Three of their group were squat. The tumanhofers seldom topped five feet, and their bodies often resembled the shape of boulders. Furry Toopka barely covered Bardon's arm with her small frame. Two male wizards had aged, and the two female wizards had not. The squire looked healthy, strong, and ready. Kale's eyes lingered on how mature and reliable her friend looked. The various minor dragons flashed a variety of colors as they flitted about.

"I believe," said wise old Fenworth, "that Wulder appreciates diverse sizes, shapes, and colors in His creation. And if He does, then who are we to pass judgment based on such criteria?" He turned to look Kale in the eye. "Let Pat be round."

Fenworth strode over to Bardon, using his walking stick, but by no means depending upon it. "Young Squire," he boomed, "I am the oldest, and by rights, should be the leader of this quest. But, as you may have heard, I am retired. So, I defer to you. I have been informed that Paladin chose you to head this party."

Bardon studied the old man's face for a moment, seeing the fatigue around his eyes and the blue tinge of his lips. He wanted to put his hand on the old man's thin arm but knew Fenworth would not appreciate that type of sympathy.

Fenworth's eyes narrowed as if he read the squire's thoughts. "Well, boy, where do you wish to go? What do you wish to do? And when do you suggest we get started?"

Bardon spoke with authority, "We shall return to the castle and endeavor to free the knights, Wizard Fenworth. And now seems to be an appropriate time to get started."

"That way, then." Fen pointed his staff in the direction they had come from and marched off, leaving the rest to follow.

Cam doused the fire Regidor had provided.

"Wait!" Fen came tramping back. "I smell soup. Delicious Regidor soup. Let's eat before we go."

Bowls came tumbling out of nowhere, aimed at each member of the party. If they failed to catch the dishes coming their way, they circled around and returned to be caught on the second try. Kale ladled up the brew. The pot emptied only when the last person's appetite had been satisfied.

Fenworth again set out abruptly, commanding the others to "step lively." Toopka scampered through the burrows, content to play chase with the minor dragons and to pick up smaller lightrocks of different colors. When they reached the trek through the forest, she slowed some. As they trudged up a mountain path, she began to complain.

Regidor picked her up, swung her around to land on his back, and spread his wings. Toopka giggled and wrapped her arms around his neck. The meech dragon took to the air and soared high, soon disappearing ahead of them.

Fenworth hollered back to Bardon. "Squire, did you say he could do that?"

"No," he answered.

"Didn't think so. Cheeky rascal. He's been a hard one to raise. Too sure of himself. Cocky. Usually right. A horrible trait in an apprentice."

They reached the courtyard of Strot's castle an hour later.

Fenworth stretched his arms over his head, and several birds flew out of his sleeves. "Exercise!" He lowered his arms, and a rabbit, a mouse, and a squirrel popped out from under the robe's hem. "Exercise is good for mind, body, and spirit." He sat on one of the stone benches and promptly went to sleep, turning into a stunted tree after the second snore. Pat scrambled out of the tangled branches and perched on top.

Toopka barreled around a corner of the building. "You're here!" she shouted. "Regidor found a door. He says it's the main entrance to the castle. But he needs the other wizards to help him get it open. Follow me." She dashed back the way she had come.

Librettowit and Bardon gently lifted the tree off the bench and carried it. Kale followed with the others close behind. A muted snore reverberated within the trunk.

Toopka skipped back to hold Kale's hand. "Do you know what?"

"No. What?"

"You can't tell this is a castle from the air. We only knew it was the right place because Regidor saw the waterfall. You can't see the statues or the benches or the walkways. Nothing! And then Regidor couldn't find the door. He had to use his forefoot instead of his eyes. He closed his eyes and walked around the mountain with his forefoot on the rock. I followed. Then he found it. I couldn't see it. He said he didn't see it, but he felt the gap in the stone. I didn't see the gap in the stone, but he showed me and showed me and finally I saw it. Hurry up."

She ran ahead.

Bardon looked over his shoulder at Kale. "You know, she doesn't seem one bit older than she did three years ago."

"She *has* learned to read a little," Kale said.

"She can be quite helpful in the kitchen," added Taylaminkadot.

Librettowit shifted his burden and said, "Emerlindians and doneels have a longer maturing period. They're considered youngsters for almost a hundred years. Tumanhofers and o'rants mature in eighteen to twenty years. Mariones' and urohms' maturation period is about the same, but their life span is considerably shorter than the other high races. Kimens mature rapidly, in three or four years. No one outside of the kimen race is sure about their longevity."

"Still," said Taylaminkadot, "there has always been something secretive in Toopka's manner. She refused to choose a day to celebrate her birth every year. And when I urged her to pick a number to say it was how old she was and start counting from that, she didn't want to. In fact, she became quite stubborn."

The subject of their conversation danced toward them, hopping, skipping, and twirling. "Come on! You're almost there."

They followed her around a hedge and spotted Regidor inspecting a section at the base of what looked like a cliff.

After placing Fenworth in the shade, they gathered around the meech dragon. He showed them the camouflaged entry. The tumanhofers and Toopka sat down to watch as Lyll, Cam, Regidor, and Kale worked to open the door. Cam assigned each wizard a range of colored threads to manipulate. Bardon scouted the area to make sure this important work wouldn't be interrupted by grawligs.

Kale had never seen such a complicated weave. She had to concentrate to keep the strands from slipping away from her. Sometimes, it was a matter of holding hers in one place while another wizard moved his strands. She smiled as she realized her mother was the best at unwinding the threads.

"Just like untangling a mess of necklaces or yarn when you're knitting," her mother said.

"I try not to let my knitting get in a tangle," said Cam.

"I rarely wear necklaces," said Regidor.

Lyll chortled and directed Cam to move his threads through a loop in Regidor's strand.

In the end, they had the colors isolated and tied off. Regidor gave a push against the door, and it swung open.

Librettowit and Bromptotterpindosset lifted Fenworth and carried him in after the others. They stood in a vast entryway with tapestries and huge oil paintings on the walls, a two-sided, curved stairway before them, and a marble floor done in many colors, much like a mosaic.

Regidor tilted his head. "Odd."

Lyll's eyes swept the room as she nodded. "Definitely."

Cam breathed in deeply and expelled the air slowly. "We must proceed with caution."

Kale felt goose bumps rise on her arms, and a shiver tingled her spine. "There's someone in the castle now, isn't there?"

"Yes," said Regidor and drew his sword.

50

In the Castle Once More

Bardon also pulled his sword. Behind him he heard the swish of metal leaving leather. He glanced at Kale and saw she had her hand in front of her as if she held a sword, but nothing was there. A quick look at her mother showed she stood in the same position. They had invisible weapons. Bardon had seen Lyll Allerion wield her sword in a fight with mordakleeps. He presumed she had trained Kale to use the weapon just as effectively.

"How many people are in the castle?" he asked.

"Hard to say," Regidor answered. "They're scattered all over this wing."

"We're in the part of the castle where the Knights' Chamber is located, right?"

"Right."

"Let's escort the wizards, Taylaminkadot, and Toopka there. Then, we'll determine who is to stay and work on breaking the spell, and who will go looking for intruders."

Regidor nodded. Bardon looked over his shoulder to see if his party was ready to go. Kale and her mother had changed into matching outfits that would not hinder their movements during a fight. Instead of the loose clothing that had been comfortable for a long hike, they now wore fitted garments of a blue material that stretched easily. Toopka clung to Taylaminkadot's hand. Cam brought up the rear. The old wizard only had his staff for a weapon, but Bardon knew he could count on Cam to punish an attacker with more than just a blow from a stick.

The mapmaker's red face and the perspiration dripping off his brow warned Bardon something was wrong.

"Bromptotterpindosset?"

"I don't relish carrying this tree up those stairs."

Bardon looked to Lyll and Kale, who flanked the tumanhofers carrying Fenworth. "Can you do something about that?"

They nodded in unison, then turned to face the tree. In a moment it floated.

Lyll smiled. "Now all you have to do is guide Fenworth, instead of carrying him."

The group climbed the right side of the curving steps. Each one moved with great stealth. The only noise came from Fenworth's occasional snore. Toopka jumped each time a snort broke the silence.

They passed down a hall with family portraits hanging on both sides, then up another stairway, this one only six feet wide and straight. Regidor and Bardon continued to lead the way. They listened at each passage that branched off from the main corridor.

At the first of these junctions, Bardon glanced at Kale. She met his eye and, by giving a small shake of her head, confirmed she did not feel the presence of another being outside their own little group. No one lurked down the hall.

Are you ready? he asked.

"Yes, I feel our connection as if we hadn't been apart these three years."

Bardon relaxed some, knowing he and Kale had entered into a state that, as far as they knew, only the two of them had ever experienced. Both alert. Both thinking along the same lines. They knew from past experience that if a fight broke out, they would react as if their movements were synchronized, thought out by one mind instead of two.

The group climbed another set of stairs and came to a third-floor hallway. Regidor mindspoke to each of them, saying they sought the room at the end of this corridor.

Light poured from the open door and made a bright patch on the dusty hall runner. The carpet's colors of burgundy red and deep green struggled to show through a layer of fine dirt. The thick pile muffled their almost silent footsteps. Bardon signaled the men and women behind to stop. With a nod of his head, he indicated that Regidor and Kale should go with him.

They crept to the edge of the door, all three tensing.

"Bardon."

The squire cocked an eyebrow, hearing Kale's voice as clearly as if she had spoken aloud.

"There's a woman in the room. She's filled with sorrow. I don't think she's dangerous."

Regidor tilted his head and suddenly relaxed. He shoved his sword into its sheath. "Granny Kye."

Bardon put away his weapon and signaled the rest to come.

He stepped into the room so as not to startle the old emerlindian. She sat at her easel and concentrated on the picture she drew. He spoke softly, "Granny Kye?"

She frowned but did not look up.

He moved closer and touched her shoulder. "Granny Kye."

She glanced at him. "There you are. I've found him. My son." She raised a handkerchief to her trembling lips. "And my other son. The one I've thought dead. Twins." She nodded toward one stonelike knight and then another. "If we don't wake them soon, they will surely be gone forever."

He knelt beside her and put his arms around her thin shoulders. "There is hope, Granny Kye. I've brought four more wizards besides Regidor, and a learned gentleman who will search this castle's library."

She nodded and rested her forehead against his chest. A little sob broke from her throat. "We're so close to saving them. We must not fail."

"How did you get here?"

"Captain Anton said it was time for us to return to Dormenae. The moonbird brought Regidor's message, but another full day had passed. The captain said we would leave in the morning, but during the night, the voices spoke to Sittiponder. He said they were most urgent. We must follow you and Regidor into the warren. Captain Anton was reluctant, but the boy convinced him. Sittiponder led the way."

"How long have you been here?"

"Three days."

His breath caught in his throat, but Bardon merely nodded. Obviously, his and Regidor's accounting of time had been influenced by the enchantment of the castle and the surrounding area.

Bardon looked at the painting of Granny Kye's two sons. Although the knights stood as they did in actuality, and their clothing represented what he could see with his eyes, the portraits revealed vibrant life. In reality the figures slumped with their chins resting on their chests. In the portrait, they were pictured as awake. Each man's eyes looked out from the canvas instead of being shut in perpetual slumber. Their expressions showed an eagerness to spring from the two-dimensional world and perhaps embrace their mother.

When Bardon stood, the son on the right seemed to watch him. A shiver ran down the squire's spine. He crossed behind Granny Kye to stand at her other shoulder. The eyes of the one knight followed him.

"Which one is N'Rae's father?" he asked.

"This one." The old emerlindian pointed to the man on the left. "Jilles. His name is Sir Jilles." Her head turned slightly, and her finger moved to the other man in the painting. "And this is my eldest son, by a few minutes. Joffa. Sir Joffa. Their father was Jofil. I thought I was very clever when I named them."

Bardon rested his hand on her shoulder and gave a gentle squeeze. "We will do our best to wake them." The portrait of Sir Joffa stared at Bardon, and now the expression held a deep sadness. The living, breathing squire gave himself a little shake to break loose of the feeling that the picture would speak if it could. He glanced up at the still, cold knight, who appeared not to breathe at all.

"Where are the others, Granny Kye? N'Rae, Holt, the boys, the guard?" he asked.

"They spend the days exploring. No one has found a way to get out of the castle. All the doors are locked. All the windows are sealed."

Behind him, he heard Lyll Allerion and Kale speaking in muted tones. He turned to see the lady wizard kneeling beside a seated knight, her head in his stiff lap.

In a few steps, Bardon reached Kale and touched her elbow. She turned toward him, and he naturally enclosed her in his arms. Her arms came around his middle, and she held on as if she would fall without his support. His embrace tightened as she melted against him and cried.

He leaned his cheek against her hair and breathed in the fresh citrus smell of her. Affection and a fierce desire to protect her surged through him. He moved his chin a fraction of an inch and placed his lips against her temple, sure that she would not notice such an insignificant kiss.

He looked at Lyll and the sleeping knight.

"Your father?" Bardon asked.

Kale nodded and sniffed. Reaching into his pocket, he brought out a handkerchief and offered it. Kale took it with one hand but kept herself tucked close while she blew her nose.

"Mother said when she heard about the sleeping knights, she hoped my father would be among them. She knew Risto had captured him and cast a spell over him. No one had seen him fall in battle. No one knew where he had gone from the last inn where she had traced him. Then she heard the rumor of Risto's mastering this sleep spell and that my father was under Risto's power. But no word as to where these men were. But she was afraid to think she had found him at last. Afraid he would not be among those sleeping here." She swallowed another sob. *"Now she has new fears. She's found him, and she is afraid we will not be able to wake him."*

Bardon turned Kale so she could see what the others were doing. *Look, Kale. Cam and Fen are at work. Librettowit already has found a reference book and is comparing what they see to the knowledge that is written in its pages. They will break the spell. I'm sure of it.*

She leaned back to look at him, and a brave, but tiny, smile lifted her lips. Bardon fought the urge to kiss away a tear that traced a path down her cheek.

He let her go, pushing her away.

"We must find the others. Pull yourself together, Kale." He turned to

Regidor, who examined the tumanhofer knight. "Reg, Kale and I are going to make a sweep through the castle and round up all the members of our questing party and return here."

"Locate the library," ordered Librettowit.

"And the kitchen," said Taylaminkadot.

"I want to come too." Toopka ran to stand at Kale's knee.

The three walked briskly out of the room. Six multicolored minor dragons accompanied them, sometimes flying around their heads, sometimes flying ahead or behind them, and sometimes resting on available shoulders, heads, or arms.

As soon as they were out of earshot, Bardon muttered, "I don't understand how they could have been in the castle for three days and never found the way out through the turret Regidor and I used."

"Don't forget," said Kale, "you had Regidor helping you. He probably did more untangling of spells than you were even aware of. It's exciting for me to watch him work."

"So your relationship as Dragon Keeper and young protégé has changed, has it?"

"Definitely. Can you imagine anyone 'keeping' Regidor?"

Toopka hopped in anticipation. "Maybe we'll find something exciting."

"We found enchanted knights, little one," said Kale. "What could be more exciting than that?"

"Treasure!"

"Actually," said Bardon, "Regidor and I saw quite a bit of valuable property, paintings and gold candlesticks, things like that."

"Any gold coins? Any jewels?"

"No."

"Well, we can look for real treasure in a box or hidden in a hole in the wall. And we could find a castle monster. That would be exciting too." Toopka shivered in imaginary fear.

"Only if we defeated it without injury to one of us."

"Oh, you and the others could protect us from anything."

"You think so?"

"Yes." She nodded her head with such a hard jerk, Bardon expected her to say, "Ouch."

Kale scratched the top of Toopka's head between her two perked ears. "Suppose you find the monster, the monster eats you, and then we come along a few minutes too late to save you."

"Then you must cut open its stomach and pull me out. I'll hold my breath till you come."

"That sounds like a slimy thing to do." Kale laughed. "I'd just as soon not deal with any monsters, thank you very much."

"Oh, I want to see a big, hairy monster." Toopka grinned and twirled, then stopped and winked at the adults. "But I really don't want to be eaten. You better come along before he chomps me."

Bardon laughed. "We'll try."

51

TREASURES

Female voices drifted up one of the staircases. Toopka darted ahead, stood at the top, and hollered, "Hi!"

Kale rushed forward, aggravated that Toopka could be so impetuous in unfamiliar surroundings. The women didn't sound dangerous, but still, Toopka's monster could be around any corner.

Bardon followed at a slower pace. Kale recognized their uniforms and greeted the two dragon riders as they reached the last steps.

"Hello, I'm Kale Allerion."

The doneel rider put forth her hand, but her eyes followed the minor dragons, first watching Metta flutter like a huge butterfly through the hall, and then Ardeo and Gymn as they swooped and dived in some game they were playing.

"I'm Lo Mees," she said, obviously forcing herself to focus on Kale. "And this is Lo Oh."

Toopka giggled, and the second rider, an o'rant, smiled down at her. "Yes, we know it's a terrible name, and I am trying very hard to earn my next rank."

"My name's Toopka. You don't see minor dragons very often, do you?"

"No," said Lo Oh. "I've only read about them in books and seen a few pictures."

"I live in The Bogs with the Dragon Keeper." The tiny doneel nodded to indicate Kale. "So I know a lot about minor dragons."

"That's very impressive," said Lo Mees.

"Not really. My friend Regidor is a meech dragon, and *that* is impressive. Have you seen any treasure or monsters?"

Lo Mees looked past her. "Now, there's a treasure of sorts, our lost leader."

They all turned to look at Bardon, who nodded.

"I'm back, and so is Regidor. We've brought people with us who should be able to break the spell over the knights. I would appreciate it if you would locate everyone and tell them to report to the Knights' Chamber. We'll have a meeting as soon as they've all arrived."

"Yes sir." The two women answered and turned around to go down the steps they had just climbed.

Kale smiled at their muffled chatter as they left. Were they enthused about the minor dragons or their handsome leader? Kale gazed at her friend. *He doesn't know how he affects the females he meets. And he doesn't much care for being impressive. Ha! Unlike Regidor, who loves attention or theatrically avoiding attention. Bardon would have loved months and months of solitude, and instead, here he is with a gaggle of questers.*

"Just how many are on this quest?" asked Kale.

"If we count your minor dragons, two dozen plus two."

"Phew! And you never liked a crowd."

"Too many people." Bardon smiled at her.

Kale picked up the next line. "Always too many people."

The look he cast her, filled with humor and chagrin, felt good. *We're friends,* she thought. *Very good friends.*

She grinned at him. "And when we successfully awaken the sleeping knights?"

Bardon groaned. "Three dozen, plus two."

Toopka hopped. "Are any of these people children?"

Kale saw a look of awareness cross Bardon's face, but more interestingly, she felt his sense of pleasure. He had a secret surprise for the little doneel.

"Yes." He patted her head. "Two are boys."

"Oh good," she exclaimed. "Boys are so much better to play with than girls."

"They are?" asked Kale. "You really haven't had many opportunities to play with anyone the last three years."

"Just when Wizard Cam takes us through a gateway for 'educational purposes.'" She looked very glum as they resumed their walk down the hall.

"Don't let her fool you, Bardon." Kale shook her head deliberately. "Cam's idea of education is a visit to a festival for cultural enlightenment or to diverse families for exposure to different lifestyles." Kale felt a sadness settle on her heart, remembering what it was like to have no real friends. "Still, it would be nice for Toopka to have one friend closer to her own age. One who is always around."

"Regidor is my friend." Her voice piped up, proving she had been listening, although she had appeared to be more interested in the paintings on the walls and knickknacks sitting in cases along the corridor. "And I'm older than him. I always will be."

She dropped to her hands and knees, wiggled under a table, and came out with a large ring.

"Look, I found treasure." She rubbed it on her yellow shirt and then held the ring up for them to see. A large square-cut emerald glistened from the ornately worked gold setting.

"I'd say that's treasure," said Bardon. "But we don't know who it belongs to. You can keep it until we find the rightful owner."

Toopka scowled as she tucked it in a pocket.

Bardon tweaked her ear as he walked by. "But somewhere in this castle is a treasure that belongs to you."

She jumped and raced past him, then turned to walk backward as she pelted him with questions. "Where? How do you know it belongs to me? What is it? Why is it here?"

"I don't know where it is. That's why we're exploring the castle. I know *it* belongs to you, because you once told me about it. It's a…" He paused. "No, I think it would be better if you discovered this treasure on your own. Why don't you turn around and look?"

At the end of the long hallway stood two boys, a blind tumanhofer and an o'rant.

Joy rushed through Kale as she realized Toopka's old friend from Vendela was Bardon's surprise. Her emotions transferred to the minor dragons, who burst into a chorus of excited chittering.

Toopka scrunched her eyes closed and turned slowly. Kale knew exactly when the little doneel allowed herself to open her eyes.

"Sittiponder!" Toopka squealed and ran to meet him.

The small tumanhofer scooped her into an embrace.

Kale took hold of Bardon's arm and squeezed. "This is wonderful. How did you find him?"

"He found us."

Kale left her arm tucked under Bardon's as they walked down the corridor.

Tiny Toopka hugged her friend fiercely. "I'm so glad you're here, Sitti." She kissed his cheek and hugged him again. Then her attention turned to the other child. "Who is this boy?"

"Ahnek." Sittiponder responded. With his arms full of the little doneel, he nodded in the other boy's direction.

"Hello, Ahnek. I found a treasure." Toopka took the ring out to show them. After flashing it before Ahnek's eyes, she pressed the treasure against Sittiponder's cheek and turned the ornate circlet slowly. "Bardon says there's another treasure here in the castle for me. I may have to give back this ring if it belongs to someone, but the other treasure belongs to me and it's one I told him about, but I can't imagine what it is because I've never had a treasure."

"You noisy bird," said Sittiponder affectionately, "quit twittering. Bardon was talking about me. I'm your treasure."

"You?" She thought a moment and then giggled. "You aren't made out of gold. You don't have jewels anywhere."

"I'm your *friend*, pebble."

Toopka sat very still in his arms. She looked at his face so close to hers, and her face grew very still. "Am I your treasure, Sitti?"

He squeezed her. "Yes, turnip seed, you're my friend. I think that's why the voices told me to come on this quest. So I could be with you."

Sittiponder and Ahnek knew where to find the kitchen, the library, and N'Rae.

Bardon and Kale followed the two boys. Toopka skipped beside Sittiponder, holding his hand. With the dragons circling above them, they moved through the hallways quickly, going down narrow stairs hidden behind doors. At one corner the two boys stopped to consult. Ahnek wanted to go left, and Sittiponder insisted they should go right. The blind boy won the dispute.

Ahnek spoke over his shoulder. "There's no sense in fighting him. He's always right.

When they walked into the library, N'Rae sat curled up in a big chair, her feet tucked under her. She looked up from a book as they entered.

"Hi! I'm Toopka." But the little girl might as well have saved her greeting.

N'Rae sprang out of the chair, sprinted across the room, and threw herself into Bardon's arms, hanging on to his neck and lifting her feet off the ground in an exuberant greeting.

Kale took a step back, thinking, *It's a good thing I no longer held on to his arm. She would have knocked me out of the way.*

N'Rae took a deep breath and leaned back to get a better look at Bardon.

"You're all right. I'm so very, very glad. We found the knights. My father is there, and so is my uncle. We've searched and searched, and none of us can find a clue as to how to break the spell. We can't even get out of the castle. We tried going out the way we came in, and that hole to the burrows is blocked somehow. A spell, I would suspect. And we're running out of food, and all Grandmother does is paint."

"Oh dear, a grown-up Toopka."

Kale, be nice. Bardon's voice popped into her mind.

"Of course, I'll be nice."

She was raised with ropma.

"That explains a lot."

Kale.

"All right. I'll be nice. Peel her off of you and introduce me."

As Bardon tactfully disengaged N'Rae's arms from around his neck and placed her a foot away from him, he explained where they had been, that they had rescued Bromptotterpindosset, and that they had brought back reinforcements.

Kale guarded her thinking. It wouldn't be prudent for Bardon to pick up her thoughts as she mused over this new development. *If I hadn't felt that kiss he planted on my head, I'd be quite irritated with my dearest Squire Bardon. I wrote him letters pages long and got back three sentences. He never once came to visit me in The Bogs. I hinted where Cam was planning to take us next, and he never coincidentally showed up.*

But that's all right. He kissed me and was naive enough to think I wouldn't feel it. Poor Bardon needs help discovering we're meant to be a couple, and I can't think of a better person to help him than me.

Kale frowned at the vivacious N'Rae. *This friendly little emerlindian had better find someone else to snuggle up to.*

Finally, Bardon introduced Kale and her dragons. The minor dragons liked the attention N'Rae gave them. Kale narrowed her eyes and vowed to give them a talking to. They immediately felt the tension in their Dragon Keeper and flew to perches around the room.

The pale emerlindian turned once more to Kale. "I am so glad you're here. I've always wanted a friend my own age, and Bardon has told me so much about you." She hesitated long enough for Kale to think, *Oh, great!*

N'Rae smiled shyly up at her. "I know you're important, the Dragon Keeper and a wizard, but I hope we can be friends."

Be nice, Bardon reminded her. *She is just what she seems.*

"She seems like she's a bit empty-headed."

Be nice.

"Oh, all right!"

Kale smiled and extended her hand. "Let's get to know each other."

⇥ 52 ⇤

Assignments

Bardon looked around the crowded room and noted the odd appearance of its occupants. Lyll Allerion sat on the arm of the chair her husband sat in. Kale sat on the floor at his feet. Two women, alive with hope and love, bracing like bookends a cold man with no feeling.

Since space was limited, others in the questing party mingled with the sleeping knights, standing next to and sitting beside the unresponsive men. Granny Kye remained at her easel, detached from the others. Jue Seeno presumably listened from the basket next to the artist's supplies.

I would love to hand over the leadership of this quest to someone else. Bardon sighed. He was obligated to fulfill his responsibilities, and he knew it. *I'll just proceed one item at a time.* He paused for a moment, surveying the other worthy leaders in the room. *Ah yes, Wulder, I see. Thank You for these people You have assembled for this task. Help me to hand bits of the burden You have placed on my shoulders into the most suitable hands.*

"Captain Anton, the wizards have opened the front door. You and your guard will be responsible for patrolling the area. I'm sure there are grawligs interested in what we are doing here. And, of course, there may be more sinister opponents lurking about. Although this fortress seems deserted, it was at one time a stronghold for evil." He paused to give Ahnek and Toopka a look of warning. Both youngsters nodded their understanding. Bardon turned back to Captain Anton. "I charge your men to hunt for food as well. There should be game on the mountainside."

The captain nodded.

"Regidor, would it be possible for you to fly out and guide our dragons to this castle?"

"It will take several hours," Regidor said. "I'll see to it first thing in the morning."

Bardon looked at Wizard Fenworth, who had dozed off and taken the form of a scraggly bush. A mouse peeked out from the long tangle of moss that would be his beard if he were awake. When Bardon looked again, the small creature had disappeared. *I wonder if that's Jue Seeno disguised as a mouse.* He shook off the distraction.

Since Fenworth was not awake, the squire addressed Wizard Cam. "What can we do to help you discover the remedy to this spell?"

"We could use assistance in the library. If you would designate workers to sort through the books and bring any to us that have to do with wizardry, that would save time and energy. We are particularly interested in tomes pertaining to living organisms and vital processes."

Bardon nodded. "Taylaminkadot, may I count on you and N'Rae to be in charge of meals?"

"It would be my pleasure, Squire Bardon," said the tumanhofer.

N'Rae perked up. "I can do that, and I'll watch after the children."

Toopka tossed the ring she'd found from one hand to the other. "We don't need watching after."

Ahnek said, "Shh!" and stood up. "We'd like to continue our explorations, Squire. We might discover something useful."

"Fine, Ahnek," answered Bardon. "That's a good plan. And when the dragons arrive, I want you to help with taking care of them. Regidor will escort them here, then they will return with their riders to pack our equipment and bring it along. You could be useful there, as well."

Ahnek beamed as he accepted the responsibility and sat down again.

Holt stirred in his seat beside a stiff knight. "Is there anything you want me to do?"

"Would you rather be assigned to the guard or the library?"

"The guard."

"Done. You'll answer to Captain Anton." Bardon surveyed the group. No one seemed to be eager to add to his instructions. "Any questions?

Suggestions?" Most of them gave slight negative shakes of their heads. Of course, Fenworth didn't respond. Neither did Toopka nor Granny Kye. "Regidor, I believe Taylaminkadot will need your assistance in providing for our evening meal. All right. Let's get to work."

They dispersed. Librettowit, with Ahnek guiding his way, led the group down to the library. Captain Anton said they would join the book search, since they wouldn't be hunting this late in the day. Kale and Bardon followed some distance behind the others.

Kale looked at him askance. "I only counted twenty-five."

"Twenty-five?"

"People."

Bardon stopped in his tracks. He took her hand and started back down the hall.

"Where are we going?"

"You need to meet someone. Kale, of all the amazing things we've seen, this is quite beyond astonishing."

He tugged her into the room and over to Granny Kye. There he crouched beside the minneken's basket, pulling Kale down beside him. "Mistress Seeno, may I have the honor of introducing a special friend to you?"

"In just a minute," her small voice came to his ears. "If I'm to meet someone new, I'd like to be presentable."

Bardon grinned, glanced at Kale, and winked.

Don't use your talent to find out who's in there. I want this to be a surprise.

"I promise."

In a minute, the cover of the basket raised slightly.

Bardon said, "Allow me," and lifted the woven lid.

Jue Seeno appeared, elaborate hat first, with round ears peeking through the velvet brim. Face next, with pointed nose and chin, whiskers quivering, and tiny black eyes inspecting Kale.

"Give me your hand, young man," she ordered.

Bardon let go of Kale's hand to offer a platform for Mistress Seeno to stand on. She stepped out with the moonbeam cape swirling about her and one of her most elaborate, colorful belts encircling her waist.

"Mistress Seeno," said Bardon in a very good imitation of Sir Dar's cordial manner, "may I introduce Kale Allerion, Dragon Keeper and wizard of The Bogs under Wizard Fenworth?"

The minneken dipped her tiny head, and Kale, kneeling beside Bardon, did her best to curtsy. She inclined the upper half of her body.

"Kale, this is Mistress Jue Seeno of the Isle of Kye."

"It is an honor to meet you, Mistress," Kale replied demurely.

Bardon observed the two women inspecting each other without really seeming to. This play of manners occupied much of the time spent at court. He didn't enjoy it there but found it rather amusing to see Kale perform the art with ease in these unusual circumstances.

Her mother has been training her, as well as Fenworth, Cam, and Librettowit. Good thing too. Who would want a woman around who only knew the crusty behavior of three old men?

Kale's light laughter flitted through his mind. *"There's Taylaminkadot, too."*

You quit intruding on my thoughts.

"Really, Bardon. Sometimes it is more difficult not to hear what you're thinking than to listen." With the introductions over, Bardon moved on to important matters.

"What have you discovered in my absence, Mistress Seeno?"

"That this castle is strangely devoid of active life forms. No cats, bats, rats, or bugs. That there is a level below the cellar that is, to me, inaccessible. That Holt is more fond of N'Rae than he should be."

As an aside to Kale, Bardon said, "Jue Seeno is N'Rae's protector."

Jue Seeno's eyes narrowed. "Are you going to send that tumanhofer back as soon as the dragons get here?"

"I'll check with Paladin's coin, but we may not be forced to expel Bromptotterpindosset from our midst after all."

"Why is that?"

"Our mapmaker met with enough 'coincidences' to be relatively assured of a universal Master's hand."

Jue Seeno was speechless, but only for a moment. "Wulder chooses to attract the most irregular people. I certainly wouldn't have bothered with such a pompous braggart."

Bardon thought it wise to change the subject. "I trust you will be actively keeping me informed of the things you observe. It's reassuring to know you're on duty."

"Of course. Now if you don't mind, I must catch up with N'Rae and that scoundrel."

He placed her on the floor, and instead of rushing out the door, she disappeared through a crack in the wainscoting.

"Shall we go search the library with the others?" Bardon asked.

Kale nodded, and he rose from his crouched position and then gave her his hand to help her rise.

As they passed the ensorcelled form of her sleeping father, she stopped and gazed down at him.

"What are you feeling, Kale?"

She turned and looked into his eyes. The depth of her confused emotions swept through him. With a pull of his hand, he drew her into his arms and for some time just held her.

Do I feel this turmoil so strongly because I, too, have never known my father? Or is it that strange bond between us that always surfaces when we're together?

"*Both, I would think.*"

I'm sorry I don't have words to say that would comfort you.

"*It's all right, Bardon. I think words are highly overrated at times.*"

He loosened his hold and looked down at her upturned face. She had particularly lovely eyes.

"Well," he said, clearing his throat. "Let's get busy doing something. Um…since words—"

"*You just missed a perfectly good opportunity to kiss me.*"

The words came into his mind with a wistful tone. He stared at Kale, whose face began to glow with a pink blush.

"You heard that!"

Yes. Sometimes it is more difficult not—

Kale placed her hand on the back of his neck. "Words are highly over—"

She didn't apply any pressure to bring his head down to hers. Bardon felt the pull from his heart, and his kiss brushed her lips just to taste their sweetness. He pulled back and saw his own astonishment flash in Kale's eyes. Uncertainty touched his feelings, and he saw the question in her expression. An explosion of delight replaced the trepidation, and Kale's face lit with pleasure. Contentment followed the joy, and he felt satisfaction bounce back from the young woman in his arms. He began to laugh, and she hugged him.

"You realize," she said, "that you have brazenly kissed me in front of my father."

He stiffened and looked down at the sleeping knight, then shrugged. "And Wizard Fenworth. And Granny Kye. And eleven other of Paladin's knights."

Bardon squeezed her and then put her away from him. "I did not expect a simple kiss to be so powerful. Kale, we shall have to use a lot of words, overrated or not, before we indulge in…"

Kale widened her eyes, mischief alive in her expression. "I agree." She giggled. "I want to be courted."

"Courted?"

"Definitely."

"And I agree. You deserve to be courted."

Bardon and Kale left Granny Kye to her portrait of her two sons and Wizard Fenworth to his nap.

"Now," said Kale as they passed through the hall, "tell me about Jue Seeno. She's a minneken, right?"

"Right."

"I want to know it all, Bardon. How is she the emerlindian's protector? Why is that handsome marione Holt a scoundrel? And there was something about a coin given to you by Paladin."

"Let's not go directly to the library. There're too many people there."

"Way too many people," they said in unison and laughed.

Bardon coaxed her toward the front staircase. "Let's go walk in the garden instead."

She tilted her head. "To talk?"

"To talk."

53

DISCOVERIES

Bardon kept an eye on his expanded questing party as the day came to an end.

Taylaminkadot fussed about the condition of the linens, but her husband overruled when she wanted to strip the beds and wash the sheets. Librettowit promised she could commence housekeeping the following day. The castle had more than enough luxurious bedchambers to accommodate them all. They did have to thump dust out of the pillows and covers.

Bardon ordered a night watch. Captain Anton insisted this was his responsibility and organized the shifts with two people on duty at a time. Holt surprisingly volunteered to do his part.

The next morning Regidor flew to the west at dawn. Several hours later he returned with the five guard dragons and Greer.

Bardon went out to greet his purple dragon. Greer's disposition was less than sunny. His squire held on to his patience and tried to make amends.

I know you don't like being left out of the action. I would have much rather had you by my side, but it couldn't be helped. The warren had huge burrows, but you would have been claustrophobic... Yes, that's a word... It has nothing to do with closets. Well, in a way it does, but not as a root word or anything.

Bardon sighed and stroked the scales under the dragon's chin. *You're not to pout... I'm serious. I need you to oversee the protection of the castle. Keep an eye out for any massing forces. Grawligs are in the area, and they had come to think of the courtyards of this castle as their own personal property... No, I don't know for sure they even recognized this mountain as a castle, but they enjoyed the gardens, the terraces, and the fountains. Listen, Greer. I don't want to be busy with other things and discover rampaging ogres pouring in the front door.*

Bardon grinned in response to Greer's sudden elation. *Yes, Kale is here... Utterly beautiful... "Utterly" is a suitable word to use with beautiful... All right, then. She's looking extremely well... That's not good, either? It would solve the problem of what she looks like if I just call her. Wait a moment, and you can see for yourself.*

The visit with Kale lifted the dejected dragon's spirits in an amazing way, but Bardon had to see to details among his charges. He could not stay to enjoy his two best friends' company.

During the early morning, Captain Anton and his men took their bows and arrows to hunt. They brought back several medium-sized wild heatherhens, plump birds known for their tender, juicy meat. Holt, who had risen a bit too late to accompany them, redeemed himself by locating the overrun kitchen garden. Even through years of neglect, the small patch of ground still had some produce to gather. The marione farm boy dug pnard potatoes and onions and brought in some scrawny herbs.

Bardon cocked an eye at Kale as Holt explained how he had overslept. In his mind, he heard her chortle. *"Scoundrel or slugabed?"*

In the afternoon, Holt and Captain Anton, with two of the guard, mounted the dragons and took off to recover the remainder of their supplies. Two guardsmen stayed behind to offer protection. They came upon a grawlig lurking around the castle and scared him off.

The dragons and riders returned at sunset. And with that event, according to Toopka, the last of any interesting activity came to a sudden end. The little doneel complained daily that no one did anything but chores and study books. The boys often escaped to explore while Toopka finished the chores Taylaminkadot had listed for her.

Granny Kye left the finished portrait of her sons propped up against a chair and moved her easel in front of Sir Kemry Allerion. She studied her subject for several minutes, then picked up her brush.

Three days later, Taylaminkadot brought a clothbound book to the Knights' Chamber.

"It's the housekeeper's journal," she said. "I looked through it, and I've put bits of paper in pages where she makes comments you might be interested in."

Bardon and Librettowit opened the book on a table and read together. After a moment, the librarian looked up and smiled at his wife. "You've done well, my darling. This is most important information."

Taylaminkadot blushed. "I'll go back to my cooking now. That's important too."

"Risto is mentioned here," said Bardon, pointing at a page. "Listen. 'That wizard is here again. Master Strot likes the man, but I think it is only because the visitor promises to help him learn more about the spells affecting the body. Master Strot wants to do good, but I think this Wizard Risto is evil. I get the shivers when he looks at me.'

"Here's another one several days later. 'To my way of thinking, the master knows more about the workings of the human body than does this awful man who smiles and is everything that is agreeable. But still, this pleasant Wizard Risto makes me cold inside and fearful.' "

Librettowit and Bardon scanned several more pages. The librarian looked up at the waiting comrades. "The housekeeper is responsible for the missing book. She says she found her master dead in his chair. She suspected Risto killed him, and she didn't want the book in the evil wizard's hands." He turned the pages back to those they had passed over quickly.

"Aha!" the librarian exclaimed, tapping an entry with a stubby finger. "Bless my little Taylaminkadot's soul. Here's the information we need in order to figure out exactly how long these valiant men have before it is too late to rescue them. The housekeeper is actively eavesdropping at this point. She doesn't trust Risto. She records a conversation in which Risto says when the Wizards' Plume that he threw into the sky has grown to a certain size and first kisses the line of discernment from the Eye of the North, the spell must be refreshed or broken."

"What is the line of discernment?" asked Granny Kye.

"A perpendicular line from the star to the horizon."

"There are still a lot of variables," said Regidor.

Librettowit patted the page beneath his hand. "Yes, but I have enough to give us a date."

The room went quiet. The librarian looked around and saw the eyes of Lyll, Cam, Regidor, Kale, and Granny Kye trained on him. His chin dropped down to his chest, and he focused on the page. Bardon heard him mutter as he calculated.

Librettowit's head lifted, and he looked with a serious frown at those around him. "Six days."

With renewed hope and a dread of time passing too quickly, the researchers went back to work. Two days later, Regidor came into the room waving a book above his head. "Here's good news and bad."

"What is it?" asked Cam, sharply.

The frown on the usually relaxed lake wizard worried Bardon more than the librarian's outbursts of temper. The time was growing short before the wizards must cast a renewal spell or instigate the process to restore the men to their natural selves.

Regidor placed the book on the table in front of Lyll and Cam, who immediately opened it.

The meech dragon smiled with satisfaction. "This is a translation guide for *Strot's Book of Anatomical Spells.* From what I gather from the words written in here, there has to be a book with the key to reversing the sleeping invocation."

Bardon rubbed his hand through his hair. "And the bad news is we still don't have that book."

The meech dragon put his hand on the opened translation guide. "I've enjoyed the brilliance Wulder has given me. Perhaps this time it will be of monumental significance. I hope that by studying the random words in this volume, I will be able to piece together Strot's method."

Cam took hold of his arm and gave it a shake. "It's worth a try. If anyone could decipher a procedure from this montage of words, you can." He slapped Regidor on the shoulder. "Get to work, young Wizard."

Regidor scooped up the book and strode across the room to sit beside Fenworth on the divan, where the old wizard had planted himself when they first arrived.

Another day passed without any measurable progress toward freeing the knights. The morning of the fourth day, after Librettowit had made his six-day pronouncement, Toopka wandered into the room. Bardon noticed her but gratefully let Kale handle the intrusion.

"Toopka, where are the boys?" asked her guardian.

"In the cellar. They're always in the cellar." The little girl plopped down on a footstool beside Granny Kye. "I don't like the cellar. It's dark and smelly. We didn't find any treasure and now Sitti and Ahnek are trying to find a dungeon. There won't be any treasure in a dungeon."

She put her elbows on her knees and rested her chin on her fists. "Taylaminkadot is making daggarts and will not let me help because she says I snitched one time too many. N'Rae is in the library with those books. The little minneken I'm not supposed to know about won't play. She never wants to play. The minor dragons have to go into the woods to find food because there are no bugs in this boring castle. I'm not allowed to go into the woods because it might be dangerous."

Her gaze shifted to Granny Kye's painting of Kale's father. She stood up and looked at the canvas and then at the palette of many colors.

"Granny Kye, could I paint too?" she asked.

The old emerlindian actually looked up from her artwork and smiled at the child. "Not today, dear."

Toopka sighed heavily but remained by the granny's side. She tilted her furry head and stared at the portrait, then at the sleeping knight.

"Isn't the picture supposed to look like the person?"

Granny Kye nodded.

"Your knight is awake, and the real knight is asleep."

Granny Kye nodded again.

Toopka leaned closer, getting her head between the artist and her easel. Granny Kye frowned.

The little doneel pointed to the background in the painting. "You've got a smudge on the wall." She leaned to the side to look around the canvas. "Oh, there is a smudge. No, that's not dirt."

She ran to the wall and crouched beside the wainscot panel pictured in the granny's painting.

"It's not here." She ran her fingers over the wood. "Yes, it is!"

"Wait!" said Granny Kye, and the urgency in her voice made Bardon put down the book he held.

Toopka pushed against the wall, and a panel moved downward six inches, exposing a gap. Toopka put her hands on the thin sheet of wood and peered into the darkness.

"It's a secret cupboard. There's probably treasure in here."

"Toopka," said Bardon, "that wood looks fragile. Don't—"

He took a step toward her and heard a crack. Instead of the panel splintering, it suddenly slipped all the way down, and Toopka tumbled head first down the hole.

Bardon raced across the room and threw himself down beside the gap in the wall. "Toopka!"

He reached into the darkness and felt nothing but rough wood.

Regidor was beside him, removing his cape and jacket. "Let me try," he said. "My arms are longer."

His wings expanded and then folded against his shoulder blades. The stylish coat he'd dropped to the floor had two large slits in the back.

"I'm all right! I'm all right!" Toopka coughed. "Really, I'm all right." She coughed again. "I got something. It's…it's only a book. What is it with this castle and books?"

Bardon looked over his shoulder and saw that Toopka had captured everyone's attention.

Kale stood at the open window. "Tell her not to be afraid. Ardeo is coming to give her some light. The others are coming too."

Bardon turned back to the hole. "Ardeo is coming. Don't be afraid."

"I'm not afraid. I'm stuck."

"Are you hurt?"

"I scraped my face and my arm." Her voice did not sound quite as brave as it had a moment before.

"Gymn is coming," said Bardon. "He'll come down and heal you."

"At least I know there aren't any spiders or leggybugs down here." Her tone had slipped to timid.

"That's right," said Regidor in a deep, reassuring voice. "No insects."

"It's kind of stuffy," she whined.

Bardon frowned. "I don't suppose there's a window you could open."

"Of course not." She sounded disgusted, which was what Bardon wanted to hear. Toopka being fainthearted just wasn't natural.

Ardeo came in through the window, flew across the room, and dropped down the small shaft.

Toopka giggled. Gymn and Pat followed in a few seconds.

The little doneel laughed. "Gymn, you're tickling me."

Kale came to kneel beside Bardon. "Gymn says your fuzzy face is very red beneath the fur."

"I'm upside down."

Kale winked at Bardon and Regidor. "Toopka, Pat has figured out how to get you out. He wants you to put your hands down on the crossbeam Ardeo is sitting on. Pat and Gymn are going to unsnag your britches. You have to ease yourself down onto that beam and then turn right side up. The other dragons are coming to make sure you don't fall."

"Tell Metta not to sing to me. I don't want Metta to sing to me."

"Why not, dear? When Metta sings to me I feel brave. She could sing a song about marching into battle."

"All right. But no baby-go-to-sleep songs."

"Of course not."

By peering over the edge of the floor, Kale and Bardon could see the activity below. As the dragons made suggestions, Kale relayed them to

Toopka. She soon sat on the large crossbeam, her feet dangling over a space that opened to the inner wall of the floors below. She still had the book clutched under her arm.

"Give your treasure to Pat and Filia, Toopka," said Kale. "They'll carry it up for you."

"It's not a treasure. It's just a book."

The minor dragons shot up the skinny shaft with the book between them. Bardon took it and handed it to Regidor.

"Is it?" asked Cam.

The meech dragon smiled. "It is!"

The room shook with cheers.

"Hey!" yelled Toopka. "Hey!"

Bardon yelled back. "You can come out now."

He heard scrabbling and looked down to see Ardeo lighting the way and the other dragons showing her where to put her hands and feet as she scaled the rough timber inside the wall.

When her head popped up in the opening, Dibl sat between her furry ears and Gymn circled her throat like a necklace.

"I had an adventure," she said as Bardon pulled her free.

"You did, indeed."

"Wait till I tell Sitti and Ahnek. They think they're going to find something in a smelly old dungeon."

Bardon kissed her cheek. "And you found something in a smelly old wall."

54

THE DUNGEON

Kale watched Bardon holding Toopka and then turned to see the other wizards huddled over the two books with gleeful anticipation. Regidor had the translation volume memorized. The older, wiser wizards would make quick work of interpreting the newly found book. Kale decided her talents would best be served relieving the squire of the little doneel.

She walked to them with her arms out. "Come with me, Toopka. Let's go spread the word that the book has been found."

"And that I found it."

"Yes. We'll even go tell the boys in the cellar."

Toopka jumped from Bardon's arms to Kale's. The Dragon Keeper put her down on her feet. "You can walk. I learned a long time ago not to carry you. I get bruises from your wiggling."

With the minor dragons flying above them, Kale and Toopka went to the library. Everyone who did not have a pressing duty to perform had instinctively gone to help search through the shelves of books.

The doneel child ran into the room, straight to Taylaminkadot. "Are the daggarts done? We get to celebrate."

"Yes, they're done. What are we celebrating?"

"I found the book! It was in a hole in the wall."

Holt and a few of the guard gave a cheer.

Bromptotterpindosset closed the book he was perusing and pushed it across the table. With a look of relief, he pulled a stack of maps from Strot's collection toward him.

N'Rae sprang to her feet. "Have they already undone the spell? Is my father awake?"

Kale shook her head and felt her chest tighten. No one had promised this miracle would happen before time ran out.

Hope. Now we have a bigger hope, but still it is hope and not fact.

She closed her eyes, took a deep breath, and practiced something Fenworth had taught her. She breathed in, remembering the promise Wulder had made in His Tomes that this world spun toward an end of His design. And she breathed out, purposefully shedding the demand in her soul that everything be made right. Right now, this very instant.

When she opened her eyes, N'Rae stood beside her. The young emerlindian gently placed a hand on Kale's arm.

"I'm sorry, Kale. I forgot that you're waiting for your father to wake up too."

"Thank you, N'Rae. I've never known him, yet it would hurt to have this chance to meet him snatched away."

Toopka bounced beside the two young women and tugged on Kale's sleeve. "Let's go. Let's go to the cellar." She turned to announce to the others in the room, "We're going to tell Sittiponder and Ahnek that I found the book."

Kale took her hand and started for the door. "Yes, we are, and the sooner, the better."

Toopka pulled her down the hallway, into the servants' wing, through a maze of rooms, and down a dark, narrow stairwell.

A shiver of dread hit Kale like an icy wind as soon as she stepped through the doorway at the bottom. The minor dragons cooed in slow mournful calls to one another. Gymn landed on one shoulder, Dibl on her head, and Metta on the other shoulder. Filia settled on one arm with Pat below her. Ardeo flew just ahead of her, lighting the way.

"Toopka!" Kale heard the fear in her own voice and wondered what was wrong in this dark basement. The area certainly smelled musty, but it appeared clean and orderly from what she could see. "Toopka!"

"I'm here." She came around the corner, carrying an armload of lightrocks. "I take as many as I can, because I think it's creepy down here." She handed the biggest one to Kale. "This way," she called as she scurried off.

Kale followed, muttering to her dragon friends. "I don't like this at all." She got the impression they liked it even less.

"We're going to get those boys and drag them up to the castle proper. This exploring for a dungeon has to come to an end."

"They're not here!" Toopka's exclamation hastened Kale's steps.

She came to the end of the hall in a storage room with wooden boxes stacked against the walls. The doneel child was nowhere in sight.

"Toopka!" she called in a hoarse whisper.

Her face popped out from behind a crate, and Kale jumped.

"Don't scare me like that," Kale scolded.

Toopka grinned and then nodded to a spot behind her. "There's a little door back here. I think you can get through it. The boys did."

Kale grunted as she moved the heavy stack of boxes farther away from the wall. She swung the waist-high door open a bit wider. Then, thinking she did not want to get trapped in any dungeon, she struggled to move those boxes against the door to hold it open.

"Come on!" urged Toopka.

Whatever had made her feel nervous when she first passed into this realm below the castle made her feel positively terrified here. Her skin crawled, and the hair on the back of her neck stood on end.

"Filia," she whispered. "Go back and get Bardon."

When the little dragon hesitated to go by herself, Kale started to send Dibl with her. *"No, you stay here with us, Dibl. I forgot your lightness of spirit gives me courage. And I need to be brave. Metta, go with Filia, and both of you be quick."*

Each dragon picked up a chip of lightrock from the stone floor and headed back the way they had come.

As she walked behind Toopka, Kale looked more closely at the structure of her surroundings. The floor and walls were chiseled out of solid rock. The cold, empty passageway had probably never been used for storage. They moved at a slower pace now.

"Toopka, do you know where we're going?"

"No," she said and stopped. "I've never seen that door before. This must be the dungeon."

"I've only been in one dungeon before, and it had rooms, not just a long passage."

"I think," said Toopka, turning an earnest face to Kale, "I'll tell Sitti and Ahnek about the book later. Let's go back and wait until they come up for supper."

"I think we had better find them and take them back with us," said Kale.

She looked at the small child in front of her. Toopka turned and stared into the dark of the tunnel with such concentration, she hardly looked as though she was breathing. Her ears usually stood at points, now they drooped. This little girl who rarely stopped moving was immobilized by fear.

"Toopka, I need you to be very brave and go back to get more help."

Toopka jerked at the sudden sound of Kale's voice. She twirled to face Kale. "You sent Filia and Metta to get Bardon."

"Yes, but I've decided it would be best if Captain Anton and the guard came. Maybe Holt, too. We may have to search more tunnels to find Sittiponder and Ahnek. I may need help. I'll send Pat and Dibl with you."

"All right. I can do that." She trotted past Kale with the two minor dragons flying as her escort. But after a few steps back, she stopped and turned. "Kale," she said, biting her lower lip, "You be careful. This isn't a nice place."

"I will. I'm just going to get the boys and come back."

She watched the blue glow of lightrock grow fainter as Toopka ran down the passageway. When she could see the light no longer, she turned to face the dark tunnel ahead.

"Just get the boys and come back," she repeated. "That sounds like a very good plan."

She walked another hundred paces. The green dragon perched on her shoulder let her know he didn't like this journey, either. A small smile touched her lips. "You haven't fainted since you were a baby dragon, Gymn. You are *not* going to faint now. But should something pop out at us at this point, you may have to revive me from falling over in a swoon."

A few feet ahead of her, Ardeo's glow blinked out of sight. Before she could call to him, he reappeared, flying toward her.

He'd gone around a corner, and around the corner was a huge cavern lit by lightrocks.

Kale sighed in relief. "That's where those boys will be."

They quickened their pace and came to the end of the passageway. It came out as a balcony overlooking a huge cavern. The walkway turned and followed the wall in a slow descent to the main floor. Kale surveyed the room and gasped. Lining the walls of the main floor stood a ring of people, slumbering as the knights slumbered in the castle above.

There must be hundreds of them. All races. All ages. The servants!

"Ahnek! Sittiponder! Where are you?"

She heard grunts but no words. She drew her weapon and held the invisible sword so that the blade pointed the way. Rushing down the ramp, she kept her eyes open and trusted Gymn and Ardeo to help her watch for danger.

When she reached the cavern floor, she heard muffled groans and sounds of struggling. She turned to see the boys being held by a tall dark figure, their hands bound behind them. Gags stopped their mouths, and ropes wound around their ankles.

Wings flashed out from behind their captor. He stepped closer, into the light, and Kale let out a startled exclamation.

"You're a meech!"

"Of sorts."

He smiled, and Kale shivered, grasping her sword's handle more tightly. She wondered if he could see it. Instantly, she regretted not protecting her thoughts from intrusion and said the words Granny Noon had taught her so long ago. *My thoughts belong to me and Wulder. In Wulder's service, I search for truth. I stand under Wulder's authority.*

She watched the meech's expression to see if she could pick up some indication that he listened to her thoughts. His face maintained the wicked grin.

He wasn't much like Regidor at all. While Regidor liked fancy clothes, this meech wore only a cloth around his waist. The muscles on his body stood out like on a sculpture, but his wings looked less developed than Regidor's. She wondered if he could fly.

The boys continued to struggle, but the meech held them away from him as if they were no weight at all.

"So," he said and tossed his head back, jutting his chin in a belligerent fashion. "The mighty Dragon Keeper has come to me. No doubt you've met your father. He didn't give you much of a welcome, I suppose."

"You have the advantage over me." Kale kept her voice even.

"Oh, quite! Profoundly so, I would say."

She ignored the interruption. "I don't know who you are."

"Well, in a way, I am Wizard Strot. And I am also a young meech dragon whose body I found particularly appealing for its youth and stamina. And I am two other wizards, so obscure I'm sure you've never heard of them."

"And do all of you have one name?"

"I toyed with several, but in the end, I decided to keep my own. I am Lord Ire. And now you know why Crim Cropper and Burner Stox have not come to claim this property as their own, as heirs to Risto's estate. Those puppies are amassing an army of creatures they hope to send to overcome me." He laughed, an unpleasant sound in Kale's ears.

"Well, I've just come for the boys. Sorry they intruded upon your living quarters. I'll take them off your hands."

He laughed again. The first one had been unpleasant. This one ripped across Kale's nerves.

"Actually, dear Dragon Keeper, I intend to absorb them. It helps to keep me young."

"How old are you?"

"Not as old as Wulder. But I know of no other than He who is older than I am."

"Pretender?"

"How clever you are."

Kale felt lightheaded, and darkness pressed in on her. *My thoughts belong to me and Wulder. In Wulder's service, I search for truth. I stand under Wulder's authority. I stand under Wulder's authority. I am pledged to Wulder. Wulder is mine, and I am Wulder's. His banner is over me. His girding is under me. His fortress surrounds me.*

Kale didn't know where the words were coming from, but she let them flow until Pretender interrupted her.

"I may not be able to touch you," he roared. "But neither can you leave. Try to move, Dragon Keeper. Try!"

Kale looked at his enraged expression. His eyes glowed. He had tossed the boys to the side, and they lay in unconscious heaps.

She tensed her right leg and tried to lift her foot. It stuck to the floor. She tried the left. It, too, remained fastened to the stone beneath her.

"You know," said the evil before her, "I don't like what Wulder has made." He waved his hand, indicating the many people who were statue-like against the walls. "I prefer to see them like this." He sneered. "I understand you have summoned more to join us in this cavern. How gracious of you to add to my collection."

"Gymn, Ardeo, go warn them not to come!"

A look from Pretender stopped the flutter of leathery wings. The two dragons dropped to the floor and lay still.

A sparkle of light seen out of the corner of her eye caught Kale's attention. A kimen stood beside Sittiponder.

Kale looked back at Pretender, but he didn't seem to see the small, lighted figure.

Kale closed her eyes.

My thoughts belong to me and Wulder. In Wulder's service, I search for truth. I stand under Wulder's authority. I stand under Wulder's authority. I am pledged to Wulder. Wulder is mine, and I am Wulder's. His banner is over me. His girding is under me. His fortress surrounds me.

55

LIGHT VERSUS DARK

Bardon strode across the mountain meadow with Captain Anton. They headed for the dragon field to check on the dragons and the rider stationed there on guard. Behind them a narrow waterfall plummeted over a cliff. Even knowing the castle was there, it took concentration to distinguish rocks from turrets, and windows from crevices. Bardon glanced over his shoulder. The sight always fascinated him.

Two minor dragons winged his way. He stopped, and Captain Anton stopped as well.

"Trouble?" asked the captain.

"I don't know."

Filia circled his head, then landed on his shoulder. Metta landed on the other side.

Bardon listened to their chatter but heard words in his mind.

"Kale has gone into the cellar of the castle and is finding it unsettling," he told the captain. "She's looking for the boys and wants me to come along."

Captain Anton's eyebrows went up. "You can mindspeak with minor dragons?"

"With these, I can. That is, when Kale sends a specific message." He stroked Metta's back and then Filia's, when she let out a jealous chirp and nudged his cheek. "I've tried it on my own, and nothing passes to me or from me to the little creatures."

"I'll go on to the dragon field," Captain Anton said, "while you go rescue the fair damsel in distress."

Bardon laughed, raised his hand in a half salute, and strode back toward the castle.

He went upstairs first, sure that Kale would want to know what progress was being made in waking the knights. The smiles on the faces of the wizards told him progress had been made. He looked closely at Sir Jilles and saw a slight rising and falling of his chest.

"How much longer?" he asked.

Wizard Cam beamed as he looked up from the young knight on whom he was working. "A matter of minutes."

"I'll stay and watch. Kale wants me to join her in the dungeon. Perhaps I can take her father with me."

He'd been in the room only a few minutes when he heard Toopka tearing down the hall.

"Help! Help!" she cried through gasps for breath. She careened around the corner and straight into Bardon's legs.

"Whoa!" He crouched to face her. "What's the matter?"

"Kale's in trouble." She panted. "The boys are in trouble. Something bad is down there in the dungeon."

Knowing her penchant for the dramatic, Bardon looked at her closely. Her alarm was genuine. He stood.

Toopka began to cry. "Kale said to get everyone. It's big and horrible."

"We nearly have the knights awake," said Lyll. "Cam and I will stay here. The rest of you go."

"I'll get the men from the library," said Librettowit. "I'll send one of the guard for Anton."

Bardon threw himself out the door and raced down the hall. He plunged down the stairs and realized all four minor dragons kept pace with him as he entered the maze of rooms in the servants' quarters. He let them lead when they got to the cellar door, and beneath the castle, he followed them to the storage room where Sittiponder and Ahnek had uncovered the half door.

He halted and took a moment to slow his breathing, to prepare his heart and mind for battle. He put his great fear for Kale's safety in Wulder's hands and petitioned for clarity of thought, for precision in his combat ability, and that his decisions would honor Wulder. He ducked through the short entryway and picked up a lightrock.

He addressed the minor dragons as he went, keeping his voice low. "I'm not used to battling with you by my side. Stay away from my blade. I don't want to be distracted with worry over your safety."

They passed a message to him, and he gathered they considered themselves seasoned warriors who would not do something so foolish. He stopped for a moment. *The influence of Kale. My skills sharpen whenever I'm around her. Where I couldn't hear the little fellows before, now I can. Thank You, Wulder, that was just the sign I needed to help me be more confident.*

He moved rapidly but with great caution. He came to a turn in the passageway and heard Kale's voice.

"Bardon, Bardon, don't come in here. Don't! Bardon?"

I'm here in the tunnel.

"Pretender's been here. He left. But I doubt that he's far away."

Pretender?

"Yes, he's in the body of a meech. Sittiponder and Ahnek are here, unconscious. Pretender knocked Gymn and Ardeo to the ground. He pinned me to the rock beneath my feet."

I'm coming in, Kale.

"No!"

You think I'm going to leave you there?

"He'll kill you. We can't fight him, Bardon."

Bardon advanced the last few steps to the cavern balcony. He bent and carefully placed the lightrock he'd been carrying on the stone ledge.

We can fight him, Kale. That's what my training is for.

He stole down the incline, his sword out and his eyes moving about the room.

Pretender is evil. He's strong and cunning. But he's not Wulder.

Bardon saw Kale crane her neck to look up at the ramp he crept down.

Her head shook in a fierce negative command, and the word "No" formed on her lips.

"Bardon, go back."

No, Kale. I hope to take vows to serve Wulder. The vows include protecting the innocent from evil and freeing the oppressed. This seems to be a good place to start.

He marched down the incline and straight over to Sittiponder and Ahnek. With the tip of his sword he sliced through the ropes that bound them hand and foot. He then leaned over and removed the gags. Neither boy stirred.

"A kimen stood over Sittiponder earlier."

He's probably still here somewhere. I have long suspected that the voices Sittiponder hears are kimens talking to him.

He stood and moved toward Kale. When he was face to face with her, he looked her in the eye and spoke in a strong, gentle voice. "You can move your feet now."

Her eyes widened, and she inhaled sharply. Without hesitation, she moved into his arms.

"How did you do that? Was it wizardry?"

"What held you was a suggestion, only a suggestion. I merely spoke the truth."

"How did you know?"

He pulled her close to him and hugged her while his eyes roamed around the room, taking in the area from this vantage point. He spoke while he sized up the strategic elements of the layout. "My studies have covered physical, mental, and spiritual laws. Yours have focused on the physical elements of Wulder's world. You can alter things you understand. You can change water into ice. You can form cloth and then change the cloth. But your training has not introduced you fully to the spiritual realm. In the spiritual there are truth and lies. And truth is the stronger of the two."

"Very philosophical." The voice rattled through the cavern.

Bardon turned to face the meech-dragon form of Pretender. He stood in an alcove, where a large tunnel led away from the main cavern.

"But," said Pretender, "your little summary leaves out many factors. For instance, the will."

"We'll get around to discussing that someday." Bardon breathed deeply, maintaining the readiness of his body to fight.

"I think not." The meech took a step closer. "You annoy me. Therefore, I choose to eliminate you."

The ground beneath their feet rumbled. The tremor grew. The sleeping figures standing around the circumference of the room fell over. Kale tried to keep her balance but went to her knees. Bardon remained on his feet.

The stone floor split open next to Kale. The crack ran from one end of the cavern to the other. The slab under Kale tilted toward the chasm, and she screamed. Bardon lurched toward her, grabbed an arm, and managed to pull her away. When the earthquake quieted, Bardon, Kale, and Pretender stood on the far side of the cavern from the balcony entrance. Much of the incline they had walked down had shattered and fallen away from the wall.

Bardon let go of Kale and faced Pretender. He raised his sword and stepped closer to the meech.

Pretender laughed. "You think I would bother to fight you myself, boy?"

Kale shrieked. "Bardon!"

He whirled to see stinger-schoergs scrambling over the edge of the chasm. The creatures crawled on thin, black, furry arms and legs. Their thick bodies supported an equally thick head. They stared out of beady black eyes and snapped oversized, sharp, yellow teeth. Tails curved up over their backs. A glistening arrow-shaped stinger tipped each tail. The creatures hissed as they approached.

One sprang at Kale. She swung her sword hand, and the beast's head rolled across the floor.

Bardon jumped to her side as the next foray of schoergs swarmed up from the black pit.

Kale and Bardon fought as one. Both trained to use their swords efficiently, they sliced and stabbed the enemy's minions, keeping the spider-like horrors at bay. Occasionally, one of the beasts made it past their blades, alive and grasping. Bardon or Kale would use a well-aimed kick to stun the creature, if not kill it outright by breaking its neck.

Two of the creatures began clearing away their dead. These two did not engage in the battle but grabbed the mangled bodies of the fallen and threw them back into the chasm.

As the creatures kept coming, Bardon had the horrible notion that the lifeless schoergs somehow regenerated down in the depths to return. He heard a shout from above and glanced up to see the balcony crowded with wide-awake knights. However, the way down from the high entrance had been destroyed. Bardon refocused on the horde attacking him and Kale.

Arrows rained from the knights' bows, slaying the black stinger-schoergs. The first assault ceased. Bardon looked up to see Wizard Cam replenish the knights' supply of weapons. Bardon realized that it would be difficult for the wizards and knights to keep an adequate barrage against this swarming mass of creatures.

His body grew weary, and he knew that Kale, too, felt the fatigue of battle. The adrenaline that pumped through him had long since worn off.

"Paladin. Oh, thank Wulder!" Kale's voice in his mind sounded as though she was close to tears.

Still swinging his sword with deadly accuracy, Bardon looked up again to see their leader at the front of the crowd of witnesses. Before him, a bridge was forming across the gap, supported by nothing that could be seen. The brief glimpse of help on the way gave him hope. He felt energy from Kale as she too recognized they were no longer in the fight alone.

In only a moment, the last bit of rock connected the balcony with the floor of the cavern. Paladin's concentrated stare left the new bridge, and he turned to the warriors.

"Slay every one," Paladin ordered. "Let not one of the abominable beasts survive." He raised his sword and led the charge across the bridge. A half-dozen knights remained on the bridge with the tumanhofers and Holt. They used the advantage of the narrow space to fight off the schoergs who tried to climb up after them. The wizards, Cam, Lyll, and Regidor, jumped to the floor of the cavern on the unoccupied side of the chasm. They knelt together with their palms pressed against the stone flooring.

Six of the restored warriors circled Kale and Bardon, allowing them to rest.

Bardon did not doubt that somewhere in the fray, the tiny minneken warrior, Jue Seeno, did her part to decrease the number against them. In front of each of the sleeping servants and beside the unconscious boys stood a kimen, their garments, made of light, shining into the darkness.

The ground began to tremble as the three wizards closed the gap created by Pretender. Soon it was too narrow for the schoergs to pass through. The attacking horde already out of the abyss continued to fight. Refreshed, Kale and Bardon joined their comrades in the final minutes of the battle. At last they stood, panting, with arms relaxed, weapons pointed to the floor, and surrounded by the slain enemy.

Kale stepped closer to Bardon, and he hung an arm over her shoulders. She leaned against him.

A roar filled their ears. As one, Paladin's brigade turned to the huge underground passage that led off from the main cavern. The smell of sulfur, a gust of blistering air, and the trembling of the ground announced the approach of something vile.

Paladin signaled them to re-form at the sides of the entrance. He stood where he was and faced the rock shaft that now flashed from within as if a violent storm rolled through the tunnel. A flash of fire heralded the entry of a black dragon, twice the size of Greer. The flame shot past the waiting warriors and engulfed their leader. When the blaze subsided, Paladin stood unharmed.

The creature lowered its head, stretched out its neck, opened its mouth, and blew. A second inferno leapt across the empty space.

"Charge," shouted Bardon, and the two lines of Paladin's warriors rushed the exposed throat of the huge dragon. The beast bellowed and threw up its head as it felt the multiple strikes. Most of the warriors lost their grips on their swords as the creature's neck rose in a mighty jerk.

"Back!" ordered Bardon, and the fighters retreated.

The fire dragon leapt to the wall and climbed out of reach as it stoked its furnace. It breathed heavily and occasionally shook its head, as if annoyed by the swords stuck in its flesh.

Paladin shouted, "Lances!"

A pile of weapons appeared on the floor. Long rods with sharp metal tips lined up between the warriors. They rushed forward and grabbed them. The beast roared and circled the wall, while the men hurled the spears at the fleet-footed dragon.

"He's enchanted," said one of the knights. "Look at him scale the walls like a tiny lizard."

Regidor joined those throwing the lances. Bardon noted that every one of the meech dragon's spears hit the mark. Holt left off throwing the lances himself and took up the task of keeping a lance ever ready for the more proficient meech dragon.

The dragon kicked a hind leg, as if trying to shake something off.

"Look," exclaimed Kale. "It's the minneken."

Jue Seeno clung to her sword. She had thrust the blade into the tender flesh behind the dragon's knee. With every one of the dragon's kicks, the minneken swung back and forth on the hilt of the embedded sword.

Infuriated, the creature leapt to the floor, using its tail to slam warriors out of the fight.

Lyll and Cam stood with their heads together. When they turned to face the dragon, their expressions showed intense concentration.

"What are they doing?" Bardon asked Regidor.

The meech studied the wizards for only a moment, then grinned.

"Good idea!" he said as a smile broke out on his face. "They are drawing all the animal's fluids into the craw that produces the flames. I think I'll join them."

The beast became sluggish. Paladin ordered, "Stand down, men, and get back," just before the heavy head slammed to the cavern floor. It breathed once more, drawing in its last breath with a shudder and exhaling a hot, fetid gasp.

Paladin walked among his men, praising their work, taking note of the injured, and giving orders. He came to Bardon's side and put a hand on his shoulder. "Well done, Squire."

Bardon bowed his head in respect before his commander.

Paladin lifted his hand and clapped it down again. "You've decided to join me, haven't you?"

Bardon raised his eyes to look into Paladin's face. Today, the ruler of Amara looked younger, stronger than when he had visited Bardon at Castle Pelacce.

"Yes," Bardon answered.

Paladin waved his hand around the room to indicate the crumpled forms of the mass of servants, all still under Risto's spell. "You will have to deal with such as these."

Bardon studied these cold, useless people, and he looked at the warriors around him. Kale and Lyll embraced Sir Kemry Allerion. N'Rae and Granny Kye had at some point crossed over the bridge from the castle cellar and now held between them the younger of the old emerlindian's twins. Bardon looked at the collapsed forms of Sittiponder and Ahnek. Toopka sat beside the blind seer, grasping his hands. In front of each and every living creature in the vast underground hall stood a kimen, solemn and watchful.

His eyes fell again on Kale, and his heart tightened with the need to hold her, to have his arms around her, to never let her go.

"Yes," Bardon said. "Each of these people is precious to someone, and all of them are precious to Wulder."

"Indeed," said his commander.

Paladin turned away from him, withdrawing his hand from Bardon's shoulder. He put his fists to his hips and surveyed those servants who'd fallen as the earth quaked. One by one, as his gaze rested upon them, their color returned, their breathing deepened, and they moved, stretching and sitting up, blinking as they looked around. Gymn and Ardeo fluttered up from the floor and sought Kale. Sittiponder hugged Toopka. Ahnek stood and turned in a circle, his mouth hanging open as he took in the wondrous scene. Those among the warriors who were injured received healing.

"Bardon," a soft voice spoke behind him, and he turned to see Granny Kye standing with her eldest twin. Her small, dark face beamed with joy.

Bardon put his arms around her and squeezed. "You have both your sons, alive and well. I'd say our quest has been successful."

"And you've gained someone as well," she said.

Bardon looked over her head to Kale, who was making her way through the crowd to him.

"Yes, very definitely." He grinned at Kale and, as their eyes met, winked.

"Oh, I'd forgotten Kale," said Granny Kye. "So I guess we should make that two someones. No, three. Four!"

Bardon leaned back to look down into her glowing countenance. He knew his face must be a mask of confusion, because she laughed.

"I'm your grandmother, N'Rae is your cousin, and, Bardon…" She eased out of his embrace so that he could face her eldest son. "Meet your father."

EPiLOGUE

The Knights' Chamber hung silent even though crowded by the entire questing party and the rescued knights. Paladin crouched before Fenworth's tree and spoke quietly to Toopka. The little girl had wedged herself in the old wizard's branches.

Bardon put his arms around Kale as she started to go forward. "Let Paladin handle this."

"Come, Toopka." Paladin held his arms out to receive her.

She shook her head. "No, he's sleeping. He always becomes a tree when he sleeps."

Paladin nodded, his eyes filled with compassion. "This time he is not asleep, but gone."

"No, no, no!"

Paladin reached in to touch her hand. He rubbed gently. "Come to my arms, child."

To Bardon's surprise, the doneel girl let go of her hold of a branch and slipped into Paladin's embrace.

She collapsed against his shoulder, and he stood, patting her back. "I know for a fact that Wizard Fenworth told you he was going to die."

She nodded, keeping her face buried.

"He is not lost to us, Toopka, but waits for us to join him in another place. Isn't that what he told you?"

She nodded again and lifted her tear-stained face. "He said he was going to go take a walk with Wulder and ask Him some things he never got figured out."

Paladin smiled. "And by now our friend Fenworth has his answers. It's all right to miss him, but do not despair. The Tomes make it clear that this is only a temporary world we live in." He hugged her. "The Tomes also give us instructions as to what to do in such a time as this."

"What?"

"Talk to the living. There are stories in this room that are just waiting to be told. Are you curious about Granny Kye's sons?"

Bardon caught his breath, and Kale squeezed his arm.

"He didn't desert you," she whispered.

He shook his head but couldn't answer past the lump in his throat. He had avoided Granny Kye's eldest son in the chaos after the battle. It hadn't been difficult. Paladin had issued orders, and Bardon sprang to obey. When they reached this room, he'd chosen to stand on the opposite side beside Kale, where she stood with her parents.

Paladin carried Toopka over to Sir Joffa, who stood next to his brother. Bardon's father had a hand resting on his mother's shoulder. "Tell us, sir," commanded Paladin, "about how you were separated from your son."

Bardon didn't want to hear this story in a crowded room. This tale was personal and shouldn't be aired in front of strangers. He stared at the man who was his father and waited. He wondered about Sir Joffa's age. Not very old, he guessed, since his skin, hair, and eyes had darkened only to a ruddy tan. The knight's eyes glanced Bardon's way for only a second, swept around the room, and then came back to rest on his son.

"I heard my brother was in trouble and decided to give aid." Sir Joffa's voice boomed across the large hall. "I set out with my fair lady and our son toward Wittoom, but we were ambushed in the Kattaboom Mountains by Risto's men. My wife was killed. The rest of the cutthroats were slain by my men and me."

By this time, Bardon had lost all trepidation over the witnesses hearing his story. He felt as if his father spoke to him and none other.

"I made arrangements for Liza's burial," Sir Joffa continued, "and spirited my son away to The Hall. I knew Grand Ebeck would take care of him for the few months I would be gone to rescue my brother, without giving away his parentage and exposing him to Risto or Stox."

He looked steadily at his grown son. Bardon returned the regard without flinching. "It is hard for me to imagine that this fine young man is the sleeping six-year-old I handed into Ebeck's arms."

Paladin turned to face Bardon. "You were old enough to remember all this, Squire, but sometimes Wulder blots out horrific memories in order to give peace to a fragile child."

Bardon felt a tug on his sleeve. He looked down into Kale's expectant face.

"Go shake his hand. Do something!" she muttered urgently.

Bardon felt released from a very long, troubling dream. He crossed the wide space and stuck out his hand to his father. Sir Joffa took it and after one firm shake, pulled his grown boy into his arms.

This can't be real. Oh, thank You, Wulder. It is real. Tears coursed down his cheeks, and he felt only joy, no shame. He heard the crowd around them cheering and applauding, but he paid them no mind.

"Now," said Paladin, "it looks like we have a happy ending, but I'm afraid there is too much still going on for us to rest." His eyes roamed the room, connecting with each of the warriors. "I have need of you all. It is true that Crim Cropper and Burner Stox are amassing a hideous army in hopes of taking over Pretender's powerful position. And although they're not attacking the citizens of Amara, their skirmishes leave our people, who are innocently caught in the fray, as casualties. Whichever side wins, the next strategic move will be to enslave Amara. It is good that these knights are now awake. We must be ever watchful and not be caught sleeping when our chance comes to stand for Wulder and righteousness."

"Hear! Hear!" shouted those in the room.

"I bless you, one and all, for your presence has returned my strength."

"What are we going to do with the tree?" asked Toopka.

"Ah yes, little one, ever practical." He kissed her cheek. "We must take care of the immediate as we prepare for the future. I am giving this castle property to Sir Kemry and Lyll Allerion. We have flushed out the evil, but if you leave a place empty, the depraved will return. Lyll and Kemry will move the tree to a sunny spot and allow it to be just what it is, a lovely tree."

"And Kale?"

"She is now Wizard of The Bogs."

"Can she do that?"

Paladin winked over Toopka's shoulder at Bardon. "Yes, with help, she can."

Glossary

Amara (ä´-mä-rä)
Continent surrounded by ocean on three sides.

armagot (är´-muh-got)
National tree, purple blue leaves in the fall.

armagotnut (är´-muh-got-nut)
Nut from the armagot tree.

astiket (a-stik´-it)
A three-team ball game played on a triangular field with three goals.

Ataradari (uh-tar´-uh-dar´-ee)
A tribe native to one of the smaller southern continents; primitive, but rich in folklore and tradition.

azrodhan (az´-ro´-dan)
Any of numerous, prolific vines, having clusters of bell-shaped flowers in various colors.

bisonbecks (bī´-sen-beks)
Most intelligent of the seven low races. They comprise most of Risto's army.

blimmets (blim´-mets)
One of the seven low races, burrowing creatures that swarm out of the ground for periodic feeding frenzies.

Bogs, The
Made up of four swamplands with indistinct borders. Located in southwest Amara.

bordenaut (bôr´-deh-not)
A mold-ripened cheese with a white rind and a soft, pale center, made from creamy milk.

borling tree (bôr´-ling)
Tree with dark brown wood and a deeply furrowed nut enclosed in a globose, aromatic husk.

bossel (bôs´-l)
Grain with flat edible chaff and seed in center.

brillum (bril´-lum)
A brewed ale that none of the seven high races would consume. Smells like skunkwater, stains like black bornut juice. Mariones use it to spray around their fields to keep insects from infesting their crops.

brouna (broo-nah)
Beaten eggs, cooked in a skillet until firm, then folded over a variety of fillings.

chigot deer (kī-go)
A large deer with tangled antlers.

cygnot tree (sī´-not)
A tropical tree growing in extremely wet ground or shallow water. The branches come out of the trunk like spokes from a wheel hub and often interlace with neighboring trees.

criantem (cree-an´-tem)
A smooth, hard, yellow cheese varying in flavor from mild to sharp.

daggarts (dag´-garts)
A baked treat, a small crunch cake.

doneel (dō´-neel)
One of the seven high races. These people are furry with bulging eyes, thin black lips, and ears at the top and front of their skulls. A flap of skin covers the ears and twitches, responding to the doneel's mood. They are small in stature, rarely over three feet tall. Generally are musical and given to wearing flamboyant clothing.

doohan (doo´-an)
A woven seat used for passengers, encased in a small chamber and mounted on a major dragon.

dorker
Large noisy bird, brightly colored, attractive to the eye, annoying to the ear.

Dormanscz (dôr-manz´)
Volcanic mountain range in southeast Amara.

druddum (drud´-dum)
Weasel-like animal that lives deep in mountains. These creatures are thieves and will steal anything to horde. Of course, they like to get food, but they are also attracted to bright things and things that have an unusual texture.

drummerbug
Small brown beetle that makes a loud snapping sound with its wings when not in flight.

emerlindian (ē´-mer-lin´-dee-in)
One of the seven high races, emerlindians are born pale with white hair and pale gray eyes. As they age, they darken. One group of emerlindians are slight in stature, the tallest being five feet. Another distinct group are between six and six and a half feet tall.

fire dragon
Emerged from the volcanoes in ancient days. These dragons breathe fire and are most likely to serve evil forces.

giddinfish
A freshwater food and game fish; usually has a streamlined, speckled body with small scales.

girder exercise
A demanding regimen of recalling actions taken during a day and justifying the decision to make such an action by reciting principles from one of the three Tomes of Wulder.

grand emerlindian
Grands are male or female, close to a thousand years old, and black.

granny emerlindian
Grannies are male or female, said to be five hundred years old or older, and have darkened to a brown complexion with dark brown hair and eyes.

grawligs (graw´-ligs)
One of seven low races, mountain ogres.

greater dragon
Largest of the dragons, able to carry many men or cargo.

grood
A basic unit of currency in Amara.

guard
A fighting unit made up of a captain and four loes.

heatherhens
Chickenlike bird having brown plumage with a speckled breast and a short tail.

heirdosh vines (hair´-dosh)
A vine with short, flat, glossy-green leaves with two white bands on the underside. The sap from the branches is poisonous. The fluid from the leaves is poisonous to a lesser degree.

Herebic continent (hair´-a-bik)
Massive continent in the western/southern hemisphere.

Himber (him´-ber)
A tribe of people who are prone to be isolationists. They value intelligence and are great inventors.

Kere (keer)
An ancient language no longer in use. This language is thought to have been used by one of the first tribes to use written communication.

kimen (kim´-en)
The smallest of the seven high races. Kimen are elusive, tiny, and fast. Under two feet tall.

kindia (kin´-dee-uh)
A large land mammal noted for its speed, strength, and endurance. Kindias are exceptionally adapted to traveling long distances with great efficiency and to surviving on a diet of nutrient-poor, high-fiber grasses. The shoulders are a foot or more taller than the hindquarters, giving the animal a slanted back.

Korskan tea (kor´-skan)
A tea flavored with citrus and spices, such as cinnamon and cardamom.

lightrocks
Any of the quartzlike rocks giving off a glow.

lo
Rank between leecent and lehman.

major dragon
Elephant-sized dragon most often used for personal transportation.

marione (mer´-ē-owns)
One of the seven high races. Mariones are excellent farmers and warriors. They are short and broad, usually muscle-bound rather than corpulent.

meech dragon
The most intelligent of the dragons, capable of speech.

minneken
A small, mysterious race living in isolation on the Isle of Kye.

minor dragon
Smallest of the dragons, the size of a young kitten. The different types of minor dragons have different abilities.

moonbeam plant
A three- to four-foot plant having large shiny leaves and round flowers resembling a full moon. The stems are fibrous and used for making invisible cloth.

moonbird
A nocturnal bird of prey, having soft plumage that allows for noiseless flight, feathered talons, large heads with large eyes set forward, and short hooked beaks. Name reflects the coloring, which resembles the surface of the moon.

Morchain Range
Mountains running north and south through the middle of Amara.

mordakleep
One of the low races, a shadowy creature with a long tail.

mountain dewdrops
Small white flowers growing close to the ground in an almost moss covering.

mullins (mŭl´-lĭns)
Fried doughnut sticks.

o'rant
One of the high races. Five to six feet tall.

ordend (or´-den)
A basic unit of Amaran currency. Twenty ordends equals one grood.

ostal greens (ah´-stuhl)
A plant in the mustard family.

parnot (pâr´-nŏt)
Green fruit like a pear.

pnard potatoes (puh-nard´)
Starchy, edible tuber with pale pink flesh.

Pordactic Period
The period of Amaran history covering two thousand years when the Pordac family ruled.

portamanca (por´-tuh-man-kuh)
Evergreen shrub having fragrant orange blossoms and whorled leaves.

Punipmats (puh-nee´-mats; notice second p is silent)
Continent of western/northern hemispheres.

quiss (kwuh´-iss)
One of the seven low races. These creatures have an enormous appetite. Every three years they develop the capacity to breathe air for six weeks and forage along the seacoast, creating havoc. They are extremely slippery.

razterberry (ras´-ter-bâr-ee)
Small red berries that grow in clusters somewhat like grapes on the sides of mountains. The vines are useful for climbing.

rock pine
Evergreen tree with prickly cones that are as heavy as stones.

ropma (rōp´-muh)
One of the seven low races. These half men—half animals are useful in herding and caring for beasts.

schoergs (skôrgz)
One of seven low races, much like grawligs, shorter, less playful.

smoothergill
Any of the marine flatfishes having a slick skin and large gills.

steppesman (steps´-mun)
A large burrowing animal of the squirrel family, covered with light brown fur. Social structure within colony resembles extended families.

stinger-schoergs
A variant of schoergs, having a scorpion-type tail instead of a prehensile tail.

thornsnippers
Tiny brown birds with bright red beaks, known to feed on thorns of various bushes.

todden barrel
A wooden container of toddens, a pickled vegetable, yellow in color and crunchy, shaped somewhat like a hand.

trang-a-nog tree (trăng´-uh-nŏg)
Smooth olive green bark.

trundle bear
A small, ferocious brown bear with enormous claws.

tumanhofer (too´-mun-hoff-er)
One of the seven high races, short, squat, powerful fighter, though for the most part they prefer to use their great intellect.

umbering
A time of refreshment, the social traditions and interaction being more important than the nourishment.

urohm (ū-rōm´)
Largest of the seven high races. Gentle giants, well proportioned and very intelligent.

Vendela (vin-del´-luh)
Capital city of the province of Wynd.

waistcoater
A deep-chested bird with a small head and short legs. The coloring of feathers suggests the bird is wearing a dark vest.

Wittoom (wit-toom´)
Region populated by doneels in northwest Amara.

writher snake (rī-ther)
A water snake, long and slender. The snake wraps its body around a victim, drags it under the water, and eats the body as it decomposes.

About the Author

DONITA K. PAUL enjoys writing, but she enjoys her readers more. Her Web site, www.dragonkeeper.us is a place where she can interact with readers, old and young.

Mrs. Paul is a retired teacher and still spends a great deal of time with young people. Although she lives in the shadow of Pikes Peak, she does no mountain climbing, preferring more sedate hobbies such as knitting and stamping. And she likes to make things she can give away.